A peculiar, almost mournful howl echoed through the chamber... within the deepest parts of the cavern s... By the echo, whatever had made... y was not far. A second wail indicate... t it was drawing nearer at incredible pace.

"What in the name of the Dragon of the Depthsss *isss* that?" whispered Kyl, stunned.

It was the call of a monstrosity, a thing that should not have survived its time in the hatcheries of the drakes, but somehow had. Only through combined effort had it been defeated last time, to go fleeing deep into the vast underground system.

A misshapen form lumbered out of the tunnels and into the throne room of the Dragon Emperor. It caught sight of the warlock and there and then Cabe knew that, as he had remembered it, so had the beast remembered him.

The monster started toward him, jaws wide . . .

Also by Richard A. Knaak

THE DRAGONREALM SERIES

Firedrake
Ice Dragon
Wolfhelm
The Shrouded Realm
Shadow Steed
Children of the Drake
Dragon Tome
The Crystal Dragon

King of the Grey

Published by
WARNER BOOKS

RICHARD A. KNAAK
THE DRAGON CROWN

WARNER BOOKS

A Time Warner Company

WARNER BOOKS EDITION

Questar® is a registered trademark of Warner Books, Inc.

Cover design by Don Puckey
Cover illustration by Larry Elmore
Hand lettering by David Gatti

Warner Books, Inc.
1271 Avenue of the Americas
New York, NY 10020

 A Time Warner Company

Printed in the United States of America

First Printing: July, 1994

10 9 8 7 6 5 4 3 2 1

Dedicated to my father,
James Richard Knaak
(1930–1993)
who was always there for me
as I pursued my dreams.

I

The riders began to collect at the outskirts of the great Tyber Mountains. They had not gathered for such a meeting in nearly two decades, and as they joined one another at the narrow pass leading into the midst of the Tybers, it was clear that none would have come even now if necessity had not demanded it.

Clad in immense, flowing traveler's cloaks that hid both face and form, the riders were a coven of gray specters astride mounts whose glittering eyes warned that they, too, hid secrets. There were no words of acknowledgment or, for that matter, even the simple nod of a head. Some of the band might, at times, have called one another brother, but the appellation was simply a matter of ceremony; there was little love lost among the riders.

When at last they were all gathered, there were those who would have set off for their destination, the sooner to end this unwelcome confrontation. One, however, chose that moment to begin pulling back the hood of his cloak. That led to a hiss from another and a low, painful, rasping reprimand.

"Not herrrre! Never herrrre!"

The one who had erred did not question his elder counterpart. He lowered his hand and nodded.

One of the other riders grunted, then urged his mount toward the path. The rest followed his example. Showing no sign of fatigue, the beasts snorted puffs of smoke and carried their masters swiftly among the mountains. Neither twisting and turning passages nor treacherous ravines slowed the group. Savage winds and slippery trails were obstacles also ignored. Though denizens not of man's world hid and watched, the riders were in no way hindered. The creatures of the mountains knew who and what the intruders were, and so remained at a respectful distance, many shivering in fear. Some simply fled in open terror as the riders approached.

None of the ghostly riders took notice of the onlookers. Their concern lay only in the vast presence looming above them, a mountain so massive that those surrounding it looked like vassals paying homage to their lord. Those of the band who had never been this close were hard-pressed not to be overwhelmed by the peak's grandeur and the power they could sense radiating from within it.

Kivan Grath. The name was old and without reliable origin, but all here were aware it meant "Seeker of Gods." No one knew the reason for the title, yet somehow it fit. The riders turned their steeds toward the peak. At this point, there was at last some hesitation from their beasts, but, unforgiving, their hooded masters prodded them on, silencing whatever protests the mounts made. The sooner the band reached its destination and completed the task before it, the sooner the riders could go their separate ways.

At the base of the vast mountain, they came at last upon that which they sought. As one, the band reined their animals to a halt, then dismounted. Their steeds secured, the hooded figures stared at the sight before them until at last one of the lead riders, known to the others for his tempestuous ways, snarled something unintelligible and stalked toward the dark cavern in the mountainside.

Buried in the side of Kivan Grath was a great gate of bronze that might have been as old as the peak itself, so ancient was its appearance. Once it had towered over onlookers, but no more. Now the gate hung awkwardly, a mortally wounded guardian frozen in midfall. Only one blackened hinge held it in place. The entire gate was a burnt memory of what once had been. Those who had been here before could recall how its surface had been decorated with a curious array of designs, but now the designs were gone, melted away by the terrible forces unleashed upon it by one mad power.

The one who had stalked forward suddenly faltered. The others did not move, as if waiting for something to happen. The tableau did not change for several anxious moments.

"Well?" questioned one whose tone was reminiscent of lapping waves. It had finally occurred to him how ridiculous he and his companions looked. "It isss not asss if we need to knock, now isss it?"

Abashed, the lead figure looked at the others, then turned once more to the gate and the pitch-dark abyss behind it. He then turned back to the one who had mocked them all. "A torch would be nice, eel!"

"Why not create our own light?" scoffed one of the younger ones, the same one who had thought to remove his hood during the ride. He held out a gloved hand. A glow formed in his palm.

"Not out here, you hatchling!" the young traveler's partner snapped. He had to struggle to make himself be heard, for, as before, his voice was barely a rasping whisper. It proved sufficient for the task, however, for the glow instantly faded away.

"There are sssome . . . *some* things that should be observed," added the one with the voice that spoke like the sea. He was visibly working to calm himself, an effort that the other riders immediately copied with greater or lesser results. "Some things that must be respected."

"There should ssstill be a torch on the inssside," gasped the whisperer. "Just beyond the gate."

Steeling himself, the foremost walked up and reached inside, his gauntleted hand running along the wall. His fingers struck something not made of stone. "I have it."

"Then light it and let us be done with this."

"You would be wise not to strain your voice," the young, impetuous one advised his compatriot, a hint of mockery flavoring his words.

Before his companion could form a retort, the others had the torch lit. The bickering figures quieted. Despite their distaste for one another, the band drew close together as they entered the battered passage. There were some fears—although none here would have admitted to such failings—that were stronger than hatred.

They walked for a short time through a tunnel that, while natural in origin, had also been improved upon by other means during the passage of time. Small shadow creatures fluttered away in vocal dismay at the intrusion of light, but the group ignored them. All other things paled in comparison to the place they had invaded.

The riders entered the main cavern.

Even in its ruined state, the cavern citadel left them in speechless awe. The interior resembled a temple, but one tossed asunder by a great upheaval. Effigies both human and otherwise lay strewn about, many shattered beyond recognition. Some still stood, frightful mourners at the funeral of their companions. Beyond them, at the focus of the chamber, was a cracked and half-buried throne atop a crumbling dais. Just before the massive stone seat, but buried by rubble from the collapsed roof of the cavern, was a wide open area where a full-grown dragon could have and *had* rested his massive form time and time again. The elder riders could recall the face and form of that reptilian behemoth. He had been a golden leviathan, the last of a line of scaled masters ruling the land called the Dragonrealm. The Dragon Emperor Gold.

A generation of men had grown since his death.

The one with the torch placed it in a location that would give them the necessary illumination for their undesired deed. Then the riders, forming a ragged half circle, knelt in homage: if not to the late tyrant, then to what he had represented.

A moment of silence passed before one rider, calmer than the rest, stepped forward and took the place where the Dragon Emperor, king of kings, would have stood. The others shuffled uneasily, but they knew that their companion sought only to speak, not to claim any right above them.

"Let the council convene." His words were softly spoken, but in the huge, still cavern they were thunder.

The forms of the riders suddenly became twisted, grotesque. They grew, and as they did their bodies became quicksilver. All semblance to humanity quickly faded. From their backs burst wings—long, webbed wings—and below those, serpentine tails sprouted. Arms and legs became clawed, leathery appendages. Already each figure was many times larger than it had been, yet the growth did not slow.

The cloaks had all been thrown aside at the moment of transformation, briefly revealing to the shadows a band of tall, dread warriors, dragonhelmed knights clad in scale armor. That image quickly gave way, however, as helms and near-hidden features melded together into monstrous, reptilian visages with long, horrid snouts and toothy maws. The scaled armor became scaled hide of colors that varied from figure to figure. There were blue, red, black, green, and at least a pair more gray than anything else. Other differences were obvious, but none more than the colors.

Where but moments before the riders had been, now the Dragon Kings stood.

The dragons stretched their vast wings and eyed one another with deep-rooted suspicion. They remained in pairs as they had since the beginning of this trek, one beast in each duo obviously dominant over the other. The lesser drakes backed up a few paces, acknowledging their lower status. One or two did this with great reluctance.

From the ranks of the dominant leviathans, a dragon of the darkest black, a sly creature with a savage scar across his throat, sneered at his emerald-green counterpart, who stood in the center. When the black dragon spoke, his voice was barely a whisper. Each word seemed a torture for the ebony creature.

"I am sssurprised that you even asked us to join together, Brother Grrreeeen! It isss not asss if you could not do asss you pleased in thisss matter!"

"We are inclined to similar notions," added a gray, preening drake, whose very tone made it clear that the "we" of his statement concerned him alone and not his companion. He plucked fastidiously at his hide, as if seeking something. In the past decade, as his interests had turned ever inward, the Dragon King Storm had begun to take on the airs of a would-be demigod. Among his brethren was a growing suspicion that he was going mad, a not uncommon affliction of drake lords. Yet, any who might have thought him a foolish sight need only listen for the iron in his voice to know that this was not a creature to be crossed. The Storm Dragon might be mad, but he was also one of the most deadly of those drake lords who remained.

The Green Dragon, master of the vast lands of the Dagora Forest, eyed them both. "*I* have always abided by the traditions."

"Enough of this bickering!" snapped their blue counterpart. His breath smelled heavily of fish, which made the black one wrinkle his snout in disgust. "We have matters to discuss which have been delayed all too long!"

Reminded of their duty, the others quieted. Green nodded his gratitude to the Blue Dragon, lord of Irrilian by the Sea, and, with a withering glance at his ebony counterpart, returned to his self-chosen role of speaker. "As Brother Blue so succinctly put it, we *have* delayed much too long in discussing this particular matter . . . *years* too long." He surveyed the group, its prominent members strikingly fewer than when last they had convened. "I refer, of courssse, to the *ascension* to the throne of the next Dragon Emperor."

Among his fellows there was some shuffling and discomfort. None of them had looked forward to this day, if only because they were uncertain as to what it meant to their kind. To some, it was an opportunity to reclaim past glory; to others, it was a final turning point. In the back of all their minds was the fear that it was all for nothing: a mere joke.

Once, it would have not been so. Once, the lands known both separately and collectively as the Dragonrealm had trembled under the iron rule of the drake race. Thirteen kingdoms and thirteen kings, with the line of Gold serving as emperor over all. So it had been for centuries, with new Dragon Kings replacing their progenitors either through the process of age or, more often, through subterfuge and deceit. A drake who became king relinquished his own name and became known by the symbol his clans had chosen so long ago in the lost past. Most were colors, said to represent the various shades of the magical spectrum. A few had gone by the strongest or most regal of the metals, such as iron or silver. One clan had even chosen the violence of nature's storms as its symbol.

The shape-shifting drakes were only the latest in a long procession of rulers who had risen to supremacy . . . and then had fallen. A few scattered remnants of some of their predecessors still existed, but most of the land's previous tyrants had faded with the lengthy passage of history. It now appeared as if the dragon folk themselves were headed into oblivion . . . and all here knew the reason why.

Mankind. Weak, clawless creatures, their race yet prospered. The Dragon Kings knew that they themselves were to blame for much of that progress and expansion. Humans had proven so useful in many ways, more than making up for the drakes' own lack of numbers. In time, their inventiveness and drive had made them indispensable to most of the Dragon Kings. Human cities had sprouted up and grown, their inhabitants loyal at first to their respective masters. But it was inevitable that as their own power grew, the new kingdoms chafed at the rule of monsters. Rebellions rose and were suppressed. Human kingdoms then grew subservient for a time, but when a new generation came into power, the cycle would often repeat itself.

Then came the sorcerers.

The *Dragon Masters*.

Human mages had always existed, and many had found their way into the services of the Dragon Kings. A few had desired to cause havoc, but ever the drake lords had kept a wary eye out for the strongest, the ones with the most potential for destruction. These were either recruited or destroyed. Some sorcerers, however, succeeded in remaining hidden from the drakes. They gathered others to them and bided their time, their only attacks being to undermine the foundation of drake rule. The Dragon Kings began to suffer a number of mishaps, small by themselves, but cumulative in effect. Despite the many mishaps, however, they did not realize what was happening. Only after many generations, when the mages decided the time was ripe for revolution and at last revealed themselves for what they were, did the draconian rulers realize the instability of their reign.

Thus began the Turning War. For nearly five years the battle was fought. For nearly five years the Dragon Kings lived in fear that they were at last to fall.

The Dragon Masters, though, had also underestimated a number of things, first and foremost the treachery of one of their number. Serving his own purpose, the traitor had killed several of the most prominent mages in the ranks, then fled before their leader, his father, could deal with him. Weakened, the sorcerers were finally defeated; but the victory was bittersweet, for in one of the final struggles, the drake lords had lost one of their own. Lord Purple, who had guided them in the actual fighting, died with the Dragon Master Nathan Bedlam. Both Purple's kingdom and the secrets of his great sorcery fell into the claws of the Gryphon, ally to the Dragon Masters. Weakened as they were, the other Dragon Kings could not oust him.

Those gathered now had long ago come to realize that the victory they had garnered in the war had been only a temporary reprieve. They had won themselves two centuries of anxiety and suspicion. When all was said and done, the empire had still crumbled. Infighting and misjudgment had done what the Dragon Masters could not.

For some time, the remaining Dragon Kings eyed one another. Then, at last, the ruined voice of the Black Dragon, he who controlled the domain of the Gray Mists, broke the uneasy silence. "Of what need have we of an emperor . . . essspecially one raised by humanssss?"

"More to the point," interjected a dusky green drake with touches of brown along his underside, "a Dragon Emperor raisssed by the grandssson of Nathan Bedlam!"

The dragon's name was Sssaleese. Some of the others looked at the new speaker, open disdain on their reptilian countenances. In their eyes, this one was not a true Dragon King but a usurper, a pretender using the devastation of the drake race to his benefit. No birth markings had decorated his egg, of that they were certain. Yet, because he spoke for a loose confederation of clan survivors who had lost their own lords, it had been decided by the majority that his presence was required if this was to succeed.

Black had not been a part of that majority. The ebony drake sneered at the other and started to speak, but Green, recognizing the potential danger of those words, quickly replied, "Worthy comments both, but it would be well for *all* to remember that it wasss our rivalries and divisionsss which brought us to our present sssorry state."

That drew the attention away from Sssaleese, but kindled a new disruption. Storm, the gray, looked mildly amused. "As we recall, the dissension was a part of life *before* the death of Gold."

"Gold wasss Gold. Kyl, his heir, will be Gold in title only. He will ssstill be Kyl." Green's gaze swept across the cavern. "In that there isss all the difference! If we but give him our allegiance, our cooperation, then will we have what we desssire!"

"I ask again," Black hissed. "What need have we of an emperor?"

Green shook his massive head. To the side, he heard Blue hiss in frustration. Blue understood what some of the others did not. The drake race was on the brink. If they did not come together soon, they faced extinction. The humans outbred them and now had clawholds everywhere. Green firmly believed that the tiny mammals now had the strength to annihilate his kind, and there were more than a few of the creatures who desired just that. Melicard I of Talak, whose father had been driven mad by the drake Kyrg, had already tried genocide. Worse, it appeared that the king of Zuu, Lanith, was massing an army and gathering what human mages of skill he could find. No one knew *what* he planned, but Zuu was a particularly disturbing point since it lay in the boundaries of the emerald giant's domain. Lanith still gave his respects to Green, but grew ever more lax in responding to questions concerning Zuu's increase in military strength.

"We need an emperor to give our kind focusss," Blue returned, speaking in a manner one might use more for a child. "We need an emperor to show the humans that we are *one*, not many!"

"Yet you would give usss an emperor raisssed by humansss," reminded Sssaleese, eyes darting to Black, who remained silent. "How could we trusssst one raisssed by a Bedlam?"

"Raised by human *and* drake." Green shook his head. "You sssee the disadvantages but not the advantagesss!"

"Could we not . . . ssspeak with him firsssst?" an almost tentative voice asked.

The assembled drakes turned as one to the blood-red figure on the edge of the inner group. Although a Dragon King, Red was fairly new into his reign, a mere two decades or so. He had achieved his place upon the death of his progenitor on the sword of yet another Bedlam, Nathan's mad son Azran. Unprepared, he had never found his proper place among his fellows. Even Sssaleese, who had clawed his way to his position, was more comfortable in the role of ruler.

"Ssspeak to him?" repeated the Green Dragon.

"Yesss . . ." Storm nodded. "We have only your word asss to his worth." The gray behemoth met Green's eyes. "We would be happier in thisss instance if we knew that the emperor-to-be isss worthy of the august title."

"A notable suggestion," agreed Blue.

Sssaleese added, "I would be interesssted alssso in the opportunity to make a judgment."

Black merely nodded curtly. Red basked in the afterglow of his success and thus missed the look the Green Dragon briefly sent his way.

"Very well," the emerald beast muttered. "I shall sssee to arranging sssuch a talk."

"The Bedlamsss will never agree to it!" gasped the Black Dragon.

"Wait and sssee! I shall do what I can." A pause, then, "And if the heir meetsss your questionsss? Then will you acknowledge his rightful place?"

The others acquiesced one by one with Black, of course, last.

"Ssso, then. The matter is settled. That leavesss but the details. . . ."

A short time later, the Dragon Kings departed through the broken bronze gate. In silence the band took charge of their steeds, mounted, and quickly left behind what had once been and might yet again be the Dragon Emperor's stronghold. They rode together through the mountains, but when the Tybers gave way to more open land, the band quickly split into pairs. Some headed in an easterly direction, others more south. Only one pair headed directly west: Sssaleese and his second.

The would-be Dragon King and his companion rode hard for more than a quarter hour, never looking back once. They rode hard until they came upon a small range of hills, in truth a stunted outreach of the Tyber Mountains. Slowing their mounts, the two drakes entered the hills by one of the narrow paths that wound through the range.

When they were well within the protection of the hills, Sssaleese turned and glanced at his companion. The other drake, as nondescript a warrior as one of his kind could be, nodded. Both reined in their steeds. Only one moon was out this night, so Sssaleese could make out little more than the outline of the other, but he was certain that his companion was pleased. The confederation lord was not so certain that he shared that pleasure.

"You are sssatisssfied with what you have learned?"

"I am. They have not changed! They blunder around, each trying to take what he can without giving up anything! My sssire never trusted them! It wasss their fighting, their *betrayal*, that destroyed him! Now they ssseek to make the new emperor a puppet who will dance to *their* tune!"

Sssaleese did not respond at first. His situation was precarious, to say the least. He needed to be on fair terms with the Dragon Kings, yet there was much potential in taking a different course, especially if it meant the favor of the one who soon would sit upon the dragon throne.

Or stand behind it, he added. If the offer his companion had made him some months back held any truth, then the true lord of the drakes now sat in front of Sssaleese. "What will you do?"

The other considered. "The meeting will be a formality. They will find my brother a sssuitable candidate. All things may proceed as I planned." The drake leaned toward Sssaleese. "Or do you have any misssgivingsss?"

The brown and green grew indignant. "We have made an agreement!"

"Yesss . . . one which allows both of usss much room for plotting our essscapes." Sssaleese's companion chuckled. "They did not recognize me! They *never* recognize me!"

"For which I am thankful! If they had known it wasss you, my life as well would have been forfeit."

"Bah! You place too much confidence in their ssstrength. They are blusssster!"

Sssaleese did not desire to pursue the conversation further. He had been subjected to his companion's tirades before. What counted to him were results, not words. So far, there had been little of the former. Yet, before he dared depart, he once more had to ask one particular question. "How do you propose to make the young heir yours?"

Once more he received the same cursed answer. "He will be."

There was no reply to that. Sssaleese shrugged. "I mussst return to my people. When shall we next meet?"

"I will contact you."

Being at the beck and call of this one irked the new monarch, who felt that he should be given some respect for the position he had worked so hard to attain. Yet he was not about to push. This was one drake he did not care to cross. "Very well."

Sssaleese turned his mount, intending to depart, when the other said, "We are kindred sssouls, friend. It isss usss against them! Their day is waning. We are the future, a place where the lack of *proper* birth markingsss does not mean one isss not fit to rule. . . ."

Sssaleese twisted around. "Let usss hope so, Duke Toma."

Toma laughed, a harsh sound that echoed in the quiet night, and confidently replied, "*Hope* has nothing to do with it, dear Sssaleese! *I* should know!"

II

"They must be mad!"

"I assure you, Cabe Bedlam, that they are very ssserious about thisss! They may not accept him otherwissse."

Cabe Bedlam stalked to the rail of the balcony and gazed down at the massive sculpted garden below. The Green Dragon, wearing the form of a tall, emerald knight in scale armor, remained where he was, red, inhuman eyes watching the master sorcerer from within the confines of a helm. The dragon crest—part of the drake's *true* visage—seemed also to watch. The drake lord kept a respectful distance at all times. Despite the human's young, unassuming face, Cabe Bedlam was a mage of remarkable power. The broad streak of silver cutting across his otherwise black hair was proof of that. All human sorcerers bore some sort of mark in the hair, either a stripe of silver or a peppering over the entire head.

Cabe turned slowly, obviously considering his response to the Dragon King's words. He looked but midway through his third decade despite being well into his fifth. That was common among those gifted with the power, but in Cabe Bedlam's case it was due to some spell his grandfather Nathan had cast long, long ago. In fact, with his jaw set and his bright eyes narrowed in contemplation, he greatly resembled his grandfather. Even the slightly turned nose was similar. The lord of the Dagora Forest had never told Cabe exactly how well he had known Nathan Bedlam, leader of the Dragon Masters. He did know that grandfather and grandson would have been as proud of one another as they both had been ashamed by Azran. The Bedlam family had ever been a fount of magical ability, whether for good or ill.

"I won't let them enter the Manor grounds," the human announced, a wave of his hand indicating both building and land. The Manor, as it was called by most, had existed for countless centuries. Green was of the opinion that the Seekers, the avian race that had preceded his own as masters of the realm, had built it, yet the bird folk did not normally devise structures so ground-based. Still, the Manor was not only carved marble; one entire portion of it was living tree. That and the many statues commemorating the Seekers were all the verification the Dragon King needed. Cabe had different notions concerning his home, and the two often argued amiably about the matter.

Whatever its origins, it could not be denied that the Manor had seen many, many masters over the centuries. Ghost images of scenes, some accompanied by sound as well, burst into momentary life, so Cabe had told him. Sometimes those images would also come in dreams. Only those with some magical tendencies were generally bothered by such. The drake knew he would not have liked living in the Manor, yet Cabe and his beautiful wife, the scarlet-tressed witch Gwendolyn, enjoyed their life here, as did the children, both the spellcasters' own and the drake young they had raised. Even the humans and drakes who acted as their servants somehow found life in the Manor enjoyable for the most part.

Although he had never said such to Cabe, the Green Dragon was unnerved by the Manor. Being what he was, he did not, of course, show any sign of that anxiety.

"I won't let them enter the Manor grounds," the warlock repeated. "They must take me for a fool." Without the Bedlams' permission, it was impossible to enter their sanctum. The Manor and the garden and woods that surrounded it all were protected by a strong magical barrier invisible to the eye. Only a select few could enter without having to request permission. The spell was ancient, a fading remnant from some previous lord; the witch and warlock had not only revitalized it but improved it as well.

"I thought, perhapsss, somewhere more neutral."

Cabe frowned and crossed his arms, wrinkling the dark blue sorcerer's robe he wore. "I don't care for the thought of surrounding myself or any of my family with Dragon Kings, present company excepted."

The Green Dragon's laugh was accented by a mild hiss. "I have never cared much for that myssself!"

Somewhere a harp began to play. Cabe's brow furrowed. He did not care for harp music, but his daughter Valea did. So, unfortunately, did the heir to the drake throne. Dragging his thoughts back to the present predicament, he tried to devise some sort of compromise. "Somewhere neutral might work, but . . . but I still have trouble with being surrounded by Dragon Kings." His face lit up. "What if the others chose a representative among themselves, someone you and they both trust? I could agree to something like that. We could meet in the Dagora Forest, if that's acceptable to you."

"If that isss your offer, Cabe Bedlam, then I shall relay it to them. I have no qualms about it. They might agree to a repressentative, but the meeting ground may be more questionable. I will try to convince them that thisss is reasonable."

"Who would you choose among them—if I may ask that, my lord?"

"There is no question," the drake lord hissed. "Black is trusted by no one, perhaps not even himself. Red is young; his opinion is still shaky. Storm . . . we fear for his sanity. None of us desire another Ice Dragon."

The name sent shivers through the mage. The Ice Dragon had been one of the eldest, most traditional of the present Dragon Kings. After the fall of the emperor, he had come to the conclusion that only a sheet of death-giving ice blanketing the entire continent would rid the realm of the human situation. Of course, it would also rid the land of the drakes as well, but the fatalistic monarch of the Northern Wastes had considered that worth the victory.

If the Storm Dragon was following the Ice Dragon down the path of madness . . . Cabe knew of at least one other Dragon King who fell into that category already, but at least the Crystal Dragon kept his insanity to himself.

"No one will trust this Sssaleese enough," continued Green, running down the list. "He was not born with the proper birth markings. That leaves but one real choice for any of us. . . ."

"Blue." Cabe leaned against a chair. "He maintains a peace of sorts with Penacles even though the Gryphon doesn't actually rule there any more." The Gryphon, whose appearance resembled that of the winged beast, had ruled Penacles until his need to discover his own past had sent him overseas to the dark empire of the Aramites. For many years he had worked to bring down the wolf raiders, as the Aramites were better known. While he was away, his second, General Toos, had ruled in his place. Now many, including the Gryphon, called the general *king*, but the tall, elderly soldier insisted he was only regent. In the eyes of loyal Toos, the Gryphon would ever be his commander.

"His sssson, Morgisss, is also a good friend of the lionbird."

"Will the other drakes accept his opinion?"

"I think that I will be able to convince them of that."

The harp music had ceased. Cabe flinched when he realized that, but then silently reprimanded himself for thinking the worst of his daughter. She was intelligent, whatever her infatuation with the exotic and unquestionably handsome heir. "Then . . . then I will agree to such terms, my lord. It'll have to take place after the visits to Talak and Penacles, however. I wish there was a way to avoid those meetings, but as you pointed out, if we get acknowledgment from two of the major human kingdoms in the east, it will make the path to the throne that much easier. I hope. Gwendolyn is in Talak now, helping to prepare things." *And with Queen Erini's aid, perhaps keep King Melicard from changing his mind about the whole visit!* "The journeys to Zuú and Gordag-Ai are still planned for immediately after the ascension, so we have no trouble there."

The Dragon King nodded. Within the false helm, the thin, lipless mouth stretched into a toothy smile. "Understand that my fellows truly have no choice; the idea of a new emperor is repellent to some after two decades of complete independence, but they also recognize the need. My race isss faltering; *you* know that. If we are to survive in the world of men, a world the Dragonrealm hasss already become, then we must unite dessspite our differences!"

Cabe smoothed his robe, trying to think of a delicate way to say what needed to be said. He could find no way but the simple truth. "There are many who think that a reunited drake race is the last thing we need. There are some who say that now that humans have the strength, it's time to deal with your kind once and for all."

"I am certain that Melicard of Talak isss one of them."

"One but hardly the worst. The Dragon Kings, again your company excepted, my lord, have rarely endeared themselves to mankind. A new emperor is to some simply a resurrecting of old evils."

For a time there was only silence, as both drake lord and sorcerer considered what they were attempting. Then, the Green Dragon said, "I never expected it to be simple, but I know it must be done. So do you, Cabe Bedlam."

"I—" The warlock's agreement was cut short by the sight of a figure lurking just within the room beyond the balcony. Cabe abandoned his position and stalked over to the entrance. The Dragon King watched but did not question.

"What is it, Grath?"

Out onto the balcony emerged a drake, but one different in so many ways from the forest lord. Whereas the Green Dragon wore the form of a hellish knight of emerald hue, this one more resembled a human. Shorter than Cabe by two or three inches, Grath had sharp, almost elfin features on a human face. His hair was short and dark green, his skin gold with touches of emerald. The young drake smiled nervously, revealing teeth slightly more pointed than that of a human. Like his elder brother, Kyl, Grath caught the eye of many women, both drake and human, but unlike the heir to the drake throne, the younger offspring of the unlamented Dragon Emperor seemed not to notice. Grath spent most of his time in the libraries. If . . . *when* Kyl became emperor, it was intended that Grath serve as advisor and minister.

Cabe had always considered it a blessing that Grath had turned out the way he had. With him to counsel his elder brother, the possibility of Kyl doing something rash was greatly lessened. Not eliminated, but at least lessened.

The drake looked nervously at his guardian, then glanced at the Dragon King. "I . . . heard . . . that my lord Green was here! I just wanted to . . ."

Cabe rescued the faltering Grath. "You want to ask him some more questions, of course." The young drake nodded in silent gratitude. For the most part, Grath shadowed his brother, but given an opportunity to talk with the Green Dragon about drake history, he suddenly became a personality. Cabe could never have believed that a drake could be shy, but that appeared to be the case. "Something strikes me, though. Shouldn't you be taking lessons with Master Traske?"

Grath almost looked guilty. "Master Traske cancelled classes but a few minutes ago, Lord Bedlam. I swear that by the Dragon of the Depths!"

"I hope he's not ill." This was not the first time of late that Benjin Traske had abruptly cancelled a session. Granted the human tutor's duties were now limited since most of his charges were nearly of adult age, but the cancellations were coming with much regularity these days. Traske was a huge man in both girth and height, and almost twice as old as Cabe appeared. The scholar had a touch of magic around him, but evidently not enough to slow the aging process. If he was not well . . .

Grath quickly smothered his guardian's concerns for Benjin Traske's health by replying, "No, sssir. He seemed healthy . . ."

Cabe dismissed the matter, deciding that he would speak with the man when he had the opportunity to do so. "If His Majesty has time when we are finished—"

"I would be pleasssed to ssspeak with you, my lord Grath," interrupted the Dragon King. He treated the other drake with deference, almost as if it were Grath, not Kyl, who was about to ascend the throne. Cabe and Gwen, while they, too, respected the younger drake's royal lineage, tried to treat Grath as a young man, not a symbol. Both mages felt it was important to give the dragon heirs some notion of normal behavior. It had been too often the case in the past that kings had been raised with no concept of themselves as real individuals. They were trained to be a power, a living incarnation. While that was necessary to a point, it also meant that they tended to lack the ability to understand the lives of those they ruled.

Whether humans had ever raised drakes before the Green Dragon's suggestion roughly two decades earlier, the warlock could not say. Cabe had no idea whether he and his wife had been correct in their decision to accept the Dragon King's challenge; they could only hope that some good would come of the years the drake children had spent growing up here.

Grath brightened at the drake lord's response.

"But first I must speak with your brother."

That brought a brief darkness to Grath's visage, but he almost immediately recovered. Bowing, he asked, "Shall I go seek him out for you, Uncle?"

The term was strictly one of respect, as was the Dragon King habit of calling one another "brother." Since the various clans rarely mixed, the Green Dragon was no more Grath's uncle than he was Cabe's. However, in the eyes of the dragon prince, it was obvious that he thought of the visiting monarch as approaching as close to the blood tie as was possible. The lord of the Dagora Forest represented everything that Grath had grown up believing in, yet, because of his secondary position, would never be unless something happened to Kyl.

All knew that the younger drake would sacrifice his own life before he would allow *anything* to happen to his older sibling.

"That would not be proper," returned the Dragon King. "As he will be my lord, it is fitting that I go to him."

Which would only serve to further inflate Kyl's ego, the mage thought. Unfortunately, Kyl had begun to develop his personality long before he had been placed in the care of the Bedlams. While Cabe and Gwen had triumphed in reshaping some edges of that personality, as a whole the heir to the dragon throne was little changed from the day he had first come to them. Still, even the few changes wrought would make Kyl a more trustworthy emperor than his sire had been toward the end.

"Do you know where Kyl is, Grath?"

"Yes, Master Bedlam."

When he saw that the drake would not elaborate, the dark-haired mage grew suspicious. "Where *is* he, Grath?"

"With Aurim."

"Aurim?" It was not the answer Cabe Bedlam had expected. He wondered why Kyl's brother seemed worried. Aurim and Kyl did on occasion spend time together, mostly because there were few others living at the Manor who were of a similar age. Aurim was also likely the only one the emperor-designate considered near his own station. Fortunately, despite the time he spent with Kyl, Cabe's eldest had not fallen into imitating the drake's royal manner. "Very well, show us the way, if you please."

They could probably have transported themselves there by sorcery, but several reasons prevented them from doing so. One was that the Green Dragon considered it a matter of disrespect to materialize suddenly before his future emperor. Another was that Cabe felt such use of the power was frivolous and wasteful; the Manor grounds were not that huge, and it was certainly no emergency.

Last, but by no means least, was the simple fear that Aurim might be attempting to use his own magic. While born with the potential to be even greater than either of his parents, he still had trouble keeping his abilities under control. Spells went wild for no reason that anyone could discover. It was sometimes a wonder that the Manor had survived his childhood. Once in a while, the young warlock would make some progress in maintaining his control, but not often enough that the residents of the area could breathe easy.

As they followed Grath through the halls of the Manor, the Dragon King said, "I apologize again for the sssuddenness of this visssit. I felt that it was important that I relay the request asss soon as wasss possible."

"You need never apologize, Your Majesty! I'm only sorry that my wife will have missed you." The Lady Bedlam had been a protégée of sorts of the Green Dragon, and that bond had remained strong despite the years. Cabe, on the other hand, while he considered the drake a friend, was always aware of the reptilian monarch's inhuman side. Whether that was the result of his own prejudices, he could not say.

Marble corridor gave way on one side to living tree. The Dragon King paused momentarily to admire the skill with which the unknown craftsmen had melded rock and plant together. As they resumed their walk, the drake lord commented, "The Manor will ever be a sssource of amazement to me no matter how much I visssit it!"

"You should rather not, thank you."

"I would rather not, thank you. Still, it is a shame we know so little of itsss hissstory. For many centuries, it lay hidden even from many of my predecessssors. To think that such a marvelousss artifact could exissst so clossse!"

Cabe hid his surprise. He had not been aware that some of the previous Dragon Kings of this region might not have known about the Manor. The warlock did not press for an explanation, but it gave him something to consider when he had the opportunity. One of his pet projects was trying to understand the ancient structure he called home, but so far his results could have all been written on the palm of his hand. The Manor had proved miserly when it came to giving up its secrets.

Eventually they left the confines of the tall structure and entered the immense garden regions behind it. The gardens were the center of life for those living in and around the Manor. Both the human and draconian servants often found reason to spend their free time here. Some even now looked up from their work to respectfully acknowledge the trio. More than a few of the Bedlams' people had made the sculptured lands their personal project, many times contributing to its upkeep even after finishing with their personal chores. There was something soothing about the gardens. The more one gave to the gardens, the more the gardens seemed to give to the person.

It had not always been so. When Cabe had first arrived at the Manor, fleeing the Dragon Kings, three drake females had tried to make a meal out of him. Then, in the garden, he had discovered Gwen, frozen in amber for more than a century thanks to Azran. Freeing her had almost killed *him*, he recalled with a smile.

The landscape was an artistic delight. Topiary animals, both fanciful and real, dotted the gardens. The sculpted animals seemed to need very little pruning. They had, in fact, looked nearly new when the warlock had first arrived. Beyond them, and the most likely place to find Aurim and Kyl, was a huge maze. The shrubbery walls of the maze rose to almost twice the height of a man. The initial part of the maze was simple, and many folk came there simply to rest. As one delved deeper, however, the puzzle became more complex, with turns growing wild and confusing. Having grown up with the maze, most of the children found it entertaining fun. Most of the adults, Cabe included, found it perplexing and confounding. If not for his sorcery, the master warlock would have become hopelessly lost on several occasions.

With Grath to guide them, they maneuvered through the dense bushes. Both Cabe and the Dragon King were silent as they followed. Each time he was forced to enter the deeper labyrinth, Cabe sought to memorize the path, there always being the slight fear that something would cause him to have to find his way out without magic. From the look of concentration he noticed when he happened to glance at his companion, the Dragon King was doing much the same.

Then, without warning, they came upon the children.

Children was an outdated term. Both the draconian heirs and the mage's own offspring were nearly all of adult age. The growth process slowed in drakes as they reached their teens, which made someone of Grath or Kyl's age resemble someone of Aurim's, who was a few years younger. Valea, a bit younger than her brother, was the only one who could even remotely still be thought of as a child, but only when she was angry. Young as she was, she was capable of turning heads and garnering admiring glances.

Which was why the tableau before him almost made the sorcerer want to reach for his daughter and drag her back to the security of the Manor.

Aurim, clad in a robe of deep, rich red, stood in the center of the small open area, hands raised. His name implied gold and, as a child, he had chosen to take that literally, forever causing his hair to shimmer like the valuable metal, save the silver streak marking him as a spellcaster. Even later attempts to change it back had failed. Cabe's son wore an expression of intense concentration on his handsome face, and the reason for that concentration was obviously the colorful display floating before him. Miniature comets of red, yellow, blue, green, and purple swirled about in a mad yet coordinated dance. At the same time, a constantly shifting array of tendrils worked to keep the comets in check. The spell was a test. Aurim controlled each and every facet of it. If he lost control of any one segment, the entire display would collapse. Outwardly, such a task might look minor to some, but only powerful and skilled mages were able to do it for very long. This one was the latest and most difficult in a series that the young spellcaster had begun two or three years back.

Had it been under other circumstances, Cabe would have taken time to admire his son's work. Unfortunately, his eyes could not help but be drawn to Aurim's audience. An audience of two, who were much too close together for his tastes.

He now saw what had bothered Grath. Kyl was with Aurim, true, but his attention was on the red-haired young woman sitting beside him on one of the maze's stone benches. Valea, a near copy of her mother, watched her brother practice. She wore a forest green gown that accented both her face and form. That was not a good sign; Valea generally preferred hunting clothes, more practical for a young woman often on the move, and only wore dresses when forced to do so . . . or when she thought she would be spending time near the drake.

If Grath and Aurim were considered handsome, Kyl was almost beautiful. He moved with a grace his brother lacked and wore richly styled clothing. In every respect he looked like an exotic, elfin lord. His shading was slightly different from Grath's, with a bit more gold in it. As the day approached for his crowning, Kyl seemed more and more to assume the royal colors of the dragon emperor. Next to him, even Aurim's blinding locks paled.

A shared joke here. A brief touch there. Everything he did was for Valea, and Cabe could see that she noticed all of it.

He was trying to control his fatherly temper when Grath suddenly called out, "Kyl! Lord Green has come to see you!"

The announcement shattered Aurim's concentration. A tiny maelstrom arose as the different segments of his spell collided with one another or went fluttering off. At the same time, Valea and Kyl straightened, both trying to pretend nothing had occurred.

As the last of Aurim's spell dissipated, Kyl rose. He was now an inch or two taller than Cabe but so lean that the difference seemed greater. There was a touch of arrogance in his smile. His eyes were burning orbs that snared a person if one was not careful. The elegant courtier outfit the heir wore was real, not a magical shaping like the scale armor of the Dragon Kings. His teeth were slightly edged. In dim light, it was possible some would not have recognized him for what he was. That illusion, however, failed each time Kyl spoke.

"Your majesssssty! How good of you to come! Forgive me for not greeting you sssssooner!"

Whereas both Grath and Ursa, the female of the trio of royal hatchlings, fell prey to sibilance only when excited, Kyl constantly suffered from it. It was a point of great annoyance to the emperor-to-be, who prided himself on perfection.

The Dragon King bowed. "It isss I who must apologize to you, my lord. Had this visit not been sssudden, I would have brought more than my own presence. I hope that you will forgive me."

"You have been my mosssst ardent sssupporter, Lord Green! That will ever be gift enough in itssssself!"

"I hope, then, that I am not disturbing you?"

Kyl casually waved off the drake lord's question. "By no meanssss! We were sssimply enjoying the day, were we not?"

It was questionable as to which of his companions the young drake was speaking to, but Valea was the one who quickly answered. "That's what we were doing, yes."

Cabe wondered if it was his own imagination that made him think that Kyl's mouth curled slightly higher when Valea responded.

"I . . . I solved the latest one, Father," Aurim added. "I told Kyl and Valea—"

"And I insssisssted that we be allowed to sssee." Kyl's tone was all innocence.

"A most impressive display it wasss, too," remarked the Green Dragon. "Now, though, if Your Majesty hasss time, there are details concerning your future which we musss discuss."

"You mean the excursion to Talak?" Kyl's mood changed, becoming tinged with distaste.

"That and more, my emperor."

"If you think the mattersss worthy of our time, then I will trussst you, my Lord Green." Turning from Cabe and the Dragon King, Kyl nodded politely to Aurim. "You will have to show me that trick again when we have more time, Aurim." Focusing his attention on Valea, Kyl reached out and dared to take her hand. As Cabe tensed and his daughter's cheeks reddened, the dragon heir leaned forward and gently kissed the hand. "My lady . . ."

Kyl released her hand after what Cabe considered much too long a hesitation. Turning back to the newcomers, the young drake eyed his human guardian and asked, "Will you be joining usss, Massster Bedlam? Your advice isss alwaysss welcome."

Refusing to be the first to break, Cabe Bedlam continued to match gazes with Kyl. "I would be happy to give what advice I can, Kyl."

"Then shall we talk here or adjourn to the Manor?"

It was Aurim who decided for them. "There's no need for you to leave! Valea and I can return to the Manor. This place is as private as anywhere else, probably more." He looked at his sister. "Mistress Belima said she'd be baking today. Perhaps it might be in order to visit her now?"

Fully recovered now from Kyl's daring kiss, Valea eagerly took up Aurim's suggestion. She turned a dazzling smile on the Dragon King. "If you will forgive us, my lord?"

"By all meansss. I have tasted the human female's meat pies. Had I known her talentsss before I offered your parents her services, she would be baking for me."

Laughing lightly, Cabe's daughter curtsied. Aurim followed suit with a nervous bow. Having grown up around royalty, the Bedlams' offspring were used to excusing themselves when the time came for important discussions. It was not as if Cabe and his wife did not believe in the abilities of the two; Valea and Aurim were usually informed as to the results of such discussions. However, where the coming coronation was concerned, it was easier for all if only those truly necessary were involved. There were times when even the master warlock and his bride did not join in, leaving the conversation strictly between the Green Dragon, Kyl, and Grath, whom Kyl always insisted be present.

The two younger Bedlams departed, Valea in more haste than was necessary. The moment they were out of sight, Kyl returned to the bench and seated himself. He looked up at the drake lord in expectation.

After a slight hesitation, the Dragon King said, "There isss a new matter we must discuss."

"You may proceed."

Cabe was amazed at the calm with which his companion accepted the royal tones of the heir. Nodding, the drake launched into the tale he had told the warlock, describing in detail the gathering of the other reptilian monarchs and their request. Oddly, despite the almost arrogant demand of the drake lords, the manner in which the Green Dragon presented it almost made it sound like lowly subjects requesting a most grand gesture on the part of their sovereign. The warlock surreptitiously glanced at the armored figure beside him. Never had he seen the Dragon King adopt so . . . so *servile* . . . a tone.

The emperor-to-be accepted it without question, although Grath, who had taken up a position behind and a little to one side of his brother, barely hid a frown. Kyl listened in silence to everything, then spent a moment or two thinking the matter over. At last, he glanced up at Grath. Something unspoken passed between them.

Nodding to himself, the dragon heir looked up at the mage and forest lord and said, "A meeting with the othersss isss not only acceptable but necesssary, asss you yoursssself pointed out, my lord." Once again, his unsettling eyes focused on Cabe. "However, Massster Bedlam makesss a wonderful sssuggestion! I like the idea of meeting with only one, the Lord Blue, assss you proposssed. It will show them that I am willing to hear them, yet will *not* bow to their demandssss!"

"I am certain that they did not mean it ssso, my liege. You mussst understand that they are only concerned for you."

Kyl's gaze leapt to the Dragon King. "I understand *their* concernsssss very well." He nodded to himself again.

The Green Dragon did not pursue the matter. Kyl's nod was a signal both Cabe and the drake lord had come to recognize. It would be futile to continue, for the young emperor-to-be would pay no more attention from here on. He had come to his own conclusions, whatever they might be, and that, in his mind, was all that mattered.

"Have you chosssen a time for thisss audience with Lord Blue?"

"After the visits to Talak and Penacles," Cabe informed his royal charge. "Too many preparations have already been made; it would not look good if we were to cancel either one this late."

A dangerous gleam appeared in Kyl's eyes, but the drake merely nodded. "You are correct, Massster Bedlam . . . asss usual. Speaking of Talak, what thought hasss been given to our entrance?"

This had been a touchy matter where both Melicard and Kyl had been concerned. The king of Talak had expected Kyl to arrive at the southern gate of the city, accompanied by an entourage, in the fashion of most human monarchs. However, the dragon heir, fully aware that he had sorcery at his command, wanted to materialize in regal but dramatic manner in the very center of Melicard's throne room. *That* had not gone over well with the lord of the mountain kingdom. Talak had lived under the shadow of the Dragon Emperor for centuries, and now that it was free and a power in its own right, the present monarch had no intention of appearing subservient to *any* drake, especially one planning to ascend to the role of emperor. Part of the task the Lady Bedlam performed even now was to find some middle ground. Cabe did not envy his wife.

"That is still being discussed," the warlock commented in very neutral tones.

"If I may make a suggestion?" The lord of Dagora waited for acknowledgment from Kyl before continuing. "It might be good to be magnanimousss for your first two visits. I shall prepare a caravan consisting of both humans and drakesss to accompany you, a large enough caravan to indicate your great status but small enough to keep the folk of Talak from running in fear." The Green Dragon paused long enough to share a smile with Kyl.

"This way, you will enter as he desires, but you will enter in glory! Thisss is not a sssimple matter; I wish I had a better suggestion, my lord, but I do not. Remember this, though. Talak will be opening itsss gates to *you* no matter how you arrive. It will be the first time they have done ssso *willingly*, and that in itself is a coup for you!"

Perhaps it was the *way* the Dragon King said it, as opposed to his actual words, for Cabe was both pleased and surprised to see Kyl accept the suggestion.

"Very well. Assss long assss it isss underssstood who it is who will be *emperor*."

Lord Green bowed. "You may rest assured on that matter."

Kyl shook his head and smiled, revealing his sharp teeth. "What would I do without the two of you? My Lord Green. Massster Bedlam. You two have been the father I lossst!"

Cabe forced back a grimace, recalling his part in the downfall of the former emperor.

Evidently he did not completely succeed, for Kyl glanced at him. "You did what you had to do and I have come to underssstand that, Massster Bedlam! The battle wasss forced upon you, after all! I bear you no animosssity. I am not my father; I am *Kyl*."

Not trusting himself to find the correct words, Cabe nodded what he hoped would appear a thankful acknowledgement. He had heard such remarks from Kyl over the years and yet still could not bring himself to believe them. There was always that hint of something in the dragon heir's tone . . .

. . . or maybe it was just his own distrust.

Grath, who had remained a silent shadow for most of the time, leaned over and whispered something to his brother. Kyl's piercing eyes widened, then narrowed. His lips curled slightly, never a good sign as far as Cabe was concerned. That smile usually preceded some sort of mischief.

"Thank you, Grath, for reminding me." The emperor-to-be returned his attention to his two visitors. "A notion occurred to me but a short time ago, a notion I meant to dissscussss with you when next the sssubject of thessse royal visssitsss arossse."

"What might that be, Your Majesty?" the Green Dragon asked, a slight edge to his voice. No one but the warlock seemed to notice it, though.

"We would like the eternal, the demon sssteed, to join usss for thisss journey."

"Y—" The Dragon King could go no farther. Both Cabe and he stared at the dragon heir as if all sense had left him.

Kyl leaned back. "Explain, Grath."

Nervous, the other young drake said, "My brother . . . my brother feels that the presence of Darkhorsssse is esssential. It deals with many situations. First and foremost is that both Queen Erini of Talak and Toos the regent of Penaclesss are familiar with the shadow steed. Not only familiar, but on good terms with him. His appearance at the meetings with Melicard and Toos should assuage any misgivings they might have over the arrival of so many drakes. No one caresss to cross the eternal's path."

"Really, Your Majesssty—"

"We are not finished yet, my Lord Green," Kyl said quietly.

Grath hissed in anxiety as he resumed. "There is also one personal but highly important reassson for the presence of Darkhorse. My brother feelsss that, in this time of forging a new peace in the Dragonrealm, peace must also be made with the eternal himself."

"It isss time for *all* animosssitiesss to die," Kyl interjected. "Even *I* mussst admit to sssome failure when it comes to the great ebony ssstallion! Now, I would offer a peace between usss! Now, I would like to be able to call Darkhorsssse *friend*!"

"Your Majesssty is aware, I hope, that King Melicard bears little love for the shadow steed. It isss his bride, the queen, who isss so fond of Darkhorse."

"All the better, then, Lord Green." Kyl's long, tapering fingers formed a steeple. "It will give the human an opportunity to make hisss own peace with the black one! Talak would certainly benefit and Melicard would earn the perssssonal gratitude of hisss lovely queen, who I know hasss alwaysss regretted the tension between her husband and her loyal friend!"

The Dragon King looked at Cabe, sending the warlock a silent appeal for help in this matter. Cabe was at a loss, though. He could see some reason behind the suggestion. Darkhorse had ever been a most deadly enemy of the drake race. At present, an uneasy truce existed, in great part due to Darkhorse's respect for the warlock's own position as guardian of the late Dragon Emperor's young. Only when attacked did Darkhorse now unleash his might upon the drakes.

Kyl had never before suggested such an overture, making Cabe suspect that perhaps Grath was responsible. Of course, the younger drake had always gotten along much better with Dark-horse than the emperor-to-be had.

"Darkhorse might not desire to come," he finally pointed out. Beside him, Green exhaled slightly. Evidently the Dragon King had decided that things were complex enough without throwing the shadow steed into the situation. Darkhorse was a matter that could wait as far as he was concerned.

Kyl did not think so. "If anyone can persssuade him, it isss *you*, Massster Bedlam! Give him my reasssons for requesssting thisss. Tell him that I know that we have not dealt well with one another before thisss and that I think it isss very much time that we made the effort."

Again there was the nod of the head, the sign that Kyl would not be swayed in this matter. He knew also that he could trust Cabe to make the request of Darkhorse. The warlock sometimes wished that the half elf who had raised him had not been so brutally honest. Cabe *would* make the request, no matter how uncertain he was as to the wisdom of it.

He could only hope that Darkhorse laughed at it. Adding the eternal to the meeting between the two monarchs threatened to replace the carefully organized affair with a haphazard, tense confrontation.

Was *that* what Kyl wanted?

"I'll see what I can do for you, Kyl. Darkhorse can be anywhere; you know that as well as I do. It may prove impossible to locate him in time, much less pass on your request to him."

"I have faith in you, Massster Bedlam." The drake rose, each movement graceful and swift, like a cat. "My Lord Green, if there isss nothing elssse requiring my immediate attention, it isss time for my riding lessssson. Masssters Ssarekai and Ironshoe have been teaching me some of the more sssubtle differencesss between handling a drake and riding a horssse." He scratched his chin. "I have been thinking of riding one of the latter when I enter Talak. Much more graceful and regal than a riding drake, albeit not nearly ssso deadly looking. I have not made up my mind which would be preferable."

The master of the Dagora Forest shook his helmed head. "No, my liege. I have said what I came to sssay. I thank you for your time and trouble."

"Not at all." To his brother, Kyl added, "Grath, I will need to sssee you later."

Both drakes bowed to their future emperor. Cabe settled for a respectful appearance. He could not bring himself to bow, no matter how agitated he sensed the Green Dragon had become upon noticing the human's action. The dragon heir did not even seem to notice. He simply turned away and vanished into the labyrinth.

After a pause, the Dragon King straightened. He looked down at the warlock. "You should bow when he leaves, friend Cabe." When his companion would not answer him, the dragon turned toward Grath. "Well, my prince. Do you still desssire to speak with me? I have a little time to spare before I must depart for my kingdom."

"If I would not be disturbing you, Lord Green."

"Of courssse not."

Cabe, not desiring any animosity to remain between himself and the one Dragon King he trusted, suggested, "My children made mention of Mistress Belima before, my lord. I can assure you that she's found time to make some of the meat pies you find so fascinating. That may be because they're also Grath's favorites, I believe." A look from the young drake indicated complete agreement. "Perhaps you would care for a light meal. I'm certain that Grath would be interested."

That lightened the mood. They all knew of the young drake's near obsession with the pies. It was considered something of a miracle that Grath remained so fit.

The Green Dragon willingly took the peace offering. "That would be quite sssatisssfactory. Perhaps I can alssso use the opportunity to convince the woman to return to my servicesss."

"You'll face the full population of the Manor if you try that, including some very adamant youngsters!"

"Then, I shall sssimply have to visit more often."

"Shall I lead us back now, Master Bedlam?" At mention of the meal, Grath had become animated again. Yet again, Cabe marveled at the transformation the younger drake went through each time he and his brother separated. It was as if there were two Graths.

He almost wished there *were*. If Kyl were only more like Grath, Cabe knew that he would feel better about the upcoming visits. Yet, it was more likely the drakes would accept someone like Kyl. Grath might just be too human for them. In truth, the warlock knew that despite his misgivings concerning the dragon heir, Kyl was more likely to be able to control the Dragon Kings than his younger sibling.

Now if only someone could control Kyl, the warlock thought, then instantly regretted even considering the notion. That was one of the dangers both he and the Green Dragon feared. Once upon the throne, *would* Kyl prove to be the emperor that was needed, or would he fall victim to the twisted advice of one or more of the deadlier Dragon Kings?

Cabe belatedly realized Grath was still waiting for an answer to *his* question. The blue-robed sorcerer waved a hand at his charge, forced on a smile, and said, "Lead on! I'm beginning to feel a bit hungry myself!"

"This way, then, Lord Green. Master Bedlam."

As they followed the drake, Cabe's eyes strayed to the empty bench. Gone instantly were considerations concerning dangers to the ascension; instead, the warlock recalled two young folk sitting much too close to one another. The image reminded him that he had a personal reason for seeing Kyl safely through the visitations and the coronation. Kyl in his role as Gold, Dragon Emperor, would be far away, so far, in fact, that he might as well be on one of the moons. Cabe knew that what he wanted was selfish and likely prejudiced, but it was more than what Kyl was that made the master sorcerer desire him far from Valea. It was also *who* the dragon heir was, meaning the mind behind the exotic countenance. Perhaps it was simply the fear of a concerned parent, but he did not trust whatever intentions the handsome drake might have for his daughter. Telling Valea that, however, would avail him naught. She was just old enough to understand and just young enough not to listen. There *were* tales, some of them with much credence to back them up, of drakes and humans marrying and raising young. It *was* possible, according to what Cabe knew. Possible but unthinkable.

Maybe I'm just imagining things. Maybe my own fears are making me see something that isn't there. Yet, Gwendolyn, too, had expressed such worries. Could they *both* be imagining it?

This was not the time for personal matters, he told himself. As dear as his family was to him, the fate of the entire realm waited on the outcome of this venture with Kyl and the throne. Whatever was or was not happening between his daughter and the drake *had* to be secondary.

Cabe hoped he would be able to remember that in the weeks to come.

III

"Well, it took some pressure from both Erini and his daughter, but Melicard has finally agreed to the suggestions made by Kyl."

Cabe, seated, nodded absently as his wife talked. Normally, Lady Bedlam garnered his full attention, if only because he adored her so. Gwendolyn Bedlam was to him a forest goddess, a fire-tressed creature of the wild. She stood across from him now, a vision in green, her hair with its silver streak rippling nearly to her waist. The emerald riding outfit she wore perfectly accented a stunning figure. Her glittering eyes matched the color of her clothes.

Seeing that she was being all but ignored, the statuesque enchantress walked gracefully toward her husband, finally stationing herself directly before the warlock in an attempt to break him free from whatever spell held his mind.

Cabe looked up. "What is it?"

"Have you tired of me after all these years?"

His brow furrowed.

She knelt by his chair, one hand touching him softly on the arm. "You're starting to find other things that interest you more than I do."

He took hold of her hand and squeezed it. "Don't be silly. Nothing means more to me than you and the children." Cabe took the hand and kissed it. "Young or old, beautiful or not, you know I'll always love you." A smile briefly touched his face. "I just hope that you'll always feel the same way."

"You shouldn't have to ask." Her own smile faded a little as she recalled what they had been discussing. "You heard what I said?"

"Melicard's agreed. It took some doing?"

"For most of it, no. He actually found the suggestion concerning Kyl's entrance to be reasonable. Where that was concerned, it was simply a matter of discussing it with his advisors. *That's*

30

what took three days . . . that, and the more delicate problem of Darkhorse."

"Darkhorse?"

She nodded. The sunlight that touched her face accented what Cabe considered perfectly sculpted features, a sharp contrast to his own plain face. He was thankful that both children had taken after her. Valea especially would resemble her mother.

"Melicard has grown more reasonable in the past few years where Erini's relationship with Darkhorse is concerned, but he doesn't like the notion of the eternal being a part of a state affair. Tensions will be high enough without his unnerving presence, so the king said more times than I care to count."

"It's understandable." Cabe tried to picture Darkhorse among the splendidly dressed courtiers. Both humans and drakes feared the eternal's power. To most, Darkhorse was part legend, a thing of shadows. It was one reason why the warlock had not been pleased by Kyl's suggestion. Darkhorse could cause the audience between the two monarchs to collapse simply by *being* there. "So has he agreed to the presence of Darkhorse or not?"

"He did. Finally. Erini and Lynnette had much to do with that. It's hard for Melicard to refuse them anything."

The warlock chuckled. "I think I understand *that*!"

She rose enough to give him a kiss, then stood. "You'd *better* understand that!"

He returned her playful smile, but other thoughts turned his expression sober. "I'm glad that's settled. Now comes the interesting part."

"You've still heard nothing?"

Cabe rose. He looked up at the ceiling, then back at his wife. "Nothing. It's been three days since I sent out a magical summons to him. Three days and still he hasn't come."

"How very odd." She put a hand to her chin. "Darkhorse is usually very prompt."

"Unless he's occupied with something. . . ."

Her expression said it all. "*Shade?*"

"I'd like to think not. I thought him over that obsession, but . . . I don't know."

Shade had been a warlock, possibly in his own way the most powerful that had ever lived. No one knew exactly how old the cloaked and hooded figure had been, but Cabe was certain that Shade could trace his origins back to the Vraad, the ancestral race of men. Shade, he was certain, had *been* Vraad.

The spell that had made the blur-faced sorcerer nigh immortal had also brought him to the edge of madness. Shade had been cursed to ever be reborn the opposite of what he had been in his previous life. Cabe had first known him as friend, but after the warlock's death during battle, Shade had returned as the horrific Madrac, one of the many splinter personalities that formed with each new incarnation. It had taken the full might of Darkhorse, who knew the ancient warlock best, to defeat Madrac.

Shade had returned again much later, but this time entirely confused, his personalities shifting back and forth without warning. Darkhorse, ever both friend and foe, had taken it upon himself to end the travesty, if only for the warlock's own sake.

Queen Erini, who had become for a time Shade's pawn, had been there at the end. Shade and Darkhorse had made their peace, and the warlock had given up his own life to prevent a disaster that he himself had been in great part responsible for creating. There and then, it should have been ended.

Darkhorse, however, had not been able to accept such a death. Shade had meant more to him than any of his mortal companions could have known. The gray mage was the only one who, in his own way, could understand the shadow steed, could comprehend the emptiness the leviathan kept buried within. There was no one else in the Dragonrealm like the black stallion, no one who could understand his longings, his fears. Immortal himself, save if killed, it was only natural that he be drawn to Shade.

Because of that, the shadow steed had spent the next several years utilizing much of his time searching for any trace of the vanished warlock. Park of Darkhorse wanted to make certain that Shade was dead, for if he was not, then the Dragonrealm risked great danger. Yet another part of the ebony stallion—and this only a handful knew—hoped that the warlock was alive, that the one creature who understood the loneliness he suffered was still there for him.

The obsession had almost cost Cabe his life. Ashamed, Darkhorse had all but abandoned his futile search . . . yet, there were times when the shadow steed would vanish to places unknown for long periods of time. No one was certain what Darkhorse did during these episodes, but the Bedlams feared that the obsession was growing again.

"What happens if we can't find him? The audience in Talak is drawing very near. Now that it's settled that Darkhorse is permitted there, it would seem a bit foolish if he was not at least *asked*."

The warlock sighed. "Kyl and Melicard will simply have to be annoyed. No one rules Darkhorse. I told Kyl I would do what I could, but I didn't promise a miracle. Even if I find Darkhorse, he might choose not to come." He shook his head. "I don't know why Kyl felt it so necessary that he be there. I don't know why Kyl does *anything* he does. . . ."

His wife came and put her arms around him. They held each other close.

"This isn't just about Darkhorse," she whispered. "This is about the same thing we always talk of."

"We tried to raise him as best we could, Gwen. Look at Grath. Look at our own children. I'm fairly confident about them, although Aurim's recklessness with magic is probably going to be the end of me soon. What *happened* to Kyl?"

"He was older, Cabe. He had already begun developing his own personality. We did what we could. Considering who he is, we've not done too badly."

"Did we? Of late, I've noticed myself thinking thoughts I'd have found reprehensible in others."

"Kyl is in great part responsible for that." The sorceress released him and stepped back. "Believe that. There are drakes here who would admit to it. As a ruler, Kyl may do great things, but as a person, his attitude lacks a certain responsibility."

They both knew that they were in part thinking of their own daughter, but neither desired to say any more on that subject for now. The two were certain . . . almost . . . that Valea was simply infatuated with Kyl's exotic appearance. She was too intelligent to think that there could be anything between them . . . they hoped.

Cabe made a cutting motion with his hand. "None of this solves the present problem. I'm going to see if I can find Darkhorse myself. The more I think about it, even if he doesn't appear in Talak, I want him to know what's going on. If anyone is planning to disrupt the event or, worse, strike out at the emperor-to-be, it wouldn't hurt to have Darkhorse nearby."

She cocked her head to one side and smiled a bit. "You know, I think this is all a *ploy*! I think you just planned this sudden little excursion so that you can escape the preparations for the journey!"

They both laughed at her joke, all the while aware that it was simply an attempt to lighten Cabe's ever-darkening mood. "Now why would I want to escape arranging and rearranging Kyl's caravan? I couldn't think of anything more entertaining!"

"Then I will go in your place, husband dear!"

"Not likely!" He took her once more into his arms. "If you leave it to me to organize this, we will be ready to depart by some time late next *year!*"

"Too true. . . ." The sorceress grew quiet, then said, "If you must go searching, you can avoid the region around Talak. I made mention to Erini that she should let us know if Darkhorse appears there."

"Then that's one place less. I have some other notions of where he might have run off to. I'm certain there's nothing to worry about." He kissed her. "This won't take long. If Darkhorse is at none of the places I have in mind, I'll leave him a sign that he won't fail to recognize. Then it will simply have to be up to him as to whether he answers or not."

"All this running around sometimes seems so futile, doesn't it? I shall be glad when Kyl is crowned so that we can at last breathe again."

Cabe forced his smile to remain where it was. "That's *all* I've ever asked."

He kissed his wife once more . . . then was gone.

As the warlock vanished, Lady Bedlam heard a knock on the door. She turned toward it and bid the newcomer to enter.

It was Benjin Traske. The huge, bearded scholar was clad in the colors and garments of his special calling—a gray, cowled cloak with gold trim on the collar and ebony robes beneath. The cowl was presently pushed back, revealing gray hair with a very slight peppering of silver. Like Cabe, Gwen sometimes thought that the tutor resembled more a condemning judge than the scholar he was. She noted also that he still wore a blade on his belt, despite such armament going against his calling. Traske had lost his family in the fall of the city of Mito Pica some years back and had always regretted that he had not had even a knife with which to protect them.

Something about his expression disturbed her. It was nothing that she could put her finger on. He seemed almost pensive, but that was not quite it.

"My pardon, lady. I thought Master Bedlam also here."

"He has left."

"I see." For a breath or two, it seemed the massive figure did not know what to say.

"I *am* Lady Bedlam, scholar. You can trust me with whatever it is you wished to speak to my husband about."

His expression became somewhat rueful. "My apologies. I did not mean to infer such . . ."

"What is it you want, Scholar Traske?"

He took a deep breath. "I realize that you have much on your mind and that I would only be further adding to your troubles, but I wish to speak to you about the excursion to Talak. . . ."

This is getting to be a habit!

The wind howled around him. Everything was white, but it was the whiteness of death, the eternal winter. Snow and ice were everywhere. A few misshapen hills, possibly only large snowbanks, dotted the otherwise flat landscape. In the distance, the warlock could see some taller mounds, but he knew it would be a waste of time to go and investigate them. If Darkhorse was not here at the very spot on which Cabe now stood, then he was not in any part of the Northern Wastes.

Snow fluttered around the silent spellcaster but did not alight on him. The same spell that shielded him from the cold also shielded him from the other gifts the inhospitable wasteland offered. Snow that sought perch on him simply faded away.

He had come here because this, of all the places that the eternal frequented, was the most likely spot that Darkhorse would have chosen to return to had his obsession taken root once again. Here, in the emptiness of the Wastes, Shade had perished . . . or so Queen Erini said. She had witnessed it all. Years later, during a quest much like the one he was on now, Cabe had been brought here by the novice sorceress, who had explained to him the relevance of this chilling place. Although he was never certain exactly why he had done so, Cabe Bedlam had imprinted the location on his mind. Perhaps at the time it had simply been because Shade had been a friend to him as well and all he had wanted to do was remember.

Now, however, it was time to move on. Darkhorse was obviously not here, and the magical signature his passing always left behind was very old, perhaps more than a month. The ebony stallion had not been to the Wastes for some time.

Where next? There were any number of locations that Darkhorse, a wanderer, frequented to some extent, but only a few he returned to again and again. Talak was one of the latter, but Gwen had seen to that situation. The Northern Wastes had been . . . a waste. Cabe had no intention of searching too many locations. First of all, chasing after Darkhorse was like chasing after a phantasm. The eternal could be anywhere he chose to be at almost any time. Darkhorse also did not tire as rapidly as a human did. Trying to chase down Darkhorse was pure folly. It was also possible that Darkhorse might journey to the Manor even while Cabe searched the countryside for his old companion. That had happened to the warlock more than once during the first few years of their friendship. He had strived hard ever since the last time to make certain that it never happened again.

There were six locations he thought worthy of searching. After that, the warlock intended to return to his home. If Darkhorse had still not answered his summons by the next day, Cabe would try a few more. If even *that* search failed . . . he was not certain what he would do then. Cabe only knew that he never abandoned a friend.

With ease, the blue-robed sorcerer transported himself to the next destination on his mental list. His new location gave him a panoramic view of a bowl-shaped valley in the distance, for Cabe presently stood atop a tall jagged hill. Cabe knew the valley, having been to it with Darkhorse in the past. The city of Zuu, from where the horsemen ruled the land of the same name, lay near the center. In the daytime, the city was impossible to see, but night would reveal a sea of light, for Zuu never slept.

The shadow steed was not here, but the traces Cabe sensed were much more recent than those at the previous site. It had been only days since Darkhorse had passed through here; that much Cabe could ascertain. He tried to trace the path the eternal had taken, but was able to determine only that it went east, which from Zuu's southwesterly location, meant most of the Dragonrealm. Still, it *was* something to go on. Two of his remaining choices were directly east. He would try them first, then head north where two of the others were. After that . . .

Again, it took only the simplest of thoughts to send him to his next destination. There had been a time when Cabe would have laughed if someone had told him he would find sorcery so comfortable a piece of his life. The young boy who had worked serving food and drink at inns would have been horrified even to think of wielding such might.

He found himself in a wooded region in the southern stretches of the central Dagora Forest. In truth, he was not at all that far from the Manor; a two-day journey by horse would see him at the boundaries of his tiny domain. However, Darkhorse did not visit this site as often as he did the first two, hence Cabe's decision to leave this one until now.

Again there was no visible sign of the shadow steed, but it was clear to the warlock that his friend had been here not too long ago. Cabe judged it to be no more than four days since Darkhorse's departure. Once again, though, it was impossible to judge exactly where the eternal had journeyed next. Darkhorse traveled either by magic or by running, and either method allowed him to move across the Dragonrealm in little time. Teleporting, however, was much harder to trace. It was one skill where Cabe was and probably always would be deficient.

He was ready to depart for the next location on his list when a peculiar sensation touched the edge of his mind. There had been magic cast here, but of a haunting sort. It reminded him of something old, yet something he should have been familiar with. . . .

It was gone. So slight had it been that Cabe was almost willing to believe that he had imagined it. Darkhorse followed a different magic—and, in fact, *was* that magic—but this was not some random trace left by the eternal. Frowning, the master warlock sought it again, but whatever he had felt was no more. Realizing how futile it would be to hunt for something that might have been the product of his own imagination, Cabe returned to the business at hand. He was tempted to depart for the Manor, but decided that it would not take that long to inspect the remaining places. It was possible that he might even find the shadow steed. Each jump seemed to put him closer.

With that thought to encourage him, he leapt to the next site.

A chill ran through him as he appeared among grass-covered ruins. It had been years since Cabe had come to this place, and over those years he had thought he had recovered from the destruction. Now, though, the sight of the broken, weather-worn rubble brought it all crashing back.

The ghosts of Mito Pica, the ghosts of his memory and conscience, danced around him.

He had been raised here. Under a spell cast by his grandfather, Cabe had remained a child for a century, maybe more. The warlock could not recall his early life, and so over the years he had come to wonder if Nathan had actually put him to sleep for most of that time. Still, whatever its elements, it had been a desperate spell, one that had been meant to save a dying baby. Its success had meant Nathan Bedlam's own death, for he had weakened himself enough so that when he challenged the Dragon King Purple, he had not had the strength to defeat the drake lord. In the end, both sorcerer and Dragon King had perished.

All thought of Darkhorse faded for a time as Cabe Bedlam drank in the macabre vision before him. Some parts of the wall that had surrounded Mito Pica still stood whole, as did several buildings. The city *could* have been rebuilt, but for some reason no one had suggested it. Yet, Cabe did not doubt for a moment that there were people living among the ruins. Scavengers for the most part, with some bandits thrown in for good measure. Possibly even a few half-mad survivors of the destruction itself. They would be old by now and probably very few in number.

After the Dragon Emperor's death, Melicard of Talak had sent his men to sweep through Mito Pica and bring any refugees they found back to the safety of his kingdom. There had actually been three or four such sweeps, so Cabe was fairly certain that all those who had desired aid had received it. Anyone living in the ghost kingdom now *wanted* to be there.

"Hadeen . . ." he whispered. Mito Pica had died because of him, and with it had perished the half-elf who had been his adoptive father. It was the other reason why Cabe had always found reasons to stay away from the ruined city. Hadeen had dedicated his life to caring for the grandson of Nathan Bedlam and his reward had been death at the claws of . . . of . . .

Toma . . .

He shivered. The voice had sounded almost like Hadeen's, yet it could not have been.

Toma . . . Cabe . . . Toma teaches . . .

Gasping, the wary spellcaster turned toward the wooded lands nearest to him. In that direction had been the home that Hadeen had built for the two of them. Almost it seemed . . . but that was *impossible.*

Toma . . . masks upon masks . . .

My son . . .

"Hadeen?" He could almost swear that the woods were *talking* to him.

Then the strong pull of another power snared his attention. The warlock cried out as he felt the force in the woods recede. He took a step toward the trees, but the second force, terribly familiar, beckoned to him, enticed him. Cabe stood transfixed, eyes darting from the trees to the darkness of Mito Pica, from where the new force seemed to radiate.

"*Hadeen*," he whispered. A rare tear ran down his cheek. There was no reply, not even a gentle acknowledgment. Whatever had called to him from the woods had grown quiet again. It was said that when elves died, their spirits became one with their surroundings, especially trees. Did that also apply to half-elves?

The shivering warlock was not allowed time to pursue the matter, for once more he was pulled toward the ghost-ridden ruins of the city. With a start, Cabe recognized what now called to him. It was not only the same as the trace he had sensed at his last destination, but also identical to something far in his past. Only rarely had the sorcerer encountered such magic, for it was a thing *not* of this world, a thing that had briefly flourished long, long ago, when godlike mages had journeyed from their dying world to this one in an attempt to escape a doom they themselves had caused.

There was Vraad sorcery here, but Vraad sorcery with a peculiar taste to it. Cabe shook his head, unwilling to believe this. First Hadeen and now yet another terrible spirit from his past. He tried to reject the notion. The touch was unmistakable, however. Only one spellcaster had wielded such strange magic.

Shade.

Cabe followed the siren trail. He could do nothing else. It was almost a compulsion, but one that he knew was his own doing. He *had* to know. Hadeen, if it had *been* Hadeen, was lost to him again, but the trail he now followed was as strong as ever.

If it *was* the blur-faced warlock, somehow alive, would he be friend or foe? Did another sinister Madrac await Cabe, or would there instead be someone like the kindly but enigmatic Simon? Toward the end, the original personality of Shade had surfaced, or so Darkhorse had said. Would it be that one? What was *that* Shade like? He *had* been Vraad. . . .

At the battered wall, Cabe paused. Part of him screamed that he should turn around, flee. Shade was more powerful than he. Yet, despite that plea, the warlock finally stepped through the broken wall. He had no choice. It would forever haunt him if he failed to discover the truth.

The first sight that met his eyes was disappointing. Weeds and more rubble. Dragon-torched skeletons of once tall buildings. Two decades of weather that had left some structures virtually unrecognizable. A skull, marking either the last resting place of one of the citizenry or a traveler who had made the mistake of thinking the ruins a safe place to rest.

There was no Shade.

The sensation had not faded. Cabe was close. He eyed the various ruined buildings, seeking the direction from which the Vraad sorcery emanated. His eyes alighted on what looked to have been an inn or tavern. He could not help smiling despite the seriousness of the situation. The first time Cabe had encountered the shadowy warlock had been where the young Bedlam had been serving ales. Shade had sat undetected at one of the far tables, watching the grandson of Nathan. He had spoken in a rather enigmatic fashion about Cabe's life, then had vanished before the serving boy could ask for clarification.

The path to the ruined tavern was filled with shattered stone and rotting wood, but Cabe chose to dare it rather than risk materializing inside. He kept his magical senses alert, but it was difficult to notice anything else in the presence of so strong a Vraadish force. The warlock could almost picture Shade sitting among the ghosts of Mito Pica, quietly sipping an ale he had summoned from the shadows.

He was nearly at the cracked and open doorway when the earth beneath his feet burst upward.

The speed with which the long black tentacles moved left him too stunned to act. They rose on all sides of him, never touching the spellcaster but instead coming together a foot or two above his head. As they touched, a green shimmer swept over the cage within which Cabe suddenly found himself trapped. The spell was one of the swiftest the baffled warlock had ever been unfortunate enough to experience. Freedom had become imprisonment in less time than it took to blink the proverbial eye.

Recovering, the warlock immediately probed his cell. What he discovered both unnerved and confused him. Other than capturing him, the magical prison meant Cabe no harm. It was simply designed to hold him where he was. He had expected some sort of death trap, but such was not the case.

As relieved as he was by the lack of any imminent threat, Cabe did not relax his efforts. Harmless the cage might be, but in the fulfilling of its basic function it excelled. Cabe searched every strand of the spell and could find no flaw. This was a cage designed to hold a spellcaster of astonishing power. The one who had designed it had worked long and hard. As he studied it again, Cabe had the sinking feeling that escape would be anything but simple. In fact, he had some doubts as to whether he could escape at all.

The warlock had to try, of course. He had no intention of idly passing the time while he waited the coming of the mage who had set the trap.

The trap's design still perplexed him. Why use traces of Vraadish magic as a lure? Few knew of the Vraad, much less their tainted power. For that matter, the trace had been a specific one, specifically that of Shade. Yet, Cabe doubted that Shade had had anything to do with this. The warlock was dead . . . as far as he knew. Somebody had simply decided to use the memory of him to bait the snare.

Which strongly hinted that the trap had been set for a particular being. . . .

Even as he contemplated that, the tenacious warlock was already at work seeking a way of escape. The tentacles themselves were not likely to break, but the place where they joined together above him might be a weak link. With intense concentration, Cabe sent a tendril of power up to the point of convergence. The tendril was thin, barely a whisper, but behind it he built up an incredible reservoir of energy. All Cabe had to do was find a slight gap in the point of connection, and then he would be able to funnel the stored power through. That, the warlock was fairly certain, would give him the opening he needed to destroy his cell.

The fault in his plan proved to be the simple fact that no such gap existed. Try as he might, Cabe could not locate a break. The tendrils had bonded together so perfectly that it was almost possible to believe that the cage had been created whole. Frustrated, the imprisoned mage continued to poke futilely about the top with his sorcery, trying to create his own gap. But even after he had exhausted every bit of sorcerous energy he had gathered for his escape, the spell controlling the magical prison remained unchallenged and unweakened.

This was the work of someone who had planned long and hard for this time. Yet how could they know that he would come here? Why such an elaborate ploy for him?

"No . . . *not* me . . ." Cabe muttered. The cold chill of reality danced down his spine. They could not have known so quickly where *he* would be, but whoever had devised this cunning trap *might* have been familiar with the ways of Darkhorse. Cabe doubted that he and Gwen were the only ones who knew that the shadow steed haunted this miserable place. Someone else must have noticed him.

There were many, not all of them drakes, who wanted the eternal for one reason or another. Most, though, would have been satisfied with destroying him . . . if such was within their power. Yet, this spell did nothing but keep one prisoner. Someone wanted Darkhorse, but for a purpose. In that, Cabe considered himself fortunate. A death trap created with the shadow steed in mind would have stood a better than average chance of killing the warlock. *He* was only human, whereas Darkhorse was . . . *Darkhorse*.

Cabe tried physical action, first pushing against the side of his prison, then attempting to tear through it. Success still mocked him. After several minutes of useless maneuvering, the weary mage finally sat down and stared at his surroundings. It appeared the creator of the sinister spell had planned for all contingencies.

Momentarily putting aside his escape plans, Cabe wondered where his captors were. Considering their effort, he would have expected them to appear the moment the trap had been sprung. Yet, as the minutes passed, no one came to claim him. It occurred to him that perhaps this might be an old spell left over from the destruction of the city, but the use of the false trail, the scent of Shade's sorcery, seemed to indicate otherwise. No one would have bothered setting such an elaborate trap in the midst of Mito Pica's downfall. Besides, Darkhorse had been to the ruins too many times for the shadow steed not to have noticed this spell before. At the very least, the eternal would have seen to it that the trap was harmlessly sprung rather than leave it for some unsuspecting fool . . . like Cabe Bedlam.

As he grimaced at his own ignorance, something that two decades of magical training *should* have had some effect on by now, Cabe suddenly became aware of the faint presence of another person.

No, he almost immediately amended, *two*. Repositioning himself, he tried to use his magic to seek out the newcomers. The cage, however, evidently muted his skills, for the two faint figures remained just that. With his magic unable to help him, Cabe resorted to simply scanning his surroundings, but a quick examination of the devastated region revealed nothing new. Everything was exactly as it had been the moment before he had been snared . . . yet somewhere out there were two nearing figures. Try as he might, the warlock was unable to discover any more.

Then, just as suddenly as they had come, the two vanished. Cabe could not feel their presence anywhere. The imprisoned mage had no time to wonder what had happened, for only a breath or two after the first pair disappeared, a third presence, more evident to his senses, popped into existence somewhere very near the warlock. Cabe glanced around the area again, but still the scene through the cage remained as it had. The new presence was nearly overwhelming in comparison to the first two, but where the others had been unfamiliar to him, this one he felt he should know.

The cell shook then, tossing Cabe around in the process. Stunned, it took the warlock time to realize that his magical prison was being probed . . . and by someone with seemingly no interest in his safety.

Had his captor come for him at last? That did not seem likely. The newcomer was inspecting the cage as if having never come across its like before. The sorcerous probes were tinged with a sense of curiosity, that much Cabe could note. He wondered, *Could it be . . . ?*

As the warlock had done before, the newcomer began to focus his efforts on the top, where the tentacles had come together. For the first time, Cabe's prison shimmered in a way he did not think was normal for it. Whatever the one on the outside was doing, it was having more effect on the magical cage than Cabe's own efforts. Yet the spell withstood the new attack. The hapless mage frowned as he felt the probes of the outsider finally withdraw. It was beginning to dawn on Cabe that he might be trapped within until he starved to death.

He moved as close as he could to the side of his prison. The scene around him remained static, yet the warlock was able to sense that his counterpart on the outside had not left.

Putting his face as close as he could to the wall of shimmering energy that ran between the tentacles, the desperate mage called out, "Hello? If you can hear me, please come closer! I mean no harm!"

According to what his magical senses told him, the other should be practically in front of him, yet Cabe could see no one. Was his would-be rescuer invisible?

He called out again, but still received no response.

With no warning, the probes of the top of his cage began anew. This time, though, there was more purpose to them. Whoever it was, he understood better now what he faced. It was clear even from within the cell that the new series of probes had one purpose in mind and that was finding a weak link. Cabe grew disheartened at that; he had already tried and failed.

The walls of his prison suddenly crackled. Tiny mites of sorcerous energy darted about the interior, forcing the warlock to briefly cover his face.

Stealing a glance upward, Cabe initially saw no change in the cell's condition. However, when he adjusted his sight so as to see the world through the eyes of sorcery, Cabe was stunned to discover that his mysterious benefactor *had* managed to wreak some minor havoc on the spell that held the sphere together. To his great regret, though, the mage also noted that the spell began almost immediately to compensate for what had happened to it. The crackling ceased and the weakened bonds strengthened again. Once more the invisible probes of the unseen mage retreated.

"No . . ." Cabe groaned. An idea blossomed even as the other abandoned his efforts. The warlock was certain that he had a way out of the cage, but he needed the newcomer's aid. If it was left up to Cabe alone, the warlock had little chance for success.

Gathering his strength, the sorcerer concentrated as best he could on the mind of the other. *Try again!* he demanded. *Try again! You must!*

Cabe continued to repeat the message over and over, but after the first few times, it was difficult not to lose heart. The trap was designed too well. Despite the power the warlock wielded, he could barely sense what was happening outside. All that Cabe knew, all that he could base his hopes on, was the fact that the other had not yet departed. Yet, if his messages did not reach the other mage, how long before that other *would* abandon the effort, leaving Cabe to whatever fate the creator of the cage had planned for his intended victim?

Above him, he suddenly sensed new effort on the part of the other mage's probes. In his joy, Cabe almost forgot what he himself intended to do, but then the thought that this might be his last opportunity to free himself urged the exhausted spellcaster to organize his mind and renew his own attack.

It was impossible to say with any certainty whether his pleas had reached the other, but Cabe did note that the mysterious sorcerer now probed with even more force than in his previous attempts. That was all that the warlock could hope for. He needed his counterpart to make at least as much progress as he had in the last attack. Cabe was not at all certain as to the intensity of his own assault from within. If his own power was not enough . . .

The cage began to crackle once more with wild energy. The warlock quickly pulled away from the wall nearest to him, realizing that the unstable spell might do him harm in ways even the creator had not planned. Cabe held off from attacking, hoping for just a bit more success on the part of his benefactor. He had to do this at the exact moment . . .

He sensed rather than saw the straining of the spell. The weak links were suddenly visible. The warlock still hesitated, searching for the moment of best opportunity.

He found it.

Cabe struck out, unleashing with pinpoint precision the full extent of his remaining power. He sensed the spell caging him weaken further and also noted the increased assault by the outsider. Encouraged, Cabe somehow succeeded in drawing further from his very being. Augmented by the physical sacrifice, his own attack grew unstoppable. The tentacles shivered and the shimmering between them dimmed. The point of connection above his head was pulled to its most taut. The black tentacles sought to keep hold of one another, but the spell had its limits, and against the combined onslaught from both without and within, it could not stand.

The tentacles tore free with a blinding flash. They wiggled madly about, wild snakes in their death throes. Cabe was awash in darkness, and for a moment he feared that he had been permanently blinded by the magical burst. Then, as his eyes adjusted, he saw that it was not the sundering of the spell that had caused him to see such darkness.

Day had become night. Somehow, although snared but a few minutes, Cabe Bedlam had missed the rest of the day.

With a last feeble effort, the tentacles tried to reform. Their power, their very existence, was already too much on the wane, however, and so they merely succeeded in flopping about once more before beginning to shrivel. Cabe eyed them carefully, lest some last trick be played out, but the tentacles continued to shrivel, becoming dried out, emaciated things that finally crumbled. The master warlock watched as even the ash faded. In the end, the only sign that the magical cage had existed at all was a series of small holes around the sorcerer.

He straightened and for the first time saw the one who had helped save his life.

"Are you all right, Cabe?" roared a familiar voice. "By the Void, the one who sought your life will find his *own* forfeit!"

A shape blacker than the night looked down upon him with glittering, pupilless eyes of ice-blue. Most would have feared what they saw in those eyes, but the warlock knew them well enough that they did not frighten him . . . *much*, that is.

The eyes belonged to a huge stallion who, despite the rocky ground, moved with silent steps toward the weary mage.

"I don't . . . don't think that they were after me! I . . . I think that they . . . they were after *you*, Darkhorse. . . ."

A devious chuckle escaped the shadow steed, echoing through the night-enshrouded ruins. "And instead they caught themselves a sorcerer!"

"I was looking . . . looking for *you*! I came here because I know you visit the ruins of Mito Pica on occasion."

"It is to remind me of the drakes." The words were said with such loathing that even Darkhorse was startled by the tone. He paused, then in a quieter rumble, added, "It is to remind me that all things pass beyond me. I saw this city built, Cabe."

It was easy to forget just how old the demon steed was. Darkhorse had even known the Vraad, although he refused to say much about them. Difficult the shadow steed might be to kill, but Darkhorse was very familiar with pain. Much of his knowledge of it had come from being a prisoner of some of the ancient sorcerers.

For lack of anything else reasonable to say, Cabe repeated his earlier words. "I was looking for you."

Darkhorse appeared to recover his spirits with the change in topic. "Ha! I know all too well! I have spent the last few hours searching for *you*, my good friend! I arrived at the Manor some hours ago, only to find the Lady Gwen rather anxious as to your own whereabouts. It seems you were due back long before."

What he saw was *true*, then. Staring up into the night sky, Cabe shook his head. "As far as I know, it's only been a few minutes since I was trapped. It wasn't until I was freed from the cage that day suddenly became night!"

"A pretty ploy! I think you were not supposed to realize how long you had been held a prisoner. I have heard of such spells, cunning things, really!"

"But what purpose would it serve?"

"What purpose?" The shadow steed chuckled. "I've no knowledge of that, save that perhaps someone did not wish you to realize that time was slipping away from you."

Time slipping away. . . . Could someone have wanted Cabe to miss the audience with King Melicard? Why—"No . . . not me. I should have remembered."

"Remembered what?"

"When I was first trapped, I wondered how anyone could have known I was here. I'd already ruled out the idea that this was an old spell left over from the destruction of the city."

"Of course," Darkhorse rumbled. "I would have noticed it before this, coming here as often as I do! In fact—*wait!*" He sniffed the air, for the moment acting much like the animal whose form the eternal had long, long ago taken a fancy to. "I smell something *familiar*. . . ." Ice-blue orbs flared. "*Shade!* I smell Shade!"

"Or something like him," Cabe cut in. "Something Vraadish."

"No, this is Shade . . . but the trace is so very old." The shadow steed dug one hoof into the ground, gouging out miniature valleys. "I am reminded of another snare, different in practice but similar in bait. One that I almost stepped into but a day or so ago. . . . "

"A day or so?" The warlock recalled one of his previous destinations. Without preamble, he launched into his experience at that site, specifically the brief trace of magic that had reminded him also of the late, lamented Shade.

When he had concluded, Darkhorse dipped his head in an equine version of a nod. "That was the very same site! That trap was not nearly so well-planned!"

"So someone *is* trying to capture you."

"And, as I have already said, trapped you instead! I little like those who presume to complicate my existence, but when they also endanger my *friends* . . ." The ebony stallion pawed at the ground. His eyes gleamed. The magical forces that were Darkhorse pulsated. "Woe betide them, Cabe! They will find that I am *not* a very forgiving soul!"

The warlock was thankful that he was not the one responsible. The enemies of Darkhorse took on the role at their own risk. Darkhorse did not forget those who thought to play havoc with him or those he counted his companions. Thinking out loud, Cabe muttered, "I wonder who it could be?"

It was the wrong thing to say.

"Who, *indeed*?" The shadow steed's laugh was mirthless. "I could think of several. Certain drakes, for instance, or even once the monarch of a particular mountain kingdom. As I said, I do not forget!"

And Kyl wants him at the audience in Talak. . . . Had Gwen told the eternal of the dragon heir's request? If yes, did Darkhorse intend to be there? If no, how was Cabe to make the request now, with Darkhorse's suspicions roused? The shadow steed might view *both* sides at the audience as possible foes; it was clear from past conversations with Darkhorse that he did not trust the emperor-to-be. Kyl was offering an olive branch, but would the shadow steed see it instead as a blade?

"We should return to the Manor," he finally said, deciding that the change in scenery would only benefit him when he asked the question. Perhaps, with Gwendolyn there to aid him, Cabe could convince his old companion to make the journey to Talak.

"Yes, the Lady Bedlam will be doubly worried if we *both* do not return." Darkhorse shook his head, sending his mane flying wildly about. "No, I would not miss it for the world!"

"Miss what?"

The eternal chuckled darkly. "Why *Talak*, of course! Was that not what you sought me out for? To ask me if I would agree to Prince Kyl's little plot and appear at the audience between Melicard and himself?"

The startled mage grimaced. "I was afraid to ask if Gwen had said anything. I didn't know what you might say."

"Well, you may rest assured, friend Cabe, that I will not miss this little party. Not at all!" That said, the demon steed straightened. "Now, let us be off before the Lady of the Amber decides to go searching for you on her own!"

The image was enough to shake Cabe Bedlam at least momentarily from his ruminations. If there were *other* traps awaiting Darkhorse, then Gwen might be in danger if they delayed any longer. Then again, something would have to be done to assure that no one else fell prey to whatever traps, if any, remained.

As Darkhorse summoned up the power to transport the two of them back to the Manor, Cabe's thoughts returned to the shadow steed's earlier words. Darkhorse looked forward to the meeting between Kyl and Melicard, but not because of any hope for peace in the Dragonrealm. Old suspicions were rising to the forefront, suspicions regrettably based in fact. As well as he had gotten on with the king of Talak for the past few years, neither could forget their initial encounter. Did Darkhorse suspect Melicard of plotting anew? The disfigured ruler of the mountain kingdom could have many reasons for wishing to capture the eternal, including a strike against the new Dragon Emperor.

That he even thought of the possibility of subterfuge on the part of Melicard suddenly dismayed Cabe. It occurred to the warlock then that his companion was not the only one plagued by suspicions. Even *he* had begun to wonder.

The world faded away as the shadow steed's spell took hold. As emptiness briefly swirled around him, the sorcerer found himself wishing that his problems would disappear as easily.

IV

Despite all, the day at last came when it was time for the journey to Talak to commence. Putting together the caravan had proved a monumental task, but under the capable direction of Gwendolyn Bedlam, it was at last accomplished. There were more than a dozen wagons, all with the long-unseen banner of the Dragon Emperor fluttering above them, servants of both human and drake origin, and an honor guard large enough to fight a war.

The last had been most worrisome. Cabe understood that the drakes did not wish to arrive at the gates of the mountain kingdom without some show of their might, but the number of drake warriors accompanying the caravan was astounding. Most of them were soldiers of Lord Green, who journeyed with his future emperor, but a few were the grown hatchlings of drakes who had served Kyl's sire. There were two in particular who stayed close to the heir, a pair of golden warriors who had been brought to the Manor at the same time as the young princes. From the first they had seemed to understand their role as bodyguards, never assuming that they were playmates. It had been amusing at first, watching adolescent warriors doing their best to protect their cousin, but watching them now, Cabe found them only imposing. He had never gotten to know Faras and Ssgayn despite attempts to do so; they did not feel their place was among royalty, which evidently included powerful mages. When with Kyl, who seemed to find them amusing, they were even more silent than Grath. Faras and Ssgayn resembled the elder drakes, but in the dark could have passed for human. Anyone who had seen them fight, however, would not be able to make that mistake. The two fought as only drakes could, with both sword and fang.

Gazing at the army he was to join, Cabe Bedlam began to wish it had been possible after all for Kyl to simply materialize before Melicard and Erini. The caravan was as unwieldy a thing as he had ever ridden with. By themselves the heir's honor guard would have ridden in orderly enough fashion, but mixed with the wagons and servants, they only added to the tension and confusion. The humans in the caravan were on edge because of their lack of numbers, the drakes because they knew they headed for the domain of a ruler who had openly hunted their kind. The horses distrusted the roving eyes of their draconian counterparts, all flesh eaters, while the riding drakes had to strive to keep up with the better-trained, more intelligent steeds.

"Such a madhouse!"

The warlock gazed down at his wife, who had come up to the side of his own mount. "I hope we can reach Talak by the appointed time. This caravan is about ten times larger than I wanted."

"But as small as I could manage to make it, what with all of the 'requirements' I was given. I hope you're not angry about my staying behind, Cabe."

"With the Green Dragon and Darkhorse to accompany us, I doubt that there will be too much trouble. You'll meet us in Talak, anyway. I wish *I* had a reason for foregoing this trip."

"Yes . . ." The emerald-clad witch glanced surreptitiously back at the Manor. Cabe, following her lead, caught sight of Valea, clad in her finest, gazing at the throng below from one of the upper windows. There was no doubt as to who it was she was searching for among the gathered drakes and humans. The warlock had to fight down fatherly fury.

"She's watched everything from every window," Gwendolyn continued, as much ill at ease with the situation as her husband. "I'm fairly certain that Kyl has seen her, but whether he has acknowledged her at all, I could not say."

"I don't know which would be worse," Cabe muttered. "I don't like him playing games with my daughter!"

"Well, this will be the longest that Kyl's been away from here. I could not let an opportunity like this pass by. Now would be the best time to talk to Valea and see if I can rid her of this nonsense."

Cabe's horse began to shift back and forth in growing impatience. The mage regained control over his animal. "I take back what I said. I don't envy you your task. I think I prefer trying to keep a caravan of anxious drakes and humans together. There are few creatures in the Dragonrealm as stubborn as our Valea! And such an intelligent girl, too."

"Yes, and unfortunately we both know where she gets it from, do we not?"

Expression innocent, the warlock asked, *"Where?"*

He was saved from Gwen's retort by the sudden appearance of Aurim. Their son was being left in charge of much of the Manor, which both pleased and frightened him. Cabe could read these emotions in the way Aurim acted. The younger Bedlam reminded Cabe of what he had been like at that age, not that that was difficult. Physically, there had not been much change in the elder Bedlam. Cabe looked only a few years older than he had been when first thrust into sorcery.

"Is there anything amiss, Aurim?" the young warlock's mother asked.

"Nothing, Mother. Just came to wish Father well."

"Don't forget that your mother will be departing in a few days." Cabe studied his son carefully. "Try to familiarize yourself with everything before that so that if you have any questions, she can answer them."

"I've only lived here my *entire* life, Father!"

"It's different when you have to manage this place," Gwen reminded her eldest. "We have an entire community here."

Aurim nodded, still a bit put out by what he thought was a lack of faith on his parents' part. Noting that, Cabe did his best to reconcile things. "I'm sure you'll do fine. We wouldn't leave you in charge if we didn't believe that."

Neither Cabe nor Gwen added that they were also leaving Benjin Traske behind to keep a watchful eye on the young mage. That had proven to be a much more difficult decision than they had expected, for the scholar had apparently assumed that he would be riding with the caravan. While Cabe had been searching for Darkhorse, the huge man had even confronted the Lady Bedlam about it. It was, so Gwendolyn had said, the first time she had seen Benjin Traske come close to anger. Only when he had heard her out did he suddenly calm. The Bedlams had always understood the protective attitude Traske had toward his charges, but they had never realized its extent until then. Knowing that Darkhorse and the Green Dragon were to accompany the heir to Talak had evidently helped much to ease the tutor's mind.

What would we have done without Benjin Traske all these years? Cabe pondered. It was chiefly because of the tutor that the first elements of the school of magic, located in Penacles, were finally coming together. The man was an exceptional organizer, and although he was not himself a mage of any strength, Traske understood the underlying theories about magic, especially after so many years with the Bedlams. His aid continued to prove invaluable. Cabe supposed that it was because teaching was teaching, no matter what the subject. A good scholar could turn his skills to almost any topic.

Gwen suddenly glanced past her husband. "Lord Green approaches. I think the caravan may be ready to leave."

"At last?" the warlock quipped. Aurim grinned. Cabe looked down at his golden-haired son. "We know you'll do fine, Aurim, but don't be afraid to ask your mother questions before she departs."

The younger sorcerer nodded.

Cabe Bedlam leaned down and kissed his wife for a long moment, which made Aurim grimace in embarrassment. Cabe chuckled.

"I regret ssseparating a family," came the voice of the drake lord. "But we are ready to depart asss soon as you desire."

"Now is as good a time as any." The warlock sighed. "Where is His Majesty?"

"Hisss mount is being readied even as we ssspeak. The horses would not remain ssstill for him and so he has decided on a riding drake."

Cabe could not blame the horses for not wanting Kyl to ride them. When mounted, the dragon heir's heritage often rose to the forefront; Kyl put his animals through paces that wore even the hardy riding drakes ragged. Horses, although swifter and with more stamina, did not have the thick hides and dull stubbornness of the reptilian mounts.

"Have a safe journey," Aurim said.

Looking up, Cabe saw that his daughter had vanished from the window, yet there was no sign of her among those who had gathered to see the caravan off. He disliked leaving without saying goodbye to Valea, but if that was the way she was going to act, then so be it. The warlock hoped his wife would be able to talk some sense into their daughter, but Cabe doubted it. Valea was in the throes of first passion, something that common sense and parental guidance had little sway over. He could only hope for the best.

"Friend Cabe, we had bessst be going."

He nodded, his eyes still lingering on the empty window. "The sooner the better."

"What about Darkhorse?" asked Aurim. "He's supposed to be going with you, isn't he?"

"It wasss agreed that the demon steed would meet usss en route," the Green Dragon hissed. There was a note of anxiety in his voice. "He hasss matters with which he must deal first."

Those matters concerned the traps the shadow steed's mysterious foe had set. Darkhorse had wanted to make certain that none still existed. He had also wanted an opportunity to search for any clue that might reveal the identity of his enemy. The eternal had agreed to meet the caravan the second night out. Swift as Darkhorse was, it did not matter where the others would be on that evening; he would find them. Kyl had acquiesced with no argument. It seemed that he was more concerned that Darkhorse be with the caravan when they reached Talak, not before.

With some reluctance, the warlock had allowed Darkhorse to go alone. He knew that a Darkhorse forewarned was proof against most threats, but there was still the fear that one of the snares might prove too much even for the eternal. If the shadow steed did *not* appear on the decided evening, Cabe was going to search for him, dragon heir or no dragon heir.

Once more he bid farewell to Gwendolyn and Aurim. Valea had still not made an appearance and he doubted now that she would. *I hope Gwen can do something about her. . . .*

He rode alongside the Dragon King as they returned to the waiting caravan. Caught up in his own thoughts, a habit he seemed destined never to break, the warlock was surprised by a comment from his companion.

"The world isss never an easy place, friend Cabe," the drake hissed quietly. "Asss much as we would like it to be so, it isss more probable that it will continue to plunge usss into one situation after another. We can only do what we feel isss bessst for all."

"Whatever that may be," Cabe agreed, amazed that the Dragon King should be so concerned and understanding. The master of the Dagora Forest was so very much unlike his counterparts, being almost human at times. Not for the first time was the weary spellcaster pleased to have the reptilian monarch for both ally and . . . yes . . . *friend*.

He glanced ahead and saw both Kyl and Grath mounted and waiting. Grath eyed them with curiosity. The emperor-to-be, on the other hand, wore an expression of regal indifference. Cabe, looking past the mask the dragon heir wore, could read the impatience in Kyl's eyes. Yes, both the journey and the audience held the promise of being . . . *interesting*.

Thoughts of the meeting in Talak mingled with worry for Darkhorse, concern for Valea, and a thousand lesser problems.

The world is never an easy place, the Dragon King had said.

That, the warlock amended, was an *understatement*.

Valea leaned against a pillar, trying to keep herself from watching the caravan as it slowly began to depart the Manor grounds. She belatedly realized that she had forgotten to say farewell to her father, but the mistake seemed minimal compared to her other loss.

He will come back this journey, but soon he will be leaving for the final time! the young witch thought, a lump growing in her throat. Soon, Kyl would be sitting on the throne of the Dragon Emperor and Valea would be a fading memory to him. On the one hand, she knew that what she dreamed was foolish, but it was impossible not to imagine what life would be like if circumstances would only permit her to be Kyl's queen. She knew her own feelings for the young drake and was certain that his were of a similar vein. Did he not make excuses to touch her hand or arm whenever possible? Did Kyl not also show her special attention whenever they were together, no matter who else was there?

Out in the yard below, the caravan continued to move. By this time, she knew that it was already too late to see Kyl one last time. Determined to prove himself, he had chosen to ride at the head of the column. It was a brave thing to do. There were men, even drakes, who wanted his life simply because of what he was.

"You are missing the departure, Lady Bedlam."

Valea gasped. Benjin Traske was standing only a few feet behind her, yet she had heard nothing.

"I apologize if I startled you, my dear."

"I was just . . . just thinking."

Traske's brow rose. "It must have been important for you to miss saying farewell to your father. The proper thing to have done would have been to see him off."

From anyone else, even her mother, the young sorceress might not have taken the reprimand. Valea felt she was old enough to do what *she* desired, even if she knew that it might be wrong. Yet the scholar had a way of speaking to her that made her feel once more like a first-year pupil. Bowing her head, the redheaded sorceress returned, "He will not be gone long. Only a few days."

"Do you speak of your father, or the young drake?"

Her head snapped back up and she started to protest.

Traske raised a massive hand. "Do not seek to convince me otherwise, Lady Valea. I have watched you grow up. I have learned everything about you. About *everyone* here. I know for how long this . . . *yearning* . . . of yours has been going on."

The young woman colored.

Oblivious to her embarrassment, the scholar went on. "I was brought here by the lord of Dagora to act as teacher to both the heirs to the Dragon Emperor and to you and your brother. I have made that my life for the past many years, Lady Valea, and so you must believe me when I say that I could not perform this task for so long without becoming aware of each of your needs and dreams." He sighed. "In truth, you are all family to me, even your somewhat arrogant paramour."

"He's not—"

"He will *need* that arrogance, my lady, so I do not fault him for it, believe me. Kyl has become what he has become because of the great mission before him. There are certain things that he in his role must be able to do. I like to think that I have prepared him for many of those things." Traske's expression abruptly softened. "Although even I would have to admit that I was not thinking he might be so drawn to one not of his own kind."

His last statement drew Valea away from the pillar. Her eyes filled with hope. "Do you mean— I mean—does he—?"

"Very much so, I would say."

Without warning, she reached out and hugged the elder man. Benjin Traske stood motionless, evidently stunned by her outburst. Only when Valea finally released him did he react, and that was simply to blink.

"Did he actually say anything?" Valea asked breathlessly.

"He . . . he has said nothing outright." Traske visibly collected himself. "But what he has . . . inferred has been plain enough for me to understand."

Still reeling with joy, Valea whirled about and rushed to the window. She leaned outside and peered at the caravan. More than half of it had already vanished beyond her field of vision. The young sorceress leaned out even further, trying to get a better view of the vanguard.

Sturdy hands pulled her back inside. "*My lady!* It would be a tragedy indeed if you fell to your death!"

She smoothed her dress, shaken both by his attempt to rescue her and by the fact that he was correct about the danger. Her control of her skills was not as sure as that of her parents. If her mother's teachings were to be believed, it would not be the first time a mage had died through simple, physical carelessness. With power came the need for caution.

"Thank you, Master Traske," she finally muttered.

"I see that I have underestimated the extent of your . . . love."

Love? It was the first time that the word had entered the situation. Even Valea had never actually thought it. Love. It must be true, she realized. Master Traske was no blind man; if he saw love, it could only be because it was there for him to see.

"*I'm in love with him.* . . ." she whispered, noticing it as truth for the first time. Why had she never thought it before? It was so obvious! What other explanation was there for the way she felt?

Then the young witch thought of her parents and how they would react if she said as much to them. "No . . . I *can't* be!"

"You are." Traske put a hand on her shoulder. The touch was gentle, reassuring. "Denying facts is a futile waste of time. My classes should have taught you that by now, Lady Valea."

"What can I do?" She could not go to her mother for such advice. Benjin Traske was the only one whose counsel she could trust. He understood the world in a way that Valea had still to learn . . . might *never* learn, for that matter. Her parents were *so* protective.

"You must wait." The scholar's voice was low, confiding. He glanced around. "If there is one thing I know, it is that one must wait for the proper moment. It is how I've led my life, Valea. You must wait. I am certain that Kyl will make known the truth before it is too late. If he does not . . ." Traske shrugged sadly. "Then, it was meant to be that way."

"But you said he *loved* me!"

"One must consider all possibilities . . . you have not been paying attention during your classes, I see." He smiled, shattering the image of inquisitor. "I doubt, however, that matters will end that way. Just listen—"

At the sudden pause, Valea looked around. She did not notice anything at first, but then the sound of footsteps echoed throughout the area.

"We will speak later, my lady. Remember what I have said. If you want something, you must often wait. It may be a long time before you—Aurim! Do you look for us?"

Valea's brother stopped where he was. She noted that he looked slightly annoyed, which meant that he had not likely heard any of what she and the tutor had been discussing. The novice sorceress silently thanked Master Traske for his discretion.

"N-not you, teacher. Mother wishes to speak with Valea, though."

The girl frowned. She knew what her mother wanted to talk to her about.

"Best that you go, then, my lady." The huge man casually squeezed his charge's shoulder as he guided her toward her brother. "If there is one authority we must always be on the best of terms with, it is your mother."

Aurim attempted a smile, evidently thinking that the scholar was making a joke. While they were rare, Benjin Traske did occasionally make the wry comment . . . most of them concerning the diligence of his students.

Unenthusiastic about the prospect of facing her mother but lacking any escape, Valea joined her golden-haired brother. Aurim made to go, but the young sorceress took the time to bid farewell to Master Traske. "If you will excuse me, teacher." She curtsied. "My thanks for your time."

He bowed in turn, always an extraordinary feat considering the scholar's girth. "I merely do my duty."

"No more stalling," her brother whispered to her. "Mother's waiting!"

Valea knew that she had been fortunate that it was Aurim who had come for her and not their mother. The elder Lady Bedlam had a way of often divining the truth that at times unnerved her children. Fortunately, Aurim was not so observant.

Steeling herself, the young witch followed her brother. She did not look forward to the talk, knowing it would revolve around both her behavior today and her feelings in general for princely

Kyl. Still, she was not completely disheartened. The unexpected support of Master Benjin Traske gave her strength. More and more his words made sense. She would listen to her mother and try her best to pretend compliance. The time would come. Master Traske had said as much, and she had rarely known him to be wrong.

She imagined herself as Kyl's bride, his empress, and . . . the mother of his offspring. Valea knew the stories; she knew that drakes and her kind had married before. There *had* been children. It *was* all possible.

If he loved her, Valea was confident that somehow Kyl would overcome all the obstacles to their love. Somehow, despite drakes and parents, they would be together.

V

The first day of the journey passed with so little difficulty that Cabe could only marvel. Kyl was actually gracious and willing to follow the suggestions of the others. It took the warlock some time to realize that the change in attitude stemmed from the heir's hidden anxiety. Kyl *knew* that he had to make the proper impression on both the humans and his own people or else he would never sit upon the throne of his sire. Now, en route to the first of a series of very crucial confrontations, the pressure was finally affecting the dragon heir.

For once, Cabe found himself sympathizing with the young drake.

The caravan came to a halt in a lightly wooded region, the northernmost traces of the immense Dagora Forest. Under the guidance of the Green Dragon himself, camp was set up. The Dragon King was doing his best to see to it that his emperor-to-be's journey was a quiet, smooth one. The warlock, however, could not help but frown as he watched the master of Dagora go out of his way to see to it that every comfort was afforded the heir. A drake lord as old and as commanding as the Green Dragon should not have had to belittle himself so. It amazed Cabe to watch. What it was in Kyl that brought out such a manner from the otherwise regal Dragon King confounded him.

Protocol demanded that he eat with the Dragon King, Kyl, and Grath. A wide tent of human manufacture had been set up for the would-be emperor, and it was here that Kyl chose to eat, the better for privacy. The young drake had eschewed bringing along chairs, instead adopting a custom from one of the western kingdoms. Seated on pillows before a low table, Cabe was uncomfortable, but as none of his reptilian companions appeared to be having any difficulty, he remained quiet.

Fortunately, the meal was short and the conversation centered mostly on the kingdom of Talak itself, including such things as trade goods, history, and people. Kyl seemed to drink in every drop of information. Grath, too, asked questions, generally picking subjects his brother had not yet mentioned. A few times, the warlock either hesitated or admitted outright that he, in all fairness to King Melicard, could not provide the drakes with an answer. The dragon heir accepted this, although Grath appeared disappointed.

At meal's end, Kyl took a last sip from his goblet, then said, "The food hasss been excellent and the conversssation very informative. I think, though, I would like to take sssome time to digessst both further. I thank both you, my Lord Green, and you, Massster Bedlam, once again for your invaluable ssservice."

Warlock and Dragon King rose. Cabe winced as he stretched his legs at last. Next to him, the drake lord executed a perfect bow. "Should Your Majesty have need of my humble self again before retiring, pleassse do not hesitate to call for me."

Cabe simply nodded in respect. Kyl nodded back, again not at all perturbed by his guardian's attitude. Grath rose to guide the two to the tent opening. He bowed respectfully to both departing guests. "My gratitude also goes out to the two of you."

Outside, Kyl's two guards straightened. The Green Dragon and Cabe walked past the watchful pair in silence, each mulling over the dinner conversation. It was not until they were well away from Kyl's tent that the Dragon King spoke.

"I am encouraged, friend Cabe. Much encouraged. Hisss Majesty asks pointed and intelligent questionsss."

Many of which seemed to originate from Grath, Cabe wanted to add. He was thankful that Kyl's younger brother was along. Where the heir faltered, surely Grath would save the situation.

"You think the audience with Melicard will be successful, then, my lord?"

"It *mussst* be! There is no room for failure! You and I both know that!"

Once more, they continued on in silence. It was not until they were among the other members of the caravan that the silence was broken . . . or perhaps *altered* was the better word.

The camp looked no different, yet Cabe suddenly felt as if someone had invaded it. He paused and looked around.

"Is something amisss?" the Dragon King asked quietly.

"I don't . . . maybe . . ."

They were in the trees around the camp.

"Seekers. . . ." he whispered to his scaled companion.

"What? Impossi—" The drake lord broke off as he, too, suddenly sensed the presence of many avian minds. One hand clenched tight.

"No!" Cabe hissed, fearing that the Dragon King would try to unleash a spell. He did not know what the birdlike Seekers wanted, but if it was to attack, they would have done so by now. Either that, or they would have fled, which would have made more sense based on the numbers that the warlock perceived. There were several of the humanoid birdfolk, but not nearly enough to endanger the caravan.

"What do they want?"

"I don't know. . . ."

Around them, several of the human and drake workers stared at the two powerful figures, most, no doubt, wondering just why it was their lords stood frozen in place. Cabe was thankful that none of them had been close enough to hear his discovery of the avian observers.

It was too dark to see the arrogant forms hidden among the treetops, but now and then the patient sorcerer heard the quiet rustle of wings. The Seekers seemed satisfied with observing. Cabe could feel no desire to attack.

"I think . . . they simply want to know a little about the future emperor."

"I shall have them shot from the treesss," snarled the Green Dragon. From his tone, he had still not come to grips with the realization that the Seekers had settled around the camp without his notice.

"Don't!" admonished Cabe. "I . . . I think we won't have any trouble from them if we simply let them be."

"*Seekers?*" The very idea of allowing the caravan and, especially, Kyl to remain surrounded by the bird folk went against the draconian monarch's notions of safety.

Cabe could hardly blame him. Still, he had no desire to start a conflict with the ancient race. Although only a vestige of their former might, the Seekers, once rulers of the land, were still a cunning and deadly foe when stirred. For now, it was simple curiosity that drove them.

Then, as silently as they had come, the Seekers departed.

Only the warlock and the drake lord noticed their withdrawal. The reptilian knight glanced down at his human companion. "Why did they leave?"

Why, indeed? "They must have discovered what they wanted to know."

"Peaceful intentionsss or not, I am putting the guardsss on alert, friend Cabe! If even *one* of the bird people returns, I will have it destroyed!"

With that said, the Dragon King whirled about and stalked away.

The mage watched him vanish into the night, silently hoping that there would be no further incident. Then, ignoring the still curious glances of the servants nearby, Cabe turned and headed toward his own tent. It would be wise, he concluded, to make a few additions to the spells he and the drake lord had cast. Stronger yet more subtle ones. There would be no repeat of the surprise visit. Next time—though in truth he hoped there would be no next time—he would be alerted to the avians' presence long before they became a threat.

Even still, Cabe knew he would sleep lightly this night. Very lightly.

To the weary mage's relief, the night passed with no return of the bird folk. Cabe had not slept well, not trusting that his newly cast defensive spells would be sufficient for the cunning avians. The nagging lack of confidence was something he had often fallen victim to in the past, and the warlock was quite aware that Aurim had inherited the tendency to doubt himself from his father. That, more than anything else, was why his son's spells went awry. Cabe hoped that one day Aurim, at least, would overcome the doubts. It was looking more and more as if *he* never would.

The caravan was ready to move on in an astonishingly short time, no doubt thanks in great part to the Green Dragon's threatening encouragement. He did not see the silent night as any sign the Seekers had meant no harm. To him, it meant that the avians intended something more monstrous later in the journey. The drake lord wanted to make as much progress as possible before that happened.

Cabe did not argue with him, deciding they were all best served by taking no chances. If circumstances called for him to step between the bird folk and the Dragon King, then so be it. He hoped it would not come to that.

The weather stayed clear, allowing them to cover much ground. There was little trouble, save an argument between a human rider and one of the drake warriors the Green Dragon had brought with him. It was the opinion of the human that his counterpart's reptilian steed was eying the horse with too much eagerness. Separating the two succeeded for a time in ending the matter, but when the accused riding drake started fighting for control with his master, his definite intention being to accost one of the other horses, the Dragon King had the drake warrior ride off and feed his mount. He was also warned that if the beast still hungered when the two returned, it would be its own master it was fed.

That this was the only incident of friction between the human and drake folk was encouraging. Even though the humans for the most part had originally come from settlements located in the lands of the Green Dragon, they had never mingled much with the drake race. Cabe's tiny kingdom had brought the two races closer together than in any part of the Dragonrealm with the possible exception of Irillian by the Sea. There, however, humans were second to their reptilian counterparts. They were treated well, but the divisions still remained. Such was not the case at the Manor. The warlock hoped that he would one day see the rest of the Dragonrealm follow their example. Even he had been amazed that the two races could work so well together.

Evening came none too soon for the mage, who wondered whether he had grown a little soft over the past few years. For the most part, he had traveled by means of either his own sorcery or the swiftness of Darkhorse. Cabe could not recall the last time he had gone on an extended journey with only true horse for transportation. He had forgotten how uncomfortable a saddle could be after two days of riding.

Thinking of Darkhorse, the saddle-worn mage wondered where the eternal was. The shadow steed was not yet late, but Cabe still feared that some other hidden trap had caught Darkhorse unprepared.

He was carefully dismounting when Grath joined him. "Master Bedlam. Can I be of any assistance?"

"Thank you, no. I'm fine."

Someone came to take the reins of his horse. Cabe gladly gave them up. Beside him, the young drake continued to wait.

"Might I speak to you for just a moment, Master Bedlam?"

The Green Dragon and Kyl had already started walking away. Cabe, seeing that he was not needed at the moment, nodded to his companion. "What do you want?"

Grath looked almost embarrassed. "The closer we come to Talak, the more uneasy *I* become. I do not mean that I fear danger, not with you, Lord Green, and soon Darkhorse to protect the caravan, but rather . . . rather I am fearful of the coming confrontation with His Majesty, King Melicard."

"Kyl's been well-rehearsed. He'll do fine." *At least,* Cabe added to himself, *I hope so.*

"It is not Kyl I am worried about. He has been trained from birth for such things. No, I fear my own lack of experience will tell. If I commit an error, it will reflect upon Kyl . . . upon *all* drakess . . ."

Worried as he had been about the dragon heir's performance, Cabe had not really considered the pressures on Grath. He had always been of the assumption that Grath was capable of doing what had to be done. When was the last time he and the others had considered the situation from the younger drake's point of view?

"Grath," he finally said, trying to choose his words for best result, "you'll do fine. I've watched you. Gwendolyn and Lord Green have watched you. We probably haven't told you lately how proud we are of your efforts. You complement Kyl perfectly. He couldn't have a finer counselor."

"If my clutch had been first," Grath said, referring to his hatching, "I would have been the heir. Yet, although I am not, I am still to fulfill a role of great importance. That is why I have always strived to know all that there is to know. If I give wrong advice to Kyl, it could cause catastrophe." The drake looked down. "To be worthy of giving counsel to the Dragon Emperor, I have striven for knowledge as if I am the heir himself, but . . . but I ssstill . . ."

Cabe put a hand on Grath's arm. "You would be as good an emperor as Kyl, Grath! When the meeting between your brother and Melicard commences, you'll do just fine. Kyl would have no other beside him. He's said so many times, remember?"

"Yesss . . ."

"We're all weary from the day's ride, so—"

A familiar presence touched the warlock's thoughts. Grath, noticing his expression, tensed and glanced around.

"Ho there, Cabe! Hello, young Grath!"

Standing where nothing but the creeping darkness of the coming night had been before, was the irrepressible shadow steed. Darkhorse dipped his head in further greeting, then trotted silently toward the duo.

"You made it!" Cabe fairly shouted. Then, collecting himself, he said more quietly, "It's good to see you safe."

"So I noticed! Ha!"

"Welcome back, Darkhorse," Grath added.

"Thank you, one and all." The huge stallion's ice-blue eyes glittered. "It was an entertaining excursion to say the least!"

The warlock's relief faded. "You found *more* spell traps?"

"Two too many, my friend! Someone was trying to ensure most readily that I was snared!" Darkhorse's voice lowered to a quiet boom. "I did not admit to you the trouble the first trap caused me. It came very close to capturing me as the other captured you, Cabe!"

Then what would I have done? the sorcerer could not help thinking.

"Of the other two snares I found, I can only tell you that they were traps of great cunning! Had I encountered one of them first, it might be that both you and I would have struggled in both ignorance and futility while day after day passed without our knowing it!"

"How did you deal with the spells?"

The eternal chuckled. "They were designed to trap, not cope with *being* trapped! Once I understood their nature, I simply *swallowed* them."

"Swallowed?" Cabe tried to picture the sight, but failed utterly.

"They were quite tasty in their own way!"

Cabe was still deciding whether or not he should ask Darkhorse to expand on his remark when Kyl appeared, trailed by Lord Green and the two guards. The emperor-to-be was still clad in his riding clothes.

"Yesss, I *did* hear your voice after all, Lord Darkhorssse! I give thankssss to the Dragon of the Depthsss that you have come back to usss whole!"

"Did you think it would be otherwise?" returned the shadow steed, an astonished tone in his voice.

Kyl frowned, as if wondering if he had offended the eternal somehow. Darkhorse was famous for his almost childlike self-confidence. "Of course not! I trussst your journey wasss little fraught with danger?"

"A little excitement! Nothing more!" Before the heir to the dragon throne, Darkhorse would want to show no weakness whatsoever.

"Good! I know that you do not eat asss we do, Lord Eternal, but I would be remissss if I did not invite you to sssup with usss thisss evening."

"I have already eaten," replied the shadow steed with a quick glance to Cabe. "If you do not mind, I would prefer to begin a search of this region. One never knows what one will come across."

"Yesss. Lassst night it was Ssseekers."

"Oh?"

The Dragon King had informed his future emperor of the previous night's incident. Cabe had wanted to make little of the incident, knowing it would only sow more anxiety, but had agreed that Kyl certainly had a right to know. To Darkhorse the warlock said, "I'll tell you everything that happened the first opportunity I have tonight."

"I would be pleased to hear!" Darkhorse gouged the earth with one massive hoof. "The knowledge of the birds' intrusion makes me all the more determined to survey the surrounding region. Your Majesty, I thank you for your kind offer! Rest assured, one way or another, we *will* speak before this excursion ends."

Kyl executed a bow. "I look forward to it, Lord Darkhorssse!"

A sardonic laugh escaped the shadow steed. "Not, 'lord,' my lord! Never is Darkhorse lord of anything, save perhaps the nothing from whence I came. I am to my friends simply known by my name; to my enemies, I am *Death*!"

The dramatic announcement was followed by another chuckle. Possibly out of habit, the drakes clustered together. Even the guards were well aware of what Darkhorse was capable of, although to their credit they remained at the forefront.

"I shall return shortly, Cabe!" roared the eternal. Before anyone could even acknowledge his departure, the shadow steed had vanished.

"We are all together," commented the emperor-to-be. "It would require a grand fool to plot mischief now!" Kyl turned to his human guardian. "Will you be joining usss at sssupper, Massster Bedlam, or will you await the demon sssteed's return?"

Knowing that Darkhorse was safe and now watched over the camp eased the warlock's tensions a bit. Some food and drink could only help at this point. "I believe I'll be joining you, Kyl."

Even as he walked with the drakes in the direction of the heir's tent, Cabe was aware that the respite was only temporary. Before long, they would reach Talak . . . and there the times would truly become interesting.

For now, though, he would enjoy the evening. After all, a respite *was* still a respite.

Aurim woke to the realization that there was someone in the room with him. He tried to be as still as possible. Through slitted eyes, the young warlock tried to spy whoever it was he had sensed.

There was no one within his range of vision. Aurim shifted in bed, pretending restlessness in his sleep. As he turned, his gaze swept the room.

Scowling, Aurim opened his eyes wide at the sight to the right of his bed.

A tall, thin man dressed in archaic robes was speaking to the air. Not a sound, however, escaped his lips. Had not Aurim known better, he might have thought he had gone deaf. He watched the man mouth words for several seconds before slipping out of bed to stand beside the silent intruder.

Up close, his suspicions were confirmed. He could see *through* the man to the window beyond.

The Manor held memories, centuries of memories, and some had a life of their own. This one was new to the younger Bedlam, but it looked similar to one his father had described. Cabe Bedlam had notebooks in which he chronicled each and every vision that appeared. Most of them remained mysteries. Over the centuries, many folk, some not human, had dwelled or passed through the Manor. Why their traces remained behind, neither the elder Bedlams nor Aurim knew. There seemed no reason for the particular time and place the visions were seen, nor the manner in which they appeared to the onlooker. Some included sound, others, like this one, were silent. The only link seemed to be that they materialized only before a mage. It mattered not whether the chosen one had any true power; as long as the person carried even a trace of sorcery within, he or she was liable to be confronted by the ghostly memories.

Aurim's spectral orator began to fade. The warlock circled the dwindling figure, curious as to why it had shattered his slumber so. He had grown up around the visions and was so used to them that, unless they burst into existence before his very eyes, he was hard-pressed to notice them. Unlike his father, the younger warlock was no longer very interested in these particular mysteries.

Until now.

What was so special about this one? It was hardly even a true shape anymore. More a wisp of smoke. Yet, it had disturbed him.

The last vestiges of his ghostly companion evaporated.

The feeling that someone else had been in the room did not.

One spell that Aurim had little problem with was changing one set of garments to another. For the most part, it was a frivolous, minor ability that had served him only when he woke up too late for his lessons. Now, however, he was thankful, for it was only the matter of a single thought to change what he wore in bed to his mage's robes. Likely it would not have mattered had he decided to forego the change, but Aurim preferred it this way. He did not want to accidentally run into one of the female servants, especially the ones near his own age, while clad in night clothes.

It was difficult to pinpoint where the trace had originated, but Aurim at last decided that the balcony was the most likely place. The trace was just a tiny bit stronger there.

Had someone been climbing into his room? Somehow, it felt more likely that, if there *had* been someone lurking beyond, that someone had remained on the balcony. Perhaps his room had simply been a stop on the way to another location.

As he walked toward the balcony, a tingle coursed through him. There was no explanation, but for a moment the golden-haired warlock faltered. Then, refusing to be cowed, Aurim pushed on. He reached the opening and carefully peered out. The warlock saw no sign of an intruder, but the hint of something lingered. Now, however, it felt a little farther away, almost as if it was coming from . . .

Below.

There *was* someone below him, someone on the path leading
into the gardens. Although he could not see who that someone
was, Aurim felt he should know the identity. He moved to the
edge of the balcony and tried to probe with his power. Sorcery
shielded the other, but Aurim did not give in. He knew that the
potential lay within him to be more powerful and skilled than ei
ther of his parents, but this was the first time the young warlock
had ever truly pushed that power to its limits. The Manor was his
responsibility as much as it was the rest of his family's.

Carefully, he sent out invisible tendrils toward the hidden fig
ure. It might only be his sister, once more pining for the drake
but if it was not . . .

His mind touched that of the intruder.

Aurim gasped. There was a familiar mind there, but underneath
it, like a second layer of skin, was *another* mind. An evil mind
and one that he belatedly realized he knew from stories. Acting
instinctively, the anxious mage tried to withdraw before he was
noticed. He had to warn the others! All these years, a monster had
been masquerading as one of their own. Tears ran down his face
How long? How long had the charade gone on?

It was then Aurim found that he could *not* break the link.

It isss not polite to intrude upon othersss, boy! came the vile
voice in his head.

He could barely move. A pressure built up against his mind, a
pressure that seemed to be trying to crush all thought. In despera
tion, the young warlock tried to call out, hoping that someone
might at least hear the truth. The devil that his father had often
told him about was *here* after all these years. Here, during this
most *crucial* of times.

"Tom . . . Toma!" Aurim croaked.

It was not enough. His voice was barely a whisper.

Aurim was overwhelmed.

He stirred in his sleep. Blinking, Aurim raised a heavy head
and looked around his bedchamber. For some reason, he found
himself expecting to see a ghost. While that happened now and
then, for the most part the memories of the Manor did not disturb
him. They were interesting to experience, but unlike his father
the younger Bedlam had never made a hobby of them.

Turning over, the warlock tried to go back to sleep. Yet, for
some reason he felt a little uneasy, almost as if something had or
was about to happen. Aurim sent out a weak probe, found the

nothing he expected, and gave up. Probably a nightmare brought on by his new responsibilities. He had not told anyone, not even his parents, just how nervous he was about overseeing the Manor, even if only for a few days. Many people, human and drake, would be looking to him for answers.

Sleep began to take hold of him. His troubles turned to mist. Even the reason he had woke seemed irrelevant. If there *had* been something involved other than a nightmare, he not only would have noticed it, he would have dealt with it. Inexperienced he might be, but he had the power.

Besides, Aurim thought as he drifted into slumber, *what could possibly happen here?*

VI

The greeting the caravan received at the gates of Talak could best be described as grandly cautious.

The gates opened while they were still some distance from them, which Cabe read as a subtle hint from Melicard that he did not fear his guests. Knowing the king as he did, the warlock was certain that was true.

Banners hung from everywhere and the sight gave pause to more than one drake in the caravan. The flag of Talak, as designed by Melicard himself, consisted of a long, sharp sword crossing the stylized head of a dragon. The crippled king had designed it during his first years of power, when he had begun his vendetta against the race that had plagued his house so long. The vendetta was at an end—so Talak's monarch had promised—but the flag remained as a constant reminder of the king's hatred.

"Talak hasss very high wallsss," Kyl commented to no one in particular. In truth, there were few kingdoms with walls as impressive as those surrounding the mountain state. They would have been even more impressive if Cabe had not been aware that they had failed to stop the drake armies.

There were other defenses now, defenses that made up for the failure of the walls. Should there be a new conflict between the drakes and Talak, the dragon warriors would find the high walls the least of the city's shields.

Trumpets began to blare. From seemingly nowhere, people from the outer villages materialized on the sides of the road leading into Talak. There was some cheering, but overall the mood remained one of caution. More than a few of the villagers eyed the members of the caravan with suspicion. Most knew little about the heir to the dragon throne, but more than a few readily identified the Dragon King who rode beside him. Responses were mixed, albeit never approaching the point of anger. That Green had generally been a friend to humanity did not matter so much as that he was recognizable as a Dragon King.

Cabe's appearance also initiated some response, most of it simple puzzlement. His robes and the slash of silver in his hair marked him as a sorcerer of some distinction and any who followed the doings of the king and queen surely had had opportunity to learn his name. Cabe even heard "Bedlam" whispered by several people. *They probably wonder why I ride with devils. . . .*

Despite the size of the caravan, the presence of so many drakes, including a Dragon King and a future emperor, and the appearance of a master mage, it was Darkhorse who elicited the most response. Trotting alongside the caravan, yet far enough away so that no one might think he was some servant of the drakes, the massive, ebony stallion could not help but draw the attention of those who, for the most part, had considered him little more than legend. A few probably had seen him before, Cabe knew. The shadow steed had visited Queen Erini too many times not to have been sighted now and then. Still, it was one thing to catch a swift glimpse of the huge, equine form and another to watch Darkhorse trot casually toward the city gates with no one attempting to stop him. A wall of silence preceded the eternal with onlookers staring open-mouthed as he passed, then babbling to one another as Darkhorse moved on. Nothing, not even the future emperor of the drakes, could outshine the shadow steed.

Which was perhaps, the watchful sorcerer concluded, one of the other reasons that Kyl had wanted him along. With so many overawed by Darkhorse, the presence of the young heir would be slightly less fear-inspiring. They would remember Kyl, of course, but perhaps not in the same light as the elder folk would recall his unlamented father.

He succeeded in using Darkhorse after all! Cabe shook his head. He hoped the eternal would not realize that.

As the caravan neared the city walls, there erupted from the open gateway a troop of mounted soldiers. In rapid succession, they lined up on each side of the road, armor glinting, lances raised in ceremonial greeting. Melicard's royal guard. There were at least fifty, by Cabe's count, all veterans.

"An honor guard," said the dragon heir. "How consssiderate of Melicard."

Cabe listened for even the slightest hint of sarcasm in Kyl's voice, but found none. The warlock's gaze again rested on the soldiers from Talak. Despite the decorative, eggshell-shaped armor they wore, these men were warriors. Strong, tenacious warriors. Contrary to the ways of many other kingdoms, Melicard's royal guard was not just for show. The guard was made up of his finest soldiers, all willing to give their lives for him.

The Green Dragon raised a mailed fist, the signal to slow but not halt the caravan. While this was being accomplished, two well-decorated commanders broke from the ranks and rode toward the royal party. They looked to be a few years older than their men but no less fit. One wore a short, black-and-gray beard that covered part of a round, wrinkled visage, while the second, clean-shaven, sported two ragged scars on the right side of his face. As the newcomers' weapons were still sheathed, the Green Dragon allowed them to ride closer.

After questioning glances aimed toward the distant figure of Darkhorse, both men acknowledged Kyl. In rather patrician tones, the clean-shaven one said, "Our Majesty's fondest greetings to you, my lord! I am Baron Vergoth and my companion is General Yan Operion. We are to be your escort to the palace, where King Melicard and Queen Erini await you. Unless you have any objections, we can lead you there immediately."

"Have preparations been made for His Majesty's retainers?" asked the Dragon King.

"Places have been set aside for everyone. We do not think that you will be disappointed."

Green looked at Kyl. The emperor-to-be inclined his head, but otherwise did not respond. The Dragon King, however, seemed to understand what the younger drake was trying to convey, for he turned back to the two soldiers and, with a nod of his own head, replied, "Then, you may lead us now."

"Yes, my lord."

Cabe marveled at the politeness of the soldiers. Not a trace of their enmity toward the drakes showed through. Kyl might have been the king of Gordag-Ai, Queen Erini's father, so well were the men of Talak behaving. *Melicard must've talked to them after Erini talked to him!*

The baron glanced at the general, who turned his steed around and immediately returned to his place at the head of one of the two columns. Vergoth signaled an officer in the other column. The soldier saluted and barked out a command. With impressive precision, the column turned to face the gateway and began rearranging itself, becoming a spearhead of sorts with the officer in the lead.

When the baron saw that his men were ready, he turned his attention back to the drakes. "If Your Majesty and Your Majesty's people will follow me . . ."

Kyl signaled for Vergoth to proceed. The Talakian soldier saluted him and turned to face the gates. As Vergoth called out the command to move, the Green Dragon raised his fist and motioned for the caravan to follow suit. Urging their animals forward, the drakes and the wizard trailed after their escort, with Darkhorse continuing to stay far to one side of everyone.

Only the column belonging to the baron moved. Cabe studied the second column, especially its commander. The general eyed the moving caravan dispassionately. He briefly met the gaze of the warlock, but then continued on with his inspection of the visiting delegation. Cabe Bedlam had met both the baron and the general prior to this occasion, but usually on state business and only for brief periods of time. Neither man actually led the royal guard, but for this visit, Erini had no doubt deemed it proper that Kyl be escorted by men of proper rank. Melicard would have chosen these two because of his trust in their ability to turn the situation around should the drakes be determined to cause trouble.

The second column had still not moved even after Cabe and his companions had reached the last man. The caravan, then, was to have an escort riding *behind* it as well as ahead. Melicard's faith in the drakes was very definitely limited.

They entered Talak.

Each time he visited the mountain kingdom, the blue-robed mage could not help but admire the peculiar architecture. Talak was a city of ziggurats, stepped pyramids often looming high in the sky. The largest, of course, would be the palace, the tip of which he could already make out. The rest of the city was only a little less impressive, however. Every gate seemed to include first a visit to a marketplace. The caravan's path took it through a people-filled, bustling combination of tents, stalls, and permanent buildings. Even the arrival of the drakes' emperor-to-be did not stop most merchants from continuing to try to hawk their wares to the onlookers and even, in a few daring cases, members of the caravan. Cabe laughed and shook his head as one woman tried to convince him to purchase a roll of gaily-colored cloth. She followed along until he was at last able to convince her he had no interest, at which point she allowed him to move on while she attempted to assault one of the human servants further back in the column.

Risking a study of the dragon heir, the warlock was interested to note the struggle going on in the handsome visage of the young drake. Kyl was fighting to keep his fascination with the city from becoming visible. His eyes, however, kept darting back and forth to admire one strange sight after another. The drake had made a few short visits to Penacles, which was closer, but had never been to the mountain kingdom. Cabe was aware that Kyl had believed Talak to be a rougher, less attractive abode. The dragon heir had expected a wind-blown, murky kingdom populated by sinister figures bent on the destruction of his kind. It was evidently becoming something of a shock to discover that these folk worshipped life and the enjoyment of it. There *had* been a period, from the years shortly after Melicard had assumed the throne to the time of his marriage to Erini, when Talak had come close to being the dark abode Kyl had expected. It was chiefly due to the queen that Melicard had not become the twisted monster his father's insanity and his own mutilation had nearly created.

They passed more and more permanent buildings, tiny duplicates of the taller ziggurats. People clad in the bright, loose-fitting clothing that was most common in Talak contrasted sharply with the armored soldiers keeping order. The crowds grew more excited as the drakes entered deeper into the city, but no one tried to create a disturbance. The warlock was pleased about that, although he knew it was all Melicard's doing. The king might be a good man, but he ruled with the proverbial iron fist.

The markets gave way to more permanent businesses, then to stately homes. The nearer they drew to the palace, the more elegant the travelers' surroundings became. This did not mean that the crowds became any thinner. On the contrary. Here were the folk who controlled much of the kingdom's commerce and politics. To them, the coming of the drakes, especially Kyl, was at least if not *more* relevant than their queen's initial arrival. Cabe recalled Erini describing her journey through Talak and smiled grimly at the notion that the aristocracy and wealthy merchant class considered the newcomers of so much more import. Of course, years ago, when the young princess had arrived, most of the powerful had expected her to take one sharp look at the disfigured king and then flee in disgust and horror. Erini had certainly surprised them.

Cabe dismissed the thoughts as the palace of the king and queen of Talak at last loomed before them.

The gates surrounding the palace grounds were open. A contingent of the royal guard, half stationed on each side of the gate, came to attention. Two heralds raised horns to their lips and announced the arrival of the visitors.

Kyl gripped his reins tightly. Cabe would have sought to encourage him, but the Green Dragon was swifter. He leaned close to the heir and pointed at the palace, as if explaining some fact about it. Cabe was not close enough to really hear, but it was clear to him at least that the Dragon King's words had nothing to do with architecture. Kyl at last nodded and relaxed his grip. Lord Green straightened again and pretended as if nothing had been amiss.

The warlock turned his attention briefly to Grath. Kyl's brother was taking in all of the splendor with much less difficulty than his elder sibling. Cabe was impressed. Grath was no more traveled than Kyl. Perhaps it helped to know that most eyes were not on him.

On the uppermost step of the palace entrance, looking calm and unconcerned, were King Melicard and Queen Erini. With them were members of the king's staff, looking not at all as unconcerned as their monarchs. There was no sign of the young princess, Lynnette, but it was not necessary for her to be here.

Melicard I of Talak was a tall and striking man. His hair had begun to turn to gray and there were lines etched into his angular features, but no one doubted his strength. He had a commanding presence; Cabe knew of few men who were not warlocks who were as overwhelming as the king. None of those few, however, could match Melicard's unique appearance.

Both the monarch's left arm and much of his face on that same side were *silver*.

In the early years of his reign, Melicard had begun his vendetta against the drakes. Two of his specific targets had been both Kyl and Grath. In order to combat sorcery that might be used to defend the hatchlings, Melicard had gone to the Seekers for aid. The avians had given him power of his own, in the form of magical medallions. Melicard had put them to good use at first. Then, during one attack, a medallion in his possession had shattered . . . discharging the stored power.

He had almost died. The injuries could be healed to a point, but the face was permanently scarred and nothing could save the arm. Seeking a semblance of normalcy, Melicard had sought out the rare, magical elfwood, a type of wood that could be trained to mimic whatever it was carved to resemble. A partial mask of the silver substance now covered every scar, even replacing most of the mangled nose. More astonishing, the elfwood arm moved with almost as much fluid grace as the original had.

The elfwood had been the beginning of the king's recovery, but his marriage to Princess Erini of Gordag-Ai had truly saved him.

The queen still looked as young as on the day she had first ridden into Talak to be the betrothed of the dark and mysterious king who ruled there. She was the fairy-tale princess come to life, with perfect features highlighting a pale, oval visage. Sun-drenched tresses almost comparable to the gold of Aurim's own head flowed behind her like a second cape. She was slim and somewhat petite, which caused more than one unknowing person to assume that the queen was a delicate, fragile person who relied upon the towering strength of her husband.

Such fools did not last long in the royal court of Talak. Erini complemented Melicard. It was Erini's love more than anything else that had made the king what he was. The queen was also not one to sit quietly and let others make decisions concerning her kingdom. Melicard and his bride ruled on an equal basis, although he would not have denied that she could sway his opinion to her thinking with but a smile.

Her ability to rule both her kingdom and her husband aside, Queen Erini possessed one more ability that made her a force to be reckoned with. Outwardly, the only evidence of that ability lay in the fact that she did not look much more than eighteen despite being more than a decade older than that. Melicard looked to be almost three times her age.

The queen of Talak was a sorceress. She had not wanted to be, but the power would not be denied. It had manifested shortly before her arrival in the mountain kingdom and had, Cabe knew, been instrumental in saving both her and the king from the machinations of Mal Quorin, counselor to Melicard and secret servant to the late, unlamented Silver Dragon. Like all other mages, she wore silver in her hair. At present, however, her crown and some subtle styling served to all but hide the telltale streak.

The king and queen waited in regal silence as Baron Vergoth led the column to a position before the steps of the royal palace. Cabe took the opportunity to once more admire the building and grounds. Melicard's palace, the largest structure in sight, was a sprawling ziggurat surrounded by a beautifully landscaped park. In the high season, flowers of all colors and scents blossomed everywhere. There were small groves of fruit-bearing trees and even a stream whose source was underground.

Despite the splendor of the grounds, the palace was by no means designed simply as a feast for the eyes. The ziggurat was well-defended, with arrow-slits as the only visible evidence. Many of the defenses were magical in nature or simply hidden. Talak itself was also protected by spells, but it was rumored that conquering the entire city would be simple in comparison to attacking the palace. Cabe could sense great power surrounding him, but he knew better than to probe. That was a good method by which to set off any of a countless number of spells. Even the warlock, who knew the king and queen well, was not privy to all of their secrets.

The caravan and its escort came to a halt. Cabe and the others dismounted. At the same time, Melicard and Erini, accompanied by their people, began to descend the steps of the palace.

Baron Vergoth led the warlock and his companions forward, save for Darkhorse, who chose to stay back for reasons no one dared ask. The two parties met at the bottom of the steps. The baron saluted his monarchs. "Your Majesties!"

It was as if the caravan and the rest of the population of Talak had disappeared. Now the world consisted only of the two small groups.

Melicard looked over the group before him, his eyes alighting briefly on first Cabe and then Kyl. "Welcome, honored guests, to our home! Welcome to Talak!"

Cabe had almost expected the Green Dragon to speak for his group, but Kyl surprised him by stepping forward. He bowed to both king and queen, adding a smile for the latter, and said, "You do usss great honor, Your Majesssty! We thank you for your hosssspitality and hope that thisss meeting between usss will be the firsssst major ssstep toward permanent peace between our two racesss."

"That we wish also," the queen returned. "But come! You've journeyed some distance to be here, and I do not doubt that many of your people could do with food and rest. If you do not object, I will have someone show your retinue to their quarters. We have set aside part of a wing just for them."

"That would be mosssst kind of you."

"As for yourselves, special accommodations have been arranged for all." Erini smiled at Cabe. "Master Bedlam will be familiar with the rooms we have given to him and I think he will be able to vouch for their comfort."

"They've been nothing less than perfection, Your Highness."

Her smile blossomed. "I am happy to hear that! Lord Kyl, if you like, I will be happy to escort you and your companions to those rooms. Then, after you have had a chance to refresh yourselves, perhaps you will join my husband and me for a light supper. The others, are, of course, also invited."

Becoming daring, the young drake suddenly reached for the queen's hand. Melicard and his men tensed, which made the drakes with Cabe also stiffen, but Kyl simply took Erini's hand, turned it palm down, and kissed the back lightly. He matched her smile with a brilliant one of his own—the type that the warlock had most recently noticed directed toward his own daughter. "You are both a graciousss hossstess and a mossst beautiful lady. I would be honored to have you essscort us. Your other sssuggestionsss I alssso find most agreeable. But name the hour for the sssupper and we shall be there."

For the first time, Cabe noted traces of suppressed emotion play across the face of Melicard. The flesh and elfwood countenance of the king briefly twitched in disgust and anger, but Melicard quickly and quietly subdued the escaping emotions. In a calm voice, he turned to the warlock and said, "While my wife escorts His Majesty to his rooms, I would like to take the opportunity to discuss a few minor details with you, Master Bedlam. If you have the time, that is."

And it would be best if I did *have the time, wouldn't it?* the mage thought wryly. He hoped that the king's temper would remain in check. Now was not the time for Melicard's hatred and jealousy to rise to the forefront.

"I'm at your service, Your Majesty."

"Fine." The monarch turned to Kyl. "My lord, I hope you find your rooms satisfactory. If there is any need we can fulfill, please do not hesitate to ask. I look forward to the supper and hope that it will be but the first step toward the peaceful relationship both of us desire."

Erini frowned to herself, then suddenly glanced past Kyl and the others. "But we are being remiss! There is one more who should be there!"

From behind Cabe came the stentorian voice of Darkhorse. "I do not eat nor do I require a place to sleep, gracious queen! Yet, if my presence is desired, I will come to your supper!"

He's offering them the chance to forego his company. Whether the eternal's reasons for making the offer were selfish or because he thought the two sides would be better able to negotiate without his presence to disturb them, Cabe Bedlam could only guess. Still, the very idea of offering the choice went against what the shadow steed had said to the warlock among the ruins of Mito Pica. Cabe wondered what the stallion had in mind.

Before the king and queen could say anything, Kyl spoke up. He looked at Darkhorse as if offended. "By all meansss, you mussst join usss! In fact, I will go ssso far asss to insissst."

"Yes," added a more reluctant Melicard, "it would be remiss not to include you."

His wife was pleased. "There! That's settled, then. Baron Vergoth, would you see to it that someone helps those with the caravan to settle in to their chambers? Also, something must be done about separating the riding drakes from the horses."

"As you desire, my queen." Vergoth saluted his lord and lady, then Kyl. "If you will excuse me. . . ."

Queen Erini separated herself from the king and made her way to Kyl's side, where she took the heir's arm. "Now, then, Your Highness, if you and your companions will follow me, I will take you to your own rooms."

Kyl was all courtesy. "You are too kind, my lady."

The two of them started up the steps, with Lord Green, Grath, and the two guards trailing close behind. Four royal guardsmen followed the party. Melicard watched them go, then turned back to the warlock. "Shall we adjourn to my private quarters, Master Bedlam?"

Cabe did not answer him at first, instead turning to where Darkhorse had been standing. "What about you—"

The shadow steed was gone. Scanning the area, Cabe could not find the eternal among the soldiers and servants.

"He vanished at some point between the moment it was decided that he would join us at supper and just now, when I turned my gaze back to you." Melicard's tone was cautious. "I will never understand that creature. Do not even you have any control over him?"

"Darkhorse does what Darkhorse chooses to do."

A half-silver frown crossed the king's unique visage. "I had noticed that. I still hoped."

The caravan and its escort had begun moving again. Cabe watched for a moment, then reminded the king, "You wanted to talk to me, Your Majesty?"

"Yes." The king of Talak looked around at his staff. "The rest of you may return to your duties."

The departure of the dignitaries left the two alone save for a second set of guards whose task it was to protect the king at all times. Melicard acted as if they did not exist. The heir to the throne of the mountain kingdom since his birth, he was very much used to the near-constant presence of bodyguards.

"This way, if you please."

Following the tall, regal figure up the steps of the palace, Cabe asked, "Has my wife arrived yet, Your Majesty?"

"I commanded those responsible to notify me the moment she does. Likely you will know before anyone else does."

That was probably true, but the warlock liked to ask, just to be certain. Gwendolyn had said she would arrive early in the evening of this very day, but exactly when had been debatable. Cabe hoped that she would appear before supper. He wanted her there if it was at all possible.

As they reached the top, Melicard casually asked, "What are your personal observations concerning this supposed emperor?"

The intrigued sorcerer arched an eyebrow. "Is that one of the minor details you wanted to discuss with me?"

A pause. "One of them, yes." The king fixed his true eye on his companion. Even after so long, it was sometimes hard to believe that the other one was not real, despite its silver shape, for the elfwood so well mimicked Melicard's original face that the false eye followed the direction of its counterpart with perfect precision. The disfigured monarch had never said otherwise, but Cabe occasionally wondered if he saw better than he pretended.

Mulling over the king's request, the warlock finally replied, "I'd be happy to give you my observations concerning Kyl."

Melicard actually appeared a bit startled. "I thank you."

The mage shrugged. "I would do the same for him in regard to you. Likely, I will whether he asks or not."

"That would be . . . fair."

Although he was able to hide it from the king, Cabe was vastly relieved by Melicard's lack of protest. Had the gray-haired ruler commanded him not to speak to Kyl, it would have created a precarious situation. Despite his position as one of Kyl's guardians, the warlock was desperately attempting to be neutral when it came to the talks between the two rulers. If either side felt that he leaned toward the other, it could only make the situation more perplexing . . . not to mention dangerous. It was even more difficult since, despite Melicard's constant formality, Cabe considered both king and queen good friends.

The question is, the sorcerer thought as he followed Melicard into the palace, *how long before I do take sides? Or have I done so already?*

He hoped that Gwen would make it in time for supper.

Kyl was pleased with himself.

"I did very well, would you not sssay ssso, Grath?"

The dragon heir stood in the midst of the sumptuous suite that had been turned over to him by the very charming queen, who had just left his company not a moment before in order to make the final arrangements for the informal supper. Had his interests not been focused elsewhere, Kyl would have utilized his full charms on Queen Erini. It was clear that she controlled her husband, so whoever controlled her could have whatever he desired. Concessions, perhaps.

"You did well," Grath admitted. Unlike his brother, he maintained a quiet, almost reclusive air. Seated in a plush, gold-and-purple chair on one side of the vast room, Grath watched his sibling continue to preen. For the first time in days they were alone, Kyl's guards having taken up residence outside the entrance to the suite.

"I wasss grace and charm. I treated our two-faced hossst with the ressspect and care that he could hardly have expected from . . . how wasss it he put it long ago? . . . from 'a blood-thirsssty lizard that sssometimes walked on two legsss'?"

"He was, I believe, talking about Toma," Grath corrected.

"He wasss talking about *all* drakesss, regardlessss of which of usss he ssspoke of at the time!" The emperor-to-be stalked toward his brother and leaned over the chair. He smiled slightly as Grath shrank back. The other drake was not frightened, merely cautious. Both of them knew how valuable Grath was to him. When Kyl had a question, his younger sibling was generally there with the answer. The arrangement pleased the dragon heir. He had the best, most loyal of all advisors, one who had no designs on the throne himself. *He would rather bury hisss head in hisss precious booksss than rule a race!*

Yes, a perfect arrangement.

"We should prepare for the supper," Grath suggested quietly. "You have to press your advantage."

Kyl's handsome face momentarily revealed anxiety. The confidence that his performance at the steps of the palace had built evaporated somewhat. It would not be long before supper. He had the advantage now, having confused King Melicard's assumptions about the new Dragon Emperor. Queen Erini was especially pleased with the elegant young visitor, of that he was confident. What, then, was the best way to further capitalize on his success? With the mountain kingdom on the very doorstep of his own domain, he needed the good will of the king and queen . . . at least until the clans of Gold were once more a power to be reckoned with. That, however, would take a few years.

Kyl studied his brother's eyes. "You have sssome possible sssuggestion. I know that look."

"I think . . . I think you should make some sort of grand gesture, Kyl."

The emperor-to-be straightened. "A grand gesssture? I thought I *had* sssimply by coming here!"

Grath steepled his hands. "I mean a *persssonal* gesture to King Melicard himself, Kyl."

A personal gesture. The elder drake could see the potential in that. Done properly, it would completely undermine the last vestiges of the human monarch's misgivings. "Tell me what you think might be a *worthy* gesssture. Tell me what you would do. . . ."

"It came to me while I was reading about Talak and King Melicard in general." Grath looked down, as if uncertain as to whether his suggestion would be worthy of his brother's time.

Kyl had no such doubts. His brother had not failed him yet. Giving his advisor a reassuring smile, the heir to the dragon throne urged Grath to continue.

The encouragement appeared to be all the younger drake needed to spur him on. Looking more excited, Grath said, "It concerns His Majesssty's father, Rennek IV, and our distant brother, the late Duke Kyrg . . ."

"Rennek and Kyrg?" Kyl could not see the connection.

The other drake leaned forward. "Thisss is what I think you should do, Kyl. . . ."

VII

The Manor was now his.

Pride and worry wrestled for control. Aurim's mother had left for Talak the night before, leaving him in charge. He knew, of course, that Benjin Traske was supposed to keep an eye on him, but even still, the Manor was now most definitely *his* responsibility.

As he walked through the garden, Aurim grew more confident. The Manor virtually ran itself. Despite all those who had accompanied his father and the others to Talak, there were more than enough people left who understood the day-to-day running of the miniature kingdom. The young warlock was there more as the symbol of authority, the final arbiter, he decided.

He felt confident enough in himself that he was willing to try a spell. Not a grand, dangerous one, but a small yet complex incantation. Aurim glanced around. There was no one nearby. The closest structures were the stables, and there Ssarekai the drake and Derek Ironshoe, his human counterpart, would have their apprentices and workers busy. With most of the animals gone, the stable masters were hoping to give the buildings a thorough cleaning out—no small feat.

The younger Bedlam held his hands before him, palms up. With his mind, he sought the forces of the world, forces he thought of as part of the natural makeup of the land but what most folk simply called "magic." The link was made and drawn upon with but a single thought; to an outsider, the action would have seemed instantaneous. Aurim knew that compared to his parents he was still a bit slow, but the potential—and to his disgust it sometimes seemed it would *forever* be only potential—was within him to be the greatest mage to walk the realm since his great-grandfather, Nathan.

The expectations people had of him were oftimes daunting, which was perhaps why Aurim still had trouble with his control. Now, however, no such fears haunted him. In the comfort of his newfound role as temporary master of the house, he was able to use his new confidence to strengthen his will.

A bouquet of flowers formed in his open hands. The bouquet was a good foot high and as wide as his body. Bright colors running the full span of the spectrum decorated the arrangement. Flower after flower blossomed, only to give way to their successors, which in turn gave way, and so on. . . .

To someone standing some distance away, the warlock's bouquet would have hardly seemed an amazing feat, considering the sort of things even a slightly competent mage was supposed to be capable of creating. It was only upon closer inspection that the complexity of Aurim's spell became evident.

The flowers were not flowers in the literal sense. Up close, it was possible to see the multitude of tiny, glittering figures constantly rearranging themselves to create new patterns. Each figure was a round, almost spherical, clown no larger than a fly. They crawled, climbed, jumped, and even flew. Aurim did not directly control each movement—no mage he had ever heard of in his mother's stories had had *that* much skill—but the young warlock did direct them in the manner in which they created the flowers. Their other actions were based on smaller subspells he had prepared in advance. The main spell, like so many others designed to hone one's concentration, had no apparent value other than visual delight, but the practice itself prepared a novice spellcaster for the time when such manipulation of the natural forces *might* mean life or death. Of course, while the practice was important, Aurim also simply *enjoyed* such fanciful creations. It was a challenge to him to see what he could design next.

He was just starting to expand the bouquet when a commotion from the stables made him dispel his creation. A roar from within hinted at one possible cause of the trouble. There were still some riding drakes and horses in the stables, and it was possible that one of the former was not taking kindly to being moved so that the stable workers could clean its pen. If it was a mother drake, then there was even more chance for disaster.

With Ssarekai and his men inside, Aurim doubted that the situation was very critical, but it behooved him to see if there was any way in which he could contribute to a speedier conclusion. He hurried to the stables, only belatedly recalling that he could have saved precious seconds by transporting himself, and cautiously entered.

"Massster Aurim! You should not be in here!"

Ssarekai himself pushed the warlock to one side just as a long, scaly tail whipped their direction. Aurim regained his balance and watched as two drakes and a short, bearded man, one of Ironshoe's helpers, struggled to keep a half-grown riding drake under some loose sort of control. The dragon men, one on each side of the beast, tugged at guiding ropes. The human stablehand, meanwhile, was attempting to use a pitchfork to prod the beast toward an open doorway just to the creature's right. Two other humans stood to the side, one of them binding a wound on the left arm of the other.

"What's wrong?"

"Nothing, my lord! Nothing!" Ssarekai bowed quickly. He and the other dragon men in the stable differed in some ways from the warriors most humans saw. The reptilian riding master and his helpers resembled, for the most part, their fiercer counterparts, but unlike the Dragon Kings and their warriors, these drakes were without crests. Instead, they appeared to be wearing round helms that partially covered the inhuman faces within. No hissing dragon's head adorned the top. Ssarekai and his kind were members of the servitor caste, a caste rarely seen, since most often servitors generally remained in or around the clan caverns.

The drake turned back to the struggling hands and hissed out a command that Aurim did not catch. The workers redoubled their efforts. Another pair of humans entered the stable. They raced to each side of the stubborn monster and joined the two drakes holding the guide ropes.

Slowly, the beast came back under control. Ssarekai hissed another command, this one evidently to someone beyond the doorway the men were trying to lead the riding drake through. There was an answering shout, then something outside and beyond Aurim's view caught the beast's attention and sent it scuttling almost gleefully through the desired entrance.

As the animal and its handlers vanished, Ssarekai hissed the drake equivalent of a sigh of relief. "I ssso much prefer horsssesss to sssuch ssstupid beasssts!"

It was strange hearing a drake speak so. "You like horses better than one of your own mounts?"

His companion smiled, revealing the predatory teeth. A forked tongue darted out and in. "People are alwaysss comparing horsesss to riding drakesss, but in my opinion, we should be comparing the ssstupid beasts like that one to your *mulesss*! Useful pack animalsss, but *ssso* stubborn! Horssses can be like that, but for the mossst part, they are quicker to learn and obey. I would choossse them over riding drakesss under almost every circumssstance."

"I seem to recall that Derek Ironshoe seems fascinated by the qualities of riding drakes," teased Aurim.

"Only asss animals of war! Massster Ironshoe wasss a cavalry sssoldier once."

By this point, it was clear that there was no need for the warlock's presence. Still, trying to give the appearance that he was as concerned as his parents were over the everyday running of the Manor grounds, Aurim asked, "How goes the cleaning, Master Ssarekai?"

The drake shrugged, a gesture more common to humans than to his own kind, but one he had picked up from his years working with Ironshoe. Ssarekai had been one of the first drakes sent to work for the Bedlams when they had been given custody of the Dragon Emperor's hatchlings. He, more than most drakes, had come to an understanding with the humans who lived here. There was no one who lived at the Manor who did not respect the reptilian stable master.

"We are, asss I sssuspected, behind in our tasssk. Master Ironshoe hasss a group ssstill working on the ssstables where the royal mountsss are kept." To Ssarekai, mounts used by the Bedlams were as royal as those utilized by Kyl or any of the Dragon Kings. It was debatable as to whom he was now more loyal. Aurim wondered whether the elder drake would depart with the others when Kyl finally left for the Tyber Mountains and his throne.

"Then, I probably shouldn't trouble you anymore. I just wanted to make sure that everything was all right."

Ssarekai nodded his head respectfully. "Your concern isss appreciated, Massster Aurim. Better to be sssafe, I always sssay."

"Father would certainly agree with that. Well, good luck to you." The warlock, his sense of duty satisfied, turned and started toward the doorway through which he had entered.

"And to you, my boy."

Aurim stiffened. There was a sudden twisting in his stomach, as if someone had thrust a blade through him and now sought to add further to the agony of that thrust. The golden-haired sorcerer remained still, trying to understand the reason for his horror. Something concerning Ssarekai? What? Ssarekai had said nothing out of the ordinary. Aurim turned around. The drake was making an inspection of one of the stalls and seemed to have already forgotten his recent visitor.

Why do I feel like this? His stomach continued to feel as if it were being twisted. A sense of dread crept over him, yet Aurim had no explanation for it. The scene before him was hardly conducive to fear. Ssarekai was the most trustworthy drake Aurim knew, more trustworthy than most humans. The warlock's only other choice seemed to be the stable, but since he had no part in the cleaning of it, for which he was thankful, Aurim could not see how the building could possibly unsettle his thoughts.

Perhaps sensing that he was not alone, Ssarekai looked up from his work. "Wasss there sssomething else, Massster Aurim?"

"No. Sorry." What could he say to the stable master? Aurim backed out of the building, unable to tear his eyes from it until he was well away. Even then, the feeling of unease continued to shake him. So occupied was he, in fact, that the youth did not notice the trio that stood quietly talking to one another at the edge of the garden until he was almost next to them.

A breathtaking maiden with long, dark hair and exotic, narrow eyes filled his vision. Her face was a dream, her lips full and inviting. The dress she wore was the color of roses and did nothing to hide the lush form beneath it. Had he not grown up with her, played with her as though she were a sister, Aurim might have been spellbound. As it was, he could only think again of the fortunate male who would someday be Ursa's choice. Peculiar as it seemed, however, that male would not necessarily care that much for her present appearance; he would likely prefer her in her *true* form.

Ursa was a female drake: sister, albeit from a different clutch of eggs, to both Kyl and Grath. She also bore the royal birth markings, which meant that while she could not be empress, the drakes not permitting such, the young female could be the mother of one. Ursa did not care about that, however. All she cared about was her best friend, her sister in all but the physical sense: Valea.

The two were together even now, but this time a third person was with them.

Benjin Traske looked up from what he had been doing and stared at him, stopping Aurim in his tracks with just that glance. Valea was partly turned to the scholar, as if the two had been in earnest conversation. All wore rather serious expressions, but whether those expressions had to do with whatever conversation he had interrupted or whether they concerned his own agitated countenance, the young warlock could not say. At the moment, that did not matter nearly as much to him as the reason for his own uneasiness. Flickering memories danced about in his mind, teasing him.

"Are you all right, Aurim?" Ursa asked, coming to his side.

"It's nothing." A face surfaced in his memory, but it was blurred and distorted.

Benjin Traske gently moved Valea aside. He walked over to Aurim and looked him in the eye. "You do not look well at all, lad."

"It's . . . night . . ." The warlock had no idea why he had mentioned nighttime, yet somehow it made sense. He tried to focus on both night and the face, trying to fit them together. "I thought I saw . . ."

"Look at me." Traske took him by the shoulders. The two matched gazes. The scholar studied Aurim carefully. "I do not see anything. Your eyes look clear. Your face is a bit pale, but nothing terrible."

The pressure on his mind faded. Aurim began to breathe easier. The memories slipped away, but they no longer seemed of any real importance. All that remained was a slight headache.

"Do you wish to lie down?"

He shook his head. "No, sir. It's nothing. Just a little headache."

The massive tutor released him. He still eyed the younger man closely. "Well, if it happens again, come to see me. A reoccurring problem is nothing to be ignored. I should be able to find some way to deal with it. You understand me?"

"Yes, sir." It all seemed rather silly now. Aurim could not even recall what had caused the headache, which was already receding.

"Do you want someone to walk with you?" Ursa asked.

He found that he was a little embarrassed by their concern. At least Valea was not fawning over him. His sister remained behind the others, also concerned but only watching. Her mind appeared to be elsewhere, but at the moment Aurim had no interest in whatever it was his sister was thinking about. He only knew that he still felt ashamed at the fuss he had just caused.

Aurim extricated himself from Ursa's hold. "I'm fine. I am. I didn't mean to interrupt you."

"Not at all, lad."

"If you'll excuse me, then?" Executing a half-bow, the embarrassed youth departed quickly, leaving the others to return to whatever conversation he had disrupted.

What was I doing? he chided himself. *Now they'll think I can't run this place on my own! Can't even put up with a small headache!*

Tramping across the Manor grounds, he turned toward the kitchens. Some food and water would do the trick. He was probably just hungry. Aurim had hardly eaten at all today. That was all it had probably been: a headache brought on by a lack of food. Considering his normal eating habits, his body had likely just not been used to so little for so long. *I'll feel fine after that! No more headaches!*

The throbbing had already all but ceased, and as for the peculiar memories . . . they were once more forgotten.

In a private conversation some minutes after the fact, the Green Dragon informed the Bedlams that he had been unprepared for the request Kyl had flung before the rulers of Talak just prior to the supper's end. Neither the emperor-to-be nor Grath had given any hint in previous conversations with him. It had startled the Dragon King as much as it had Melicard.

It had startled Cabe equally as much, although he had been able to hide his surprise better than most of the others. Only Darkhorse, who simply shook his head, and Grath, the only one with whom Kyl *had*, perhaps, discussed his decision, had seemed fairly calm about the matter.

The heir to the dragon throne had requested the opportunity to perform a special ceremony, one that he had claimed was long overdue. It was to be a private but formal ceremony, with wreaths and a speech of apology to both the city and its rulers. Kyl had claimed that he wanted to prove once and for all that the sins of the father would *not* be ignored by the son.

What was most stunning about the request was that the dragon heir desired to have this special ceremony take place before the burial chamber of Melicard's *father*, Rennek.

At first the king had been dumbstruck. Then he had stopped just short of calling the notion something that certainly would have raised the threat of war between the two races. At last, he had looked to his queen for guidance. Erini had simply put one slim hand on his elfwood arm and nodded. That had settled it for Melicard. If Erini thought the idea had merit, the king could not argue. This was a situation where Cabe had known that Melicard would be unable to trust his own judgment. The warlock was rather surprised that the queen had so readily agreed to it, but he, like the king, trusted her intelligence.

That had been last night. By now, late in the morning, the entire castle, perhaps even most of the kingdom, would be astir with rumors. When exactly the ceremony was to take place was still undecided, but the master warlock hoped that it would be soon; if the event was delayed more than a few days, then Cabe feared that . . . well, to be truthful, he had *no* idea what might happen, just the feeling that something *would* happen.

"What could've possessed Kyl to make such a daring move?" he asked his wife as the two spellcasters walked the grounds of the palace. Unlike most visitors, the Bedlams did not require an escort. That did not mean they were not watched. Cabe could sense eyes on him: eyes, and weak, inexperienced probes. Melicard had himself one or two mages now, it seemed, but neither were of any high level of skill. The warlock knew that Gwendolyn had also noted them and found the probes almost as amusing as he did. With a simple spell, either Bedlam could have left the hidden mages following a false trail for the rest of the day. As guests, however, it would have been bad form. Melicard was only acting in the manner of all cautious rulers past and present. He was by no means either the most paranoid or the most troublesome.

"I am curious as to that myself," the Lady Bedlam finally responded. "That even Lord Green had known nothing about it bothers me a little. I understand that Kyl did not need to consult anyone, but such an act should have, I think, made him think about doing so. You saw Melicard's face."

"Every variation."

"Yes, well, we can thank Erini for his relative calm toward the end. Melicard's parents have always been a touchy subject. Rennek IV was not the best of rulers, evidently, but he had a soft place in his heart for his son."

"And too fragile a mind," added Cabe. Ahead of them, he heard the laughter of a child and the sound of the queen's voice.

"It *is* a clever suggestion," the crimson-tressed enchantress admitted. "Now that Melicard has gotten over his initial confusion, he should be able to see that himself. It allows Kyl to show his willingness to admit to the terrors committed in the name of his sire, while at the same time it enables the king to show his people that he is strong enough to have the respect of the new emperor of the drakes. That no one but we will witness it makes no difference. Word will get out and that will be sufficient."

"Providing it ever takes place."

She grimaced. "I think I will urge Erini to convince her husband that it should take place either tomorrow or the day after that. Most likely the day after; with the formal reception this evening, tomorrow would make everyone feel hurried for time."

Cabe looked at her, a wry smile spreading across his plain features. "Exactly who runs this kingdom? You? Erini? Lynnette, perhaps?"

Gwen had no chance to respond to his jest, for suddenly both of them became aware of the sound of soldiers running. The sound came from the same direction where they had both heard the queen and her daughter playing not a moment before.

No word passed between the two, but suddenly Gwen no longer stood at his side. Cabe hesitated only long enough to ready himself, then also vanished.

He materialized in the midst of spear points and sword tips. More than a dozen guards surrounded the scene, with yet another contingent arriving even as the warlock drank in his surroundings. Erini stood to one side, a small, delicate-looking girl holding her hand and two massive guards shielding them both from possible danger. Darkhorse stood near the center of the circle the soldiers had formed, but it was not the eternal at whom the weapons were pointed.

A drake cowered before the captain of the guard. Darkhorse was on the dragon man's other side, looking more curious than wary.

"Pleassse! I meant no—"

"Be silent!" The captain struck the drake across the false helm. Cabe noted the lack of crest; the prisoner was one of the servitors, not a warrior. That did not mean that the drake was not capable of killing, but it did make it unlikely. They were generally not very aggressive for their race, even in dragon form.

It seemed doubtful that *any* of the drakes would be so foolhardy as to attack one of the royal family, even as a dragon. True, any one of the draconian visitors had the potential to become one of the legendary leviathans, but in Talak that was more likely to mean death to the shapeshifter than to his prey. It was reasonable to assume that Melicard had planned for such circumstances; the king would never have allowed the drakes in otherwise. And prior to the departure of the caravan, Lord Green had made certain to remind his folk that even an accidental transformation meant punishment . . . possibly at the discretion of Melicard himself.

To most drakes, Melicard was a demon in human guise. Cabe had been confident from the start that none of the reptilian race would risk themselves so.

Which brought up the question as to what had happened *here*.

"Captain, I command you to stop that."

The guardsman looked at his queen, rather befuddled that she would give such an order. With evident reluctance, he lowered his hand. "But Your Majesty—"

"Stay here, Lynnette," the queen whispered to the slim, ivory-skinned child. The young princess, despite her appearance, was no fragile flower, but this was one time, Cabe saw, that she would obey her mother without question. Erini stepped past the two reluctant guards and confronted the captain. "I gave you a command."

Her words were spoken softly, but the soldier nonetheless paled. He saluted and stepped back.

The queen finally seemed to notice the Bedlams. "I am glad the two of you are here. Do you recognize this drake?"

Cabe thought he did, but Gwendolyn spoke before he had a chance to commit himself. "Osseuss, isn't it?"

"Y-yessss, my lady!"

"He was trying to sneak up on the queen and the princess!" snapped the captain of the guard.

The drake shook his head. "Nooo! No!"

"Lies!" The soldier made to strike the drake again, but a glance from Erini made him falter. "My men saw him creeping around the trees, Your Majesty! Creeping around the trees and watching you and the Princess Lynnette!"

"And *me!*" rumbled Darkhorse. "Come, come, Captain! Do you think one drake is any threat to *me?*"

Even under the chilling gaze of the shadow steed, the veteran warrior remained steadfast. "I was doing my duty!"

"And very well," soothed the queen. "I thank you for your concern, but I have my doubts as to the danger posed by this particular drake. Tell me, Osseuss; why did you come here?"

The dragon man glanced at the Lady Bedlam, who nodded to him and said, "Tell the truth."

Keeping one eye on the captain, Osseuss explained, "I wasss losssst. The landsss, they are ssso beautiful, ssso well-kept! I wandered, then realized that I had become turned around. I thought I knew the way back, Your Majesssty, but found myssself here inssstead! I grew fearful, knowing that I wasss where I wasss not meant to be, and when I sssaw you and your daughter, my heart pounded! I was certain that I had condemned myssself by not paying attention!"

"Why is that?"

"A *drake* near the bride of Melicard the Terrible? Only for the royal party isss that posssible! For the ressst of usss, that is surely sssuicide!"

Judging from the guards' expressions, it was clear to Cabe that Osseuss was correct in that assumption. These men were ready to kill the servitor simply because he was what he was. To be fair, Osseuss *should* have known better, but if men could be foolhardy, then so could drakes. In some ways the races were too similar.

Queen Erini looked at the Bedlams. Gwen studied the cringing drake for a moment longer, then said, "I will vouch for him. His duties at the Manor concern the care of the gardens there. Osseuss has always been one of the most loving caretakers. I will definitely vouch for him."

"So will I," Cabe added in support. Unless Osseuss was a cunning mage comparable in power to the trio of spellcasters before him, his story was genuine. While neither Cabe nor his wife had delved into the drake's thoughts, it was simple enough to read the truth in the emotions radiating from the mind of the servitor. There was true fear there, fear mixed with confusion and self-recrimination.

The guardsman was still not convinced. "But *Your Majesty*! We can't just—"

"Are you questioning the word of our guests, Captain? If so, you will also be questioning mine, because I find I agree with them in this matter."

As if that was not enough in its own right to crush what protest there was left in the officer, Darkhorse added, "And if you question the word of my friends, then know you that you also question *my* word!"

Seeing that there would be no more interruptions, the queen did the unthinkable. She held out her hand to the prisoner. He stared at it for several seconds, trying to decide what she intended. When it was clear that Erini did not plan to withdraw the proffered hand, Osseuss reluctantly took it. He rose, then executed a perfect bow.

"Can you find your way back on your own now?"

The drake hesitated. His reptilian eyes continued to flicker between the queen and the captain. A forked tongue darted out and in as he nervously considered her question. "I . . . I am not sure."

"I would give you an escort, but I think that emotions run too high for that at the moment."

"*I* will return him to his companions."

Everyone looked at Darkhorse, whose attitude so far had been surprising. He had sided with a drake and now offered to see that same drake back to safety. It was almost amusing. Osseuss was at least as fearful of the eternal as he was the guards.

"Are you certain you wish to do that, Darkhorse?"

The ebony stallion chuckled. "I thought I had just said so! Do you doubt *my* word, Your Majesty?"

"Never." The queen smiled. "Thank you, then."

"I am your servant!" Darkhorse trotted up to the still-anxious drake. The captain of the guard—and the rest of the guards, for that matter—retreated as the shadow steed neared the prisoner. "Come with me, dragon!"

Osseuss looked to his master and mistress for confirmation.

"Go with him," Cabe responded. "There's nothing to fear."

It was clear that the servitor could have argued that point, but he nonetheless obeyed the warlock. The circle of guards gave way for the duo, the nearest soldiers wisely deciding to lower their weapons as Darkhorse trotted by.

Erini watched the strange pair depart, then summoned the recalcitrant officer to her. "I want you to know that your loyalty is commendable, Captain. These next few days *will* be difficult for all of us. Caution is good, but we must never lose control."

There were many things that the guardsman probably wanted to say in response, but this was his queen and so he could only obey. The captain saluted her. "I understand, Your Majesty."

"You may resume your duties, then. I wish you the best of luck. This *will* be a taxing situation for you and your men, but I have every confidence in your abilities."

"Thank you, Your Majesty."

The captain organized his men and led them off in record time. Only four soldiers still remained, the personal guard of the queen herself.

"I thank you, Erini," Gwen said when the captain was gone.

"It was a mistake; I saw that, too. I was glad that you were there to verify it for me, however. My skill at sorcery will never be as great as either of yours."

"Yours is formidable enough. You have done us proud." The queen had been the Bedlams' first student and, so far, their most promising. The handful of spellcasters that had been brought to Penacles were, for the most part, folk who would never be able to do much more than light fires with a glance or lift small objects into the air. There were one or two who might go beyond that, but so far no one who had the potential to even remotely approach the power of either the witch or the warlock.

This did not mean that such did not exist. Cabe could count four whose powers were adequate at the very least. Three of those worked for King Lanith of Zuu. The other was a wanderer, a blond beauty who had used the name Tori and who had, at one point, attempted to seduce Cabe. Considering the way these four had turned out, the sorcerer wondered whether or not it was a good thing that so few others of any measurable might had appeared so far. The present crop of spellcasters was not by any stretch of the imagination a shining example of what a new age of sorcery might offer the world. Too many people already feared those like the Bedlams, who had done them no harm at all. If more like Lanith's lackeys appeared, the reputation of sorcery would only be tarnished further.

Queen Erini had blushed slightly at the compliment. "I thank you for your confidence in me, Gwendolyn." Her expression changed almost immediately. "But enough about that. I am glad that both of you are here. If you will excuse me for one moment. . . ." She turned back to her daughter and the remaining sentries. "I believe it is almost time for your lessons, is it not, Lynnette?"

The little princess made a very unladylike face, but under the queen's steady gaze she finally nodded. "Yes, Mother."

"I thought so. Then you had best be on your way—" Erini raised a hand as her daughter started to run off. "*Not* like that and *not* without some company. Also," she added in softer tones, "it would be nice if I could have a hug first."

Smiling, Lynnette rushed over to her mother, who leaned down and took the girl in her arms. They held one another tight, then Erini reluctantly allowed her daughter to slip away. Lynnette curtsied to the two mages, then returned to the guards. One pair followed the princess as she started back toward the palace.

Queen Erini sighed as she watched her only child depart. "It gets hard to watch them grow up so fast! I remember when she was but a baby!"

The Bedlams were quiet but sympathetic, understanding all too well the sensation the queen was experiencing.

"Enough of that!" The slim woman looked at her two old friends. "I am glad you happened along, because I have need to talk to you. Melicard has agreed to the ceremony taking place soon after the formal reception but has not set a specific day and time. Do you have any suggestions?"

Cabe looked at his wife, who smiled back at him. Turning her gaze back to the queen, the Lady Bedlam replied, "We were *just* discussing that very subject before we heard the soldiers!"

"And what did you decide?"

The warlock could not resist. "My wife the royal counselor thought that the day after tomorrow would be best. It would allow a day of calm for all of us after the excitement of tonight's reception."

Erini could not hold back her smile. "The royal counselor may be correct. I was thinking along the same lines. What time of day would the royal counselor suggest?"

"To be fair," began Gwendolyn, giving Cabe a piercing but playful stare, "I think the royal counselor's *husband* should contribute on *that* matter."

"And what do *you* say, royal counselor's husband?"

Unschooled in the eccentricities of proper royal behavior, Cabe had no idea what time of day would be appropriate for such a solemn ceremony. Thinking of his own preference, he hesitantly answered, "In the morning?"

Erini considered this for quite some time. Cabe hoped that he had not erred in some way. Better to face an angry Dragon King than try to muddle his way through the idiosyncrasies of the monarchy.

"Yes, the morning might work. I have always thought that there was something captivating about the first few hours of the day, something touching the soul."

The warlock relaxed.

"I will take your suggestions to my husband. If he finds them agreeable, then they will be presented to Lord Kyl and Lord Green." The queen hugged them both. "Thank you, both of you. I always know that I can depend upon your sage advice."

"We're glad to help in any way we can," Cabe returned. Gwen echoed his sentiments. Erini was a good friend.

"The day after tomorrow," repeated the slim monarch. "In the morning. Early, so that the wonder of a new day will touch us all . . . those of us who can *appreciate* morning, that is."

"How fare the preparations for the reception this evening?" asked the Lady Bedlam, changing the subject.

"Everything is moving swimmingly. I have been planning for this day since it was first suggested some time back. The food will be ready. The ballroom is being prepared even as we speak. All the arrangements are proceeding exactly as I hoped." Some of the queen's high spirits faded. "Now, if only the *guests* could be so obliging. Not everyone thinks that peace with drakes is a good thing."

Drakes eating and drinking alongside the cream of Talak's leadership. Cabe tried to hide his own anxiety from Erini. It was one thing to have a private supper between the two rulers, but the reception invited so many new and unpredictable elements into the situation.

"I'm sure that they'll—"

"*Erini!* Are you all right?" called a frantic voice.

They turned to see the king come rushing across the lawn. Behind him and having difficulty keeping pace with the distraught monarch were Baron Vergoth and Melicard's personal guard.

"It is all right, Melicard! I—" The queen had no chance to say more, for the tall form of her husband suddenly enveloped her.

"I just spoke with the guards protecting Lynnette! Curse those drakes! I'll have the whole bunch of them slaughtered, with that snake who would sit on the throne beheaded before the entire city!"

"*Melicard!*" Erini's eyes were wide with fear, but fear for her husband and her people, not for herself. "You will do no such *thing*! Think what that would mean! The rest of the Dragon Kings would see no choice but to fall upon Talak with their full combined might!"

"I do not care!"

"But it was a *mistake*! The drake did nothing! He was lost and happened to wander too near. The sentries saw him and mistook his presence for a threat, but he was only trying to find his way back to the others. If anyone was in danger, it was *him*! Just ask Cabe or Gwendolyn."

Melicard turned his unsettling gaze toward Cabe, who was forced to steel himself when the unseeing, elfwood orb fixed on him. "What is she saying?"

"The truth," the warlock responded. He did not allow the king any time to argue. "It was a servitor drake. They're more inclined to work than assassinate. This one was scared out of his wits. Your guards did their duty," he added, not wanting to sound too recriminating, "but in this case they had nothing to fear."

"Where is this . . . lizard?"

"Darkhorse led him back to the others. Both my wife and I will vouch for the drake, Melicard."

"As will I, husband." The queen forced the hesitant ruler to look at her again. "It was *nothing*. Perhaps the guards still worry because they are not used to even the presence of a drake in the city, but they were wrong if they told you that I was attacked."

The king stilled, but the tension had by no means left him. *Why did this have to happen now?* wondered Cabe.

Baron Vergoth dared speak. "Shall we locate this drake, my lord? Question him ourselves?"

Melicard stared at his bride. Erini gave him a look of defiance. "No, Baron. Not this time. It seems we were mistaken."

The aristocrat looked rather disappointed, but he nodded.

"Thank you," whispered Erini. She hugged her husband, then gave him a light kiss. "And thank you for your concern."

"I would give up all of Talak if it meant your safety."

"Let's hope it will never come to that, then, shall we? I think the people deserve better."

With some effort, the king turned to the Bedlams. "I thank you two for your assistance in this matter. I also apologize for any inconvenience that this may have caused you."

The sorcerer would have liked to have said something concerning the fact that the one who had suffered the most inconvenience was the drake Osseuss, but such a bald statement would not have sat well with the king. Instead, he replied, "I hope that this doesn't make Kyl more reluctant."

Beside him, Gwen gasped. For once, he had thought of the ramifications before she had.

Melicard, too, saw the possible consequences. "I will have a most sincere message relayed to the Lord Kyl. You also might inform him of my regrets, should you see him before the messenger does."

"As you wish." Cabe was too relieved about Melicard's acquiescence to point out that he was hardly at the beck and call of Talak's master. "I'm glad that everything is back to normal."

"*Nothing* will be back to normal until those drakes are gone," the lord of the mountain kingdom snapped. "Even after that happens, I doubt if we will ever be able to relax! For the sake of my family and my people, I hope that I am wrong, but the history of the drakes, at least during *my* lifetime, has been fraught with nothing but troubles."

"Hopefully," interjected the Lady Bedlam, "this visit will alter that."

"Yes . . ." Melicard squeezed his wife hard, but his eyes never left the mages. "I hope it will, but you would all be wise to remember what I said earlier: if I find any proof, *any at all,* of a threat to either my family or my kingdom, I will take the drakes, no matter what the cost, and execute each and every one of them . . . beginning, I think, with *Lord Kyl.*" Melicard released Erini and began to turn toward Baron Vergoth and the guardsmen. "Now if you will excuse me, I have a reception to prepare for."

The king, trailed by his men, stalked away, leaving in his wake three silent, thoughtful figures.

VIII

Throughout the day and into the evening, various folk in the kingdom of Talak were greeted with an unsettling sight. Before them they would suddenly find the dread legend known as Darkhorse. The demon steed appeared in the alleys of the dankest parts of the city, the open fields of the surrounding countryside, and even among the silent ancestors of the king laid to rest in the royal necropolis. Those who stayed around long enough to observe the shadowy form might have noticed how the glittering, blue eyes of Darkhorse took in everything, as if the legendary creature was seeking something. Yet, whatever it was, Darkhorse did not appear to find it. Through the day and into the evening the shadow steed searched, reluctantly foregoing his quest only when light finally gave in to darkness.

There was, after all, a reception he had been requested to attend.

If things are going so well, then why does it seem as if everyone in the room is about to burst from tension?

Cabe sipped his drink and watched the proceedings. Kyl, flanked by Erini and Melicard, was being introduced to various members of the kingdom's aristocracy and civilian leadership. The king knew the importance of maintaining a balance between the two groups. In Talak, the divisions between the aristocracy and the upper-class merchants were less strict than they were in some kingdoms. Living under the continual shadow of the Dragon Emperors had a way of drawing people together. That, however, did not mean that the two groups did not constantly attempt to gain some advantage over one another.

Kyl was not a lone drake among humans, however. Next to the monarchs were both Grath and the Green Dragon. Grath followed every introduction with avid interest, while the Dragon King kept a wary eye on everyone. Further back, an honor guard consisting of a dozen drake warriors, Faras and Ssgayn first and foremost among them, stood at attention, willing to take on the entire palace if need be. While outnumbered by the Talakian guardsmen, Cabe had no doubt that the drakes, if given the opportunity, would be able to wreak great carnage in defense of their lords.

As a sorcerer of renown, Cabe had not needed to dress for this occasion, but Gwendolyn had insisted on it. Therefore, the mage now wore a dark, dignified outfit akin to those once worn in the courts of Mito Pica. Cabe considered himself a survivor of that kingdom, his foster father having raised him in the wooded lands surrounding the city. The outfit consisted of dark blue pants and coat and a high-collared shirt of gray. Black, shin-length boots completed the conservative suit. In truth, the suit would have been considered conservative even in Mito Pica, for the sorcerer had decided to forego the more decorative aspects of his former kingdom's tastes. Even doing that, however, did not make the suit anything a proper mage should wear.

The Lady Bedlam, however, was by no means so reserved. She was clad in a dazzling gown of emerald and pink that had many of the elite of Talak looking a bit on the shabby side. Cabe could not think of another woman in the ballroom who was more beautiful, more resplendent, than his wife, an opinion he suspected was shared by many of the male merchants and aristocrats, for some of them seemed almost as attentive to her as they were to either their monarchs or the drake heir.

Yes, everything *seemed* to be progressing smoothly, but now and then Cabe would catch a frown or a surreptitious glare among those gathered. Just enough to keep him tense.

The last of the introductions were made. After a short conversation with the king and queen, Kyl turned to Lord Green and said something. The Dragon King shook his head, but Kyl was adamant. At last, the Green Dragon nodded.

Kyl signaled to Grath, and the two began to walk unprotected among the Talakians.

"I don't know whether he's amazingly brave or simply majestically foolhardy," said Gwendolyn as she rejoined Cabe. "We had best keep a careful eye on him."

"He does wield power of his own."

"Yes, but this *is* Talak."

His wife had a point. If ever there was a place where the people would be prepared against dragon tricks, it was the mountain kingdom. "What's he hoping to accomplish by doing this?"

She took a sip from her goblet. "That only Kyl and maybe Grath know. Kyl *says* that he wants the people to really know him, to understand that he should not be feared the way his father was."

"The Talakians don't fear him as much as they hate him." It was a sweeping statement, even Cabe would have been willing to admit that, but it held more than a grain of truth. The most evident hate was that of the older soldiers and aristocrats, the ones who could still recall the days before the last Dragon Emperor's death. Baron Vergoth could be numbered among those, although he was much more expert at hiding that hatred than many of his contemporaries. The warlock did not care for the way the baron's eyes followed the dragon heir. Had looks truly been able to kill, Kyl would have been dead now, a blade in his throat. Vergoth, fortunately, was too loyal to his king.

"Where is Darkhorse?" the Lady Bedlam asked suddenly.

"I don't know." Cabe could sense his presence somewhere in Talak, but could not fix on one location. Still, it seemed as if the eternal was suddenly making his way to—

There were shrieks from just beyond the king and queen. Both human and draconian sentries readied their weapons, prepared for the worst. Kyl, speaking softly to an elegant if somewhat plain-faced countess, turned slowly toward the direction of the cries.

The shadow steed had finally made an appearance.

That there was not more panic was due to the earlier presence of mind of the queen. Erini had very carefully warned her subjects of the coming of the legendary creature. Most of those gathered here had long been aware of her peculiar friendship with the creature from the Void, and while many of them were aghast at such a relationship, it was well-known that Darkhorse had saved the lives of both the king and queen.

Still, one could not blame anyone for becoming startled at the abrupt materialization of a huge, ebony stallion. Two women fainted and several more guests, both male and female, looked ready to join them. Darkhorse, as usual, ignored the effect his arrival had had. He trotted across the marble floor, his hooves making no sound and leaving no marks. When he finally stood before Melicard and Erini, the eternal dipped his head in both greeting and respect.

"My greetings to Your Majesties," he rumbled.

His respectful attitude toward their monarchs helped settle in part the nerves of the other guests. A few even eyed the eternal with satisfaction. The warlock sipped his drink again, thinking *they see Darkhorse as an ally of Talak, a weapon to use against the drakes.* He glanced at Kyl, who also seemed quite pleased that Darkhorse had come to the reception. The emperor-to-be was quietly studying the reactions of the Talakians. Grath whispered something in his ear that made Kyl smile and nod his head. *Is this what you wanted, then, Kyl? To make Talak feel that it has nothing to fear from the new Dragon Emperor because they've got allies such as Darkhorse to aid them if need be?*

If that was the case, then Kyl was even more devious than Cabe had imagined.

Things slowly returned to something resembling normal. It was almost humorous to watch some of the guests constantly look from the dragon heir to the eternal and then back again. This was likely the most unusual reception any of the Talakians had ever attended. It would make for tales to tell. As the warlock continued to observe, he saw that with Darkhorse's presence now an accepted thing, people were beginning to approach Kyl. The handsome drake was less of a shock compared to the eternal. Now he was simply exotic. True, his teeth were a bit sharp and he spoke with the characteristic sibilance of his kind, but the rest of his appearance made him worthy of any royal court.

He had already charmed most of the women he had talked to, but this time Kyl was careful not to aggravate the men who were with them. For the most part, the young drake was in his element and whenever it seemed he might falter, Grath was there to whisper in his ear or even add a rare word of his own to the conversation.

Yet, Cabe still did not feel confident about the night. Perhaps it was simply because this was Talak, hated enemy of the drakes. . . .

You share my fears, then? came a voice in his head.

He knew that it was Darkhorse, but it still gave him a start. Gwendolyn looked at him, but Cabe only smiled and made a comment about the wine. If Darkhorse desired to talk to him alone, then he would respect the shadow steed's wishes . . . to a point. There was little the sorcerer hid from his wife.

You may tell her what you wish when I am through. I certainly have nothing to hide from the Lady of the Amber, remarked the great stallion. Darkhorse was one of the few who still called Gwendolyn by that title, but he was careful not to use it in her presence. For roughly two centuries, she had been kept sealed in a prison of amber, the legacy of Cabe's mad father, Azran. The Lady of the Amber was almost as great a legend as Darkhorse himself, but few knew that Gwendolyn Bedlam was the same woman.

What do you want?

Several yards away, Darkhorse continued to speak with Erini. It was astounding the way he could hold two conversations at the same time without ever becoming confused. *I have found something of interest . . . or perhaps I should say that I found* nothing *and find* that *of interest!*

Cabe held back a sigh, hoping against hope that this was not to be one of the eternal's murky explanations. There were times when the shadow steed could leave him more befuddled than informed. *What exactly are you talking about?*

There is no trace, no sign, of the sort of sorcery such as what was used to bait the traps that almost snared me and did *capture you!*

That did not surprise Cabe, and thus should not have surprised Darkhorse. *I haven't noticed anything and I doubt that there is anything to notice. Melicard knows better, Darkhorse! He wants peace, too. The days of genocide are over.* Cabe *hoped* they were. *You should have told me that you were looking for some sign of guilt. I could have told you that Melicard is innocent.* Erini *could have told you that!*

To the naked eye, there was still no hint that the eternal was doing anything other than conversing with the queen. Yet, in the sorcerer's mind, the shadow steed practically roared with impatience. *But that is what I mean! Of course you cannot sense any trace, but neither can I ! Me! I should be able to find some trace; no one knows the Vraad . . . or especially* Shade . . . *as well as I, yet I find absolutely no evidence here!*

It *was* to be one of the stallion's murky explanations. *And that means?*

Someone else is responsible.

As worldly as the eternal was, he somehow still retained a childlike attitude in many things. Cabe *hmmphed,* but fortunately Gwen did not notice. *There* are *others who despise or fear the drakes. Zuu, for example.*

No, it was not Zuu. I have been there.

Cabe still had no idea as to how Darkhorse could be so certain about his findings, but he knew better than to argue that point. *Well, there can't be too many remnants of Shade's legacy, can there?*

I do not know. With that, the eternal broke the link.

So that's what he's been doing, the warlock mused. *Using his invitation to make a thorough check of this place.* Cabe was glad that Darkhorse had found nothing in Talak. It would have crippled the possibilities for peace if Melicard was discovered returning to his old ways. Not only that, but it would probably have also meant the end of his marriage to Erini. That bothered him almost as much as the threat of a return to war.

Cabe despised the intrigues of government. Sorcery was so much simpler, so much more straightforward, in comparison.

"What do you suppose is happening there?"

Gwen's question concerned a young noble who was speaking with Grath. They appeared to be having a somewhat heated discussion, at least where the human was concerned. While what Grath was saying was not audible, the drake's demeanor indicated reason and calm. Yet, each word seemed to incense the noble.

Stepping between his brother and the human, Kyl muttered something to the Talakian.

The noble replied.

Kyl, hissing loudly, started to swing a fist at the man.

"Trouble!" Gwendolyn breathed.

Before either of them could move, Grath took hold of his brother's arm and prevented the blow from landing. Unfortunately, the noble took the aborted assault as excuse to draw a ceremonial knife from his belt. Even from where he stood, Cabe could see that the blade was as well-honed as any normal knife.

"Jermaine!" Melicard called. "Stop!"

Both the king's men and Kyl's honor guard began moving toward the struggle. Neither Bedlam could get a good enough view of those at the center to dare a spell. It was possible that the wrong reaction would leave either the dragon heir or the noble open to attack. The death of either would shatter the peace, no matter what the original reason for the argument.

Jermaine, the noble, slashed at Kyl. Grath's hand blocked the attack, but not without incurring a jagged cut. One of the courtiers behind Jermaine grabbed the noble's other arm. Jermaine struggled free, then took a step toward his adversary.

The entire situation threatened to get out of hand . . . if that were any more possible. The two honor guards had already taken up positions around the combatants, old hatreds causing both of them to choose their own kind. A full-scale battle was brewing.

"I'm going to try to pick Kyl out of there!" Gwendolyn hissed. "I don't understand why the fool hasn't done so himself!" Although the warnings against using drake magic were supposed to apply to the emperor-to-be as well as his retinue, it was doubtful that Melicard would have held Kyl responsible for using his sorcery in self-defense. Still, perhaps the drake felt it was safer to fight by hand rather than risk the defenses of Talak.

Then, just as it seemed that everyone was converging on the battle, a blast of thunder shook the entire room. It was so intense that everyone froze, many perhaps thinking that an earthquake or siege had commenced.

"Children, children! Behave yourselves *now!*"

It was Darkhorse. His stentorian voice echoed throughout the room.

"Milady," he continued, now looking at the queen, "I regret to say that I may have cracked your floor down to the foundation! For that, I do apologize."

Queen Erini was barely able to hide a smile. She nodded to the shadow steed. "You are forgiven, I think."

"My gratitude for that." The ice-blue, pupilless orbs focused on the king. "Your Majesty, the situation is now in *your* hands."

Melicard reacted immediately. His expression unreadable, the lord of the mountain kingdom marched toward the struggle. Two courtiers held the noble named Jermaine by the arms. Kyl and the others watched in silence as the tall king stopped before them and stared.

"My Lord Kyl, I hope you will forgive this distasteful display. It should never have happened."

The dragon heir exhaled. The fire in his eyes faded. He eyed the noble, then his brother. Something passed between the two drakes. To the king, Kyl replied, "It isss underssstandable, Your Majesssty! Mossst regrettably underssstandable."

"I will have someone see to your brother's hand."

"Let *me*." The queen stepped forward. There was a murmuring among the guests.

"The wound is slight," argued Grath. "There is no need."

"Nonsense!" Erini took the drake's hand. She inspected the wound, then cast a disappointed glance toward Jermaine. The noble had the good sense to look at least a bit ashamed.

It would have been simple for any spellcaster of reasonable strength to heal the flesh wound. Grath himself could have done so, given a little time, but Cabe understood what the queen was doing. Talak was responsible for the wound and so Talak, in the form of Queen Erini, would heal it.

Meanwhile, Melicard had turned on the young noble. "Have you anything to say, Jermaine? What was this all about?"

Jermaine's mouth moved, but no sound came out. One of the courtiers holding him cleared his own throat and quietly said, "If I may, Your Majesty; I think it was a misunderstanding."

Pulling his attention away from the queen's ministrations, which had already caused the wound to seal, Grath announced, "Yes, that was all." Curious eyes turned his way. "A very great missunderstanding. We were discussing the future relationship of our two kingdoms—"

The king raised a hand, silencing the drake. "That will be sufficient. I know this lad and I know how he thinks." The disfigured monarch paused. "I know very *well* how he thinks. Baron Vergoth!"

The baron stepped out of the assembled throng. "Yes, my liege?"

"Will you see to our unruly guest here?" The king indicated the petulant Jermaine.

"One moment, Your Majesssty," interrupted Kyl. "What do you plan to do with him?"

The two lords confronted one another. In level tones, the king asked, "Did you have some particular punishment in mind, Lord Kyl?"

"I had *no* punishment in mind. I undersssstand hisss way of thinking. There isss much reason behind it, consssidering the passsts of our two racesss. I would rather hope that you will take that in mind and treat him accordingly. Better to work to break down old hatredsss rather than reinforce them. The latter will only ssslow the peace we both desssire."

Melicard stared at the drake as if seeing a different person there. He visibly mulled over what Kyl had said. "I cannot very well reward him for shaming Talak, but I understand your point. Very well." Melicard turned to Jermaine. "You know what I could have done to you for endangering the kingdom?"

"Yes, my liege. I . . . apologize for everything. I would make some restitution."

"You will. I'll see to that. I will have you work to help make this peace real, lad. We cannot let it be said that Talak was incapable of changing when the chance was offered to it. We're not merely speaking of peace with the drakes, you fool, but also with the other human kingdoms. Who would trust us if you had more seriously injured—possibly even *killed*—one of those to whom I have granted protection under a banner of truce?"

"I had no intention of killing him, Your—"

"Which excuses nothing." Melicard folded his arms. "Baron Vergoth and some guards will escort you from this palace. Tomorrow afternoon, you will return here, at which time I will tell you how you will make amends for this. Is that clear?"

Jermaine went down on one knee, his eyes downcast. "Yes, my liege."

The king turned to Vergoth. "If you please, Baron?"

"Aye, Your Majesty."

The impetuous noble was led silently off. The other guests whispered among themselves. Cabe read a variety of emotions among them. There were many who felt that the king had been more than generous, considering the importance of the affair, but there were also several who revealed sympathy for Jermaine. The warlock made a mental note of the names and faces of the most conspicuous of the latter just in case.

Once more, King Melicard turned to his special guest. "I apologize again, Lord Kyl, for this disastrous incident. Despite what *anyone* might imagine, such behavior will not be tolerated. The next one who shows such colors will not benefit from your good will."

"I undersssstand and appreciate your wordsss, Your Majesty."

"He is healed, Melicard," Erini informed her husband just then. She held Grath's unblemished hand toward the king so that he could see for himself.

"Very good!" The king raised his arms to the assembled folk. "My friends! This incident is at an end! Please return to what you were doing! There is still food and drink!" Melicard nodded toward the emperor-to-be. "There is still a peace to plan."

Slowly, the guests spread out again. Kyl and Grath joined the king and queen, who were on their way to thank Darkhorse for his timely assistance. Gwendolyn looked at Cabe. He nodded his understanding. The crimson-tressed enchantress followed after the monarchs. Conversations sprouted up elsewhere. People began to relax, albeit not too much. The drake and Talakian sentries returned to their assigned positions, but not without last glances toward one another.

For all practical purposes, the reception returned to normal, though every conversation now tended to revolve around what had happened. Drinking also slowed as many became fearful that a drop too much would cause them to say the wrong word to the young drake lord.

"That was very fortunate, friend Cabe."

The warlock looked up into the half-concealed face of the Green Dragon. He had completely forgotten about the Dragon King. Now he wondered where the drake had been during the altercation. The emerald warrior had taken no part in the event, not even when the life of his lord had been in jeopardy.

"It could not have happened better than if we had planned it," the drake went on. "The moment Melicard stepped forward to put an end to it, I realized that it would be better if I remained behind. Let the king of Talak take responsibility. The significance of that would not be lost on the other guests . . . and how *true* that turns out to be! Yesss, things have moved to cement the ties between our two races!"

"I'm just glad that no one was hurt."

"Of course!" The Green Dragon looked slightly offended. "I would not have wanted that, either, but I had confidence in the outcome of the sssituation."

Cabe was glad that one of them had been so confident. There were times when, despite the years he had known him, the warlock found the Dragon King an enigma. The mistake, he suspected, was trying to see the drake's desires in terms of human ideals. There were similarities, but also significant differences. *Very* significant differences, at times.

The sorcerer took a sip from his goblet and let his eyes wander toward where Talak's rulers and the future Dragon Emperor were speaking with one another. Kyl had been raised among humans, but while he more resembled one of Cabe's kind than something akin to the Dragon King, he was still a drake . . . wasn't he?

Was he *neither*? Kyl and the others had been very young hatchlings when the mad Dragon Emperor had fallen, young enough to still be influenced and molded to other ways. Knowing that the only way for them to survive—and for his own race to continue as a power equal to the rising humans—the Green Dragon had taken it upon himself to create this unusual situation.

It had not been an easy task. There had been many humans and even some drakes who had threatened the young heirs over the years. The avian Seekers had actually even kidnapped them once in an attempt to use them as leverage against the Ice Dragon. Yet, despite all the dangers, despite those who still sought to end the possibility of a new Dragon Emperor, Kyl had grown to adulthood. However, no one, not even Cabe, was certain as to what the young drake would be like once he assumed the throne. How much of his personality was influenced by his guardians and how much was influenced by his race's history?

"The ceremony will top this visitation off grandly," the Dragon King was saying. "It wasss an excellent suggestion, would you not say, friend Cabe?"

Only half aware of the conversation, the ebony-haired mage nodded. "It was."

"It wasss Grath's idea, you know. I only dissscovered that this day."

"Grath's—" Cabe stirred, but before he could say anything more, the Green Dragon had turned from him.

"Excuse me, Massster Bedlam, but my emperor desiresss my presence."

"Grath's idea?" whispered the spellcaster. It made sense the more he thought it through. The ceremony had not seemed like the sort of notion Kyl would have come up with on his own. He was intelligent, there was no denying that, but such a personal display was not generally his way. Grath . . . now that was more reasonable.

He caught sight of the younger drake, ever near Kyl's side. Now and then, whenever the emperor-to-be looked hesitant, Grath would speak. In fact, Cabe now noted that Grath generally spoke *only* when necessary. He was like a shadow of his elder sibling.

Two emperors. The drakes would be gaining two emperors, not one. Taking another drink, the sorcerer was glad that at least *one* of them could be trusted.

The Dragonrealm needed such an emperor if it was to have peace.

Two days later, in the early hours of the day, the drake emperor-to-be journeyed to the necropolis in which were buried the kings and queens of Talak. He was accompanied by Cabe, Gwendolyn, Kyl, the Green Dragon, and, of course, the royal family. Darkhorse was not with them, having said that there were things to which he had to attend. A contingent of the royal guard had escorted the group to the tall, iron gates of the vast cemetery, but Melicard had ordered them to follow no further. The necropolis was a sacred place, a place of final peace. Here the king demanded that his ancestors and those others buried here received the quiet they deserved.

The day was as Erini had said it would be. A light mist lent a sense of tranquility to the morning, putting everyone into a contemplative state of mind. Even Kyl seemed changed. He was subdued, perhaps thinking about his own heritage. In some ways, his background was much like that of Melicard. Both their sires had been driven mad, then had died because of that madness.

Despite his differences with the young drake over the Bedlams' daughter, the warlock could not help but feel some sorrow for Kyl . . . and Grath, for that matter. He also felt relief that they did not hold him responsible for the Dragon Emperor's madness. After all, Cabe had only been defending himself.

They were led through the cemetery by the master groundsman, a surprisingly young if pale man with white hair. Cabe had expected an ancient cadaver clad in black, enveloping robes, but the groundsman, while indeed clad in dark, respectful clothing, would have belonged among the courtiers at the reception save for the short, eagle-headed staff he carried.

"He is new," Queen Erini whispered to the Bedlams, "but his family has held the post for the past two centuries. Roe knows and reveres this place as much as anyone could. His own family rests nearby, as is only just, considering the care they have given this place."

On the queen's other side, Princess Lynnette stared at the surrounding mausoleums and tombs with childlike fascination. She had been here many times before. Melicard had insisted that she come to know the history of her family the moment she was old enough to understand. Lynnette had little fear of the necropolis, which had surprised Cabe until the petite princess had told him that she could never be fearful of a place where so many members of her family watched over her.

The tomb of the kings and queens of Talak was actually a series of interconnected mausoleums that had gradually spread across much of the necropolis. Cabe had actually expected a massive ziggurat, but the low, flat structure before him was by no means inferior to the pyramid of the spellcaster's imagination. Elaborate gargoyles stood watch over the doorways, the latter of which were flanked by thick, marble pillars bearing the royal crest. Talak was unique in that its human rulers had risen more or less from one family line. The people of the mountain kingdom had been very loyal to their monarchs.

The master groundsman led them to the grand entrance of the structure, a more recent addition that enabled one, so the guide said, to find their way to any of the crypts, including the most ancient. As they approached, however, Cabe heard a slight rustling from all around them. He was suddenly alert, his powers already gathering for whatever stalked them.

A band of armed and hooded men appeared from within and around the entrance.

No magic that the warlock could detect had been used to camouflage them; these men were simply adept at concealing themselves. The warlock had never seen an armed force in a cemetery, at least not before now. They were not of the royal guard, for instead of the eggshell breast plates, these men wore chain mail under their cloaks. The sentries, a full dozen, resembled to Cabe avenging wraiths risen from the grave. They eyed the newcomers blankly, somehow radiating a sense of dread power. Cabe was surprised to sense a bit of power among them. So far, that power had not been used, but it was potent enough that he remained wary.

The master groundsman raised his staff. "Stand aside for King Melicard I, the Queen Erini, Princess Lynnette, and their most respected guests!"

The guards did not move despite the command, and it took the warlock little time to realize why. He doubted that drakes had ever sought entrance to the necropolis before, much less the royal crypts.

Roe waved his staff at the reluctant guardsmen. This time they obeyed, albeit casting distrustful glances toward the drakes in the party. The master groundsman waited until they had stepped aside, then turned to his charges.

"My liege, I must apologize for this behavior."

It was Kyl who replied, "Pleassse, King Melicard! Assure him that I undersssstand the hesssitation."

"Again, that is most gracious of you, Lord Kyl," Queen Erini said. She looked pointedly at Melicard, who nodded.

"Lead on, Roe," the king commanded, putting an end to the incident.

The groundsman led them up the steps and to the doors, which opened up as the party reached them. A pair of gray sentries stood at attention behind the doors. Cabe found the situation rather ironic. Melicard had left his soldiers at the gate in respect to the dead, at least so he had indicated, but the monarch had failed to mention that his ancestors had protectors of their own, protectors with sharp weapons and secret magic.

If the party had expected a dank, frightful tomb, they were disappointed. *It's almost as if we were walking through the libraries of Penacles!* was the warlock's first thought. The corridor connecting the various crypts was clean and, if not well lit, at least sufficiently illuminated. Cabe wondered if the rest of the necropolis was so well preserved.

"This way," announced the keeper, pausing to point to a corridor to the party's left. They followed him down the new hall, passing empty spaces in the walls that were obviously reserved for the future. Cabe shuddered and saw Gwendolyn do the same. Neither Erini nor her daughter seemed bothered by the reminders of their mortality, perhaps because they had come here so often that the crypts no longer held any anxiety for them.

The corridor was short and ended in a stairway leading into the earth. Roe began to descend, with Melicard close behind. The

Green Dragon also had no qualms about the descent, but Kyl and Grath both froze. Then, the emperor-to-be stiffened and literally forced himself down the steps. Grath hesitated only a bit longer. The queen and her daughter followed after them.

Bringing up the rear allowed the two spellcasters to take a moment to ready themselves. The enchantress squeezed Cabe's hand, took a deep breath, and started down. Grimacing every step, he shadowed her, trying not to think about the sort of hole they were entering.

The remainder of the trip was thankfully short. The names and faces carved into the stone plaques became more recent until at last the party confronted the final resting places of Rennek IV and his wife, Queen Nara, who had died many years previous to her husband.

It should have been darker, for a single candle was all that was burning when they arrived, but the master groundman's staff proved to be a surprise—the head glowed brighter the darker the path became. Thus it was that the illumination available to them was almost as great as if they stood out in the open air.

Before Kyl was permitted to begin, the king had a ceremony of his own. One day each week he journeyed to this place, often with his family beside him. A wreath already hung over each of the stylized images of his parents, wreaths fairly fresh, since Melicard had been here four days prior. Nonetheless, the king removed the wreaths by hand, then reached into a sack he had been carrying. From it the monarch of Talak brought forth new wreaths, which he then placed where the previous pair had hung. Melicard then stepped back and knelt before the two plaques.

He spoke, but was so quiet that no one else could hear what it was he was saying. Cabe did notice the queen silently mouthing words, tears running down both cheeks. She, at least, knew what her husband was saying.

After several minutes, the king rose. There was a hint of moisture on both cheeks, which disconcerted the warlock a little since the one eye was only supposed to be a carving. The magic of elfwood, however, was a mystery to even the most learned. There was argument as to the extent of its ability to mimic life. Over the years, Cabe had come to the opinion that elfwood did *more* than mimic.

Now at last it was Kyl's turn.

He signaled Grath, who carried a bag similar to the one the king had been holding. The younger drake reached into the bag and pulled out, not a wreath, but rather two bundled packages about half the length of his forearms. Grath gently opened each bundle, revealing what at first appeared to be a pair of roses. He held out the roses to his brother, and as the dragon heir reached for them, they caught the light.

The roses glittered. The sight was breathtaking. Only now did those gathered realize that the scarlet flowers were not real, but rather *sculpted* from some magnificent crystal. In every detail did they match or, as impossible as it seemed, surpass their real counterparts. It was almost possible to believe that sniffing one of the sculpted roses would reveal a tantalizing fragrance.

No one spoke as the drake stepped forward and placed one rose before each of the two plaques.

Straightening, Kyl broke the silence. "May thesssse lasssst as a sssymbol of both regret and hope, King Rennek, Queen Nara. Long after the beauty of a true rossse would have faded, let the not ssso cold beauty of thessse pieces show my pain at what my kind hasss done to thisss kingdom. Let it alssso symbolize my promissse to the lords, both passst and pressssent, of thisss mountain kingdom that the days of terror are now forever passst. I cannot remake all of what wasss losssst thanks to my sssire and hisss predecesssssorsss, but I shall do what I can; that I ssswear in memory of all of you!"

There was more after that, much of it concerning regret to Rennek in particular for the atrocities of Kyrg and Toma, who in the name of their sire and emperor, had been willing to do most anything, no matter how vile. Kyrg had paid the penalty at the siege of Penacles and no one had seen Toma in years, but the memories of the terror the duo had spread remained vivid to those who had been involved, including Cabe. Kyl's words faded as the warlock pondered the evils of the drake dukes and their master. He knew that he would not rest easy until he was certain that Toma had followed his brother and his emperor to oblivion.

The young drake finished. It was an elegant and worthy speech, no matter what the true reasons behind it. The king was too intelligent a man to fall prey to pandering, but it was impossible for him not to be affected by something such as this. Erini had tears in her eyes.

Kyl turned to Melicard. "I hope I have acted with sssensitivity toward your esssteemed progenitorsss, my lord. If you find the rosesss not to your liking, I will replace them with sssomething elssse."

"The fire roses were . . . appropriate," replied the king. His voice shook a little. "I've not seen such beautiful work in years."

"The skill isss almossst lossst. A ssservitor in the Manor knew how to make them, but had not done ssso since coming there. When I was made aware of sssuch skill, I had him make thessse two with the original intention of them being given as farewell giftsss to your lovely queen, but that changed when I dissscovered I had no proper token to bring to thisss ceremony. I hope you will forgive me, Queen Erini."

"Of course I will. They shall have a place of honor down here, Lord Kyl," the queen said, her eyes still a bit moist. "I will see to it."

"I thank you. Perhapsss when I return to the Manor, I will be able to convince Osseussss to make another pair for you."

"Osseuss?" Erini glanced at Cabe and Gwendolyn. "A good thing then that we were able to prevent a terrible injustice. It would be a tragedy for the world to lose such an artisan!"

Cabe, who had never been aware of the servitor's talent and wondered how Kyl had come to know, had to agree. The roses had been the crowning touch to the drake's performance, a perfect complement to the carefully crafted, yet emotion-turning speech he had given. Even Grath and the Dragon King had been touched by it. Roe was staring at the dragon heir as if seeing him for the first time.

There was nothing more to be done here, but it was several seconds before Melicard appeared able to organize his thoughts. His eyes darting back to the roses, he commanded, "Have someone watch these closely, Roe. I want nothing to happen to them. I also want you to personally devise the best way to keep them safe here. They must *never* leave."

"Yes, my liege."

Again there was silence. At last, Erini seized control of the situation from her husband. "I think it's time we return to the palace. I have arranged for a midday meal in the gardens. I hope that will meet with your satisfaction, Lord Kyl?"

The drake bowed. "Mossst assuredly, Your Majesty."

"Good! Master Roe, if you would be so kind as to lead us back to the gate?"

"As you wish, my queen. Please follow me, everyone."

The master groundsman started down the corridor, Melicard and the others following. Gwen took Cabe's arm, both of them more than happy to be departing this place. They waited while Kyl, Grath, and the Green Dragon followed the royal family, then fell in place behind the drakes.

As the party wound its way toward the steps, the Dragon King suddenly looked back at the warlock. He said nothing and but a moment later returned his attention to the trek. With the only true light emanating from the staff that young Roe carried, it was a struggle to see the expression on the half-hidden face within the dragonhelm, but Cabe was almost certain that he had read in the eyes of the drake lord a deep sense of satisfaction at the outcome of this ceremony. Things, as the Dragon King had put it at the reception, could not have happened better than if they had planned it.

Strangely, the warlock could find no comfort in that thought.

IX

They're back! Valea's heart rose as she heard the rattle of wagons and the voices raised in cheerful greeting. Ursa, sitting beside her, glimpsed the expression on her companion's face, but said nothing. Valea knew that the drake was aware of how her human friend felt about her brother. Ursa herself associated little with either male. Drakes were more divisive; females tended to associate with females and males with other males, save in matters of mating, of course. That was changing as living among humans affected the drakes here, but the change was a slow one that would need generations.

Ursa had never spoken against Valea's desires, which the young sorceress had decided meant that while she might not approve, the drake was also not going to interfere. That was probably for the best. The novice witch would have felt terrible if the friendship the two had developed over the years was destroyed by this.

She waited for Ursa to rise, but when the drake made no move to do so, Valea finally flung herself from her chair and rushed to the window. For the past few days, she had spent nearly all of her free time either in her chambers or in the gardens—anywhere that allowed her seclusion. Other than Ursa and the very understanding Benjin Traske, she found the company of others to be cloying, especially when that other was Aurim, who seemed to think that while he was in charge he was their father and mother combined. Around other folk she could not let her thoughts drift, could not dream of Kyl and the future she wanted.

Now she did not have to dream. Kyl was back . . . and in triumph, of course. Valea had expected no less from him. She peered out the window and watched as the caravan entered the Manor grounds.

There he was! Riding at the forefront. Father and Lord Green rode with him, Valea's mother and Grath close behind. Kyl was in high spirits. Everyone seemed to have a smile on their faces, although her father's was slight. Even Darkhorse was there, but the eternal's presence did not thrill her as much as it had when she had been younger. She still loved the shadow steed's company, but being what he was, he could never understand the emotions coursing through her. It was very likely that if she told him of her dreams, of her belief that Kyl might flout everything and make her his bride and queen, Darkhorse would act just like her parents. Everyone knew that he despised drakes.

"Do you see them?" asked Ursa, finally coming to the window.

"Yes! There they are!"

Her alluring companion followed Valea's gaze. "Things certainly seem to have gone well."

Ursa's perfect profile caused a brief twinge of jealousy in the young witch. She was aware how beautiful and exotic the drake seemed to males of both races. Then she consoled herself with the thought that to Kyl *she* was exotic. He was used to the magical splendor of female drakes and Ursa was, after all, his sister. Besides, was it not to Valea that Kyl paid the most attention? If he did not think her beautiful, then he would not have continually pressed for her favor.

Before he left for Penacles, Valea hoped to make the handsome drake admit his love.

"I want to go downstairs!"

"To be there to greet your parentsss?"

Her intention had been to be where Kyl could not fail to see her, but Ursa's pointed question struck home. Valea was not on very good terms with her mother and father. The long and very boring lecture her mother had given to her just before departing for Talak had only underscored that. Now would be the best time to start mending that relationship. She loved them both, and even though they were wrong to think so badly of Kyl and her, Valea did not want to lose them. It would be terrible enough when they discovered that their protests had gone for naught.

A horrible notion occurred to her as she and Ursa departed the room. What would happen if Kyl did *not* acknowledge her? What would she do *then*?

It was too monstrous to imagine. Besides, Scholar Traske had almost sworn an oath to her that Kyl returned her love. Somehow, their love would come to pass. Kyl would be able to make it so. After all, as Dragon Emperor, he would be wielding more power than any other single being. He would *make* everyone accept her as his love.

Valea did not question her extravagant dreams. To her, that was the way things would occur. To have the future follow any other path was unthinkable.

They were down the stairway and at the outer doors of the Manor before she even realized it. The short trip down the steps and across the grounds to where the rest of the Manor's inhabitants stood cheering passed even more quickly.

She chose a location ahead of the slow-moving caravan. A gap opened as people realized she was there. Valea halted as she reached the forefront, then tried to pretend that she had not run most of the way. Ursa joined her a moment later, looking just a little dismayed at the behavior of her friend. Valea ignored her completely, for Kyl was just riding into view.

He was talking with the Dragon King when suddenly his eyes swerved her direction. Valea fought down her emotions, not wanting to seem like a giddy little girl. The Dragon King followed Kyl's gaze, but what he thought was insignificant to her. She was only interested in the handsome figure riding at the forefront.

Kyl smiled at her. Valea vaguely noted a greeting from Grath.

The riders reined their mounts to a stop. Stable hands rushed to take control of the animals. Kyl and the others dismounted, including the young Lady Bedlam's parents. Steeling herself, Valea did not go directly to the drake, but rather greeted her mother and father first.

Of course, Aurim was already there. He had just finished hugging their father and was now doing the same with their mother. Valea was a little annoyed; trust her brother to be ready and waiting. She had wanted to be first, the better to impress upon them her desire to heal the rift that had spread between the three.

Father saw her first. He gave Valea a hesitant smile, which she returned. Truly, she hated arguing with them. It would have been so much easier if they could have gotten past their old prejudices and accepted her choice. Perhaps there was still time.

"Valea." The blue-robed mage hugged his daughter. Without a word being spoken, the rift was suddenly closed. Cabe Bedlam could not stay angry at his daughter. Her father was like that. He had always been the easier of the two to deal with, the most willing to bend. That was not to say that he was not stern with her at times, but it was generally easier to sway her father than her mother.

The enchantress was already with her, arms encircling her daughter. Valea returned the warm greeting, adding a smile nearly identical to that of her mother. Whereas Aurim and their father somewhat resembled brothers, Valea had long ago come to grips with the fact that she and her mother would forever seem more like two nearly identical sisters. It was, admittedly, a tiny bit annoying to think that a male, especially Kyl, might find the elder Lady Bedlam more attractive, but fortunately that did not seem to be the case with the drake. He had already proven which of the Bedlam women he preferred. Besides, everyone knew that her parents were inseparable.

"How have things been?" her mother asked.

"Well enough." There really was not more to say, but parents never seemed satisfied with such short responses. "I spent most of the time at my lessons or with Ursa." There was enough truth in that answer to make her feel as if she had not been lying. Telling her parents that she had spent the last few days thinking only of Kyl would have quickly reopened the chasm.

"Welcome back, my lady."

Valea had not realized that Ursa had followed her this far. She momentarily feared that her friend would betray her by expanding on the truth, but then Ursa simply repeated her greeting to Valea's sire. The Lord and Lady Bedlam returned the drake's welcome, which then seemed the end of the matter. The novice witch breathed a little easier.

Cabe Bedlam turned to talk to Aurim, no doubt wondering how her brother had fared in his role as lord of the manor. Valea desperately sought some reason to leave her mother. She wanted the chance to welcome Kyl back before he vanished to his rooms.

It was too late. Glancing in the drake's direction, she saw that he, Grath, and Lord Green were already starting to walk away, the heir's shadows, Faras and Ssgayn, close behind. Perhaps it would have been better after all to risk her folks' ire by greeting Kyl first. Now her one opportunity was lost.

Then, the heir to the dragon throne looked her way.

The smile was there again, the smile that was just for her. Kyl did not pause, but the smile and the look in his eyes told Valea that he *would* see her before long.

Scholar Traske spoke true! she thought, barely able to keep her pleasure hidden. Her mother, though, was talking to one of the servants about some household matter and therefore missed the brief struggle. Even had the Lady Bedlam noted the flush of pleasure spreading across her daughter's countenance, it was probable that she would have assumed that it had to do with her own return.

None of that truly mattered now. The novice sorceress had confirmation. Kyl truly *did* care for her.

"If you do not have need of me at thisss time, I would like to return to my kingdom immediately, my lord. There are duties I, too, must attend to."

Grath nudged Kyl, whose attention had been on Cabe Bedlam's fiery daughter. Pausing, the dragon heir gave the drake lord an understanding nod. "By all meansss, Lord Green! You of all here do not need to ssseek my permission!"

"It would be improper otherwise. Although the formalities must still be observed, you *are* my emperor. If there wasss any doubt, it was dispelled by your excellent behavior in Talak."

Kyl basked in the compliment. "Thank you for sssaying ssso. When shall we be graced with your company again, Lord Green?"

"I shall return before it isss time to depart for Penacles, be assured of that. Asss to the exact day, that I cannot say."

"There isss no need. Let me sssay before you go, that I am ever appreciative of your loyalty and guidance."

The Dragon King bowed. "I do what I must, Your Majesty."

Kyl and Grath watched as the Green Dragon departed, then continued on their way to their chambers, the two drake guards ever maintaining a respectful distance behind them. The heir turned to his brother. "Without Green'sss sssupport, none of thisss would have been possible, would you not sssay so, Grath?"

"It would have certainly been more difficult, but you would have overcome it, brother."

"With your aid, perhapsss. I mussst again commend you for the wordsss and gift you sssuggested for the ceremony. They were perfect! Hisss Majesty King Melicard wasss overcome! I will have hisss sssupport now!"

"I merely made recommendations, Kyl. It was your execution of them that made it work." Nevertheless, there was a smile on Grath's visage.

"What would I do without you at my ssside, my brother?" The dragon heir put a companionable arm around his brother's shoulders and smiled. "Talak wasss a sssuccess! Penaclesss will alssso be a triumph! With ssstrength from both drake and human elementsss, no one will quessstion my right to sssit upon my father'sss throne!"

"They would be foolish to do so now," commented Grath. His face hardened. "But sssome will. There are always a few."

"Asss long asss they are not ssstrong enough to caussse me any worry, Grath. You will sssee to that, will you not? I could trussst no one elssse ssso."

The younger drake nodded thoughtfully. "As you wish, Kyl. Asss you wish."

A formidable figure abruptly loomed before the drakes, but his presence brought slight smiles, not scowls, from Ssgayn and Faras. Grath immediately bowed in respect, and even Kyl could not resist a slight nod of his head. Benjin Traske had that effect on others, especially those who had been his pupils.

"I'm glad to see you back, lads," rumbled the scholar. "I would have greeted you and the Lord and Lady Bedlam sooner, but I was ensconced in my chambers and did not know that you were back until a servant informed me."

"There wasss no need, Ssscholar Trasssske," Kyl returned. "But it isss indeed kind of you to come to usss now. I am sssorry that you could not be with usss in Talak. Your fine inssstruction made all the difference, I mussst sssay."

Traske chuckled. "You sound very much like the diplomatic monarch, Kyl, and I thank you. It pleases me to think that I might have had some small part in your success. A tutor always likes to see his pupils excel. When you have the opportunity, I would love to hear of your experiences."

The thought of impressing his former tutor was enticing, but Kyl was a bit weary from the long trip. Besides, there were other things he needed to prepare for, not the least of them being a chance encounter with Valea. Of course, Kyl never left chance encounters to chance; he and Grath made them happen. The handsome drake had a suspicion of where the Bedlams' daughter would be for the next hour or two, and he intended on stumbling on her at some point during that period.

As ever, it was Grath who stepped in to solve his dilemma. It was *always* Grath. Who else could it be? "I would be happy to relate our tale to you, Scholar Traske! It would give me the chance to ask you a few questions that I have about the mountain kingdom. I wasss amazed by it!" He waved his hands as he exclaimed the last. "Would that be satisfactory to you, Master Traske?"

"I would be delighted. You have time now?"

"I will make time. I've questions that cannot wait."

"You should first perhaps make certain that your brother has no need of you," Traske reminded Grath. "This is a crucial time for him. Your trip to Talak might be a thing of the past, but there is still Penacles to consider and the Dragon Kings afterward."

Grath had always been the scholar's most avid student. Kyl knew that the heavyset scholar enjoyed conversing with his former pupil. Grath also enjoyed the conversations, especially since Traske was a fount of information. Whenever there was a question that the younger drake could not answer—and those seemed to be becoming increasingly fewer—he would turn to the human who had taught them.

Had it been within his power, Kyl would have offered Benjin Traske a place in his empire, if only because between the human and his brother, he would have had the best counselors that any ruler could hope for.

Why *not* ask him at some point? The human had no plans once his role at the Manor was finished. His only pupils were Aurim and Valea, but Aurim was nearly finished with his lessons and Valea . . . well, perhaps that would be the final factor. Valea would need friends. There would be Ursa, but the witch would need more than one companion.

When Grath returned from this conversation with the human, Kyl would present the suggestion. His brother would know best whether they could trust Benjin Traske to be loyal to them when the time demanded it.

"By all meanssss, he may go, Ssscholar Trassske! I have no need of him at thisss time. I have many things to attend to that will keep me busssy for the next few hourssss. If I have need of my brother, I know where to find him."

"My gratitude, Kyl." Benjin Traske bowed his farewell. Grath did the same, a barely perceptible nod following.

Left alone with Faras and Ssgayn, which was almost the same as being completely alone, Kyl contemplated his next move. He needed but a moment to refresh himself. It was true he was weary, but not weary enough to forget the importance of letting the exotic young witch know that he had not forgotten her. The glance he had been able to give her would keep her hoping, but it would be wise to follow with an actual meeting, even if it included her parents. All that was essential was to make her think that he had spent the entire visit to Talak thinking of her, which was, at least, half true. Valea was a prize he and Grath had worked long and hard to obtain, and Kyl knew that she was at last within his grasp.

She was both beautiful and a pleasure to be around, which only served to make each encounter that much easier for him, but those facts were secondary next to her greatest asset to the drake.

Valea was a Bedlam, a scion of the most powerful line of sorcerers. She was the daughter of Cabe Bedlam and the Lady of the Amber, an enchantress of vast might. The young witch had not yet displayed more than a fraction of the extraordinary power the line was known for, but everyone knew that the potential in her was possibly as great as it was in Aurim. If not, she could still pass the power of the Bedlam line on to her offspring.

His offspring. It *was* possible for the two races to interbreed, although how that could be was a question not even Grath was able to answer. Kyl knew that it was true only because his brother had come across evidence—evidence which Master Bedlam seemed to know about, too.

He realized that he had not moved from the spot where he had been standing when Grath and the scholar had left. Precious time was being wasted. Turning to his two shadows, he hissed, "Well? What are you two waiting for? Come!"

The two draconian warriors, looking properly chastised, hurried to keep pace as the dragon heir moved on. He would have to dismiss them before he located Valea. There was nothing romantic about two scowling lizards, which, in his opinion, was what the duo resembled. Kyl was quite pleased with his more human looks, mingled as they were with his draconian origins to create a unique, provocative appearance. Grath was the only one who resembled him at all, but even his brother's looks were more rough-hewn than his own.

She could not fail to want him. All that really stood in his way was her parents, but Grath had assured him that they would be no trouble whatsoever.

Kyl had been careful not to ask how his brother could be so certain. He simply had faith that loyal Grath would do what had to be done . . . whatever that might be.

Things were at last calming down, and none too soon as far as Cabe Bedlam was concerned. The caravan was being dismantled and the Manor itself appeared in fine order. Aurim had only had control of the Manor for a short period of time, but the warlock was aware of how many things could go wrong in just one day. It was a wonder that the place was not more chaotic. Sometimes he thought that the ancient edifice itself watched over those who lived in it, much the way the Dragonrealm seemed to watch over its people. Yet, the mind of the Dragonrealm, assuming it had one, was a rather perverse one, for it seemed to take fondness in thrusting Cabe and his friends into one danger after another whereas the Manor simply seemed protective.

The Green Dragon had given his apologies and had departed only minutes after returning with the caravan. Cabe understood; the Dragon King had neglected his own realm for much too long already. Gwen and their offspring—it was growing impossible to call them *children*—were in the gardens talking about Talak, Darkhorse also adding a word here or there, but mostly just enjoying the companionship of his mortal friends. Aurim and Valea loved visiting the mountain kingdom, if only because the spectacle of the Tybers looming in the background was breathtaking. They also loved the strangeness of the city, having lived much of their lives in the relative calm of the Manor.

Cabe had left them in order to organize some notes Aurim had given him. One of the few peculiar things his son had reported to him was a sudden increase in the number of hauntings by the memories of the Manor. At first, Aurim had simply ignored them, but when three sightings had occurred in the same day, all suffered by the younger Bedlam himself, he had started to make a list. Almost all of the hauntings had occurred in the last three days, a record eleven. One had appeared as recently as last night. All but two had involved Aurim; the others had been seen by Valea.

Most of the visions were familiar ones. The archaic wedding ceremony. The Seeker landing on the terrace overlooking the gardens. A closed book with the symbol of a tree on it . . . which had always puzzled Cabe since it did not exist in the old library. A being who resembled a wolfman, probably of a race that had preceded not only the Dragon Kings but the Seekers and the Quel as well. All of these had been registered by the master warlock, some of them many times. But Aurim had experienced *three* first sightings as well, images that, especially in one particular case, his father would not have expected.

A Quel had stalked through the halls. Aurim had never seen one, but knew of them from his father's tales. The huge, armadillolike race existed only in the very southwest of the continent, their once mighty empire reduced to a few ruined, underground enclaves. Cabe had never known them to exist this far east, although it made sense to think that at one time their empire had covered much of the continent the way the drakes' or the Seekers' had.

The massive, armored figure had been swinging an ax at something, but what it was Aurim could not say. He only knew that the beastman had been frightened out of his wits, and the last image of the Quel had been that of the monstrosity falling on his back in terror.

Sometimes it was sobering to think of all that must have happened in this place. Cabe had little desire to know what had attacked the Quel as long as it no longer existed to threaten his own family.

The second image had been barely glimpsed, but in his scribbled notes Aurim had described what sounded to Cabe vaguely like a sword slicing through the air. What that was supposed to represent, the sorcerer did not know. It was different from other images in that his son had sworn that, being so nearby when it had materialized, he had actually *felt* a slight wind as the blade had moved. To Cabe's recollection, no other ghostly memory had ever proven even the slightest bit tactile.

Even that paled in comparison to the final new vision. It was the first of its kind that any of them had ever come across, and its existence shattered every theory that the master warlock or his wife had ever devised concerning the ghostly images.

Aurim had seen his *father*.

Cabe had joined the ghosts of the Manor.

The image was a very recent one. That, too, was unsettling. Aurim's description of the short scene had registered in the elder Bedlam's memory. It had taken place but a few days prior to their departure for Penacles. The occurrence had not been of any significant moment as far as he could see. It was merely Cabe using a knife to cut open a srevo, one of the lush fruits often found in the markets of Penacles and long a personal favorite of the sorcerer. Cabe was not one to use his power for something so simple as cutting up fruit. He considered such misuse both wasteful and criminal. That day, however, the black-haired mage wished that he had broken his cardinal rule.

Aurim's description of what had followed was exactly as Cabe recalled it, save that much of the surrounding scene was missing. The vision revealed Cabe holding the large, round fruit and making the first cut. Then, as he had readied one half for another attack with his knife, something had caught his attention, making him turn as he lowered the sharp blade. In real life, that something had been Benjin Traske, come to ask a question about the then forthcoming trip to Talak. The interruption itself had been minor, but the warlock, eyes turned away, had cut into his thumb.

He still remembered the pain. The wound had not been deep, but surprise had amplified his agony. Cabe had no qualms about using sorcery to repair even the most minor injuries, particularly those causing him torment, and had healed it almost immediately. By the evening of that same day, he had forgotten all about the incident.

For some reason, though, the Manor had not.

And why is that? he wondered. The spectral images had never made sense to him. Why would the ghost of such a trivial incident be created? What logic did the Manor follow? *Is there any logic? I keep assuming that there has to be, but who knows who built this place? They might've been mad, for all I know!*

The situation was certainly insane enough. Cabe slumped back in his chair, willing to admit that after all these years he was no closer to understanding the magical citadel than he had been the first time he had entered it. It reminded him of the fact that the structure would probably still be standing long after he and his children had become nothing more than . . . *memories?*

A movement behind him quickly dispersed all thought of the Manor's eccentric ways. Cabe pushed his chair back and turned, expecting one of his villagers. His eyes bulged as what should have been an impossible sight stood before him.

It was a drake warrior. His eyes searched the room with avid interest. He wore a cloak, and the dragon's head crest on his helm was one of the most extravagant that Cabe could recall. The drake's red eyes seemed to burn. His coloring was dull green mixed with touches of gold.

It was a drake warrior, one known to Cabe Bedlam.

It was Duke Toma.

Although to the warlock it seemed as if his reflexes had slowed almost to nothing, still he succeeded in gathering his power and striking at the deadly drake before Toma even seemed to notice him. A whirlwind formed around the reptilian invader, a funnel of dizzying speed that affected nothing else in the room, for its object was Toma and Toma only. At Cabe's silent command, the tornado seized the sinister drake and threw him to the ceiling.

That is, it was *supposed* to throw him to the ceiling.

Toma stepped through as if not even noticing the whirlwind. His eyes still darted left and right, never seeming to focus on his foe. Cabe pointed a finger at the draconian figure's armored chest. Sleek, black tendrils formed around the deadly duke's upper torso, tendrils designed to pin the drake's arms to his sides.

The tendrils tightened . . . and continued to tighten *through* Toma's body.

"What—" Daunted but not defeated, Cabe began to rise from his chair. At the same time, Toma's piercing eyes turned his way . . . and continued past, at last focusing on the wary sorcerer's desk.

Only then did Cabe Bedlam realize that, if he stared hard, he could just barely make out the door *through* the chest of the drake.

An illusion? I'm fighting an illusion? He stumbled closer, still not positive that this was not a trick. Toma seemed to walk toward him, although after a moment Cabe decided the horrific duke was actually walking toward his desk. The warlock stepped to one side, studying the figure as it went past.

There was something familiar about the illusion. It was not a proper illusion, for if it had been, he would not have been able to see through it. Toma was a phantom, a ghost.

Ghost or not, the drake seemed very familiar with this chamber. He walked quickly to the shelves that held Cabe's personal library, works that the warlock himself had gathered over the years, as opposed to the ancient library elsewhere in the Manor. As the specter searched the shelves, Cabe struggled to understand the madness happening before him. This was either a very elaborate hoax, a trick played by Aurim, perhaps, or . . .

Toma began to fade away. There was no warning. His form simply began to grow murkier and murkier and his movements slowed until they came almost to a halt.

It was the final confirmation. Everything about the ghostly drake screamed only one possible answer.

The Duke Toma before him was nothing more than one of the Manor's phantom memories . . . and that could only mean that the deadly drake had paid a visit to the one place the warlock had believed was forever safe from him.

Toma in the Manor. It seemed impossible, but the proof was *there*. How, though? How could the draconian renegade have made his way past the defenses of the ancient structure?

There was also the question of *when*. Perhaps it was an old memory from the time when no one had actually lived in the Manor, a time when Gwendolyn had been a frozen prisoner in Azran's amber cage and a trio of sinister female drakes had usurped the fabled place. The original spells protecting it *had* begun to deteriorate. Darkhorse had been unable to enter, but Cabe had stepped through without even really knowing what had happened. Of course, at the time, he had been bedazzled by the temptresses' beauty, not realizing that he was to be their meal.

Could Toma have been here back then? It seemed a far more sensible conclusion, yet that reasoning held flaws, terrible flaws. The first and foremost of those was what the drake had been doing. Toma had walked to the desk, which was an addition of Cabe's. The chamber had originally been devoid of any trace of furniture or other contents. Also, the monstrous figure had been inspecting the shelves, his eyes lingering on particular tomes.

The shelves and their contents were *also* additions made by the warlock. Before that, the wall had been bare.

He could not deny it any longer. Duke Toma had been in the study chamber searching through the knowledge that his rival had gathered over the years. How long ago, though? It could still have been years—but if so, why had the drake never struck at them? If there was anyone Toma desired to see dead, it was Cabe and Gwen.

Gwen . . . Valea and Aurim . . . Suddenly the warlock grew fearful for his family.

He had to know.

" . . . as I've said before, Valea," his wife was remarking as he appeared in their midst. The trio paused in their conversation, eyes widening at the unexpected visitation.

"You're all . . . right!" Cabe gasped, relief bubbling over. In truth, he had expected to find them prisoners of the drake . . . or even worse.

Gwendolyn was on her feet instantly. She put her hands on his shoulders and looked him in the eye. "Cabe! What's wrong?"

Seeing them there, all concerned about his well-being, made his fears now seem laughable. Yet, Toma *had* invaded their sanctuary at some point in the past. That meant that there had been a threat to them . . . and, in fact, there might still be. The drake had never been one to pass up a golden opportunity.

He exhaled, forcing himself to relax. Only when he was certain of his control did the sorcerer permit himself to speak again. "Toma. It was *Toma*."

"Toma? Where?" The emerald-clad enchantress warily scanned the grounds around them. Valea and Aurim looked worried but not panicked. Like their mother, they prepared themselves for the worst.

"Not here. Not now, Gwen. I don't know when he appeared, but at some point in the past, Toma somehow invaded my study."

"How do you know that?"

Cabe indicated Aurim. "When I went to the study with the notes Aurim had given me, the ones about the hauntings . . . "

"Your pet project."

He nodded. "I was just considering the last one, the image of myself. I felt a prickling . . . or something. All I know is that when I turned around, *Toma* was standing behind me, eyeing the room the way a dragon eyes fresh meat. After looking around, he stalked toward the desk and the shelves above it."

"And then?" No one seemed to be breathing. Anticipation had made slaves of his family.

"And then . . . " He shook his head. "And then I realized that the Toma I saw was another of the Manor's living memories!"

"A very timely one, if it was. You are certain that it was not an illusion? Not some trick?" It was clear that Gwen wanted that to be the case.

"No illusion . . . or rather, yes, it was, but only if you count the Manor's ghosts as such. This was one of those! I know the difference between them! Toma *has* been here before, Gwen. Not only that, but he had time to search this place thoroughly, I think."

The sorceress released him. Her hands, Cabe saw for the first time, were shaking. "It *has* to be an illusion! How could he have succeeded in passing the barriers? Only we can let anyone in or out!"

The warlock looked at his family. "I don't know."

"What should we do?" asked Valea. Duke Toma had always been something of a nightmare monster to her, like the creatures children thought lived under their beds. To find out now that the nightmare had invaded their very sanctuary . . .

The master warlock thought it out. "We have to search this place using our power. We have to carefully go over everything and every place. We——" He blinked. "Where's Darkhorse?"

The shadow steed had been with his family when last he had left them, and that had not been very long ago. Darkhorse was the only one other than his wife and offspring that Cabe would have trusted with all of this.

"He asked permission to depart only a few minutes ago." Gwen was perturbed. She, too, realized how useful the eternal's skills would have been for this deadly matter. "He was anxious, as if he had somewhere urgent to be. It was fairly sudden."

Was there a possible connection? Cabe was not certain. He hoped that Darkhorse would have informed him if there was some danger to them. The shadow steed was generally not that carefree with the lives of his friends. *Maybe it had something to do with the traps . . . and maybe there is a connection!* Darkhorse, however, had departed before the warlock's encounter with Toma's specter. "We'll have to do without him, then. He could be anywhere. The search will be our responsibility and ours alone."

"What are we looking for?" asked Valea.

He wished it was possible to leave her out of this, but Valea's power was needed. Even with the four of them working in concert, it would take the rest of the day to scour the Manor grounds. "Quite frankly, I don't know."

"We *have* to search, though," Gwendolyn impressed upon their daughter. "Toma was . . . *is* . . . a vicious, cunning creature, the epitome of every terrible tale ever spoken about the Dragon Kings! You know what we have told the two of you about him. Toma was so treacherous, so *dangerous,* that he became a renegade even among his own kind! He has never forgiven the fact that, had he received the birth markings Kyl was born with, *he* would have been Dragon Emperor."

The young witch's mouth opened and her face grew pale. "Do you think . . . do you think that he might try to hurt Kyl?"

Cabe disliked the intensity of her emotions. She had not only not forgotten her infatuation with the drake, but it seemed that somehow it had even *grown* in their brief absence. That, however, was a matter for another time. All that mattered now was discovering whether Toma had left behind a legacy of his visit.

It bothered him that the drake had been so bold to wander the Manor as freely as the image seemed to indicate. Toma was arrogant, yes, but to go stomping around in his full glory? What was the drake plotting? Had it been madness that had made him so daring?

He also could not help but wonder why the Manor had happened to reveal the image to him at this particular time. Toma would be interested in the coronation; there was no doubt about that. Perhaps Kyl *was* in danger. *Immediate* danger.

Or is he maybe in league with that demon? Should I confront him about it? There was no proof, however, and it would have been unfair to condemn the young drake without such proof. If anything, Kyl was probably in danger. Still, until they knew otherwise, the affair would have to be handled with caution.

His wife had come to the same conclusion. "Kyl may be in danger. *All* of us may be in danger. This is Toma we are talking about." She paused, paying particular attention to Valea's reactions. Cabe knew that she, too, was thinking of their daughter's interest in the handsome heir. "Which means that we must keep this to ourselves for now."

"To ourselves?" Clearly, Valea did not like that.

"The more that know, the worse the danger. Toma may have some allies among the drakes here. I hate to think that way, but it could be true. The four of us need to do this on our own."

"I still don't know what we're looking for!"

"Neither do we," Cabe reminded her. "The only thing I can say is to look for anything out of the ordinary . . . as far as the Manor goes." He raised a hand in warning. "If you *do* notice anything, though, I want you—and that goes for both of you—to find *us*. Whatever Toma might have left behind would be very deadly. I have faith in your skills, but believe me when I say that even the Dragon Kings fear him."

"Do we start now?"

Cabe and Gwen considered their daughter's question. The enchantress finally nodded. "We do not seem to have any choice. It might be that there is nothing to fear, but I, for one, will not be able to relax until I know that we are safe."

After a moment, Valea nodded her agreement.

Throughout the conversation, Aurim had remained quiet. Cabe had paid scant attention to that fact until now, originally believing that his son had simply been mulling over the possible threat they faced. Now, however, he noticed the peculiar expression on the younger Bedlam's countenance, as if his son were trying to recall something of import. "Is something wrong, Aurim?"

The expression faded. Aurim briefly looked annoyed with himself, but then even that expression faded as determination took over. "Nothing, Father. I'm ready to begin whenever you like."

Cabe wanted to sigh, but held back. *He* most certainly was not ready. Nonetheless, they had no choice. He tried to sound confident as he began, "Then this is how we start. . . ."

X

Valea doubted that Toma had bothered with the stables, but her father had insisted that she search them regardless of that doubt. In truth, she was certain that it was *because* Toma would not have come here that her parents had chosen her to be the one to investigate the stables. Her mother and father had chosen to search all of the more likely spots. Aurim, too, had been relegated to probing areas of the Manor grounds where the drake had most likely never set foot. On the one hand, the young enchantress appreciated her parents' protectiveness, but on the other hand, she also resented it. After all, she was a grown woman now, was she not?

Standing to one side of the nearest stable so as not to draw so much attention, Valea began her search. Tendrils of magic visible only to her own senses snaked over and around the building next to her. Unimpeded, they began to sink into the walls and ceiling, hunting. If there was anything unusual in the stable, she was confident that she would find it. Of course, since it was highly unlikely that there *was* anything to find, the novice sorceress found it impossible to become very excited about her work.

As she had expected, her initial search brought nothing significant to light. The horses used by the Bedlams were stabled here. It had seemed as likely a target for Toma as any of the other structures here, and the fact that she found no trace of the renegade's passing only served to strengthen her belief that this entire location was a waste of her efforts. Still, the witch knew that if she failed to search the stables thoroughly, it would be on her head if Toma *had* left something behind, something that might later endanger her family.

"Ssseeking a place of sssolitude, Valea?"

She gasped in surprise, then silently reprimanded herself for her reaction. Her probes faded as her concentration broke, but Valea hardly cared.

From behind the stable emerged Kyl. He had changed from his traveling clothes into a fresh outfit—a sleek, dark green piece that happened to be one of her favorites. The high collar and the lack of any lighter colors to contrast the darkness made the drake seem a man of deep mystery.

He had worn it for her; she was certain of that. It thrilled her to think that Kyl had gone to such trouble.

"I found myssself ressstive after I had cleaned up and ssso I decided to take a walk," Kyl continued, shortening the gap between them as he talked. "When I reached the ssstables, it occurred to me that a ride might be in order. Then, I caught a glimpsse of you and recalled that I had never properly greeted you after our arrival."

"There was no need." It was a struggle for her to sound calm. Inside, Valea was again a maelstrom of emotion.

"There *wasss* need, though. It wasss unforgivable."

Only an arm's length separated them now. The young witch waited for Kyl's strong arm to bridge that gap, and for a breath it seemed it would, but then the drake's hand continued beyond her to brace against the stable wall. It was not what she had hoped for, but the action still left the two of them so very close. All he had to do was lean forward a little.

"Talak wasss fassscinating, Valea! Ssstrange and beautiful! You have ssseen it before, I know, but I wish you could have been there to sssee it with *me*."

She was beyond words.

Kyl seemed not to notice . . . or perhaps he only pretended. Valea could not say. "Sssuch splendor! Sssuch majesssty! King Melicard isss rightfully proud of hisss kingdom. He hasss a loyal following, a magnificent city, and mossst beauteous queen."

Jealousy pricked Valea. Erini *was* beautiful, a true fairy-tale princess. She also looked little older than Kyl. With Talak so close to the citadel of the Dragon Emperor, there was no doubt that the demands of his throne would bring the handsome drake and the queen of the mountain kingdom together fairly often.

She realized that she should say something. *Anything.* "She loves him very much, you know."

It was not what Valea had meant to say. She was certain that her cheeks were crimson now.

"She doesss, indeed." Somehow, the drake had lessened the distance between the two of them even more. Valea was struck by contending choices. One part of her was afraid and wanted to step back. The other part of her wanted the last remnant of the chasm closed. "It wasss ssstrange, though. Talking to her, being around her, I found mysssself thinking of *you*, Valea."

Her reaction to this declaration infuriated the young Lady Bedlam. As if acting under some impulse of their own, her feet moved, propelling the maiden *backward* three or four steps until she was beyond the stable wall and out in the open.

To her vast relief, Kyl did not look repulsed. He followed her, albeit stopping at the corner of the building. The special smile that he reserved just for her was there. "I thought about you mossst of the time I wasss there, Valea. I like to think that you were alssso thinking about *me*."

Even having heard all that she had, Valea could not believe her good fortune. "Then, it's true? It's as Benjin Traske said?"

Now Kyl looked puzzled. "Ssscholar Traske? What hasss he to do with thisss?"

Valea took a deep breath. This was it. He had all but said the word, his fear that she would reject him probably the reason he had not taken the last step. She would do it for him.

Slowly, hesitantly, Valea began, "Scholar Traske . . . he said that . . . he said . . . "

Cabe probed the library one more time. There was no trace of any hidden spell or physical trap. There was not even any sign that Toma had ever been in this room.

The warlock sighed. He had been carefully inspecting each room of the Manor, and although he was still not even half finished, much of the day had passed. So far the results of his thorough search had yielded nothing. Unfortunately, with Toma that did not mean that the drake had not been here. The duke was a master sorcerer who had often in the past surprised even those who had thought that they had known his limitations. His skills were far more versatile than those of the more traditional Dragon Kings. Toma dared to do things that no one else did, which made him the wildest of wild cards. He had more or less vanished after the terror of the Ice Dragon, but now and then rumors of his activities surfaced. However, so far as Cabe had been able to tell, the rumors had never proven to bear any truth.

Which, of course, did not mean that Toma had been idle all these years.

Cabe wondered how the others were doing. None of them had contacted him, but he tried not to be paranoid. If something *had* happened, he would have known.

The constant probing was making his head throb. Cursing under his breath, the warlock decided to get a breath of fresh air. He stepped out of the library, crossed the hall, and made his way to the nearest window. A minute or two of relaxation was all that the sorcerer needed. It was odd how small, fairly simple spells could often take more out of the caster than huge, earth-shaking ones.

Leaning out the window, Cabe surveyed his tiny kingdom. Somewhere, possibly even beneath his very feet, there might be a clue to whatever Toma had done while here. Studying the bookshelves had revealed nothing. Perhaps there was nothing to find, not even a trap of some sort, but the warlock could not risk that chance.

His eyes alighted on a crimson-tressed woman standing next to one of the stables. It could not be his wife, who searched the lower floors of the Manor, which meant that it had to be Valea. Cabe recalled that she was supposed to be searching the stables, but at the moment, she was simply standing there. Why?

He had his answer when Kyl stepped part of the way out from behind the stable wall.

The enraged sorcerer did not even wait. He was gone from the window and next to the stable in less than a breath.

"Valea."

At the sound of his voice, she froze. Whatever his daughter had been about to say died on her lips, probably a fortunate thing in his opinion. Even Kyl looked satisfactorily guilty for a change.

"Father, I—"

"I gave you a project to do, Valea. A very important project. Have you finished it?" Cabe tried his best not to let his anger show through, but even he was aware of the harshness tinging his words. Kyl's eyes flickered, but other than that there was no sign that the drake might have noticed. The warlock had no doubt that he had, however.

His daughter's expression told him the answer to his question even before she replied. "Not yet." Her cheeks were crimson. "I only paused for a moment . . . I . . . I'll get back to it now."

Curtseying to Kyl, the young witch rushed off. Cabe's anger drained away. He had embarrassed his daughter. Granted, the search was of the utmost importance at this time, but that was not why the warlock had come down here. He had come down here because his daughter had been alone with a . . . with a *creature* . . . that had designs on her.

It could have been handled differently, but when it came to his family, the master sorcerer could not always think straight. Now, he and Valea were at odds again—and his actions had most likely pushed her further toward the drake.

"There isss sssome major project underway, Massster Bedlam?" Kyl asked politely, his entire person radiating innocence.

"More of an exercise, Kyl." The warlock now wished that he had thought of some better excuse, but for most of those living at the Manor, calling the search an exercise would have been sufficient. Cabe had been too concerned with beginning the hunt to think about what Kyl or Grath, who understood the ways of sorcery, might conclude from the Bedlams' peculiar activity. *Two decades and I still think with the cunning of a serving boy!* It could not be helped, though. Kyl might suspect, but unless he was somehow in league with Toma, he would be able to do no more than guess.

"Ssso sssoon after our return? We have only just arrived!"

"I felt it was necessary, Kyl. Didn't Scholar Traske ever surprise you and the others with sudden tests or projects of his own?"

The drake verified his supposition with a grimace. "Massster Trasssske had an amazing talent for the unexpected tessst. Yesss, I sssee your point."

It was doubtful that Kyl actually did, but the warlock was happy to let it go at that. Kyl would think whatever he wanted to think. Once the search was ended, it likely would not matter very much. Whether any trace of Toma's passing was found or not, Cabe's family was now warned. Toma would not find entry into the Manor so simple the next time he tried.

What did he want, though? That's what I would like to know!
The obvious motive concerned the very drake before him. Cabe
realized that he would have to speak to the Green Dragon as soon
as the Manor was considered safe again. The Dragon King would
want to know what had happened. He might also be the best one
to handle the delicate matter of questioning Kyl. For all he disliked the heir's manner, especially toward Valea, the warlock *was*
concerned about the drake's well-being. Toma could offer the
emperor-to-be nothing; therefore, the renegade sought to *take*
from Kyl.

It was tempting to warn the young drake even after he had
commanded Valea not to do so, but Cabe persevered. Best to wait
for the Dragon King. The lord of Dagora would better know what
to do about his nephew.

"I shall leave you to thisss, then," the dragon heir was saying.
"I apologize if I interfered in sssome way. I happened by, sssaw
Valea, and sssince I had not yet greeted her since our arrival, I
thought it polite to do ssso now. Again, Massster Bedlam, my
apologiesss."

"It's nothing, Kyl."

"That isss very kind of you to sssay. I shall trouble you no
longer, then, Massster Bedlam." With that, the drake bowed and
quickly departed.

Cabe watched him walk off, more certain than ever that he had
just interrupted something important between his daughter and
Kyl. He hoped that whatever it was had not gotten out of hand.
*Only a few more weeks and he'll be far enough away that she can
start to forget him.* It would be wise, he thought, to take Valea
and Aurim to some of the more peaceful human kingdoms, such
as Penacles or Gordag-Ai. Let them meet more people their own
age. There were a few at the Manor, but unfortunately, here
Aurim and Valea were considered the young lord and lady of the
house. That was why the drakes had become their closest friends
over the years; the others considered the two their masters as
much as Cabe and his wife were.

Yes, it would be wise to do some visiting after Kyl assumed his
throne. Penacles especially seemed a good choice.

That was still weeks away, however, and in the meantime,
Cabe would have to continue to watch his daughter. It might have
been easier on him if she had at least chosen Grath; the younger
drake had always seemed kinder, more sensible. Less *deadly*. He
was thankful that Aurim, at least, had not gotten involved in any

romantic entanglements. At this point, the master warlock was not so certain that he could have handled yet one more situation.

Which reminded him that there was still a search to complete. Toma was, by far, the most immediate danger to everything. They had to make absolutely certain that neither he nor some legacy remained within the boundaries of the Manor. Cabe knew, however, that even if they found nothing, he would still be unable to relax. The mere presence of the renegade had shattered his sense of security. Not even his home was safe.

Something will have to be done to put an end to your legacy of terror, Toma, the sorcerer thought as he prepared to resume the hunt. *And if it would cost me my life to see that accomplished, I'd gladly give it if only it meant that you were never able to threaten my family again.*

He meant every word, he truly did, but Cabe hoped that it would not come to that.

Unfortunately, with Toma involved, there was a very good chance that it *would.*

Darkhorse moved swiftly through the forest, darting in and out among the trees with an ease no earthly steed would have been able to imitate. The shadow steed squeezed between trunks or overran fallen trees that would have daunted any true horse. Darkhorse barely noticed. He, like the Bedlams, was on a hunt, but in the eternal's case, there was a trail. It was slight, so *very* slight, but it was the first true clue that he had discovered.

Darkhorse had picked up the trace at the site of one of the spell traps. He had not thought to search for this particular type of trail, having been more consumed with the obvious scent. His adversary had been a clever one, using the traces of Shade's sorcerous mark to cover the true one. Now, however, the shadow steed knew what to look for . . . in part because he suspected who was responsible.

Oddly, though, the trail was now sending him in a direction he had not anticipated, toward a destination that had to be false. The ebony stallion rode on, though, determined to let nothing, including personal trusts, cloud his judgment.

I should have come across him by now! he thought. *There is no possible way that I could have passed him by!*

Nonetheless, the next several minutes revealed no sign of his mysterious quarry. The eternal finally paused and surveyed his surroundings. There was little that should have been able to evade his senses, but more and more Darkhorse wondered whether he had somehow missed what he had been searching for. The trail was fading before him. Had he been duped again?

It seemed so. Several more minutes of searching proved the futility of his hunt. The trap maker had covered his path all too well.

"So be it!" rumbled the eternal. "I will waste no more time on this!" Still, he could not help pondering his failure as he turned and renewed his run through the forest. Darkhorse did not like mysteries, or at least mysteries that he could not solve. Perhaps it was time to visit Penacles. The Gryphon was there, and although he no longer ruled the so-called City of Knowledge, still he had access to many sources of information there, including the fabled libraries underneath the very city itself. *Perhaps the lionbird can pluck some useful knowledge from the libraries' contrary contents!*

Whoever had created the libraries of Penacles had to have been a madman. All the great knowledge of sorcery was said to be found there, written down in one great tome or another. The difficulty lay not only in *locating* the proper volume, but making sense of the insane script within. The knowledge of the libraries usually came in the form of some peculiar riddle or nonsensical passage. Why that was, no one now knew. Still, if there was anyone who could solve those conundrums, it was the Gryphon.

Feeling much more pleased with his situation than he had felt but moments before, Darkhorse increased his pace. He made no sound as he ran and his hooves left no mark on the uneven ground. When it was his whim, he could do both, but for the most part Darkhorse preferred to move as a ghost. It would have been simpler to transport himself to Penacles, but the shadow steed loved to run. It seemed to clear his thinking. Besides, a few minutes more or less would not matter. Darkhorse was so swift that he could cross miles in seconds if he chose. He did not run so fast now, but even still it would take him little time to reach Penacles.

His path took him across the trail that the caravan had taken in order to reach Talak. Darkhorse vaguely recognized it, although he had not joined the party until further north. At first, the eternal ignored it, set as he was on his destination, but then the presence of many inhuman minds made the powerful stallion come up short.

He wasted no time looking around. If they chose to, his new companions could keep themselves well hidden among the treetops. Instead, the shadow steed kicked at the ground, raising a cloud of dirt and loose vegetation, and roared, "Play no games with me, birds, or I will knock your roosts down one by one until this part of the forest is nothing more than a field!"

There was the rustling of leaves in the treetops—rustling that the light breeze around him could not have caused.

A man-sized creature burst through the foliage and alighted onto one of the larger, lower branches. He was shaped more or less like a human, but in every other way resembled a bird of prey. The newcomer snapped his beak once at the eternal, then cocked his head to the side so as better to see the huge stallion.

"What do you want, Seeker?" Darkhorse shifted so that he looked directly up at the avian. "A challenge? A threat?"

The Seeker pointed a taloned hand toward the southwest and squawked.

"Aaah, so very enlightening!" snorted the stallion. He kicked at the ground, digging huge ruts in the dirt. "And why is it I should go that way?"

An image of a tree in summer, its crown green and full, formed in his mind. Under the protective foliage, was an area of cool shadow. It seemed to be this that the avian desired to emphasize, but Darkhorse was puzzled by it. What did the base of a tree, a shaded area, at that, have to do with—

Shaded? Shade?

The Seeker's eyes informed him that he had correctly guessed the answer.

"A tree and *shadow*. How perfectly *obvious*." He hated communicating with the bird folk for this very reason. With humans, the images were more direct. Cabe Bedlam would have seen an image of the blur-faced warlock himself. However, Darkhorse's mind was different from that of any other creature in this world. Using such clues was the only way the Seekers could communicate with him other than pointing. They had no written language, at least not one that anyone understood. The shadow steed was thankful that he had little congress with the creatures. Of course, much of that was due to the fact that the Seekers were, in general, more devious than helpful. If they wished to help him now, it was only because it served their desires, too.

Again the Seeker pointed southwest.

Was he trying to say that *Shade* was there? That seemed highly improbable. Even Darkhorse had come to the conclusion that the warlock was long dead . . . but then what did it mean?

Not Shade, then, but perhaps the one who had used the memory of the warlock as bait to catch the eternal?

It could be that this was also a trap, but the shadow steed's curiosity was piqued. Caution warred with that curiosity, with the latter at last triumphing. The eternal started off in the direction in which the avian had pointed. He shielded his thoughts, however, not wanting the Seekers to know just how little he trusted the bird folk. Should they have a snare prepared, they would find him more than ready for it.

The male who had pointed the way flew ahead several yards and alighted onto another branch. When Darkhorse was near, he again pointed.

"Are you to be my guide, then?"

The Seeker nodded, then fluttered off ahead once more.

So the trek continued. Much of the trail was straight, which raised his temptation to rush ahead without the avian. Darkhorse decided against that, however. The Seekers had planned long and hard, he supposed, so the least that he could do was not disappoint them . . . yet.

He could hear the fluttering of many wings above him. A full flock of the bird people were trailing after him. Darkhorse estimated that there could be no more than twenty, including his guide. That seemed a fair combat to him.

Once again, his guide located a new perch. Darkhorse sighed audibly, hoping that the bird man would understand that he was tiring of this chase. The avian again pointed, adding an annoyed squawk to emphasize the importance of the situation . . .

. . . and then the trees were full of warring Seekers.

The eternal stopped and quickly gazed skyward. Through the tangle of trees, he watched in amazement as a second band of the bird folk attacked those who had been shadowing him. Claws raked across chests. Beaks strong enough to crack bone tore flesh. Now and then, a small but potent spell was unleashed and some combatant would wither, burn, or simply fall to its death.

A savage squawk brought his attention back to his guide. Despite the chaos above, the Seeker was *insisting* that he proceed.

Darkhorse, however, had decided that he would not. Things had become a bit too confusing. Seekers *never* fought Seekers. It was unheard of. "I think, perhaps, my friend, that I will decline your guidance from here on!"

As he began to turn away, the avian leaped for him. Out of the corner of his eye, Darkhorse saw that the Seeker now held something in one taloned hand. The shadow steed doubted that he wanted it to come any closer than it already was.

The bird man was swift, but still too slow in comparison to his attempted prey. Darkhorse dodged the grasping claws. Under other circumstances, he would have stayed where he was and laughed as the Seeker was trapped within him. Many over the endless centuries had described the eternal as a living hole from which nothing that was pulled in ever again emerged. It was a very accurate description. Drakes, humans, beasts, Seekers . . . how many there had been Darkhorse could not say. He did not care. Those who sought to harm either him or his companions deserved no mercy. They would fall forever into the abyss that was the shadow steed, who was very aptly called a child of the empty, endless Void, the place in which he himself had been spawned.

This Seeker, though, was a danger as long as he was able to wield the mysterious object. Darkhorse knew that no creature would be so foolish as to attack him unless they believed that they could defeat him, and while stupidity was a trait among many races, the Seekers had always struck him as a little more intelligent. That meant that whatever his adversary held, it promised nothing but harm to the shadow steed.

Rising up again, the lone avian eyed him. It was clear that things were not going as the Seeker had originally intended. He glanced skyward, where his companions were clearly losing, then back down at the shadow steed. At last, with a squawk that somehow relayed frustration and anger, the bird man turned and began to fly back in the direction from which he and Darkhorse had come.

His flight was short. The limbs of the nearest trees bent in a manner no wind could have made them bend, suddenly blocking the swift avian's path. The Seeker, moving with the intention of quick escape, struck the heavy limbs head first. There was a cracking sound that had little to do with the branches themselves.

The limp form tumbled to the mossy ground, where it lay a twisted, still shape.

Darkhorse did not even wait for the Seeker's body to strike the ground. He started to back away, eyes scouring the visible world and senses formed in the Void searching those worlds beyond. It occurred to him that he could no longer hear the combatants above, surely not a good sign. Still, the eternal was not fearful. It had been too long since he had been faced with a proper challenge.

"Come, come!" he roared, still unable to locate the foe by either set of senses. "You wanted Darkhorse and so you shall *have* Darkhorse! *All* the Darkhorse you could ever want!" The eternal roared with mocking laughter.

He felt something pass his way, but the sensation was brief. Darkhorse glanced that way, then turned his head the opposite direction as he felt yet another presence on his other flank.

"Skittering like mice, are you? Perhaps I can shake you from your holes, then!" The shadow steed raised a hoof and brought it down hard on the forest floor.

There was a crash of thunder and the land around him shook as his hoof struck the earth. Birds flew off in panic while Darkhorse laughed, taunting his foes.

Then . . .

It had the stink of Vraadish sorcery, as great a stink as the eternal had ever known. The shadow steed drew in just a little, slightly disconcerted at the intensity of it. Vraadish sorcery was a legacy of another world, battered, maimed Nimth, the place from which the ancestors of humans had come after nearly destroying it with that very power. Yet Nimth was sealed off, the barrier between this world and that one stronger than ever. Darkhorse had been there when the way had been closed.

The eternal sought to back away from the foulness, but found he could not move. Gazing down, Darkhorse stared in astonishment at his hooves, which were several inches deep in what seemed to be *molten grass and earth*. The land still retained the form of the forest floor, but it moved like quicksilver. Stunned, the ebony stallion still had the wherewithal to attempt to free himself. With effort, he pulled first one hoof free, then another.

A gleaming tentacle snared one of his free limbs. Horrible, shocking pain coursed through his very being. The stallion's shape grew distorted as his control of it slipped. One leg grew too long. His head drooped as if melting. Ripples ran across his torso. Fighting the agony, Darkhorse regained control, but was unable to restore himself to his proper shape.

Another tentacle snaked around a second limb. This time, he saw what it was. It was not a beast of some sort, but rather a whip, a weapon. Darkhorse followed the length of the horrific weapon back to a slight shimmering in the air. Even as he watched, the shimmering coalesced into the form of a cloaked figure. The shadow steed's first startled thought was to imagine that Shade *had* returned from the dead, but then he realized that this was not the warlock but some human minion, for a quick glance the opposite way showed that an identical figure had materialized there.

There was something familiar about the trap, but it took the struggling Darkhorse a moment to recall what it was. *The whips! I know these whips!*

They were toys of the Vraad. Darkhorse knew them *very* well, for it was with whips like these that the ancient sorcerers had guided him. These whips and other foul toys.

Had it been only the eternal and the whips, Darkhorse was certain that he would have been able to triumph easily. The molten soil, however, slowed his counterattack by seizing his limbs again and again. Darkhorse gave up trying to maintain his shape, deciding that he stood a better chance of success by returning to the amorphous form that had been his until the sorcerer Dru Zeree had stumbled into the Void and discovered him.

Like melting wax, the huge stallion's form sagged and dripped toward the ground. His head became almost indistinguishable from his body as the two began to fuse together. His legs were twisted things with the consistency of molasses. Only the two icy orbs that were his eyes remained as they were.

He was little more than a blob of darkness when it became clear to him that even now the whips and the earth maintained their holds on him. Shock at last became tinged with fear when Darkhorse also discovered that he was now trapped in his present form. He could neither complete the transition to living shadow nor return to his equine form no matter how hard he fought to do so.

As the eternal fought futilely to regain control of himself, a third cloaked figure shimmered into being before him. Darkhorse saw the clawed hands of a drake emerge. His attention then became fixed on a small object cradled in the hands of the hooded dragon man. A box. An old—no, *ancient*—box with a pattern on the top that the shadow creature could not make out clearly from where he was trapped.

It was not until the drake opened the lid that Darkhorse recalled this particular toy of the Vraad. For all he knew, it was the very same box which the Vraad Barakas Tezerenee had turned on him.

Although he no longer had a mouth, still Darkhorse roared. He struggled as he had not struggled since last he had seen such a

box, since last the maw of such a monster had been opened wide
so that it could receive him.

His struggling went for naught. He felt the pull and knew that
the link between himself and the box had been made. Despite the
inevitable, however, the eternal continued to fight. He could *not*
go there again!

The box was stronger. A black stream, the essence of Darkhorse, flew toward and into the devilish container. All the while
the shadow creature roared, but there was no longer any hope.
Darkhorse continued to flow until all of him had entered the
Vraadish device.

The drake shut the lid, silencing his scream.

XI

No trace of Duke Toma was found. The next several days passed
without incident, save that specters of the Manor continued to appear in burgeoning numbers. Every member of the Bedlam family
experienced at least one, with Cabe taking the brunt of the ghostly
assault. Not a day went by that he did not witness two, sometimes
three, manifestations. Most he was familiar with, but again there
were the new ones. He himself experienced the unsettling sight of
watching his image cut into his thumb.

The Toma image reappeared only once. It followed the same
pattern as before, then vanished. No one observed the blade
Aurim had described in his notes.

The journey to Penacles was mere days away now. The short
span of time between the visits to the two human kingdoms had
been intentional from the first, but now Cabe wished that he could
have another week to prepare himself. Toma's mysterious invasion still bothered him. Worrying about the renegade drake and
his continuing concern over the way Valea was acting around Kyl
combined to make the sorcerer too weary even to think about the
journey ahead.

Thus it was that when an emissary of Penacles arrived unex-
pectedly at the borders of the Manor grounds, Cabe Bedlam al-

most refused him entry. Only when he discovered who that emissary was did he agree to let him pass through the invisible barriers that protected his domain.

They met in the garden, the warlock immediately bowing in the presence of his old friend.

"I am no longer king, Cabe, so please stop that; it's rather embarrassing."

"Toos would be glad to turn the throne back over to you, Gryphon."

"Too true," the former monarch of Penacles returned. The Gryphon was, in his own way, as fascinating a being as Darkhorse. Manlike in his general form, he otherwise shared much in common with the Seekers, especially his countenance. The Gryphon, who had no other name, resembled the very creature of legend. His visage was that of a predatory bird, in this case a majestic eagle. Yet, the eyes were closer set, falling somewhere between bird and human. The lionbird, as he was nicknamed, also bore the aspects of the feline part of the creature he so resembled. His mane was thick and long and only at the bottom did it taper to feathers, although that sometimes changed depending on his mood. Underneath the cloak and loose clothing he wore, the Gryphon's form was more animallike than one first suspected. His legs were jointed like those of a cat, and on his back were tiny stubs, vestigial wings. The Gryphon's hands were more human than those of the Seekers, but his claws were as sharp as a cat's, at least on his remaining eight fingers.

Cabe eyed the maimed hand out of the corner of his eye. It was a legacy, a magical wound from the war that the Gryphon fought overseas. The war had gained for him a bride and their two children; yet it had taken away so much as well, stealing from him the eldest of those children, the warrior-child Demion. All knew that the lionbird would have rather lost both hands or even his own life than his eldest child. As it was, he and the cat-woman Troia now doted on their second son.

"Your visit's a surprise, but a pleasant one, Gryphon. I have to admit, though, that I don't know why you're here."

One of the servants brought them drinks. The Gryphon thanked her for the goblet, then raised it to his mouth. As he did, his features blurred, becoming those of a handsome, somewhat older man with fine patrician features. The transformation startled the servant, who almost dropped the wine. She scurried off before the

Gryphon could lower his drink and apologize. His features had already reverted to those of the eagle.

"I forget sometimes that there are so many outside of Penacles who are not used to me."

"I think it was just the suddenness of the change. Drakes change, too, but it takes them more time."

"Perhaps." The Gryphon paced the terrace as he thought. Like the predator he was, the former mercenary could not sit still when disturbed by something. He did, however, manage to pause when he spoke. "I'm chiefly here because Toos wants to hear how things went in Talak."

The warlock gave him a conspiratorial smile. "I'd think that Penacles would already know more than I could relate."

"He was especially interested in your personal observations," responded the lionbird, ignoring Cabe's comment about the spies that Penacles no doubt had spread throughout the mountain kingdom. Of course, Talak had its own spies in Penacles just as they likely had them in Gordag-Ai and Zuu. Spies were a favorite pastime of rulers.

"About the entire visit or something in particular?"

"Both, actually. Let us start with your view of the stay itself." The lionbird took another sip of his drink, again momentarily transforming his features.

"Gwendolyn should be here for this." The warlock looked around, but there was no sign of his wife. He projected a summoning, but the only response from her was that she would come when she was able. Cabe decided to leave it at that. The Lady Bedlam and the Gryphon were old comrades of a sort, both being survivors from the days of the Turning War, although they had not met then. If the enchantress chose not to be here, it was not because of any lack of love. The Gryphon and his wife were as dear to her as Erini.

"My visit must be necessarily short, Cabe. I understand if the Lady Bedlam cannot be here. She could never cause me affront."

The lionbird had always struck the warlock as the sort of monarch that he had hoped Kyl would become. Sadly, the young drake had chosen among his own kind for guidance, but fortunately he had at least chosen the Green Dragon as one of his mentors.

Cabe launched into a detailed description of the journey and their stay in Talak. Mention of the Seekers made the Gryphon's mane ruffle in concern, but the emissary asked no questions. The lionbird was visibly surprised at Kyl's handling of the untrusting Melicard, especially the request for the private ceremony acknowledging to the lords of Talak the travesties performed in the name of the Dragon Emperor.

Cabe was about to point out Grath's influence in most of those situations when he felt the presence of his wife's mind within his own.

Cabe. I tried not to disturb the two of you, but would you please come to Aurim's chambers?

What's wrong?

I am really not certain. She broke the link.

"Something is amiss, Cabe."

The warlock eyed his guest. "You know?"

"You grew slightly distant and your gaze drifted. I have studied sorcery for far too long not to recognize that you were communicating with someone, likely the Lady Gwendolyn. If she feels that something is important enough to create the need to summon you, then I can only assume it is nothing good."

Rising, the warlock could only marvel at the Gryphon's guesswork. "You assume right. I'll explain later, but for now, if you'll excuse me—"

"Nonsense!" The Gryphon also rose. "If there is something wrong, Cabe, I don't plan to sit by." He unsheathed the claws of one hand. With his regal bearing and his polite manner of speech, it was sometimes easy to forget that the figure before him could be every bit as savage as his namesake.

"All right, I won't argue. You could be right." The warlock took hold of the Gryphon's arm. "We're going to Aurim's chambers."

"Lead on."

The transfer was immediate. Cabe and the Gryphon looked around, searching for any sign of danger. The room, though, appeared completely normal, save for the pensive expression on the face of Gwendolyn Bedlam.

"Always a pleasure to see you, my lady," the Gryphon said, bowing as gracefully as was possible for him.

"I apologize for not greeting you, Gryphon." The emerald enchantress continued to look slightly anxious. Every few seconds, her eyes would turn from them to gaze at some random location in the chamber. "I'd planned to, but first I had wanted to talk to our son."

" *Aurim?*" Cabe noticed that their son was not in the room, but before worry could overwhelm him, his wife shook her head.

"He's all right, Cabe. I haven't summoned him, yet, but I do know where he is."

The warlock relaxed. "Then what's the danger?"

She put a hand to her chin and stared into space. "I am not absolutely certain if there even *is* any danger, but . . . but when I stepped inside, I noticed something that unnerved me." Gwen blinked, then spread her arms. "Tell me what *you* sense. Both of you, if you don't mind, Gryphon."

"Not at all."

Cabe cleared his thoughts and sent out a probe. At first, the room seemed no different. Aurim's presence was everywhere, which was to be expected in a place that he frequented so much. There were other, older traces, but they were so faint as to be inconsequential. Besides, the sorcerer recognized them. They could not be what his bride had wanted him to notice.

He briefly touched the presence of the Gryphon, vaguely noting the differences in their magical signatures. Since that, too, was quite obviously not what he was hunting for, Cabe moved on. He wondered again what exactly it was Gwen had noticed and contemplated asking her, if only to better aid his search.

Barely had the warlock thought that when he discovered the answer. It was an answer he could have done without.

The trace was barely noticeable. He had to concentrate hard to keep from losing the tenuous trail.

"What is it?" the Gryphon asked from beside him. His probe, too, had located the trace, but he did not recognize its origins.

"It feels as if . . . as if . . . " Cabe did not want to complete the sentence, as if that would make it not true.

"It tastes of Toma, does it not?" the enchantress demanded, arms folded tight. Like her husband, she also wished to deny it.

"*Toma?*" The former mercenary's voice went cold. "Toma? In the Manor?"

Hearing the hatred, Cabe quickly added, "Not now, but sometime in the past."

"But how?" demanded the Gryphon. "How could that murderous lizard have gained access to your domain?"

"We have no idea, Gryphon," the Lady Bedlam replied. She explained how they had come to know the startling truth. The lionbird listened in awe, and even Cabe felt chills as he relived seeing the renegade duke standing in the doorway of his study. Gwen went on to describe the careful search they had made of the Manor grounds, a search which had yielded nothing for all their hard work.

"But then how do you explain this?"

"The trace is very faint. I cannot explain why I noticed it, but I can see how it might have been missed before, especially since Aurim practices his spells in his room. You can feel his overwhelming presence here, can you not?"

The Gryphon nodded. The room was very much the young Bedlam's domain.

"What worries me is that this might not be the only evidence that we have missed."

Cabe had not thought of that. True, it was unlikely that he and Gwen had missed any such trace, but what about the areas that Valea and Aurim had been searching? He recalled where he had interrupted Kyl and his daughter. "We should probe the stables again . . . just in case."

"If I may be permitted, Cabe, perhaps I could do a search of my own."

"There's no need for you to—"

"Please. We have been through that before, haven't we?" The Gryphon turned to Gwendolyn. "What say you, my lady? Will you permit me to attempt a spell of my own? It promises a very thorough scrutiny of this place."

There was no hesitation on her part. "Do it. I want to be able to rest easy. I want to know."

The lionbird nodded. Without another word, he closed his eyes. Cabe could feel the stirring of power.

It was as if the Gryphon were everywhere at once. A force radiated from him, a force that spread throughout Aurim's chambers and continued on, unimpeded by any physical presence. It moved beyond the outer halls and the balcony, out beyond the very Manor itself.

The inhuman mage grunted. Next to him, the warlock sensed a renewed push that expanded the Gryphon's spell farther and farther beyond the Manor walls. The terrace was engulfed. The stables. The outer buildings, where most of those who served the Bedlams lived. Even the gardens were enveloped. The lionbird's claws unsheathed and sheathed as he worked to maintain his concentration. The spell did not require that much power, but it did require concentration if it was to be effective, especially since they were searching for what were likely very thin traces of the duke's former presence.

"The spell's reached the barriers," the Gryphon finally announced. "It can go no further without your permission."

"Let it go just beyond, if you will."

"A wise thought, Lady Gwendolyn." The inhuman sorcerer did just that. "My spell now covers the surrounding forest for almost fifty yards in every direction."

"Do you sense anything?" Cabe asked, fascinated.

"A moment." The Gryphon's voice grew distant. "This is a spell that works slowly, and by doing so more thoroughly searches. Let me . . . " He nodded to himself. "Yes, that does it. There are ancient traces of sorcery in this chamber, but they're so old that we need not worry about them. *Curious!* Did you two know that an aura surrounds this edifice? A very *strange* aura."

Both Bedlams knew of the aura of the Manor. It was, as the Gryphon had exclaimed, a very curious aura. Even Gwen, whose knowledge of such was far more complete than Cabe's own, had never experienced anything like it. However, they had long ago come to realize that whatever surrounded the Manor meant them no harm and had left it at that.

"I don't think Toma was in this room," the lionbird continued. "He reached in with his power. The trace comes from beyond, somewhere in that direction." He raised a taloned hand and pointed.

Following the Gryphon's direction, the warlock went to the balcony and peered outside. His eyes narrowed as he found himself looking down at the stables.

A figure stepped out of the nearest building, the one most directly in the path the Gryphon had indicated. Ssarekai. The drake seemed intent on heading toward the Manor, but then paused. After a moment's deliberation, Ssarekai turned his gaze upward. His eyes widened just a little as he met the stare of the sorcerer.

Cabe acknowledged him with a slight nod. Ssarekai dipped his head in what might have been an abortive bow and scurried on.

"Did you see anything?" Gwen called.

He turned back. "Just the stables. The stables and Ssarekai."

The Gryphon, meanwhile, had moved on. "I sense Aurim and another with some talent for sorcery. Not Valea; she's elsewhere. The drakes are everywhere." All drakes had inherent magic, although it varied greatly from one to another. "But no other telltale marks of the renegade save the trace in the study, of which we are already aware." He paused. "Yet . . . "

Both humans tensed.

"Nothing. I was wrong. Too hopeful, I suppose."

In one respect, Cabe found himself disappointed. Yet, if the Gryphon discovered nothing else, that did mean that the Manor was clean of all but this one trace of Toma's taint.

"There are some other odd sensations emanating from the Manor and the grounds, but they all seem to be a part of what makes this place what it is...."

A faint noise near the doorway caught the warlock's attention. He turned quietly, so as not to disturb the lionbird's work, and saw Benjin Traske. The massive scholar had one hand on the knife he always wore on his belt and the other on the arched doorway. He appeared startled at the presence of the Gryphon.

Cabe put a finger to his lips. Traske, recovered from his surprise, nodded once. He did not enter, but simply remained in the doorway.

"Some of your human servants have the natural potential for sorcery, did you know that? It's been suppressed."

"I shall have to look into that when we have more time," Gwen replied.

"I can let you know which ones at some point in the future." Slowly, the Gryphon turned. He did not stop turning until he had performed three-quarters of a circle. "I think . . . that's all. I find no other vestiges of his work. They might have dissipated beyond the spell's abilities, but at the very least that would mean you had nothing to fear from them. I can find no spells or traps anywhere."

The mood in the chamber lightened. Cabe noted that even Benjin Traske, who could not have understood what was being done here, relaxed.

Without warning, the Gryphon opened his eyes. The spell dissipated with astonishing speed and simplicity. "As near as I can tell, the Manor is safe. I cannot promise that the spell was perfect in its execution . . . "

"I am quite satisfied, Gryphon." A very relieved Gwendolyn moved to the lionbird's side. She put her arms around him and leaned forward to kiss him in gratitude. Cabe noticed that the former monarch managed to transform his monstrous features into the more handsome, human ones before the enchantress' lips touched his cheek. Even knowing that the sorceress loved him and that the lionbird loved his own mate, the warlock suffered a twinge of jealousy.

He extended his hand and gave the Gryphon his own thanks, adding, "It was fortunate that you arrived today. This will mean that we will be sleeping a lot easier again."

"You've done much for me in the past, both of you." The Gryphon, however, did look pleased. As he shook Cabe's hand, he finally noticed the figure in the doorway. "Benjin!"

The huge figure performed one of his miraculous bows. "Lord Gryphon."

"Will we be seeing you in Penacles when the heir comes? I would like to show you some improvements we've made with the school. I would like your opinion."

"I cannot say, my lord."

The lionbird's feathers and fur ruffled in growing annoyance at those around him. "Must I keep repeating myself? I am no longer king of Penacles! I have *no* title!"

"Only in your own mind," countered the Lady Bedlam. "You might have refused to take back the throne, but everyone, including Toos, agrees that what you did for the kingdom when you did rule there deserves respect. You *are* the special counsel to the regent, aren't you? That in itself infers some sort of title. I know that Troia wouldn't mind that."

He sighed. "I give in. There are those who believe that I am unusually stubborn, but Toos would still have me resume the throne even after all the time since my return to Penacles. Now *there* is stubbornness!" The Gryphon waved away what to him was a most distasteful subject. "You are not traveling with your former pupil to Penacles, Benjin?"

"That is for my lord and lady to decide."

The scholar gave no indication of his feelings one way or the other, but somehow his words made Cabe feel guilty for having left the man behind on the journey to visit Talak. Glancing at his wife, he saw that she, too, was having second thoughts.

"I think that something can be arranged, Scholar Traske," the enchantress finally conceded. "We'll talk later."

"Yes, Lady Bedlam." Benjin Traske's somber demeanor gave way to growing curiosity. "Lady Bedlam, what, if I may ask—"

"We'll talk about *that* later, too."

"As you desire." Bowing once more, the tutor departed.

"What was that you said about him coming with us to Penacles?" Cabe asked his wife. "I thought that he would be staying here just as he did when we journeyed to Talak."

"First, we really had no right to make him stay here last time. You and I both know that. Traske could have traveled with you if he so desired, but he chose not to rather than argue with us. Arguing is not his way. Second, he really should have the opportunity to see his work in Penacles . . . and I have decided that I shall stay home for all but the most essential days of the visitation."

The Gryphon did not take this news well. "Troia was hoping that you would come with the others. She does not feel as comfortable around the people of Penacles as she does around you, Gwendolyn."

Considering his mate's feline tendencies, Cabe did not find that at all surprising. The attention that she received as the former king's bride did not help the matter any. Troia was not used to being such a center of attention, and now that she had a small child to rear, it bothered her even more.

The Lady Bedlam smiled, thinking of the cat-woman, but still said, "I promise that I will see her when I do arrive, Gryphon. I remained behind when Cabe traveled to Penacles because I wanted to help the children prepare for being masters of the house, but on that score I no longer have any worry. You know what still bothers me, though. I'm sorry, but even the thoroughness of your spell can't completely shake the fear from me concerning Toma's invasion. I *need* to be here, can you understand that?"

Cabe certainly did. Had he been given any choice, he, too, would have remained behind. One of them, however, had to go to Penacles. Had his wife been the one forced to make the journey, she would have spent most of the time fearing for their home, their children, and all those whose lives depended upon them. Cabe himself would certainly worry, but knowing that the enchantress was watching over everyone would ease much of his fear.

The Gryphon also understood her concerns. "Then I will pass on that message to Troia."

"When time permits, I *will* come for a more extended visit; I promise her that."

"And she will hold you to that." The lionbird chuckled and clasped his taloned hands together. "Now, I regret to say, I must depart. There are some other tasks I must perform before I transport myself back to Penacles." The distinctive human/avian eyes widened. "Aaah! What a fool I am! Before I forget again, will the eternal be coming to the gathering? I know he joined you on your trek to Talak, Cabe. Will he also do so when you bring to us the Gold Dragon's heir?"

Thinking back, the sorcerer could not recall whether or not he had ever discussed Penacles in particular with Darkhorse. They had mostly talked about the mountain kingdom. Still, Darkhorse was always more welcome in the court of Toos the Regent than he was in that of Melicard. Cabe saw no reason why the shadow steed would not make the journey. "I would think that he would be there, but no promise was made."

The Gryphon laughed at that. "Then I shall warn Toos to be ready for him! The shadowy one, for all he is known in Penacles, still makes most of us jump! If he could only be taught to appear in a less dramatic fashion than is his wont, things would be so much quieter."

"If I see him, I'll be certain to pass on that suggestion." Having seen the reaction of the Talakian guests to Darkhorse, even after Melicard's warnings, Cabe had no desire to witness a repetition.

"Good! Then if the two of you might be willing to lead me to the edge of the barrier spells . . . "

"I could simply transport us there," reminded the warlock.

"I think that I can spare the two of you the extra few minutes . . . unless you fear my close proximity to your lady?"

"Not as much as you should fear the claws of *your* lady if she learns about that close proximity," Cabe countered.

"Yes, there is that."

"We would be delighted to walk with you, Gryphon." The scarlet-tressed sorceress took hold of the lionbird's arm.

With Cabe leading, they departed Aurim's chambers. More at ease, the trio's conversation turned to more pleasant things, such as the activities of the Gryphon's second child or the school of magic. Cabe had hopes for the future of the school; while its initial students seemed destined to be minor spellcasters at best, the openness in which the school operated was making the people of Penacles more comfortable with the concept. None who showed any promise was refused a testing, and none who took the test could claim that they had not been treated fairly, whatever their place in society. That was another reason both Bedlams desired the chance to return more often to the City of Knowledge. It behooved them to do whatever was in their power to keep the school a place that folk everywhere would admire, not fear. It was not merely for their own sake; it was for the sake of their children and other mages to come.

The Gryphon was describing the practice sessions of a student whose impatience rivaled that of Aurim when the young warlock himself appeared in the hall. With him was Ursa, who seemed to be supporting the Bedlams' son.

The brief interlude of peace was immediately shattered as parental concern seized control. Stepping toward his son, Cabe asked, "Aurim, are you well?"

The younger Bedlam glanced up. Embarrassment colored his cheeks. "I slipped and struck my head, Father. It's nothing, really."

"Merely a large lump and a maddening headache," Ursa added with a wry smile. "I still don't know how he did it."

"I wish *I* knew, so that I wouldn't do it again!"

"Where did it happen?" Perhaps it was because of the discovery that they had made in Aurim's room, a discovery that Cabe was still debating about mentioning to his son, but the warlock needed to know.

"At the beginning of the maze. It was such a good day that I'd been practicing in there instead of here. I supposed I was still thinking about the spellcasting and just misstepped." The young warlock shook his head. "Everything pounds now!"

Cabe was disappointed. For reasons that were not yet clear even to him, he had almost expected that his son's accident had taken place in or around the stables.

"Then, there's no sense in you standing here," admonished Gwendolyn. "Ursa, if you would see him to his room, I will be back in a few minutes."

"Certainly, my lady. I will stay with him until you return."

Aurim did not like being treated so. "All I need to do is lie down, Mother. There's no reason to worry."

"I will be the judge of that. If you please, Ursa?"

The beauteous drake led the feebly protesting Aurim away, his mother's gaze remaining on the pair until they were well on their way.

"A fine boy," remarked the Gryphon, but his tone hinted that his thoughts were, in part, on another boy long dead.

"But very stubborn," insisted the Lady Bedlam.

"I, for one, am not surprised."

She took the comment for the compliment it was supposed to be. As they moved on, the enchantress added, "It is not the *worst* trait he could have."

"Not by far. Will you be bringing Aurim and Valea to Penacles when you make your extended visit?"

Cabe's wife considered that. "It might be a good idea. With Kyl, Grath, and Ursa gone, the Manor will certainly seem empty for the two of them."

"The Manor will seem empty to you, too, won't it? After all, many of those who live here will be leaving with them, won't they?"

"Many of the drakes will be leaving, and some of the humans, too, but some of those are returning to the domain of the Green Dragon, who originally brought them to the Manor. Actually, anyone, either human or drake, who desires to remain behind is welcome to do so. I have hopes that most will."

They had reached the staircase. The Gryphon glanced at Cabe, who had been silent for the past several moments. The warlock had been listening, but he had also been brooding over his earlier notion concerning the stables. He could not say why; after all, the Gryphon's search had yielded nothing, and if there was anyone other than Darkhorse whose power Cabe respected, it was the lionbird.

"I hope you and your entire family will dare to take some time to visit us after Kyl is ensconced on the throne of the Dragon Emperor, Cabe. Things should be much more peaceful by that time, and I think that Troia may not desire to travel much out of the city. Not, at least, for several months." There was a twinkle in the lionbird's arresting eyes as he saw comprehension slowly creep into his hosts' countenances. "I would say that Troia will be showing very soon."

"Another child? How wonderful!" The sorceress hugged the Gryphon.

Cabe, forgetting all else, reached forward and shook his old comrade's hand again. "Was that the true reason you came?"

"Oh, the others were good, too, but I decided to save the best news for last." The Gryphon tilted his head a bit. "I would be happy with a female this time, but another male would be loved just as much!"

"I'm amazed that you kept the truth hidden from us so long."

"I wanted to tell you when I first arrived, but I had sworn that I would save this news for last, it being the best possible news there could be!" He laughed. "I tell you, there is no reason that Toos could give me now that would make me take the throne back from him! I intend to enjoy the coming peace by watching all my children grow up while Troia and I make up for all the time the war kept us from truly enjoying one another."

"We shall have to visit you the moment after Kyl has ascended to the throne, no later than that!" exclaimed the Lady Bedlam. She and Cabe both knew what children meant to the Gryphon and Troia. For all his warlike past, the lionbird adored the young, but that fact had not been noticed until he had met his mate.

"Kyl . . ." The Gryphon squawked and shook his head. "I am more than happy to be free of the curses of monarchy, but if that's what he desires, may he rule long as long as he rules fair. I wish him the best of luck, of course." He shrugged, and when he spoke again, some of the joy created by the announcement of his forthcoming child gave way to consideration of another child's impending future. "But I hope that he may *never* have need of it."

XII

Unlike the city of Talak, Penacles, situated to the southeast of the Manor, was a place of tall towers, many of them topped with majestic, pointed spires. It was also a land of gardens, reminding those who had journeyed from the Manor of their home. The gardens were everywhere and ranged from small plots of earth in the center of the bazaar to huge, rolling landscapes toward the eastern part of the kingdom.

Cabe could hardly believe that this day had finally come. It seemed as if the past few days had dragged slowly by. Preparing for this second visit had been only a part of the problem. Cabe and Gwen had also had to cope with the nagging fear that they had missed some legacy of Toma's. There had also been the more realistic problem of Valea, who stared after Kyl at every opportunity. Somehow, Cabe had kept the two apart save on occasions when they were all together, but he knew that after Penacles something permanent would have to be done. Because of Kyl's rank, the warlock had forborne from directly confronting him on this issue, but no more. This was one situation that could not go on.

Penacles had known no overseeing Dragon King for well over a century, not since the Gryphon and Cabe's own grandfather, Nathan, had brought down the Dragon King Purple. The Gryphon had then ruled here until his long-hidden past had forced him on a journey across the seas and into the dark empire of the Aramites. While he fought to bring down the wolf raiders' regime, his most trusted aide, General Toos, also known as the Fox, had ruled in his place . . . and had proved quite an impressive monarch in his own right. Still, even after roughly two decades as lord of Penacles, fiery-haired Toos still insisted he was only holding the fort until his king came to his senses. Hence the tall, narrow ruler's nickname of Toos the Regent.

After Talak, Kyl did not seem as awestruck with Penacles, although that did not mean that the dragon heir was not fascinated. He drank in the wonders of the City of Knowledge. The dizzying heights of the many towers most impressed him, for Cabe noticed the young drake eye them again and again. Grath, too, was amazed. The Green Dragon and Benjin Traske, on the other hand, seemed oblivious to the beauty of the ancient kingdom. Of course, they had been to Penacles many times before.

Things were going well, but Cabe could not shake his uneasiness. He felt that he had a good reason, though; one of his party was missing.

Darkhorse had never promised that he would also accompany them to Penacles, and it may have been that the shadow steed felt it unnecessary since Toos was a much more reasonable ruler than tempestuous Melicard. Certainly, both the former and present monarchs of Penacles were on fair terms with the eternal. Kyl would not have impressed them by maneuvering Darkhorse into journeying with him to this place. The eternal would have understood that, too.

Still, Cabe had expected *some* word from the massive stallion. That this had happened virtually on top of their discovery of Toma's intrusion was likely why the warlock was so bothered. It was not as if Darkhorse had not disappeared without explanation before. The eternal was governed by no one save himself.

"Is that the palace?" Grath asked him, leaning close so as to be heard over the trumpets and the crowds.

Cabe shelved his thoughts and studied the structure looming ahead of them. "Yes, that's it."

He knew why Grath had asked him. The palace of the lords of Penacles was a sharp contrast to that of the kings of Talak and also, in fact, to the city of Penacles itself. With so much beauty everywhere else, it was surprising to first-time visitors to discover that the palace resembled nothing more than a great stone fortress. The walls were a drab, unadorned gray and the only entrance was a massive iron gate. Huge marble steps that seemed to go on forever led up to the palace. There were no decorative columns, no gardens, and no statuary save the lone marble figure of a gryphon in flight. The last had been a gift to the lionbird from some of the citizenry during his long and productive reign. Toos had left it where it was as one more reminder that he was *not* king.

The honor guard that had been provided for them led the caravan directly to the palace. As in Talak, they were met at the steps. Toos was there, accompanied by the Gryphon, four officers who were a part of the regent's personal staff, and a small honor guard. The former general had never taken a queen, although in the past year he had begun to court one or two women. Despite his resemblance to a man entering his latter years, the vulpine monarch had at least a good fifty years left of life. That was because mixed in with the graying red hair—red hair that had once made Cabe joke that Gwen and the regent might be very long lost cousins—was a streak of silver. Toos, like Cabe, was a mage, but in the former mercenary's case, the magic apparently manifested itself as an uncanny ability to outmaneuver his opponents, be it on the field of battle or in the intrigue-laden courts of Penacles. The only other sign that Toos was a man of magic was his age. A sorcerer could live to be three, and in some cases, four, centuries old. Toos was already well beyond the normal life span of a human.

"Welcome, Lord Kyl." The voice was strong and, while formal, still quite different from the practiced tones of the aristocracy. There was also a look in the regent's eye, a look that hinted of humor.

"Greetingsss to you, General Toosss," replied the young drake, executing a bow. The two then shook hands.

Cabe held back a smile. The heir, possibly with a little reminding from Grath, had remembered that Toos did not care to be called king or lord. The regent considered himself a soldier and so preferred to retain his rank.

"Your journey went well?" asked Toos.

"Quite well, thank you. I had forgotten what a wondrousss land Penaclesss wasss, or what a fassscinating place the city proper isss."

"You're not referring to the block of stone behind me, I hope," commented the regent with a foxlike smile.

Kyl was momentarily taken aback by the openness of Toos. The young drake had met the human on occasion over the years, but not for quite some time and most often for only a few minutes. Cabe had warned him about the general, reminding him that Toos had been a mercenary and warrior for far longer than he had been lord of a mighty kingdom. Even the warlock, who had known Toos since the days when the angular commander had led the defenders of a besieged Penacles against the invading dragon forces of the Dragon Emperor, could not always adjust to the man's mercurial style. As a soldier, Toos had constantly kept his adversaries off guard, the better to defeat them swift and sure. The style had suited him in his present role as well.

"The palace isss very—"

"Functional. The inside is not much of an improvement, although the grand ballroom and the royal court are decorative enough, I suppose. We'd best leave it at that." Again, there was the foxlike smile. "Now, Lord Kyl, if you will allow my staff to see to your people, we shall end this greeting and instead save our breaths for climbing these steps."

The drakes were not at first certain as to how to take the almost flippant manner of their host. The warlock smiled slightly. Toos *had* changed since their first introduction.

Grath whispered something to Kyl, who eyed the steps. The emperor-to-be nodded, then replied to the waiting Toos. "Yesss, the sssuggessstion hasss merit, General. *Much* merit."

Snapping his fingers, Toos sent two of his officers to deal with the caravan. Then, waiting for Kyl to step up beside him, the general led the way. Everyone soon saw the wisdom of the regent's words. The climb was exhausting, even to those who had been prepared for it. Progress slowed the higher they climbed, but at last the party reached the top of the steps.

Toos glared at the path they had just tread, grumbling, "That you can blame on one of your own, Lord Kyl. Someday, I must do something about it."

"I said that for years, Toos," retorted the Gryphon. "You would have to tear down everything here, though. That would be a massive undertaking."

"Each time I climb those steps, it becomes more and more tempting, I'll say that."

Cabe surveyed the others and found to his surprise that, other than the sentries, who would not think of showing their exhaustion, the only one who appeared unaffected by the climb was Benjin Traske. The warlock stared hard at the massive tutor and finally had to ask, "Are you well, Benjin?"

"I have always believed in maintaining both the mind *and* the body, Lord Bedlam."

"So I see now." He shook his head. With a minor spell, the sorcerer could have reinvigorated himself easily, but like Talak, Penacles had its special defenses. Some remained from the days when the Dragon King Purple had ruled, and others from the reign of the Gryphon, but there were also a vast number of new spells protecting the city, placed there at the regent's request.

Toos looked over his guests. "If we're all ready to continue, I've planned some food and entertainment. Lord Kyl, have you ever witnessed a living chess game before?"

The young drake's eyes were wide with curiosity. "I mussst sssay that I have certainly not." He glanced down at his brother, who shook his head in equal confusion.

"Then I think that you have a treat awaiting you. If you'll all follow me?"

Penacles had been at peace for years, their neighbor to the east, mist-enshrouded Lochivar, having been quiet since the Gryphon had nearly dealt its master, the Black Dragon, a mortal blow. The darksome lord of the Grey Mists still lived and ruled, but it was said that he could barely speak and that his powers were waning.

That meant that Penacles had an army that trained and trained, but had no enemy to fight. While Toos looked forward to peace as much as most other folk did, he believed in maintaining a strong force. One never knew when times might change. Therefore, it had behooved him to find some way in which his men could keep their skills paramount.

War games had solved that problem, at least where his soldiers were concerned. Each month, various units would maneuver against one another in the nearby hills and valleys. Men who excelled in skill and ingenuity were rewarded. The soldiers also kept wary, for it *was* possible to be injured. Officers worked to see that such injuries happened as rarely as was possible, though.

Yes, Toos had solved the problem of keeping his men at their best, but he could hardly join them on the field, however much he would have wanted to do so. There was the risk that something might happen to him, either by accident or due to some assassin. No ruler who desired to survive dared believe that there was *not* an assassin lurking nearby. Simply because the Black Dragon had made no new assaults on the kingdom in years did not mean that he had withdrawn his spies.

From his long years as the Gryphon's second, the vulpine soldier had picked up a fondness for chess, especially its constant demand for reevaluating one's strategy. Simple chess had been sufficient for some time, but then, while visiting the magical libraries of Penacles with the Gryphon, the bored regent had commented on his need for something further.

"To my surprise," Toos said to his guests as he considered his next move, "the *gnome* spoke up."

The libraries of Penacles were a magical wonder dating back possibly beyond the present city. No one knew much about them save that they were larger than should have been physically possible, some corridors stretching for what seemed miles underground, yet apparently movable, and accessible only through a wondrous tapestry hidden in the palace.

The libraries also had a librarian . . . or perhaps many, although if the latter was the case, then all of them were identical in form. For as long as either Toos or the Gryphon could recall, they had always been served by a small, squat, completely hairless gnome wearing a robe much like that of a mage. All one had to do was tell the gnome what one was searching for and the odd little figure would locate it. Rarely, however, did the gnome offer words of advice.

Toos made his move and continued. "He suggested a field, a life-sized board, and living champions to do combat. I scoffed at the idea at first, but . . . " The general indicated the area just before them. "You see what I've done."

In what had once been a small arena where human slaves had fought for the personal amusement of the Dragon King, there was now a black-and-white pattern of squares, each approximately three feet by three feet. There were viewing boxes on each end of the board, providing seating for perhaps two dozen people apiece.

On the board, or sitting off to the sides, were soldiers clad in armor representing the various pieces in the game. These were the game's living chessmen . . . and women, too, since not only did each side need a queen, but female soldiers had been a part of the army of Penacles since the days of the Gryphon's reign.

Cabe took his mind off of the game to observe the lionbird himself, who was the general's opponent. The first time the warlock had been invited to witness the tournament, he had come fearing that the regent had finally fallen prey to his power and had become a decadent tyrant. However, after watching the game and learning the rules behind it, he had come to enjoy it himself.

The chessmen were volunteers. Over the years, it had become a bit of prestige to be a combatant in the chess tournament. Unlike the true board game, a chess piece was not removed simply because another piece had captured it. Instead, the two warriors had to duel, utilizing their skills while remaining within the two squares involved. Fighters were removed if they lost or if they attempted to truly wound their adversaries. It had become a matter of honor for most soldiers involved to win as cleanly as possible, as the best were often chosen for a place in the royal guard.

At the moment, Toos was in grave danger. His rook, his last line of defense against the Gryphon, had just fallen in combat against the other's knight. The rook, a man armed with a mace and shield, had been disarmed by the knight, an armored figure also using a shield, but instead of a mace had wielded a broadsword.

"I knew that would happen," the regent muttered. "Luck of the draw! He's current champion among the champions!"

The game ended three combats later. The rule involving checkmate particularly fascinated Cabe. First the player would have to assure that his opponent's king had no escape. That was the same as a normal game of chess. However, in the general's variation, the checking pieces then had to do battle with the beleaguered monarch. It was possible for the king to free himself from checkmate if he could eliminate every opponent involved, but he had to fight all of them; he could not move to safety after defeating the first adversary.

The drakes, especially Kyl and Grath, were eager to direct the game themselves. The Dragon King had already played on one or two of his previous visits, so he offered to stand aside and let brother go against brother. Toos repeated the differences in the rules from normal chess, then chose their pieces for them. Chessmen were always chosen by lottery, so that no player could ever come to trust too much in his warriors. It made for a more balanced game and, in fact, after the countless battles the Gryphon and Toos had played, the lionbird was up by only seven victories. Of course, if there were ever two opponents who knew how one another thought, it was the two former mercenaries.

While the regent guided Kyl and the Green Dragon, who had always had a fondness for the human game, coached Grath, the Gryphon made his way back to where Cabe and Benjin Traske sat watching the opening moves. As usual, Faras and Ssgayn took up a spot near the dragon heir, which made for some crowding as the general's own guards insisted on watching the drakes.

"They will be quite occupied with this game," the Gryphon commented as he joined the two humans. "This might be a good time to visit the libraries."

"For what reason?"

"I'm doing some research, trying to see if I finally understand some of the methods by which the libraries pass on information. I'm certain now that long ago something happened that distorted the original function of the place. I thought that I might save my next visit for when you were here. Do you wish to come?"

"I'd be a fool to say no." As the Manor was the warlock's pet project, so were the libraries the Gryphon's. Both researchers had achieved about the same amount of success so far . . . meaning very little. If the lionbird had finally made progress, Cabe wanted to see it for himself.

"Good!" The Gryphon paused, then eyed Traske. "Benjin, you've never been in the libraries before, have you?"

"No, my lord."

"You *haven't?*" That startled Cabe. "After all these years?"

"I blame Toos for that!" The former monarch of Penacles shook his head. "Toos has never trusted the libraries . . . and who can blame him? You and I were virtually the only ones he would allow to enter until fairly recently, warlock. The old fox rarely even visits them himself!"

Cabe had known the last, but not that Toos had been so restrictive. Surely, Benjin Traske, whose expertise had helped create the school of sorcery, deserved that much trust. Once again, he was reminded of the paranoia of the monarchy.

"Well, I think that it's time the scholar was given permission to visit them," the Gryphon commented with a glance toward the regent. "You may certainly join us, Benjin."

"Thank you, my lord." The calm veneer momentarily twisted into a look of extreme pleasure. Then, apparently remembering himself, Traske quickly reverted to his more stolid, scholarly expression.

As they rose to leave, Cabe could not resist quietly commenting to the Gryphon, "I thought that you no longer ruled this kingdom."

"You may consider me king emeritus for the time being."

"Perhaps you'd better hope that Toos will consider you that."

The Gryphon chuckled, an incongruous sight, considering his features. "My old comrade-in-arms would be happy to consider me king of *anything*, just so long as he can relinquish the throne to me!" He pretended to shudder at the thought. "Now, come! We really should give Benjin all the time we can in the libraries!"

They left the drakes and the general to their game. The Gryphon led his companions back into the palace and through its halls. As the visitors had noticed on their initial walk through the gray edifice, the inside of the palace was little better decorated than the outside. A few pieces of art, most recent and all of them reminiscent of war, dotted the halls here and there, but for the most part the palace interior looked as if the architects had left their project undone. Only when they passed the grand ballroom was there a radical change. Cabe glanced inside as they passed by and marveled at the bright, glittering array of crystal and gold decorations. After the rest of the building, the sight of the ballroom was almost jarring.

On and on they walked. Cabe began to wonder why the Gryphon had not chosen to transport them there. Most likely it was because the lionbird preferred physical activity and considered such use of magic frivolous. While this pattern of thought was much akin to the warlock's own way of thinking, this particular trek was one where he would have happily made an exception.

At last they came before a doorway beside which two huge, iron figures stood, roughly hewn warriors that, like the palace, seemed to have been abandoned before they had been completed. The Gryphon signaled his companions to halt. He continued on for several paces until he stood no more than two yards from the center of the doorway.

"Well? Will you let us pass?" the lionbird asked.

What happened next made Benjin Traske gasp and clutch the hilt of his blade, an action which, in retrospect, Cabe realized might have endangered all of them.

One of the iron figures slowly turned its head toward the waiting Gryphon. The other looked not at the lionbird, but rather at the two behind.

The warlock took hold of the scholar's arm and whispered, "Make no false moves, Benjin. If they perceive you as a threat, they might attack. You'd be surprised at how fast they can move!"

"Iron *golems*," the tutor muttered, still stunned. "I have heard of such, but only in old stories."

"Did the stories mention what they could do to those they were sent against?"

Traske did not release his blade, but he made no other move, which was perhaps the best that Cabe could hope for.

Oddly, the Gryphon was still waiting for the doors to be opened. The golems continued to stare at the trio, as if uncertain what to do.

"You *heard* me. The three of us will enter here; is that understood?"

Very slowly, the golem watching the former monarch returned to its original stance. As its head swiveled back, the creature rumbled, "You may enter."

"Thank you *very* much." The Gryphon waved the other two forward.

The doors suddenly swung open of their own accord. Beyond was a chamber that, like the ballroom, was a contrast to the stark simplicity of the regent's palace. That was because the chamber before them had once been the Gryphon's very room, his private sanctum in the days when he had ruled Penacles.

With careful steps, the three entered the chamber. Cabe noticed that the other golem continued to observe the Gryphon's two guests. He could not recall the last time that the iron monsters had taken such interest in him. Then he realized that it must be Traske in whom the metal man was interested, for the scholar had never been permitted entrance before.

Benjin Traske still clutched his knife hilt, but he had almost forgotten the golems. Now he was busy inspecting the room that they had entered, his eyes quickly fixing on one ornament in particular, a skillfully woven tapestry hanging on one of the walls.

"I still use this place on occasion, although for the most part my stays last only the day. Troia would never forgive me if I left her and Zeras alone overnight. Since we live not that far from here, I cannot blame her. Mostly, I use this chamber when I'm researching the libraries."

The doors suddenly swung closed and as they did, they revealed two more of the metal colossi standing guard inside. Cabe had seen these two often enough, but for the first time that he could recall, they were watching the Gryphon's guests closely.

Leading them to the tapestry, the Gryphon explained its importance to the scholar. "This is the only way—the only way we know of—that one can gain entrance to the libraries."

"The detail is fantastic!" whispered Traske. "And it appears to be very ancient. I have never seen such a style before."

"We don't know *how* old it is, Benjin, but it may be from the first Dragon King. No one is certain."

Traske squinted. "But . . . this is present-day Penacles! That cannot be right!"

"The tapestry is quite magical. It always shows the kingdom as it presently is. We could watch a building being torn down, return to this chamber, and find that it's also vanished from the image."

"How does it help us journey to the libraries? I do not even see them."

"You have to know how to look for them, Benjin. Where the libraries are concerned, you won't see an actual building. Instead, there's usually a symbol of some sort. It varies now and then. Sometimes it's a book, other times it might simply be a cross or star. Knowing the tapestry as I do, I merely have to search for something that is out of place." The Gryphon studied the image. "And I think . . . that's certainly a strange choice!"

"What is it this time?" Cabe asked.

"See for yourself." Their host put his finger next to the mark, then shifted to the side so that the others could look at it.

Just under several buildings in what was the eastern edge of the city was the symbol. Cabe had never seen its like in all the times he had watched the Gryphon use the tapestry, and its very pattern disturbed him.

Benjin Traske peered at it. "A very stylized version of a dragon, is it not?"

"It is. That's not the symbol you find on each tome in the libraries, though. Looks very familiar."

"It should," whispered the warlock. "Kyrg and Toma both used it as one of their banners."

"I'd *forgotten* that! Of course!"

Cabe frowned, suddenly filled with tension. "I don't like that coincidence. This could mean that Toma somehow gained access to the libraries." Traske, who had finally been told of the drake's other intrusions frowned at this. "He could be in there *now*."

The Gryphon nodded agreement, but added, "I can't see how he could have gotten into the libraries, but then he did get into the Manor. There may be danger in the libraries. Perhaps you should stay here after all, Benjin."

The scholar looked disappointed but understanding. "If you think I should."

"If nothing's wrong, then we'll immediately return for you. Now, if you could please step back ten paces?" He waited for Traske to obey. Then, placing his finger directly on the symbol, the Gryphon began to rub it. As he did, Cabe moved next to him.

The golems, the chamber, and Benjin Traske began to fade away. Only the tapestry remained the same. It was as if a great fog were building up, a fog that somehow did not affect the duo or the artifact.

The Gryphon continued to rub. Quickly the chamber and all in it vanished, only to be immediately replaced by the dim image of a corridor and countless shelves. Within seconds, the image became distinct. The last vestiges of blurriness faded away before a full minute had elapsed since the transfer had begun.

Cabe and his companion stared down both directions of the corridor. All the great books were in place and everything was as neat as was possible. Yet, once before a drake, the fatalistic Ice Dragon, had somehow obtained entrance to this magical place. The warlock wondered if that intrusion had at last been repeated.

"That's odd," commented the Gryphon.

"Seems quiet to me."

"Yes. Absolutely quiet. *Where* is the librarian?"

The hairless little gnome was nowhere to be seen. Always he, or perhaps another exactly like him, appeared to those arriving in the libraries. This time, however, it was as if the vast structure had just been abandoned.

"Maybe he was too far away for once." Even Cabe doubted his suggestion. The gnome should have been awaiting them.

The Gryphon continued to scan both ends of the corridor. "I think that perhaps we'd—"

Cabe glanced at his companion. The lionbird was staring past him at something far down the passage. The warlock turned and saw that the gnome had at last made an appearance.

The crooked little figure stood no higher than Cabe's waist. Somehow, despite his size, he had always impressed the mage as a creature not to be trifled with. The notion had always lingered despite the fact that the gnome had never made any hostile gesture toward any of them.

"I am afraid that the libraries must be closed to you for a time, former lord of Penacles."

"Closed? That's ridiculous! They've never been—"

The sudden silence filled Cabe Bedlam with fear for his companion. He tore his gaze from the gnome and looked at the Gryphon . . . but found *no one* beside him. Immediately, he turned his attention back to the ominous little figure. "What have you done with him?"

"He is back in the chamber, as you will be, too, Bedlam." The creature sighed. "Your family will insist on disrupting my existence for all eternity. I have never seen such a consistent streak for falling into trouble as your tree bears."

"What does that mean?" The gnome had known some of his ancestors? Cabe doubted somehow that the librarian was speaking of Azran or Nathan. He suddenly had the suspicion that this gnome was incredibly old.

"Your line will probably be the death of me yet . . . or rather *again*. By laws that I myself put into effect, fool that I was, I can tell you nothing more save that the face of your terror is before you often."

It was a warning as twisted in riddle as any other answer given by the tomes of the libraries. Cabe wanted to demand a better answer, but before he was able to say anything—

—he was back in the Gryphon's old chambers.

"Cabe!" The lionbird grabbed him by the arms as if to assure himself that the robed warlock was real. "What happened? Where were you?"

"Being told puzzles by the gnome. I do know one thing; not only has he existed for as long as the libraries, but he seems to have met a few of my ancestors over that time."

"Did he explain what he meant by that nonsense about the libraries being closed?"

"I *think* he did." Cabe repeated his short conversation with the crooked little figure. When he was finished, the Gryphon and Benjin Traske both looked as confused as he felt.

"It suggests something about Toma, I would think, but with so much else going on, there could be other meanings. How typical of the libraries."

"Whatever the meaning, he indicated that there would be no more information or aid. I gathered that he *couldn't.*"

"We shall see." Returning to the tapestry, the Gryphon raised a clawed hand with the intention of rubbing the libraries' symbol and returning to the hidden edifice. However, midway to the ancient artifact, the lionbird halted his hand.

"What's wrong?"

"The symbol . . . it's *disappeared!*"

The warlock could scarcely believe that. Trailed by Benjin Traske, he joined the Gryphon in his search. The dragon symbol had not only disappeared, but there was no new symbol to replace it. Even if Cabe had somehow missed it, he knew that the sharp eyes of his companion would not have. The Gryphon knew every detail of the tapestry and every nuance of its function.

"I didn't think that was possible!" muttered the former monarch. "It *shouldn't* be! He has to obey! The libraries serve the lord of Penacles or whomever he permits access to it. The libraries know that Toos has given me leave!"

Cabe considered that. "Perhaps that's why we can't enter now. Perhaps the libraries are somehow serving Toos or you by doing this." He suddenly thought about the visions that had appeared in the Manor. Was it, too, trying to warn or protect those who lived within? "Is that a possibility?"

"A very peculiar possibility, but, yes, one that might be worth contemplating." Still bristling, the Gryphon glanced at the third member of their party. "I apologize, Benjin. This was hardly expected. Perhaps next time that you are here we will be able to make the journey."

"I am patient, my lord." Although his face was bland, the scholar's eyes again revealed his disappointment.

"Then let us return to the others and see how the game is progressing." Despite his attempts to be cheerful, the Gryphon was clearly still upset about this development. Never had the libraries defied him so.

By the time they returned to the arena, the game was almost in its climax. Cabe and the others joined Toos, who stepped away for a moment to speak with them.

"It's Grath's turn. He's trying to find a way out of his predicament, but I think it'll be checkmate in a few moves. He was threatening to beat the young emperor-to-be, but then his luck turned. Made some bad moves. Misjudged his champions' opponents. There's no way the king can fight his way out if he's cornered, which he will be soon enough." He glanced back to make certain that Grath had not yet moved. "Lord Kyl will hardly need my help now."

"How well do they play?" asked the Gryphon.

"Early in the game, I would have said that Grath could have given either of us trouble, but now I'd have to say that both of them are good players who still have to learn. Lord Kyl looks to be the better of the two."

A warrior on the field moved. The general excused himself and returned to the game, but Kyl was already commanding his knight forward. Toos remained next to the dragon heir just long enough to discuss the move, then left the young drake to his own efforts.

"Not the move that I would've made, but it'll bring the battle to an end soon enough. The Gryphon informed me earlier that he might bring you to the libraries. Is that where you were? Did you enjoy them, Scholar Traske? I don't believe that you've ever been to them."

The Gryphon answered for them. "We were *forbidden* entrance, Toos. The gnome said that the libraries were closed to us!"

It was evident that the regent did not believe what he was hearing. "That's *preposterous!*"

"True, but it happened."

"Tell me everything."

They did. Toos listened in disbelief, shaking his head when they were finished.

"Madness!" he snarled. "I'm inclined to take this as a sign that we should cancel this entire affair, but that's out of the question. Perhaps it's so many drakes nearby. There's not been this many dragons in the land since the siege led by Kyrg."

The others had not considered that fact . . . or, at least, the warlock had not. He eyed the Gryphon who was nodding thoughtfully. "That, too, is a possibility, but I think that there's no doubt that Toma is somehow involved. Cabe's conversation with the librarian was a murky one at best, but I feel that that's what it concerned."

"Well, I think that I'll try to see if they'll let me enter, though I doubt it. In the meantime, you can rest assured that measures will be taken in this matter."

"We know that we can trust you to do that. Toma may try to get near to our young emperor-to-be, so perhaps you might want your people to keep a special watch on him."

"Oh, believe me; they are."

An exclamation of triumph informed them that the game was at an end. As expected, Kyl had emerged the victor. Grath waved his congratulations from where he sat. Behind the younger brother, the Dragon King put a consoling hand on Grath's shoulder.

"We should inform Lord Green," Cabe suggested.

Toos studied the drake lord. "Yes, I'd thought of that. I'll do so this evening, when we discuss the final details of this visit. You all know that there's the required reception so the aristocrats and merchants and such can feel impressive. I'd also planned a ride out to where two of our best units are having their field exercises, but it might be best to postpone that. I'll have to see what the lord of Dagora thinks about it."

Kyl chose to join them then, which ended the conversation. The young drake was elated with his victory. "Did you all sssee? What a fassscinating game! I shall have to devissse sssomething akin to it once I asssume the throne! What a marvelousss passstime!"

"I'm glad you enjoyed it so much," returned Toos, pretending that nothing was amiss. "There will be opportunity to play again, of course, but I'm sorry to say that for now matters of state must take my time. If you will excuse me, I think the Lord Gryphon will be happy to show you the armory. Penacles might be called the City of Knowledge, but we have amassed quite an interesting array of armaments, too."

Kyl's eyes were bright with eagerness. He had not yet calmed down after his victory. "Yesss! I would be delighted!"

"Excellent! There are also some last arrangements to be made for the events of the next few days, arrangements that will be passed on for your approval later this evening. I hope you'll find your time here well spent."

The regent bid them all farewell, including Grath and the Dragon King, who had just rejoined the party. Grath, too, looked exhausted from the game, but he seemed slightly less enthusiastic. Considering the outcome, Cabe did not think the younger drake's attitude at all surprising.

"An excellent game, Your Majesty," the Dragon King commented.

"Yesss, it wasss! Lord Green, when I am emperor, I would like your help in creating a version of thisss tournament for our own kind."

"I will be happy to be of ssservice, although I fear our warriors might be a little more inclined to blood than these humans were."

That did not seem to bother the heir at all. In fact, the warlock thought that he looked much too hopeful.

"If Your Majesty is ready to depart," the Gryphon interrupted, "the royal armory requires a short ride."

"Armory?" questioned the Dragon King.

"It isss sssupposssed to be fassscinating, Lord Green!"

The drake lord acknowledged Kyl's words. "You will certainly enjoy it, my liege, but I must request you permit me to stay behind. I mussst really see how things are progressing with the rest of our caravan. We want no incidents such as happened with the artisan Osseuss. I would like to make certain that everyone knows what they are and are not permitted to do."

Kyl was not about to miss the armory. He waved away the Dragon King. "Of course, you have my permission. You will report to me later?"

The Green Dragon's tone was neutral. "Of course, my emperor."

Once again, it amazed Cabe to see how willingly the Dragon King bent before the young heir. Green truly had to want this peace to work, for there could be no other reason for his willingness to suffer Kyl's bouts of lordliness. The warlock sincerely doubted that he could be so understanding.

The matter dismissed from his thoughts, the eager young heir turned back to the Gryphon. "We may depart whenever you wish, Lord Gryphon."

"Thank you." Kyl did not notice the slight touch of humor in the lionbird's tone, but it was all Cabe could do to keep from smiling. "Lord Green, if you'll join us for a short time, I will find you a proper escort to lead you to your chambers."

"That would be sssuitable, thank you." Even under present circumstances, any drake who walked alone in Penacles risked danger. Not as great a danger as in Talak, but enough that such a risk was not to be taken.

They had only just begun walking when Cabe felt someone touch him on the shoulder. He turned to find Grath behind him, which startled the sorcerer a bit, since the younger drake always seemed either at the side of his brother or next to the Dragon King.

"What is it, Grath?"

"Master Bedlam, is Darkhorse coming? I think Kyl was expecting him to be here. He will not disappoint us, will he?"

"I don't know. I haven't talked to him since we returned from Talak." Realizing that, the mage's earlier worries came back multiplied. It *had* been quite some time since he or anyone had seen the eternal. Had something happened?

The young drake's thoughts apparently mirrored his own. "Do you think he's all right?"

"He should be. Darkhorse has a tendency to turn up at the most unexpected times. He'll likely materialize in the midst of the reception, just like he did in Talak."

That brought a brief smile to Grath's handsome face, but then the smile slipped as he said, "I hope nothing's wrong."

The conversation ended there. Moments later, Grath drifted back to his brother's side.

Try as he might, the warlock could not stop thinking about the shadow steed. He was certain that Darkhorse had continued on with his investigations into the mysterious traps some unknown enemy had planted.

Unknown enemy? With all else he had been blamed for, could not such cunning, magical traps have been set by *Toma*? It made perfect sense to Cabe, although he was willing to admit that he was paranoid when it came to the renegade. Still, it would explain a lot.

Darkhorse in the claws of Toma. . . .

XIII

The headache had not gone away even after several days. Aurim calculated that by now his father was spending his second day in Penacles. His mother planned to leave tomorrow, but not if Aurim was not well. Aurim had insisted that the headache was nothing, which was something of a lie. However, the throbbing in his head was nothing compared to the thought of looking weak.

It was a peculiar headache. For the first day, it had seemed like any other, but after that, the throbbing had taken on a strange quality. It was as if something was trying to break free. Each day seemed to weaken whatever held that thing back.

For reasons he did not understand save perhaps that it might end the pain, Aurim felt as if he *wanted* the mysterious force to burst free.

Eyes open, he stared at the ceiling of his bedchamber. His mother had suggested that he take an afternoon nap, something that he had not done since he was five. There was no arguing with the Lady Gwendolyn Bedlam, however, and so Aurim had retreated to his room. To his surprise, he had actually slept. Unfortunately, when he woke it was to find that the headache was, if anything, worse than ever.

He rolled over and stared at the balcony. Aurim found himself drawn to it for what must have been the dozenth time since he had stirred but minutes before.

Groaning, Aurim rose. Whatever fascinated him about the balcony drove him almost as crazy as the headache did. *Maybe if I look outside, that'll make it stop!* He hoped so. Aurim was certain that he could overcome the headache, but not the headache *and* this peculiar compulsion.

No great revelation came to him as he stepped out. Still, the breeze that touched his face calmed him a little. He leaned on the carved handrail and peered down. People, both human and drake, went about their businesses. Off in the distance, Aurim could make out his sister and Ursa. *Probably pining for Kyl!* he thought with a snort. Kyl was his friend, but Aurim doubted that any relationship between the drake and his sister was a wise thing. Try telling that to *her*, though.

The throbbing continued unabated. Trying to keep his mind from it, Aurim continued to study the areas below. Perhaps if he took a walk through the maze. That always soothed him. If his mother had no need for him, he would do that. The garden maze had been his own personal world when he had been tiny: a fantasy realm where he had sometimes fought heroic battles and other times simply sat and enjoyed the peacefulness.

He looked to his left. The stables, as usual, were fairly active. Some of the horses were being walked. Two figures were inspecting the hoof of a bay. One of them straightened, shaking his head. Ssarekai.

Ssarekai.

"Toma . . . " he whispered, not realizing what he had uttered until a moment later. When he became aware, Aurim's countenance paled. He did not remember everything, but he remembered something.

Toma! That night I woke . . . the stables . . .

"Ssarekai?"

He did not even recall transporting himself, but suddenly Aurim was standing before the drake. The bay whinnied and tried to shy away from him, but the stable hand who had been conversing with Ssarekai managed to maintain his hold.

"Master Aurim! You should never—"

"What *happened*, Ssarekai? What did he *do*?"

The drake looked at him as if the warlock had gone mad. Perhaps he had, but Aurim did not care. He only wanted some answers to the horrible memories suddenly filling his head. Without thinking, he reached for the servitor and pulled him close. Ssarekai did not struggle, perhaps recalling that as a mage of great potential, his young master could have as easily thrown him across the span of the Manor grounds.

"You were with him! Somewhere below my chambers! You were with Toma!"

He had never seen a drake blanch before, but Ssarekai managed to do just that. The drake shook his head and his tongue darted out and in. He was so frightened that his sibilance became even worse than Kyl's.

"Not sssso, Massssster Aurrrim! Not sssso! I would neverrr have anything to do with that rrrenegade, that monssssster!"

"I saw you! I also saw him—" *Saw him do what? Do something, but I can't recall what it was Toma did!*

"I know nothing; I sssswear that by the Drrragon of the Depthssss!"

"Aurim!"

He ignored the call, his concern only for an answer to the scene replaying in his head. It was like reading the same page of a book over and over. He saw—or rather had *sensed*—the two of them below. Ssarekai himself the warlock could not really recall noticing, but he *had* been there; Aurim knew that now. Ssarekai had stood in silence while something had happened to Toma, a spell that the renegade himself had cast.

"Aurim!" This time the voice would not be denied. A hand clamped onto his shoulder to emphasize that fact.

Abruptly aware of what he was doing, the young sorcerer released his grip on the drake. Ssarekai hissed in relief, then stepped back just enough to be out of reach. Everyone was staring at Aurim . . . including his mother.

She almost seemed ablaze. The enchantress took hold of her son by the arms and looked him straight in the eyes. Under that gaze, he could not turn away.

"Listen to me!" she demanded. "Do you know what you've been doing?"

Much of the fight left him. He had come close to using his power on a trusted retainer, on someone who was a friend. He had been about to unleash his power without any thought as to the consequences.

"Do you know now?"

Aurim nodded. Only then did it become possible for him to look away. In a voice much younger, he whispered, "I'm sorry."

"I'm not the one to apologize to."

He understood. Turning around, he faced the still wary Ssarekai. Two stable hands were half-supporting the drake. "I'm sorry, Ssarekai! I really am!"

His extended hand was at first greeted with a stare. Then, the drake slowly extended his own. The two clasped hands. Ssarekai even smiled.

Although everyone else had begun to relax, Aurim was still anxious. His mother must have noticed, for she again drew his attention to her.

"Now tell me what happened, Aurim. Think it over carefully and answer me as best as you can."

Taking a deep breath, Aurim related his tale, beginning with waking up and feeling the urge to go to the balcony. The emerald sorceress's eyes burned when he mentioned suddenly recalling the presences of Toma and, belatedly, Ssarekai. What they had been doing, he could not remember. Aurim only knew that something had been happening to the renegade.

When his story was finished, Gwendolyn Bedlam turned to the unnerved Ssarekai, who had spent the last several seconds shaking his head in denial of his young master's condemning statements.

"You've been with us since the beginning, Ssarekai. I won't judge you without first hearing what you have to say."

"I am innocent of thissss, missssstressss!"

"Calm yourself." She touched him on the shoulder, touched him gently so that he could know that she was not going to harm him. "Tell me."

Hissing, the drake sputtered, "I remember nothing of the fantastic tale Massster Aurim related! I would *never* deal with the likesss of that monster Toma! Never!"

Gwen glanced at Aurim. "What night was this? Do you remember *that*?"

He tried hard to recall. The best he could give her was a period of time spread across four days.

Again, Gwen questioned the drake. "Do you recall anything about those nights?"

Ssarekai looked even more distressed. "Missssstressss, I generally sleep very ssssoundly at night. I recall nothing of thosssse nights!"

"Nothing?" Her hand slid an inch or two across his shoulder.

"Nothing."

"I know what I saw!" Aurim exclaimed. Now that he had remembered, it amazed him that he could have ever forgotten. How had it been possible, unless . . . unless Toma had cast some *spell* on him?

Toma in his mind. He recalled *that* now, too.

"His mind has been tampered with."

His initial thought was to believe that his mother was speaking of him. Only when he realized that she was looking at Ssarekai did Aurim understand.

"The spell is very subtle," the enchantress went on. "And unless we were looking for it, it would be almost impossible to notice. I'd wager you have something akin to it in your own mind,

Aurim, but because of your power, the spell could not affect you as thoroughly as it did Ssarekai."

The drake should have been pleased to have verification that he was innocent of the young warlock's accusations, but discovering that the renegade had toyed with his mind had quickly destroyed that brief pleasure. Still, Ssarekai was not the type to let his fears rule him. "Can you remove it, Mistress Gwendolyn? I would remember whatever shameful thingsss the monsssster had me do ssso that we can begin tracking him down!"

She concentrated on him, seeming to stare into the drake's very soul. However, after more than a minute of this, a minute which to Aurim felt as if it were an hour, the enchantress shook her head. "No, not now. He's somehow bound it to you. It will take more effort, more study. I think I would prefer that my husband or perhaps the Gryphon worked with me."

"What about me, Mother?" asked the young warlock. They had always talked about his potential; why not let him prove himself here and now?

"I know what you're thinking, Aurim, and it's true you have the power, but this is a spell crafted by a black mage far more experienced than you. With time, you'll likely be able to do this without anyone's aid, but this is a predicament requiring long mastery of sorcery."

"I understand." He did, too. Duke Toma no doubt knew a thousand different ways to tangle his spell so that removing it would likely tear apart his victim's mind. Aurim did not wish to be responsible for Ssarekai's death.

It then occurred to him that the drake was not alone in his predicament.

"Mother, what about me?" His voice shook just a little. "I have the same spell on *me*."

Her voice was calm, but her expression hinted at her great concern. "I know, Aurim. I thought about that the moment I realized I could not remove the spell on Ssarekai. However, you should bear one thing in mind. Your ability to focus and use your power far exceeds that of Ssarekai. The fact that you recall anything—and I suspect you've been struggling to do so for days—proves that your own mind is fighting back. It could very well be that this is the beginning of the spell's unraveling. You could recall everything else that happened that night at any moment."

"The headache *has* lessened."

"As I thought it might have. We shall have to see what happens now. This is something that must be monitored carefully."

"Will you still be going to Penacles?"

"I don't know." She eyed both Aurim and Ssarekai. "There are different options, and all of them should be weighed first. I should contact your father, however. Although what I can tell him that won't simply add to his worries, I don't know. If you could only recall more . . . with so much going on in Penacles, I hate to add this. Worse yet, the formal reception is this evening, and once again I've promised to be there." Lady Bedlam uttered a mild curse, which still managed to startle a few of those who had gathered around them. "Cabe has the right of it: this land *does* seem to like nothing better than to complicate and endanger our lives!"

Aurim could only nod grimly. She would get no argument from him on that matter. As far as he was concerned, the Dragonrealm had chosen them to be players in some game. The moment one crisis seemed past, yet a new one would come to life. His father found it all very frustrating and had mentioned quite often that he hoped the peace would mean an end to that game.

Head still throbbing, Aurim's only question was what the land would *do* with its pieces when the game was over.

"So the devil has been busy, has he?"

The Gryphon's words rang in Cabe's ears. After much deliberation, Gwen had contacted him and described what had happened to their son and Ssarekai. The warlock was, of course, concerned for the drake, but he could not help being more fearful for his son's life. Toma particularly hated anyone of the name Bedlam; unraveling the spell blocking Aurim's memories might kill him . . . and none too pleasantly, either.

His wife had wanted to bring both victims to Penacles, but then both of them realized that doing so would leave the Manor with no one to keep an eye on it. With Toma's whereabouts unknown, that might be as good as inviting him to wreak more havoc. Neither Cabe nor Gwen planned on leaving Valea in charge; she was not yet old enough or skilled enough to take on a drake as experienced as the renegade. The warlock was wondering whether even *he* was prepared for the drake duke.

"I wish Darkhorse was here," he muttered to the figure standing before him. The two of them had retired to the Gryphon's chambers as soon as the sorcerer became aware of Gwendolyn's mind touching his own.

The news had not been good. That Toma had dared to do what he had done to Aurim and Ssarekai disgusted Cabe. He was only thankful that the renegade had not done worse.

"I've got to go home, Gryphon! I've got to do what I can to help free my son of that spell. There's no telling *what* might happen otherwise!"

The lionbird nodded. "I understand completely, Cabe. You know that."

His statement made the anxious sorcerer feel a little guilty. The Gryphon had lost a son already; Aurim was still alive and healthy.

"We'll have to explain to Toos and the others. I'll also need to get word to Troia."

"You're coming, too?"

The human/avian eyes stared coldly at him. "Did you think I would abandon you on this? Whatever aid I can offer is yours. You should know that by now."

He had been hoping for his old friend's help, but it was good to be reassured. "I can't thank you enough."

They both rose. The Gryphon patted the warlock on the shoulder. "We've always been there for each other and for each other's family. There's no need for thanks. I owe you as much as you think you owe me."

Cabe differed on that, thinking of how the former monarch had shielded a young, confused man running from the hunting armies of the Dragon Emperor. From that moment on, he had considered himself forever in the lionbird's debt.

Their news was received with both dismay and shock. Benjin Traske insisted on returning with them, his deep concern for the mage's family touching Cabe's heart, but the warlock refused, knowing that the scholar was needed in Penacles more than ever. Without Cabe there, it would be up to Traske to aid the Green Dragon in watching over Kyl. Benjin Traske finally gave in, but only with great reluctance.

Toos, of course, approved of their departure. He leaned close and added, "Your children, warlock, are my children too, as are the Gryphon's. It would pain me dearly, son, if anything happened to any one of them."

The drakes, too, were adamant that Cabe return to the Manor. Kyl, like Benjin Traske, also wished to return in the hopes that he might be able to do something for the young warlock. The Green Dragon and Grath reluctantly convinced him to do otherwise, for which Cabe was grateful. He was surprised at the heir's shock at what had happened to Aurim; his son and the drake were evidently dearer friends than he had imagined. The sorcerer had been convinced that Kyl generally associated with Aurim in order to be near Valea, but the concern he read in the drake's visage told him otherwise. It made him just a little uncomfortable to realize that he might have misjudged Kyl, at least in part.

"Things will be fine here, Cabe," Toos concluded. The regent waved a dismissing hand at them. "Go! See to your son and Ssarekai. Good horseman for a drake, that one. He doesn't deserve Toma's games any more than Aurim does."

"We shall do what we can for both of them," replied the Gryphon. "As soon as we are able, one of us will return with news." He turned to Kyl. "Your Majesty . . . "

"Formality isss not necesssary now, Lord Gryphon. All I desssire isss that you do for my friend what you and Massster Bedlam can!"

The others nodded their agreement. Cabe laid a hand on the lionbird's arm. "Ready?"

"Of course."

They were all waiting in the largest of the Manor's underground chambers. The first time Cabe had been down here, many years before, he had expected to find dungeons. To his relief, most of the rooms evidently had been used for storage. There were traces of old magic, but the spells had either been fairly simple or had been cast so long ago that no danger remained. As for the largest chamber, the table and chairs he had discovered in it indicated that its last use had been as a council room or something akin.

Aurim and Ssarekai sat in chairs in the middle of the room. The table had been moved away, no doubt at Gwendolyn's request. The party looked up as Cabe and the Gryphon materialized.

"Was there any difficulty?" the enchantress asked her husband.

"None save that everyone wanted to give what aid they could."

"I'll be sure to thank them when I can." Her gaze shifted to the figure beside Cabe. "For now, I want to thank *you*, Gryphon, for coming."

"As I keep telling your mate, my lady, there is no need to thank me. We are family."

"I wish everyone would stop talking as if I were about to die," interjected an apprehensive Aurim.

"No one is going to die, Aurim," Gwen replied, walking over to the young man, "but you know that Toma's left something in your head. We can't help but feel a little anxious. I know it doesn't help to hear that. Just rest assured that there's nothing Toma's done that we can't untangle."

"I hope," Aurim muttered.

"Aurim!" Gwendolyn Bedlam stared down at her son.

The Gryphon raised his hands in an attempt to calm everyone. "Please! We should begin as soon as possible. Make no mistakes, this is going to take the rest of the day and likely tomorrow, too."

That made the young warlock grimace. "*That long?*"

"I'm afraid so. You won't have to sit there the entire time, though. First we have to see what's there. Then, we have to see how we can get rid of it."

"Let's do it, then," added Cabe as he joined the Gryphon.

"What about the reception?" asked his son. "Won't you miss that?"

"Toos will give our apologies." The Gryphon sighed. "Now, please, Aurim. You have to remain silent for this."

Next to Cabe, Gwendolyn whispered, "I wish Darkhorse was here! I think that with his peculiar brand of sorcery, he would stand a chance of unraveling this spell by himself."

The warlock nodded. He decided it was not the time to express his concerns about the eternal. Darkhorse had been missing far too long for his tastes.

"Let me look first," the Gryphon suggested. "Once I have an idea what is there, I will know better how to proceed." He met Aurim's nervous gaze and chuckled. "I should thank you, young warlock. You have no idea how bored I am at receptions. Before your mother contacted us, I had just resigned myself to looking forward to five or six hours of empty talk and stuffy faces. It really was kind of you to drag me away from such wonderful entertainment."

Aurim smiled, which Cabe suspected was the Gryphon's intention. His subject more relaxed now, the lionbird summoned his power. Although they could not see his probe, the others could sense the spell progressing.

Forced for the moment to wait, the warlock thought over his old comrade's words. More a creature of action than speech, the Gryphon despised affairs of state. But at the moment, Cabe would have preferred nothing more than fighting boredom at the royal reception in Penacles. At least that would have meant that his son, his entire family, was well.

His reverie was shattered by an intake of breath by the Gryphon. "Well, what do we have here?"

Everyone leaned forward. Anxiety spread once more across Aurim's pale countenance.

"What is it?" Cabe asked.

The Gryphon sighed, then looked at his companions. "This is going to take much longer than I had hoped." If it was possible for a creature with a beak to grimace, then the lionbird had done just that. "We seem to have run into a problem."

XIV

Grath observed the reception from his usual place a bit behind his brother. Penacles he found more fascinating than Talak, possibly because Penacles was a kingdom built to honor knowledge, one of Grath's personal gods. The young drake prided himself on his mind. He had already discovered that the majority of adults, be they drake or human, were his inferiors in terms of intellect. Grath did not hold that against them, though. He was certain that he had been born with a superior brain. After all, had not his dam, his mother, once been a part of the clan Purple, the dragons that had ruled Penacles before the Gryphon? All knew that Lord Purple had been the guiding force in the Turning War, not Grath's sire, the emperor. Had he not died in mortal combat with Master Bedlam's grandfather, Grath was certain that the Dragon King would have eventually seized control from Gold, the emperor.

Hatchlings were not supposed to know their mothers. All were raised in a communal setting with the matriarch overseeing everything. Grath, being who he was, had had little trouble in tracing his background. It prided him to know that his mother had come from the most intelligent, the most cunning of the dragon clans. That did not mean that he did not appreciate his late sire. If not for Gold, Grath might have never been born. He owed the late Dragon Emperor for that, if nothing else.

Toos was introducing them to yet another functionary. Grath waited for Kyl to perform his peacock routine, then bowed when it was his own turn to exchange greetings. His brother was every inch what one expected from the heir to a throne and Grath took great pride in that, for he felt that he above all others was responsible. Kyl followed his instructions to the letter and performed as well as any trained dog. That he did not realize what was happening, Grath could forgive him. Kyl was intelligent, true, but hardly on the same level as his younger brother. At least he was intelligent enough to realize how quickly he would flounder without his brilliant, loyal counselor by his side.

It's not who sits on the throne that rules, Grath's mentor had told him. *It's the one who has his ear.* The truth of that was plain for him to see. Queen Erini truly ruled in Talak. Her husband could deny her nothing. Here in Penacles it was the same. Toos the Regent—a fairly knowledgeable human, he was willing to concede—ever listened to the counsel of the Gryphon.

Grath admired the Gryphon, who pretended he no longer ruled but in reality did. The young drake had once dreamed of being emperor himself, but now it made so much more sense to stand behind the throne. If things changed and it became necessary to step forward, the support would be there.

He had the best of all possible worlds awaiting him.

It would have been preferable if Master and Mistress Bedlam or the Lord Gryphon were also here. They were clever enough to appreciate his skill at handling his brother, even if they did not realize the extent of that handling. Grath had been warned to stay some distance from them, especially his soon-to-be former guardians, but this was one point on which he and his mentor differed. The Bedlams were his family, too, and he saw no difficulty in maintaining a balance between the two aspects of his life. Besides, was it not planned that Valea would join Kyl after he assumed the throne? Better to keep on good terms with her parents for when the time came to convince them of the inevitability of Valea's departure for the caverns of the Dragon Emperor.

That did not mean, of course, that he would not be willing to destroy them if it proved necessary for the success of his plans.

Something caught Grath's attention. He shifted his gaze from the attractive young human woman curtsying before his brother and discovered that Lord Green was trying to gain his attention.

Turning to Kyl, he whispered, "Lord Green desires my attendance."

His brother nodded his permission, never taking his eyes off the woman. Grath forced away a condescending smile as he left his brother. More so than him, Kyl had a fondness for human females. It had made planting the suggestion of seducing Valea that much easier. Kyl actually enjoyed her company, although that was not going to stop him from flirting with others. Grath was more dedicated; when her dashing emperor finally tired of her, Valea would find Grath waiting. She was everything he desired in a female: exotic beauty, a mind, personal strength, and, best of all, the power of a Bedlam.

The dragon king looked impatient by the time Grath joined him. He respected Lord Green very much, even if the elder drake seemed a bit too subservient to his brother. Yet, the Dragon King also found much time for him. How ironic it would be if the tall, hellish knight knew the truth. That was one problem that Grath had not yet solved. If the Dragon King discovered what the young drake was involved in, it would mean having to do something that Grath did not find appetizing.

It won't happen, though. I have control now! I have become the kingmaker, the power behind the future of the entire Dragonrealm.

"How isss he doing out there?"

"Perfect, of course." Grath thought that the Dragon King had become too nervous of late, as if anything could go wrong at this point. The meeting with Lord Blue, the Dragon Kings' chosen representative, was a foregone conclusion what with Grath to coach Kyl through it. Soon, Kyl would renounce his name and take on the mantle of Gold, Dragon Emperor.

"I do not like thisss." The Green Dragon was more sibilant than usual, a definite sign of excessive worry as far as Grath was concerned. "The Bedlams are gone and the Gryphon with them. The demon steed is also missing. Our defenses are weakened."

The Bedlams had sent word just prior to the reception that they would be unable to attend. The cunning spell attached to Aurim's memory had so far defeated their best efforts. Toma had planned well when he had devised that one. Grath could not help but admire the spell's obvious complexity. How many were there who could so cleverly befuddle his guardians?

"Things will be all right, my lord," he answered dutifully. "We are in Penacles, after all. There is no better guarded kingdom than this one save Talak, and yet there we faced much more resent-

ment. Here, people already accept us . . . to a point, of course."
Grath hoped to find reasons to make future excursions to the City
of Knowledge before necessity demanded that it be returned to
drake control. Since the latter would not take place for some time,
he did not feel too concerned.

His eyes suddenly focused on a fantastic figure entering the reception. Here was one whom Kyl would find most appealing, he
thought. *And so do I,* the young drake was forced to admit.

There was no one in the Dragonrealm like the Lady Troia, mate
of the Gryphon. She had met him across the sea, at the beginning
of the revolt against the Aramite Empire. She was lithe and graceful, yet still a predator, her tawny color in keeping with her feline
appearance. When she smiled—a bit uncertainly, he thought—her
slightly pointed teeth reminded him of a female drake. She also
had talons that were supposed to be every bit as deadly as those of
Grath's race.

If not for his desire for Valea, Grath would have been tempted
to see what a flirtation with the cat-woman would have revealed.
Likely his dismemberment, if what they said about her love for
her mate was true. Still, he doubted that knowing that would stop
his brother from trying. Kyl *had* to flirt. It was one trait of his
that, while frequently useful, Grath was as yet unable to completely control.

"I would have thought that the Lady Troia would have remained home with her child sssince her mate hasss been called
away," muttered the Green Dragon. "She should not be here."

"Why?"

"She isss with child," responded the Dragon King, as if that answered everything. Grath tried to puzzle it out, failed, then decided that it was not worth his time.

"Perhaps she has a message from the Gryphon. Perhaps the
Bedlams and he are preparing to return to Penacles."

Lord Green looked at him, but said nothing. Grath decided
there and then that he would mention to Kyl that perhaps it would
be an excellent notion to allow the Dragon King to return to his
own domain. The drake had worked hard to bring them to this
point, but it was clear that he needed some rest.

Without warning, the Dragon King started toward the
Gryphon's mate. After a moment, Grath followed, in great part
because he wanted to see Lady Troia up close.

The cat-woman noticed them coming and, unlike most of those attending, gave them an open smile. This did not surprise Grath, who was aware that one of the Gryphon's closest comrades during the war against the Aramite Empire had been the very scion of the Blue Dragon, a great drake warrior called Morgis. Through Morgis, Troia had perhaps become more used to the drake race than anyone else at the reception.

"It's . . . Lord Green . . . is that the way to say it? I always forget."

The Dragon King executed a slight bow. "That is one of the accepted forms of address."

"Would you prefer 'Your Majesty'?"

"With my emperor present, it does not strike me as proper. 'Lord Green' isss perfectly fine."

She looked him over. "If you were of a more bluish tint, I'd swear that you were Morgis."

"We do tend to look much alike to your kind."

Another very feline smile spread across her fascinating face. Grath realized he had not yet bowed and quickly did so. Seeing her hand near enough, he followed his impulse and took it in his own. To the Lady Troia's flattered amusement, he kissed it.

"Not all of you look the same. You've become a daring one, Grath. Do you stalk the same prey as your brother?"

It took him a moment to decipher her comment. When he had done so, the young drake smiled. "Kyl does well enough for both of us, my lady."

"I'm sure he does."

"What brings you to the reception?" the Dragon King asked without warning. "Are your mate and the Bedlams returning?"

Her smile changed to a frown. "I only wish. No, they're still hoping to solve the riddle. The Gryphon contacted me long enough to let me know that they would not be returning this evening. Cabe and Gwendolyn don't plan to cease their efforts until their son and the drake with him are free of this Duke Toma's spell." Her light, short fur began to bristle. "He sounds as foul a creature as the Senior Keeper D'Rak!"

Grath had no idea who this D'Rak had been save that by his name he had been an Aramite, a wolf raider. Lord Green, however, nodded his agreement. Grath made a mental note to ask the Dragon King about D'Rak and wolf raiders in general. Their empire might be in ruins, but a number of their ships still prowled the seas as pirates. Desperate men like that might be willing to bargain their services to a great power.

"I decided that with everyone else gone, it would be a good idea for me to be here. If there's trouble, I'll be around to lend a claw." She unsheathed a handful of deadly talons impressive even by drake standards.

"But you have children of your own to be concerned about," insisted Lord Green. "Both your son and the one within you."

The young drake could not detect any swelling. Of course the gown prevented a better examination.

Troia laughed, an enchanting, throaty sound. "Your concern is appreciated, Lord Green, but I come from a sturdy people. I fought in battle only days before our first child, Demion, was born. It was not by choice, but it gives you an idea of how resilient my folk are. The way I am *now* will by no means slow me, I can promise you that! There is almost a full month to go. As for our other son, I have good people watching him." She glanced past him at where the regent and Kyl were standing. "Would you excuse me, Lord Green? I want to ask a favor of Toos before I forget."

"Certainly, my lady."

They both bowed as the cat-woman moved on. Grath watched her walk with renewed appreciation for females, then recalled himself. It would not do to be so coarse among present company. What he did reflected as much on his brother as what Kyl himself did. Still, he was amazed that she could be so far along. What he could see did not in the least remind him of any of the pregnant human females he had seen.

His gaze drifted to Lord Green, who appeared rather preoccupied. The elder drake stared as the Lady Troia joined Kyl and Toos. For some reason, Grath doubted the Dragon King's interest centered around the cat-woman.

"Grath, have you ssseen your tutor lately?"

The question caught the young drake by surprise, but he quickly recovered. "Scholar Trassske is not one for receptions, my lord. He felt it would be best if he retired to his chambers. I believe he isss studying the progress of the school of sorcery. The Gryphon planned to take him to visit it the day after tomorrow."

"He may have changed his mind, but feels uncertain about arriving so late. Go and see whether that isss the case."

"But—"

"Do it, Grath." The Green Dragon walked toward Kyl and his companions, preventing any further protest the younger drake would have made.

Grath hissed quietly, incensed by the Green Dragon's tone and attitude. He was *not* a servitor to be talked to so. He was the brother of the new Dragon Emperor, not to mention that emperor's counselor. The Dragon King should be treating him with *deference*, not indifference.

Still, as much as it rankled him, Grath chose to obey. Lord Green had been good to him for the most part and was still a necessary ally. He would forgive the Dragon King his mistake this time, but if it happened again, Grath would remember for the future. *Patience and memory are important driving forces,* his mentor had said, *allowing one to survive for years until the time is ripe for vengeance.*

As usual, it all made perfect sense to him.

Lord Green wished him to find Benjin Traske. Very well, then, he would find Benjin Traske. It would give him the opportunity to ask a few questions that had arisen this evening.

The walk was a long one, and at other times he would have contemplated sending a messenger, but Grath knew that this once it would be better if he obeyed the command to the letter. He walked through the halls, unaccompanied but not alone. Toos had indicated that this night no escort would be necessary for the drakes, but that did not mean that security had been relaxed. Tonight, sentries lined the major corridors, the regent's precautions against assassins and possibly wayward drakes. Grath admired their order and steadfastness as he walked. Too many drakes still underestimated their human counterparts, but he did not. Underestimating your opponents was the best way to open yourself to utter defeat.

There were guards even in the corridor outside of the chambers that had been set aside for Grath and the other visitors. Again, it was supposed to be for their own safety, but he was certain that the regent had also ordered the soldiers stationed here in the hopes that it would discourage his draconian guests from wandering off to where they were not desired. The rooms he sought were furthest down the hallway. He walked past the remaining sentries, faced the door, and softly rapped on it.

The door swung open without preamble. The face of the tutor appeared. "What is it, Grath?"

Disconcerted, he still managed to reply, "I was sent here by Lord Green. He thought that you might yet make an appearance. He insisted that I personally go to you and ask if that might be so."

"The Dragon King insisted that you come for me?"

Grath nodded.

The massive figure stepped out into the hall. He was clad in the robes of a scholar, making it appear as if he were just about to begin class. The nearest guards glanced the tutor's direction, but when they saw who it was, they immediately resumed their statuelike stances.

"Did he say why he wanted to know?"

"No, Master Traske," replied the young drake after a quick look at the sentries. "He simply insisted I go, then walked over to where Kyl and the regent were standing."

"Did he now? I'd not planned to be there, but if Lord Green is so interested, it would behoove me to come."

That was somewhat of a relief to Grath, who was not certain how the Dragon King would have reacted if he had returned alone. Eyeing the guards once more, Grath asked, "Would you prefer that I wait out here while you prepare yourself?"

A brief smile spread across the bearded face. "Yes, that would be good of you."

Benjin Traske slipped back inside. Grath took up a place just to the side of the door and watched the guards. They did not even so much as twitch. These were veterans, men who had fought in battle. The young drake hoped that no reason would arise that would force him to fight one of them.

The door opened but a minute later. The scholar, slightly neater but overall looking much the same as he had a moment before, stepped out into the hall again. After making certain that the door was secure, he turned and began marching down the corridor.

Throughout most of the journey back, the large figure beside Grath said nothing. The drake attempted questions once or twice, but they were met with short, unenlightening responses. Grath gave up and concentrated his efforts on keeping up with the other. His companion was setting a swifter pace than he had expected, almost as if there was some urgent need to appear at the reception as soon as possible. He would have liked to have asked if there was some reason for the speed, but if one of the sentries overheard, it might make for some misdirected conclusions.

As they neared the ballroom, Grath noticed that the reception had grown much quieter during his absence. He wondered if perhaps something had occurred that had made Toos call an early end to the event. If so, it could not have been anything terrible, for the few voices that he did hear seemed as unconcerned as he would have expected.

"Is something the matter, boy?"

"No . . . nothing."

A soldier opened one of the doors for them. Grath nodded in the manner of a superior to a servant, but his cool demeanor was shattered by what he saw in the ballroom.

It would have perhaps been more appropriate to say what he did *not* see. More than half of the guests had vanished. Small groups clustered here and there, but the bulk of those who had come to meet the new Dragon Emperor were gone. As were, Grath realized in a quick, anxious survey of the ballroom, Toos, Lady Troia, The Green Dragon, and Kyl.

A heavy hand clutched his shoulder. "Where did they go, Grath?"

"I don't know! They were here when I left."

The massive, robed figure looked around. His eyes alighted on a trio of elderly men wearing robes like his own. "Wait here a moment."

Grath was tired of being commanded by everyone, but he did as he was told. The scholar marched over to his counterparts and immediately questioned them, ignoring their annoyance over his rude interruption of their conversation. One of them made a reply that Grath could not hear, a reply which was then apparently supported by a nod of the head from another in the trio. Benjin Traske gave them a curt response, then returned to the waiting drake. His expression puzzled Grath; it looked as if his companion was suffering a number of conflicting emotions, none of them good.

"They are outside. The arena. Some tournament. I was not told *anything* about this."

"Tournament? You mean the chess game?"

"Yesss . . ." The huge man came to a decision. "Come, Grath. We do not want to be late."

"What are—"

Grath's question died abruptly as his companion glared at him. Clamping his mouth shut, he followed the other through the ballroom.

* * *

Toos watched the game unfold with uneasiness in his heart. There was no reason for him to be anxious, not with the safeguards that he and the Gryphon had implemented for this visit, but simply having the drake heir out in the open like this, with not even a roof to protect his head, made the regent uncomfortable. The night sky was dark, there being no moon out. He kept imagining Seekers or some other airborne danger circling above, biding quietly until the proper time. A part of him knew that it was paranoia, but another part argued that there was a basis for his fears.

His entire *life* was a basis for those fears.

Kyl, with the subtle aid of Toos himself, was playing opposite Baron Vergoth. Toos had confidence enough in Vergoth to know that the aristocrat would do his best to see to it that his royal adversary looked good. As to whether the baron would actually allow the young drake to win, the regent could only guess. Baron Vergoth was an intelligent man. He was capable of judging what results would best serve Penacles.

The dragon heir was actually doing fairly well against the much more experienced Vergoth. Either that, or Vergoth was much more skilled at manipulating the game than Toos had ever imagined. Both players were fairly even at this point. Vergoth had a slight advantage, but it was one based more on the strength of his champions than numbers. Through sheer circumstance, the baron had drawn some of the best of the guardsmen who played as pieces. Fortunately, Kyl had a few masters of his own.

In point of fact, the young drake's knight was about to defeat Vergoth's pawn. This particular combat had gone on for more than the normal two or three minutes. Since they were confined to a single square, duels by champions often ended when one player was forced beyond the boundaries. In this case, both men had succeeded in remaining in place. However, the knight had finally beaten down the defenses of the baron's pawn and had the man only inches from the back edge of the square.

A final blow ended the battle. Spectators applauded as the pawn stumbled backward, not only stepping out of bounds but also falling on his back. It was as clean a victory as any. Clean and without any bloodshed. Toos was aware that some of his guests would have liked to have seen blood, but that was not the point of the game. Anyone exhibiting more than a little fondness for what little blood was spilled was not invited back for quite some time. Most learned from that. To earn the regent's disfavor was something few desired.

Kyl was considering his next move. Toos leaned forward and whispered, "Beware Vergoth's bishops. He likes to put them into play fairly quickly. Likely when he does, he'll go for your knight using both of them."

A slight nod was all he received in response from the young drake. Kyl already understood just how unorthodox the baron's playing was and appreciated his host's guidance. However, how the drake chose to counter the move was entirely up to the emperor-to-be himself.

With his part done for now, the tall, narrow regent studied the assembled guests. Still nothing out of the ordinary, but the same sense of uneasiness that had allowed him to survive decades of mercenary work insisted that something was amiss. Kyl glanced at the Green Dragon, who stood off to one side with the draconian sentries. The Dragon King had them spread out and ready for immediate action. There had been room enough for them behind the heir, but the Dragon King had insisted that they would be of more use out in the open, where they could better watch over the entire area. As it was, the two bodyguards who always accompanied Kyl stood behind both the heir and the regent. Toos, who was a good judge of warriors, thought they looked capable enough, if somewhat distant. *But then, they're drakes, aren't they, Toos? You know them only from across the battlefield, not from the same side.* It was strange to have drakes at his back, but the regent's own bodyguards also stood behind the master of Penacles and his guest. Toos had the utmost confidence in his own soldiers; they had ways of dealing quickly with treacherous drakes.

And Toos had a few tricks of his own.

A disturbance near the entrance caught his attention. He turned to see Grath and Benjin Traske. The scholar tried to hide it, but it was clear to the trained eye of the former mercenary that he was upset about something. Even if Traske's face and form had not indicated anxiety, Grath's own evident nervousness was enough to garner the regent's concern.

Time passed, the game went on, and still nothing happened. Toos wondered whether the danger was all in his mind, but whenever he looked around, he felt somehow vindicated in his beliefs. Grath, the Green Dragon, Traske ... wherever he looked, the regent found faces whose concern matched his own. It was as if they were all waiting for something to happen, something that *should* have happened by this time.

Kyl hissed. The wary general shifted his gaze immediately to the heir, but the drake's reaction was at the loss of a valuable piece and not because of any danger. Kyl glanced his way. "If hisss championsss can defeat my king, I am lossst!"

Pulling his thoughts back to the game, Toos saw that his royal guest's summation was correct. Vergoth had two men, a knight and a rook, in position. Another rook stood nearby. All the baron had to do was give the command, and that piece would put the drake's king into checkmate. Kyl's man would then have to fight each piece until he had either defeated all three or had fallen to one of them. Sizing the soldiers up, Toos was willing to give the heir's man one, maybe two combats, but fatigue would prevent him from salvaging the game for his player.

Kyl's king carried shield and mace and knew well the advantages and disadvantages of each. As Baron Vergoth commanded his second rook forward, the champion readied himself. Under the rules that Toos had formulated, Vergoth could choose any of the three with which to begin. Kyl's man had already positioned himself so as to face the knight. Toos nodded; it was the same opponent that he would have chosen. To the regent's amused surprise, however, Kyl's adversary chose instead to use his first rook, the least of his three champions. There were a few murmurs in the crowd, but most did not comprehend what Vergoth was doing. The regent did, and the knowledge brought the shadow of a smile to his foxlike features. Vergoth, very much the politician, was giving his opponent as much aid as he possibly could. The game was already his, but if Kyl's man could defeat at least one rival, then so much the better for the heir's showing. The closer the game appeared to be, the better the dragon heir would feel.

Weapons clanged as the rook took on the king. Champions were ofttimes given the option of choosing their own weapons, and so this was a battle of mace against scepter, the latter in reality simply a more elaborate mace. Both men struck hard at the shields, each hoping to knock the other's defense away or at least open a hole. People cheered, and not a few bets were placed on the outcome. As an old soldier, Toos had no qualms about betting as long as it was kept under certain limitations. Now and then he liked to make a bet himself. The years had given him a practiced eye when it came to the art of war.

The rook tried to get his mace under the king's shield in order to lift the latter away, but the drake's champion turned the trick against the younger soldier, pushing down with his full mass. The rook's grip loosened on the mace as the weapon was pulled down. Wasting no precious time, the king struck with his own weapon, almost getting around the other's shield. His opponent struggled to free his mace even as the king attacked again, but the elder champion would not permit that. Changing tactics, Kyl's man suddenly turned his assault from the rook's shield to the imprisoned mace, bringing his scepter down on it.

Several people gasped, thinking that the king intended to crush the hand of his opponent, a move that Toos would have condemned. The general, however, understood what the champion was doing. As the mace came down, the rook, obviously stunned by what he thought was happening, pulled his hand back as if bitten. The mace continued to come down, but midway it suddenly shifted. Instead of striking where his adversary's hand would have been, the king brought his scepter down on the upper shaft of the other mace. Had the rook realized that his hand had never been in danger, he could have used that moment to seize the wrist of Kyl's champion and possibly balance out the odds. As it was, the rook was now weaponless. The king knocked the loose mace far away and wasted no time pressing his attack. The bout ended but seconds later, to the sounds of great cheering.

Kyl was hissing, but Toos recognized his reaction as one of extreme pleasure. The heir had half-risen out of his chair, the better to view the battle. As Vergoth's knight stepped forward, the young drake rose more. A slight frown escaped the regent; he hoped that the heir was not given to bloodlust like some drakes. Toos looked around for Grath and discovered that neither he nor the scholar had moved from the doorway. Unlike Kyl, the younger drake still appeared more apprehensive than anything else. He was glad to see that Kyl's brother, at least, was not given to bloodlust, but he also wondered what worried Grath so. When the opportunity presented itself, the general intended to talk to the lad about it. Perhaps doing so would clear up some of his own mysterious anxieties.

"Thisss one will be much clossser!" remarked the dragon heir to his host.

Forcing himself back into the game, Toos agreed. "You must be prepared to accept it if your champion loses, Lord Kyl. The knight's very skilled."

"I am prepared, General. I do not give up hope jusssst yet, though. If I losssse, I lossse; if victory isss sssalvaged, ssso much the better."

The statement pleased Toos, more because of the way it was said. Kyl's tone indicated he meant every word. *Perhaps I've mis-judged him. He might be more level-headed than I thought.*

His attention was again diverted, this time by the Green Dragon, who signaled to Grath and Benjin Traske to join him. The Dragon King had a goblet in one hand, though, and when he shifted position, the better for those he was signaling to see him, the hand with the goblet bumped against one of his guards.

The goblet slipped from his hand, its contents spilling on the floor. The draconian soldiers nearest to him converged on the fallen cup.

Snapping his fingers, the regent summoned one of his own men. The man saluted and waited for orders. Toos pointed at the huddled figures. "Get someone over there now. His Lordship might need something to clean himself off with. Make certain not a spot remains and give the Dragon King whatever other aid he desires."

"Yes, sir."

Kyl, still standing, had not noticed what was happening. His own attention was fixed on the two combatants. Toos blinked. He could not even recall the beginning of the bout, but the drake's champion and Vergoth's man had obviously already been at it for several seconds. The skill of the knight was already telling, how-ever, for Kyl's king was beginning to lose ground. The general scratched his long, narrow chin. He had expected better of the king, but that was the way of the game. The soldiers who took part did not play the same way twice. One time, they might seem unstoppable; other days, they might fall after only a few blows. It was part of what made his variation on the game of chess a much more interesting one in his opinion.

The sense of danger again pervaded his being. Yet, surveying the scene, Toos could find nothing amiss. Servants had not yet reached the Dragon King, who, surrounded by his own soldiers, was virtually invisible. Kyl and the scholar were wending their way toward the lord of Dagora, but they appeared to be safe. What could—

As it had happened so many times in the past, he saw what was to be. No one, not even the Gryphon, truly understood the work-ings of the former mercenary's limited yet potent magic. Toos himself did not, for he had never met another in whom the power had so focused itself in one direction. Had he been asked to transport himself from one end of the arena to another, the regent would have been unable to comply. Had he been asked to levitate a sword, even that would have been beyond him. Yet, despite this seeming lack of skill, he had one of the most unusual gifts of sorcery, one that had saved his life time and time again.

He had heard of only one mage skilled in prophecy: Yalak of the Dragon Masters, who had once created a crystal egg that could show images of possible future events. Knowing prophecy had not prevented Yalak from being murdered by Azran Bedlam, however, which was why Toos had always been careful to cultivate his ability and had shared its full secrets with no one, not even the Gryphon. He had always felt guilty about that, but what was done was done.

The image came at its own chosen time, just like all the others. He had only time to gasp at its implications and marvel at the audacity of the one behind it before he became aware that the true event was *just* taking place.

It began with the striking of the two champions' weapons against one another. The mace of Kyl's king was knocked from the warrior's hand and, before the startled eyes of the many, flew almost unerringly toward the astounded heir. As it neared, however, it was clear to most that it would fall short. Kyl took a step back, but did not otherwise protect himself from the misshaped projectile.

Only Toos knew that the true threat was only now coming into play. Leaping toward the drake, he cried, "Get down!"

The former mercenary reached Kyl just as the draconian guards stirred to life. Perhaps they had not heard his cry, or perhaps they felt that it was their duty to protect their master, not his. Toos only knew that he had barely thrust the dragon heir to the floor when a massive, armored figure shoved him aside, causing the general to spin in a half circle.

Something hard and swift thudded against his back.

He thought at first that the mace had somehow managed to fly over the arena wall, but then a fierce pain wracked the general's chest and it was all he could do to keep from collapsing there and then. Grimacing, the regent forced open his eyes, which he could not recall closing, and peered down. To his surprise, Toos saw no sign of the wound that should have been there. Then, as his legs began to buckle, it occurred to him that the entry point had to have been from the back. The bolt, or whatever the assassin had used, had not quite pierced him all the way through.

The world spun around. Toos fell to his knees, which did nothing to alleviate the agony. Around him he knew that there was panic. Someone called out to him, but it was as if they were receding even as they spoke.

He knew he was dying. For once, his magic-wrought ability to outmaneuver his foes had worked against him. He *had* beaten the assassin, for Kyl must certainly still live, but it had *not* been the general's intention to make himself the new target.

Sloppy, Toos thought. *Been away from the field too long. Shouldn't have listened to those jackanapes! Next maneuver, I go out with the men . . . get myself back in shape. . . .*

Things grew hazy. Someone was in front of him. Toos tried to focus. The figure coalesced into that of the Gryphon, but that was nonsense, the regent knew. The Gryphon was with the Bedlams.

He chuckled, which caused him to shake as renewed pain coursed through him. Toos tried to speak to the imaginary Gryphon, but all that escaped his lips was blood. Putting one last great effort into his attempt at speech, he told the apparition, "It's . . . yours again . . . "

Toos closed his eyes, knowing that the meaning of his words would be clear. After so many years of trying, he had *finally* found a way to force his old commander to reassume the throne. It was the Gryphon who had made Penacles what it was. Toos had simply been its caretaker while the lionbird recovered from his great labors. Now, however, the regent's work was done. It was time to move on.

A sound caught his attention. Horns. He had little trouble recognizing the notes; it was the call to arms of his old company, the one in which he had first followed his commander.

Rising, Toos the Fox unsheathed his sword and went to join his old comrades in one last, glorious battle.

XV

"They've killed him, Cabe. . . . " The Gryphon snarled, his claws unsheathing and sheathing. His entire body quivered with unreleased fury. His mane bristled as the lionbird struggled to maintain his control. "They *killed* Toos!"

Cabe Bedlam stared in horror at the grisly tableau before him. The regent of Penacles lay face forward in the Gryphon's arms, a scarlet blossom of blood across his back. The bolt had penetrated so deeply that it had nearly burst through the rib cage, if the warlock was any judge. It was a wonder that the old mercenary had lived even the few moments he had. That he had done so had made the situation that much more tragic, for Toos had lived just long enough for the Gryphon to return, then had died almost in his former commander's arms.

When the Gryphon had looked up from his so-far futile attempts to free the minds of Aurim and Ssarekai and cried out about danger in Penacles, his companions had been stunned. Cabe knew that his old friend kept some sort of link with both his mate and his former officer, but not even the warlock had known how strong or immediate those links were.

The lionbird had not even paused to explain. He had asked permission to leave, received it, and had vanished, leaving the Bedlams to recover their wits on their own. Naturally, Cabe and his wife had followed as quickly as they could, but even then it had been too late.

The arena was in chaos. Guests ran about in full panic and there were shouts of "Assassin!" from all corners. Toos was sprawled on the floor of one of the boxes used by the chess players. Kyl was gone, evidently spirited away by his two bodyguards. Around the fallen regent and his former commander stood a wary and fearful group of human soldiers.

Cabe had never seen the Gryphon this distraught. It was clear to the warlock that he would have to handle matters for the moment. "Which way did the bolt come from?"

One of the guards pointed upward and to his right. He added, "Our men already give chase, Master Warlock! We shall have them before the hour is ended!"

The mage was not so certain. "Have you discovered how they got so close?"

The sentries looked frustrated. The spokesman slowly replied, "No, Master Warlock. . . . "

"This . . . smells of . . . of magic," Gwen commented. Cabe glanced at her. There were tears streaming from her eyes, but there was also a hardening in her face. He knew that his own visage now held a similar cast.

He made a decision. Too much time had already passed. "You stay here with the Gryphon, I'll—"

Cabe was interrupted by a group of pale guardsmen. Two of them carried bundles. An officer, a captain by rank, gave the Gryphon a half-hearted salute, which the lionbird did not even notice. Cabe signaled the officer his way.

"You know who I am?"

"Yes, Master Bedlam!"

"You can tell me everything. Have you found them?"

This last caused the captain to grimace. "In a matter of speaking, my lord. . . . "

"*Please*, Captain. . . . " begged one of the men. In one hand he carried a glove that appeared to be full of some substance. The Bedlams glanced at one another, then Cabe indicated that the officer should explain his words.

Swallowing, the captain indicated the bundles two of his men were carrying. "I think . . . uh . . . I think this is all that's left of them, Master Bedlam."

"What?" For the first time, the Gryphon acknowledged the presence of the newcomers. Still clutching the form of his old comrade, he glared at the captain and added, "What do you *mean*?"

"One of the men s-saw it, Your Majesty." The captain had the bundles brought forward. He also signaled the man holding the one glove to join them. "The assassin . . . he . . . he was . . . my lord . . . he was *crumbling*! Darion saw him and Darion doesn't lie, Your Majesty!"

"Aye! I'll swear to it, my lord!" added one of the guards laden with a bundle. The burly soldier looked around as if daring someone to contradict his words. "It's truth!"

"Explain in more detail," encouraged Gwendolyn Bedlam.

His arms filled, the guard called Darion used his chin to indicated his captain. "He said it all! I saw the man . . . it *was* a man, lordships—ugly and bearded. Looked like a northern type maybe. All I really saw was him look my way, then his eyes, they went wide, they did." The veteran hesitated, still unnerved by the sight. "Then . . . then, he just went to pieces, like he dried out and crumbled to *sand*!"

The captain took over. "Your Majesty, we brought all that was left of him. Some others found a second figure, but he . . . he was already dust."

The Gryphon looked up to his two comrades. "Could you . . . do you think you can verify . . . ?"

Gwendolyn nodded. Without a word, the two spellcasters took the bundles from the grateful warriors. The third man held out the filled glove toward Cabe.

"What's this?" the warlock asked.

"It's one . . . uh . . . it's one o' them, lordship."

Cabe almost snatched his hand back, but if the guards had forced themselves to bring back some of the remains, it behooved him to do what he could with it.

The enchantress inspected her bundle. "What about the weapon? Where is it?"

There was something stiff in Cabe's bundle. Gingerly, he opened up the cloth, which appeared to be some sort of glittering cape folded inside out, and discovered a crossbow. Oddly, there were no more bolts to go with it. "I've got it here."

"These will need a more thorough examination later," Lady Bedlam commented, her interest in discovering the truth for the moment overwhelming her sorrow, "but there is something we can do now."

Both of them were already at work. Those who had gathered around watched in wary curiosity. To the eye, all that the two did was pass a hand over each bundle, Cabe also repeating the process for the glove and its grotesque contents. He gasped as his fingers traced patterns over the glove. It was as the guard had said; this had once been human. He could tell no more about the unfortunate assassin save that whatever had killed him was no ordinary sorcery.

"This . . . is . . . *strange*," was all his wife could add at first.

From where he squatted, the Gryphon cocked his head. There was an unhealthy look in his avian visage, Cabe thought. "You said 'strange.' How so?"

"It reminds me of . . . " She looked at her husband for aid.

"We both know what it reminds us of." The warlock hesitated, but when he saw the further tensing of the Gryphon's body, he decided that a swift response was the better choice regardless of what results the truth might then bring. "It reminds both of us of Darkhorse. It bears his trace."

"Or something akin to him," interjected the enchantress. There had once been a time when Gwendolyn Bedlam would have been the first to call Darkhorse demon, but now she was his champion. He had saved the lives of all the Bedlams more than once.

"There is nothing we know of in all the Dragonrealm that is akin to Darkhorse." Yet it was clear that the lionbird did not think the eternal was responsible for the day's tragedy. He looked down at the still form in his arms and in a much gentler voice added, "But perhaps he, like old Toos, has become a pawn."

"He's still missing," whispered Cabe, his blood going cold. He had feared that the shadow steed had been captured by the one who had set the magical snares, and now it seemed that that fear was likely a thing of substance.

The Gryphon started to rise, but could not without leaving the body of Toos lying alone on the cold floor. Freeing one hand, he waved the nearest sentries over. "Take him gently. Bring him to his bedchamber and have the doctors clean him up as well as they can. I also want a pair of you to take these bundles and bring them to my rooms. They should be guarded until I have time to more thoroughly inspect them. I shall give you further orders when you return."

The ease with which leadership shifted from the murdered regent to the former king did not surprise Cabe Bedlam in the least. The Gryphon was legend and the regent had always made it quite clear that he would have gladly stepped aside at any time. There was also inherent in the lionbird's manner a natural sense of command, one which made others willing to follow him. He was, the warlock concluded, meant to be a leader, and now, despite his best attempts to forever discard such a role, it appeared as if the Gryphon once more had a kingdom to rule.

With great care, the guards slowly lifted the body of Toos from the floor. The Gryphon, rising, watched each and every movement. Under such a baleful gaze, the men dared not fail in maintaining their holds. No one desired to test the wrath of the distraught monarch.

Two of the men who had brought the remains of the assassins took both the bundles and the glove back. Cabe was not sorry to give up the gruesome objects. The Gryphon was welcome to do what he wished with them as long as it helped them discover who was responsible for the death of Toos.

When the guards and their terrible burden were out of sight, the Gryphon at last returned his attention to the mages. From the crowd still gathered emerged his mate, Troia. She moved past the Bedlams and enveloped her husband in her arms. The cat-woman was well aware of the place Toos had had in the Gryphon's life. The tall, cunning general had been family, a brother in spirit if not in blood.

Taking hold of his wife, the Gryphon looked at Cabe Bedlam. There was now a cold calm in his voice that did not bode well. "I want the one behind this, my friend. Was it . . . do you think it was *Talak*?"

"There's no proof one way or the other," Cabe quickly responded, the notion of a war between the two powerful kingdoms filling him with horror. "And I don't think that it was Melicard, Gryphon."

"I *know* it isn't," added Gwendolyn. "Erini would never forgive him, and he cares more about her love than he does his old vendetta."

"Then it seems to me," growled the lionbird, unsheathing his claws again, "that it must be *Zuu*. They would gain in a war in the east."

Cabe put a hand on his friend's free shoulder. "Before you do anything, you'd better make certain. We're *so* close, Gryphon! Toos would've advised caution; you know that."

At first, the angry monarch simply stared at the warlock with his unsettling avian gaze. Then, some of the anger faded. The Gryphon nodded. "You are correct, of course. There are others who would benefit by what happened today. It's . . . it's hard to recall that Toos was not even the target; it was Kyl, after all."

"Kyl!" gasped the enchantress. "We haven't even seen how *he* is!"

"Then go to him, friends. I've lost a dear comrade, true, but the young drake's faced death up close." The Gryphon looked around at the gathered guards and functionaries. "Besides, I think that there is enough here to keep me occupied . . . for a lifetime, even."

"Will the guards have taken Kyl back to his suite?"

"That would be most likely, yes." The lionbird sighed. "And good luck with him. I cannot say what effect this may have on the heir; we will have to watch him closely."

The warlock agreed. "Once we know a little more about how Kyl is faring, one of us will have to search for Darkhorse. More than ever I fear that he's in grave trouble."

"I think you are correct." With a shake of his head, the Gryphon added, "Why is the process of peace always so violent?"

Cabe had no answer. Instead, he simply wrapped his arm around his wife and asked, "Are you ready?"

"Yes."

Their surroundings altered. The scene of the regent's assassination became the extravagant chambers put aside for the visiting emperor-to-be. Several draconian guards leapt to action as the pair materialized, but the Green Dragon, standing to one side of the room, signaled for them to relax.

Kyl sat in a tall, cushioned chair next to his bed. At first he stared ahead, but upon the Bedlams' sudden arrival, he turned to the mages. His eyes gleamed with a combination of anger, confusion, and fear. Grath stood beside him. He looked at the two spellcasters with an unreadable expression.

"They tried to *kill* me!" the heir to the dragon throne abruptly spat. "They tried to have me *assssassssinated*!"

"Did they catch the assassins?" the Dragon King asked in a quieter, calmer voice.

"The assassins are dead. They either killed themselves or were killed by whoever sent them."

"Ssso no one claimsss to know, then. Convenient." Kyl looked to his brother, who only shrugged. The heir leaned back, his hands gripping the chair arms tight. "I want to go back to the Manor."

"There are still—" began the Green Dragon.

"I want to go back *now*!"

Under the circumstances, Cabe could not really blame him. Kyl had been confronted with the ugliest of all aspects of rule: the desire by someone to remove him from the throne even before he was allowed to sit on it. The only reason that they had not succeeded was due to the quick but unfortunate interference of Toos.

"Kyl, I hope you don't think that Penacles was responsible for this—"

The handsome face twisted into a look of incredulity. "I think it pretty clear that it wasss not, or at leassst that it wasss nothing to do with the lamented regent, but the fact remainsss that I am not sssafe here!" Kyl's hands were shaking. He turned to the enchantress. "Missstresss Bedlam! Will you allow me entrance to the Manor?"

Gwendolyn met Cabe's gaze. "It might be for the best right now."

"Someone should stay at the Manor, anyway," he returned. "It might be that Darkhorse will still turn up—"

"Darkhorse?" asked the Green Dragon in a confused tone.

"He's missing. It may be that he's fallen prey to the same forces behind this assassination."

The Dragon King's only response to that was a low hiss and a nod.

"Will you take usss, then, my lady?" Kyl asked again, more plaintively. "Myssself, my brother, Faras and Ssgayn, and Lord Green?"

The Green Dragon straightened. "With your permission, my liege, I would like to conduct my own invessstigations into this terrible event. Between Massster Bedlam and myself, I think then that we shall have most probabilities covered."

Kyl was clearly on the edge of collapse. He waved a dismissing hand. "Then by all meansss, go. If you can find the fiendsss resssponsible for this disssasssster, then so much the better . . . but I want them brought before me."

"Of course."

"If I may," said a voice from behind Cabe. "I would like to return to the Manor with the others. I can serve no true purpose here."

The Bedlams turned to find Benjin Traske standing next to a small wall table. He had been so still and quiet that the warlock had not even noted his presence, an unnerving thing to Cabe. Still, it was not as if he had been consciously searching for the man.

The emperor-to-be gave his former teacher a cursory glance. Kyl now seemed only half-aware of what was around him. "If you musssst. I don't care. I jussst want to go back *now*."

Traske bowed, then joined his two former students.

Cabe hugged his wife goodbye. As they pulled one another close, he whispered in her ear. "Keep a very good eye on Kyl and wish me luck. This could be more complicated than we imagined."

"What are you saying?" she whispered back. "Was Toma responsible for this, too?"

"I don't think he's any more responsible than Talak or Zuu is. I . . . I have some strange suspicions." Cabe released her without explaining further. She looked him in the eye, then finally accepted his enigmatic response. The Lady Bedlam knew that her husband would not long hide things from her. If Cabe did not want to tell her now, it was only because he did not have much to support those suspicions.

Stepping away from her husband, Gwendolyn Bedlam joined the two drakes and the scholar. She waited just long enough to assure herself that they were prepared, then, with one last glance at Cabe, vanished with her charges.

The remaining drakes looked to Lord Green for guidance. He seemed to consider their position, finally commanding, "Rejoin the rest of the caravan. Someone will be there to take command before long." Facing the warlock, he asked, "Friend Bedlam, do I have your permission to have sssomeone take charge of the caravan and return with it to the Manor?"

Cabe had not given that part of the situation any consideration, but he realized that they could not just abandon the drakes and humans in Penacles. "Yes, I think that would be fine."

"You have your orders, then," the Dragon King told the guards. "Be certain that you have a human esssscort, however, and by all meansss, do not become involved in any altercation with our hosts here. Those who do and survive to tell about it will *not* be pleasssed that they did. I will guarantee that."

"Perhaps we had best escort them as far as the arena, Your Majesty," the warlock suggested. "With tensions the way they are at this moment, we don't dare let any of your people wander around without guides."

"Yes, that would be best."

As it turned out, their return to the arena was uneventful. The Gryphon was still there, as Cabe had rightly assumed. He was talking to two warriors clad as champions of the chess game. Brow furrowing, the curious sorcerer stepped up his pace.

Noticing the mage's return, the lionbird dismissed the two combatants. He acknowledged the Dragon King but focused his attention on Cabe. "I have been speaking with the two warriors who did battle when the assassination occurred. They told me one or two interesting things."

"What would those be?" the drake lord asked before Cabe could speak.

Looking at both of them, the lionbird replied, "During their battle, at the moment just prior to the attack, both had difficulties keeping their grips on their weapons. The man who wore the armor of king, especially, claimed his weapon seemed to have a life of its own. He reports that it fairly flew out of his grip and headed straight for where the heir and Toos stood."

"It fell several feet short, if I recall," commented the Green Dragon.

"Yes, it did. The timing is too good, however. At the very least, the flying weapon was a decoy, I believe, designed to draw the attention of the victim and those around him. No one would be watching. The assassins would then strike . . . and die. Someone invested much sorcery to make this work, but they underestimated poor old Toos." The Gryphon blinked. "How is the emperor-to-be doing?"

"He requested to be brought back to the Manor," Cabe replied, judiciously avoiding mentioning the manner in which Kyl had put the request.

"No longer trusting Penacles and its ability to protect him, eh? I cannot blame him. My Lord Green, Cabe, I'll tell you now that any agreements made between Toos and the drakes will be held to. I will see to that—" the lionbird sighed "—as the ruler of this realm."

"That isss good to hear."

The king of Penacles bristled, but it was not due to anything the Dragon King had said. "I will not let Toos die in vain. He wanted peace more than I did. I will do anything I have to to see that peace succeed." He closed, then reopened his eyes, visibly trying to keep himself calm. "But you desire something. How may I help?"

Cabe quickly described the situation, emphasizing his need to hunt down Darkhorse before any more time had passed. As much as he tried not to think about it, the fear that it was already too late to save the shadow steed nagged at him. The warlock was aware of how many times in the past he had underestimated Darkhorse, for in truth the eternal was more powerful than he, but knowing the shadow steed and how willing he was to go charging into the fray, Cabe could not help worry that each time Darkhorse vanished would be the last any would see of him. Darkhorse had the capability of living forever—as long as he was not destroyed.

The Gryphon wasted no time once his friend had explained. He quickly summoned one of the general's aides and ordered him to lead the drakes to the caravan.

"I will go with them and arrange their departure," suggested the Dragon King. "When I am through, with your permission, I will depart for my own realm. It may very well be that through my own methods, we shall overcome Toma'sss plotting yet."

"You think that Toma did this?"

The drake's eyes burned red. "I do."

"I wouldn't have expected him to use such methods. He is more likely to move behind the scenes."

"Then, if it isss not him, I may also discover that." The Green Dragon bowed to both Cabe and the Gryphon, then joined the draconian soldiers. "Rest assured, I, too, want this peace to succeed."

As the drakes followed the aide, the monarch of Penacles rubbed his beak. "An odd farewell, but then, I've never completely understood drakes."

"I think that they have the same problem with us."

"Yesss. . . . Cabe, where will you search?"

The warlock kept his face neutral. It was too early to tell anyone of his suspicions. "I have a few places in mind. I knew where Darkhorse planned to be at certain times after he last departed the Manor. I'll check them first."

"He may be dead . . . like Toos."

"Then I'll find the one who did it."

The Gryphon's unsettling eyes seemed to twinkle. "You had best find him—or them—before I do if you hope to have anything left." He toyed with his talons, extending them to their full lengths. "I do not intend to hold back this time."

Recalling how hard it had been for the lionbird to "hold back" when he had been tracking the murderers of his firstborn son, Cabe shuddered. He hoped that it would not come to that. If the Gryphon lost control, there was no telling what he might do.

Evidently, the lord of Penacles was thinking much the same thing. He almost glared at the warlock, but managed to prevent himself. Instead, he simply turned a little away, his eyes shifting to nothing in particular, and said, "The sooner you leave, the more chance you have of saving him."

Cabe did not need another hint. He bowed to the former and present ruler of the City of Knowledge, then vanished.

Valea was with Ursa and Aurim when her mother returned with Kyl and the others. The trio, along with a nervous Ssarekai, had finally abandoned the underground chamber, assuming that it might be some time before their parents returned. Aurim was the first to see the newcomers as they materialized in the front hall of the Manor.

"They're back!" he pointed out to the others. "But Father's not there and . . . and Kyl and Grath are!"

They hurried to meet the returning party, Valea with conflicting emotions. Fear stemming from the knowledge that *something* had happened in Penacles intertwined with relief that Kyl was safe. She started to greet him, but the expression on his handsome visage made her pause. It was both cruel and confused. Even Grath showed signs of anger, although he hid them much better than his brother. Scholar Traske revealed nothing.

"What is it? What happened in Penacles?" asked Aurim, his own problem not even a concern to him at this point. "Where's Father?"

"Your father is all right," Lady Bedlam replied quickly, so as to relieve some of her family's fears. "He searches for Darkhorse, who's missing." Her face grew more somber. "You should all know . . . Toos the Regent was killed during an assassination attempt on Kyl."

"Gods!" The young warlock shook his head.

Ssarekai swore an oath by the mythical Dragon of the Depths. Valea could scarcely believe what she was hearing. Her relief at finding Kyl safe gave way to her grief for the towering old soldier. He had been like the grandfather she had never had—and who would have wanted *Azran* anyway?—giving her presents and tolerating her questions about the war years.

In the midst of their grief, Kyl suddenly snapped, "If he had not died, it would have been *me*, inssstead!" He straightened his clothing and tried to look unruffled. "If you will excussse me, Lady Bedlam, I desssire greatly to return to my roomsss."

"I quite understand, Kyl."

The drake had not even waited for her response. Already turning, he snapped his fingers at Grath and his bodyguards. "Come with me!"

With the dragon heir in the lead, the drakes departed the still-stunned group. Valea found herself just a bit put out by Kyl's attitude, although, admittedly, he had been through much today.

"How do you feel, Aurim?" Benjin Traske asked suddenly. His question first struck the novice sorceress as incongruous to the situation at hand, but then she recalled that the massive tutor had been in Penacles. He would know more about the events that had taken place there than the progress, or lack thereof, of the Bedlams' attempts to free the minds of her brother and Ssarekai.

"The same," her brother remarked halfheartedly. It was clear the news about dear Toos was far more important to the young Bedlam.

"I see." Traske turned to Valea's mother. "My lady, perhaps it might be good if I left your company for now. This is a matter for you and your family, and I can perhaps be of better use to Lord Kyl. I do not doubt that he is going through a conflict of his own."

"I should go to him—" the enchantress began.

"You are suffering also, madam. Your family knew the regent better than I. I mourn his death, true, but not near as much as you. I think that you should explain things to the young here. I will do what I can for my former pupil."

"Thank you. In truth," responded Gwendolyn Bedlam, "he probably would listen to you more than he would either Cabe or myself."

An uncharacteristic smile spread across the scholar's bearded countenance. "It pleases me to hear you say so." He performed a bow. "My lady . . . "

Ursa suddenly looked anxious. "Scholar, may I go with you? He isss my brother."

He hesitated. "At this point, young lady, it might be better if you waited. Let me do what I can. Too many new voices might drive the emperor-to-be to further distress. He needs a guiding hand at the moment."

Valea thought she knew the true reason why Benjin Traske did not want Ursa along. Ursa did not really get along with Kyl. One of Kyl's greatest faults, subconscious or not, was that he saw the females of his race as inferior creatures. The courtesy he freely gave to Valea, the young drake only forcibly gave to his own sibling. It was a strange double standard that she would never understand. Valea had tried to question Kyl about it, but it was one subject he refused to discuss.

Her mother looked as if she wanted to speak in Ursa's defense, but Valea's friend acquiesced before she could do so. "You are right, of course, Scholar Trassske. Will you let me know how he is?"

"As you desire." The tutor bowed again, this time taking his leave immediately after. Valea wondered if other households were as abrupt as hers. Throughout her life it had always seemed as if people were in a hurry. Everyone was always rushing someplace.

She, too, wanted to be there when the scholar told Ursa how Kyl was faring. It was purely for selfish motives, she knew, but she was aware that the kind of tragedy he had faced could change him permanently. Valea feared that those changes would put them farther apart from one another.

Her mind returned to poor Toos. She felt guilty that she should be so concerned about Kyl when the regent had died saving his life. *I wonder how the Gryphon is taking it? They were good, good friends. . . .*

Lady Bedlam was doing her best to maintain control. She said, "Why don't we go to the drawing room? I think it would be wise to be as comfortable as possible while we talk. This situation is hardly over. We are going to have to be wary for some time."

They all understood what she was saying. Valea knew that where there had been one assassination attempt, there might be others.

The enchantress began to lead them away, then paused when she realized that there was still another member of the party. The drake Ssarekai had remained behind after the others had left. Valea liked him; he hardly seemed like a dragon at all. *How left out he must feel right now!*

"Ssarekai? You are welcome to join us, you know. Don't think that you aren't family after all these years. You've gone farther than many toward making cooperation between our races work."

The stable master had been staring down the hallway Benjin Traske, Kyl, and the drakes had used. With effort, he shifted his gaze to the sorceress. "I thank you deeply for thossse wordsss, my lady, but I have let too much time pass. There are dutiesss that I realize I must see to before it isss too late."

"Very well. We have not given up on the spells that bind you and Aurim. I want you to know that they are still priorities with us."

The drake shrugged. "I have had it this long; I think that if Master Aurim can wait, then so can I."

Valea's mother swore an oath, so upset was she. "There's always too much happening at the same time! These spells *should* be removed as quickly as possible!"

"They don't seem to be harming us, Mother. I can wait, too." Aurim's face was pale. "Besides . . . I need to hear what happened. I need to hear about Toos. How did Toma sneak assassins into Penacles? How does he find his way into everywhere?"

For some reason, this made their mother pause. At last the fire-tressed sorceress admitted, "Your father thinks it might have been someone else who plotted the assassination. He hopes to find out more. . . . " She hugged herself, obviously worried. "I pray that he doesn't find out more than he planned."

The others nodded, Valea making her own private wish concerning her father's safety . . . and the rescue of Darkhorse. At least, she thought, the assassins had failed in their goal; Kyl was alive and well.

She would have to see him at first opportunity. He would certainly not turn *her* away. As selfish as she knew it was for her to think so, Valea could not help wondering if perhaps this tragic event would be what finally brought them together. She would be good for him, especially now. Kyl would not have to fear for her; Valea had the power not only to protect herself but to further augment the heir's own magic. Between them, no assassin, however well armed, would stand the slightest chance of success.

Not even Toma, she decided.

Grath had a great desire to slap his brother's face again and again until the idiot calmed down and thought properly once more, but he knew that such action would only see him dismissed from Kyl's side. That would ruin everything that had been planned.

The death of General Toos had been a tragic loss, both politically and emotionally, but Grath had long ago learned to put the worst aside, leaving his mind clear for thought. He would miss the regent, miss him much more than his mentor would, of course, but overall the human's death had been worth the price. After all, if not for Toos, Kyl would be dead and Grath would be forced to take his place. It was much too soon for that. Perhaps later, once it was clear that the power of the Dragon Emperor was secure.

Of course, first he had to free his brother from the shock and paranoia Kyl now suffered.

"They tried to kill me, Grath! Thossse missserable humans! I should overrun them all when I am emperor! They cannot be trusssted, the furry ssscavengers . . . but . . . " Kyl's face twisted into an expression of extreme uncertainty. "The regent gave hisss *own* life to sssave mine! I would have been *murdered* but for him!"

Faras and Ssgayn exchanged glances that Grath noted out of the edge of his eye. They were beginning to question both their emperor-to-be's sanity and his bravery.

He put a brotherly hand on Kyl's shoulder. "Now isss not the time to think about all of this, Kyl. The best thing to do right now is rest. You *need* rest. In only a few days, the Blue Dragon, representing the other Dragon Kings as well, will arrive in the Dagora Forest. He will want to question you. This will be your moment."

To his astonishment, Kyl pushed him away. "I don't care about the drake lord! If they cannot accept me asss emperor already, then I will *make* them come to me on bent knee!" A frightening glint came into the drake's eyes. "Could it be that Blue or one of the other hesssitant oness sssent thosse killers? They *do* all have their human agentsss, do they not, Grath?"

The last thing he wanted to encourage was a fear that the recalcitrant Dragon Kings might be trying to kill Kyl. True, it was a possibility that he had considered—only minutes before, in fact—but that was something that could be dealt with once Kyl and he gained the power of the Dragon Throne. The drake lords would be less inclined to attempt the assassination once his brother was officially their master.

Grath exhaled, trying to gather his thoughts together enough to give Kyl some sort of reassuring answer. The chaos in the arena had not been nearly so draining as trying to keep his brother in line. *And he is to be the emperor?*

He was still trying to decide what to do when there came a heavy knock upon the door. Faras stalked toward the door, weapon at the ready. Kyl, Grath was ashamed to see, actually drew back into his chair.

The guards tensed. Faras opened the door.

Relief washed over Grath as he saw who it was who had dared to join them.

Kyl looked up at the newcomer, still wary. "Ssscholar Trassske. You desssire something of me? I am rather busssy at the moment."

"So I see," remarked the tutor with obvious sarcasm. Grath knew that his brother had never heard the figure before him speak with such impudence. "Busy falling prey to your fears when you should be using them to strengthen you. A ruler must learn to control his weaknesses and make them work for him."

"I don't have time for your sss—"

Grath allowed himself a brief smile as Kyl broke off at the look on the massive figure's face. At last there was someone who could make his brother see sense . . . and who else was better suited?

Benjin Traske ceased glaring at the heir to the dragon throne just long enough to deal with Kyl's bodyguards. "Leave us."

To Kyl's astonishment—but not to Grath's—Faras and Ssgayn bowed and hastily retreated from the chamber.

The dragon heir rose, intending to command the two to return, but Traske stepped directly in front of him. Kyl, trying to back away, fell into the chair.

"Things are moving much too swiftly now, but we can compensate. The death of the regent, while unexpected, does nothing to change the fact that you *will* be emperor in only a very short time. You survived the assassination, and now it will be almost impossible for whoever was responsible to attempt something else. I will see to assuring that."

"You will see to that?"

"In whatever way is open to me, of course," Traske corrected. "What is more important is to consider the next step you must take on the road to the throne. If I may suggest—"

This made Kyl laugh harshly. "Teacher, you are a human I admire, I freely admit that. Your advice I would generally find good, but you could not possssibly undersssstand what I am going through. You do not undersssstand the *challenges*, the myriad *pitfalls*, that I face in asssssuming the throne of my kind."

"Perhaps I understand more than you imagine. . . ."

"You would have to live through it yoursssself. There isss no other way to undersssstand it ssso well."

Benjin Traske started to speak, then paused in consideration. At last, he simply said, "I can see that for now I am wasting my time here."

He was leaving. Grath could not believe that. Here was the one being able to drag Kyl back to his feet and he was leaving without having even tried. "Teacher—"

Benjin Traske shook his head. "No, Grath. I will waste no time here. I can see that Kyl needs time to let his thoughts cool." The huge figure loomed over the heir. "Then, Kyl, you and I will talk again. Much longer, this time."

The heir had already slipped deeper into his chair. "I have no desire to do so."

"You will." Traske's tone was such that Kyl could not help but straighten. It was the voice that had kept both drakes highly attentive throughout their lessons. It was a voice that brooked no disagreement, one that Grath knew his brother had not yet learned to control completely and probably never would.

Benjin Traske turned to leave, the issue of Kyl's permission negligible under the circumstances, but then paused. He glanced first at Grath, then at Kyl, to whom he added, "You will be emperor. You will be strong. We will see to that."

The dragon heir glanced up. His gaze did not leave the figure of the scholar until Traske had closed the door behind him. Then, Kyl simply turned to stare at one of the walls. Grath remained where he was, silent as the night. When Faras and Ssgayn returned, he indicated silence, then pointed where he wanted them positioned. They obeyed him without a sound.

Kyl continued to stare at the wall, but from where Grath stood, it was possible for the younger drake to see the look on his elder brother's visage. Still brooding, but now Kyl was at least thinking. It was the first stage to recovery.

"Grath? What do you think of our esssteemed tutor?"

How to phrase it best? Grath hesitated, then responded, "He came here to see you made emperor, brother. He is not the kind to let years of work go for naught. When he says that you will be emperor, he means it."

"Ssso I felt." The dragon heir hissed. "I sssometimesss wish that Toma had sssucceeded our sssire after all. *He* would have brooked no threat from asssasssin or king, human or drake."

"There isss much to admire in Toma," Grath ventured. "He was loyal to our sire."

"Ssso I was thinking."

The young drake smiled at such a response, but only because his brother could not clearly see his face. Faras and Ssgayn could, but they were of no consequence; they knew their places.

"Perhaps, when you are emperor, you will be able to arrange to talk with him."

The notion made Kyl blink. "I could do that, couldn't I?"

"As emperor, who would stop you?"

"Who, indeed?"

Behind the emperor-to-be, Grath allowed himself another smile.

XVI

Cabe frowned as the night aged. The evidence he had hoped to find had failed to turn up, but still the warlock could not abandon his suspicions. He *wanted* to, very dearly in fact, but some part of him forced the mage to push on.

Twice already he had contacted his wife and the Gryphon. There had not been much to report from either side. Thanks to a private conversation between Benjin Traske and Kyl, the heir had at least calmed down. He remained secluded in his chambers, however. Gwendolyn reported some lingering signs of his earlier nervousness, but it appeared that Kyl had his fear under control. There was nothing else to report from the Manor. Aurim and Ssarekai were still afflicted by the mysterious spell Toma had cast upon them, but so far it had not affected anything but their memories concerning the renegade.

The news from Penacles was little better. Order had been restored and most in the kingdom seemed perfectly satisfied with the return of their former monarch, but the lionbird had been forced to admit that the spells of searching that he had cast upon the remnants of the two assassins had revealed nothing new. He had, however, promised the warlock that he would keep the garments under guard until Cabe or Gwen had the opportunity to study them thoroughly.

In a wooded area near the northern edge of the Dagora Forest, Cabe sat on a high rock contemplating the lack of success on everyone's part. Even he had not had anything to report. It had been his decision to continue the search through the entire night if necessary, for, in his mind, each second he delayed meant more danger to Darkhorse. Fortunately, he could revitalize himself for a time through the simple use of sorcery. Cabe did not like substituting magical energy in the place of normal rest—it was a danger in the long run for *many* reasons—but he did it rarely enough that now would not cause him trouble. What *did* bother him was the possibility of finding his last clues as useless as the others. Then, the only choices left to him would be to confront the source of his suspicions, or forget the matter—and Darkhorse—forever.

He could never do the latter, but the former unnerved him almost as much.

Exhaling, the warlock floated off the rock and slowly descended to the ground, where he landed in a standing position. Cabe surveyed the area, seeing it well despite the darkness. For once, he had dared to adjust his eyes to better see at night. As much as Cabe disliked altering any portion of his form, especially something as sensitive as the eyes, the missing Darkhorse deserved at least *that* much effort. The warlock was willing to give his life, if that was what it took to save the ebony stallion.

I should've sensed something! What am I missing? What, indeed? Cabe had tried to follow Darkhorse's trace, but so far it had led him nowhere. It was as if his last few days had been erased from—

Then it at last came to him. He cursed himself for a fool. *I should've seen that before! And people think of me as a master sorcerer! I'm a* novice, *that's what I am! A wet-behind-the-ears, all-knowing, first-day novice!*

The traps set for Darkhorse had been designed in a variety of manners, but one consistent trait had been the creator's use of one bit of sorcery masking another. What better way, then, to cover the trail of the shadow steed by use of the same, or rather, *similar* technique?

Tensing, the spellcaster reached out and looked at the world anew. There were different levels of vision, and while Cabe made use of both the mundane and magical, he did not usually utilize all of the latter. He could not remember a time when he had been forced to reach beyond the most common of the magical dimensions. Cabe *had* viewed the world from every level, but only for practice. He had never had to truly make use of them until now.

In the first shifting, the land around him became fluid, but everything still held its basic shape. Trees and rocks wiggled like overfilled water sacks, yet did not burst when he touched them.

The night sky was blue. Lines of force, the same forces that Cabe's body drew upon when he utilized sorcery, crisscrossed everywhere. Colors were askew, with green things now red and brown things now yellow.

Unfortunately, for this realm, everything was as it was meant to be. There were no variations that would have signaled the necessary aberration that Cabe was hunting.

He tried the next level beyond. Now, the night was green and everything, including himself, was pierced by a thousand tiny blue lines. The fact that all else was normal by human standards did nothing to keep him from becoming disconcerted by the strands. He was almost grateful to see that there was no evidence of the masking sorcery on this level.

His third attempt gave the warlock the ability to see the world as a land of glittering spheres. Each time something moved, be it by its own choice or simply the touch of the wind, the tiny spheres went flying hither and yonder. The landscape also glittered, making it appear that the trees, rocks, and all the rest had been formed out of volcanic glass. It was one of the most exotic and most beautiful of the magical planes, and Cabe made a note to himself to view it again when things calmed down.

There among the beauty he finally found the black trail. To his eyes, it appeared as a jagged scattering of black glass. In some places there lay only a single piece, but still there was enough to follow. Cabe reached out with his power, which in this level was represented by a gleaming blue stream, and linked himself to the trail.

It was childishly easy to follow it through a series of hops. Each time he materialized, the warlock expected to find some difficulty, some barrier, but there was none. Cabe began to fear some trap, but if there was one, it was so subtle that it escaped his careful monitoring.

On the twelfth hop, he came across the hooded figures. The suddenly still warlock did not know exactly where he was, although the region reminded him of somewhere near the ruins of Mito Pica, but *location* hardly mattered now. What did matter was that he had no doubt whatsoever he had found the ones he sought.

As he saw the world, the dismounted riders were mounds of black steel among the glass trees. The images disconcerted him until he shifted his vision back to night sight. Even then, however, the silent figures were ominous shapes. They wore cloaks identical to those of the assassins, huge things that only now and then revealed the race to which their wearers belonged.

They were men *and* drakes. Three of the former and two of the latter, all seated around a fire that was little more than embers and so gave some heat but hardly any betraying illumination. It was a surprising but not unbelievable sight, and whether it confirmed his suspicions, Cabe could not say.

Shielded by a pair of tall oaks, the silent mage surveyed the group. One of the humans seemed to be in charge. He muttered something to one of the drakes. In the drake's hands was a small box that, at first, the warlock's gaze passed over. Only when he belatedly sensed the strangeness of it did he probe the object. To his surprise, it resisted his best attempts to unveil its contents, but what he learned about the container made him shiver.

It was Vraad . . . or at the very least, based on Vraadish sorcery. It was by far not the first artifact he had been confronted with over the years. In the short time that the alien magic had thrived in this world, millennia before, it had certainly left its mark, the warlock thought. A *black* mark, in his opinion.

Suddenly, he had a horrible feeling he knew what the box contained.

"We wait, then," grunted the leader. "I can have a little more patience."

Wait? For who? For the assassins? That seemed peculiar, considering that the two had clearly been intended to die regardless of their success or failure. Was the leader then waiting for reinforcements, or was someone else planning to join them?

A quick but cautious search of the surrounding region revealed no other intruders. The warlock came to a decision; he would have to strike now lest he lose this one chance. Cabe had no doubt that he had found what he was searching for, and so in his eyes waiting only threatened to lessen his opportunity to take the foul container without a greater struggle.

He knew that there was magic about the riders, but could read nothing more. They might have enchanted daggers or be untrained but lethal mages. It might even be their cloaks alone, which he had already discerned had some spell interwoven in them.

Magic or not, it was time to act. Reaching out, the warlock sent tendrils of power toward each of the figures. With any luck, the battle would be over before any of the five noticed what was happening. A simple sleep spell, one that should be effective regardless of the sorcery he sensed. Surprise was ofttimes a more useful tool in magical combat than all the power of an archmage. Surprise mixed with caution, that is. There were many instantaneous spells that he could have unleashed, but Cabe wanted to take no chances. It was *his* way. If this failed, then he would be more direct, more instinctive in his attack.

He encountered no barriers, no protective spells. That made sense. Unless one was very skilled, protective spells tended to be noticeable. This was not a party that wished to be noticed, as the pitiful fire had already indicated.

Slowly, each tendril took its place. Cabe found himself sweating. He wanted to hurry the spell through, but was aware how such impatience had a tendency to backfire. There might still be some sorcerous shield in place that he had not noticed.

Still the hooded figures seemed unaware of what he was doing. The ease with which his plan progressed worried Cabe. Despite his vast power, he always expected the worst to happen. If he was wrong this time, so much the better, but until then . . .

Before he realized it, his spell was finally ready. When he chose to, each tendril would strike the head of the figure before it, unleashing the unstoppable command to sleep. He had drawn enough power into the making of the spell to down five times the number of riders before him. That, unless he had miscalculated horribly, would be sufficient to overcome each.

So why are you waiting? Having no good answer to the silent question, Cabe Bedlam unleashed his spell.

Two of the men and one of the drakes collapsed.

The human leader and the drake who held the box rose. Their hoods kept their faces all but obscured, but Cabe could read consternation in the dragon man's movements. The human, however, was furious.

An armored hand shot forward as the leader pointed directly at the warlock's hiding place. *"There! He's there!"*

Shifting his prize to one hand, the drake pointed a taloned finger.

One of the oaks burst, sending tiny spears of wood flying. The warlock folded himself into a ball as the deadly shower enveloped him, his robe making a seemingly insufficient shield against the storm of tiny but lethal spears.

"Give me the box!" growled the leader as the fearsome rain poured down. He pulled out a short sword. "Go and make certain that he's finished!"

The drake thrust the container into the human's hand and stalked toward the curled figure, his speed increasing the nearer he came. When he finally stood over Cabe, the drake raised one hand high in preparation of a new spell. The hand glowed with pent up power.

Cabe materialized behind the leader just as the huddled form exploded at the dragon man's touch.

The drake went flying backward, stunned. The warlock's simulacrum had not been created to kill; Cabe desired prisoners, not corpses.

He reached out for the leader even as the explosion rocked the immediate vicinity, yet somehow the hooded man sensed him coming. With astonishing dexterity, the leader swung the blade behind him, almost severing the warlock's hand from his arm. Cabe barely pulled back in time, yet still he managed to release his spell.

The outline of the hooded figure flared white, but the man was otherwise unchanged.

"Yes . . . I *am* protected against your little tricks, magic man, but are *you* protected against *mine*?"

Still clutching the box in his other hand, the armored leader advanced on Cabe. This close, the warlock's enhanced vision allowed him a better view of the armor beneath the robe. It was dented and worn, but there was no mistaking the familiar ebony armor. His foe was, or rather had been, a wolf raider.

Their empire was all but a memory, but that did not mean that the Aramites, the wolf raiders, were also. They still held pockets of the neighboring continent and their ships now prowled the seas as true pirates. Even in the Dragonrealm, half the world away, there were remnants. This one might even have been part of the large force that had attempted to build a new powerbase on this continent. Those wolf raiders had been defeated, but more than a few had no doubt escaped the cataclysm that had befallen the army in the southwesternmost region of the Dragonrealm. Reports of survivors being captured in various places all over the continent had been verified. It was, therefore, not so surprising after all to find one here. Somehow the Aramites seemed to have a hand in almost every plot that touched the lives of Cabe and those he cared for.

However this one had come to be here, Cabe knew that he could not let him escape. The warlock backed away as the raider advanced, but that was not something he could continue for very long. In fact, he did not have to. The surprise of discovering what his adversary was had finally faded and now Cabe was prepared to finish the task at hand. The Aramite could not be allowed to escape with the box.

"I've not worked for so long to have you destroy everything!" snarled the wolf raider. Suddenly his sword's reach was longer than it should have been. Although the blade missed the sorcerer by a good arm's length, still there was suddenly a slash in Cabe's robe. The raider's sword had some limited magical ability. What *other* tricks did the man have hidden beneath his robe?

Enough was enough. If he could not affect his adversary directly, then Cabe was prepared to work *around* him.

The leader swung again, this time leaving not only a small rip in the sleeve of the warlock's garment but also a thin, red line across Cabe's lower arm that stung almost enough to make the warlock forget what he was doing.

However, as the Aramite pulled back his weapon for another vicious cut, a tree branch suddenly got in the way of his sword arm. Cursing, the hooded attacker pulled his arm around, but his swing was ruined. He sidestepped the tree, but then another branch caught him in the face.

"Dogs of war! What is—" The rest became unintelligible as yet another branch shifted, despite the direction of the wind, and struck him soundly in the unprotected throat.

Upturned roots caused his advance to falter. As he stumbled, the raider almost dropped the box, but at the last moment, he managed to retain his grip That was his only success, however, for now he could not manage to lower his sword arm. Worse yet, the blade itself was now tangled in a mesh of smaller, intertwined branches above the raider's head.

Cabe allowed himself a slight smile at the sight of his handiwork. His adversary had blundered directly into it. In fact, it had almost been too easy. The warlock had never truly been in danger. It was an odd sensation, so easily defeating the threat. Cabe kept expecting some last-second trick by either the trapped leader or some henchman still in hiding, but inside he knew that no trick would be coming. Each passing second left the raider more and more hopelessly entangled. Already he could no longer move.

One time I garner a quick and easy victory and I can't be satisfied with that! He tried to shake the doubts away, but failed. Sighing, Cabe decided to simply ignore them. The doubts could not take away the fact that he had won.

Walking over to the imprisoned leader, Cabe reached out and pried the box from his helpless hand. "Thank you."

His prisoner said nothing.

Cabe looked close, utilizing his enhanced vision to study the one before him. He did not recognize the man, but he had the look of an officer. Aramite officers were, to his bitter recollection, deceitful monsters with sadistic streaks. One of them had killed the Gryphon's firstborn. That one was dead, but Cabe knew that the lionbird would find this one of almost as much interest.

"Tell me about this box, wolf raider." He held the offensive artifact up close to the Aramite's scowling face.

There was a peculiar look in what Cabe could see of that ugly visage. With a rough, humorless laugh, the leader replied, "You'll have to find out about it on your own, spellmonger. It'll be my last gift to you and yours."

It was too late by the time the warlock reacted.

With a gasp, the imprisoned raider began to shake. His entire form convulsed, so much so that he almost shook free of the binding branches. That was not the man's intention, though. Cabe tried to counter whatever spell was upon the raider, but the same defensive measure that had prevented him from directly attacking blocked these spells as well. What it did not block, however, was the thing killing his prisoner, which to Cabe meant that the source lay somewhere *within* the Aramite's body.

"Drazeree!" muttered the warlock, calling upon a legendary and possibly blood-related hero/god of the age of the Vraad. What Cabe witnessed now was worthy of the foul Vraad and possibly would have revolted even a few of them.

The guards had spoken of the assassins literally crumbling to ash. He could only assume that this was the same spell, for it seemed unlikely that anyone would devise two such similar horrors.

The Aramite grew ashen-faced. His clothing, with the exception of the cloak and the armor, appeared to crackle and break. The raider laughed, but the laugh quickly became a gurgle as first the man's teeth and tongue, then his entire *jaw*, fell away.

Without warning, the decomposing figure slipped free of the branches and slumped to the ground. A terrible mound of gray flakes formed around his diminishing body. Now, there emerged no sound from Cabe's hapless prisoner. The appalled spellcaster doubted that the man was still alive. The graying skin crumbled off of the raider's face, followed without pause by the skull and hair.

Cabe turned away, too sick to his stomach to watch the final moments. In little more than the blink of an eye, he had watched a living creature be reduced to dust.

By the time he had recovered enough to look again, all that remained of the leader was his cloak, partly tangled in the tree branches, empty bits of black armor . . . and an unsettling mound of dust. He forced himself to sift through the remains, but there was no sign of what had protected his adversary from his spells or what had finally killed the wolf raider. In fact, there was not much of anything. No clues. Nothing.

Then it was that Cabe Bedlam recalled the other hooded figures. His stomach recoiled, but he had no choice. He suspected what he would find, but that did not mean he did not have to look.

It proved to be as he had feared. Of the others, even the drake who had fallen for his trick, there remained nothing but bits of armor, metal objects, the mysterious cloaks, and foul piles of ash.

Had they willingly let this be done to them? He could hardly believe so, despite what the leader had said, and despite the words that had given credence to the notion that the Aramite had been responsible for this entire plot. He was aware that he was grasping at straws, but too many things had fallen into place easily while others had not.

The warlock studied the carved exterior of the box as if it could give him some of the answers he craved.

To his surprise, it gave the two most important answers of all. Both he desired, but one he would have preferred not to have known.

The box was what he had feared it would be. An artifact so ancient but still capable of the evil for which it had been created. Exhaling, the weary sorcerer cautiously touched the front. At least it had not been designed to confound. Opening it would be the easy part, possibly the *only* easy part from this point on.

Cabe turned the box so that it would open away from him. Then, taking a deep breath, he pressed the lock and lifted the lid back.

The scream shattered the night and almost caused the warlock to drop the box. A black cloud burst forth from the box, a black cloud darker than night.

"I am *free!* Free!" A mocking laugh followed, a laugh almost as horrifying in its own way as the shriek preceding it.

The black cloud sprouted long legs and a tail. A head, at first twisted and unidentifiable, grew from the front of the cloud, while at the same time the tail rose in the back.

Darkhorse coalesced before him, the shadow steed's hooves more than a yard from the earth below.

"I am free!" he roared. The eternal looked down and the ice-blue orbs that were his eyes widened at the small figure below and before him. "Cabe!"

"Darkhorse, I—" He had no chance to finish his statement, for the shadow steed was suddenly whirling about in the air, eyes seeking. "Where *are* they, Cabe? Where are those misbegotten vermin who have dared reintroduce me to my worst nightmare? I will draw them in and let *them* taste eternal emptiness! Where are they, Cabe?"

"They're dead."

At first the shadow steed did not believe him. He snorted and darted toward the nearest cloak, not yet realizing what it represented. Kicking it aside, the eternal studied with confusion the ash beneath. "What is this dust?"

The spellcaster closed the box and placed it in the folds of his robe. He would deal with the box in prompt order, but first he had to calm the maddened stallion. "That's all that's left of them, Darkhorse. I saw it happen to the leader."

"No! I *will* not be denied! I cannot be!"

He kicked at the cloak, then trotted to one of the other piles. Watching the huge form dart about in the darkness, Cabe was torn between letting things end here or voicing his beliefs. To him, the box was the deciding point between taking the struggle here at face value or seeing the wolf raider and his men as the pawns they might be. In the warlock's eyes, the Aramite and his henchmen had died so that someone else would remain anonymous.

Unfortunately for that someone, Cabe had not fallen for the ploy.

Suddenly the eternal loomed over him. "It's true, then? My captors are dust?"

"All of them." Cabe almost winced as he told the lie. "It wasn't a pretty way to go, Darkhorse. I think you can be satisfied that they've paid."

The shadow steed snorted. "I will *have* to be, I suppose." He cocked his head. "I wonder what they wanted of me. How long have I been a prisoner?"

It had not even occurred to the sorcerer that his friend knew nothing of the dire deeds that had transpired since his imprisonment. Cabe swallowed. "There's much you've missed, Darkhorse. Too much."

Some of Darkhorse's fury abated. "Your tone is not one I find I like, Cabe. What is it? What's happened?"

The tale spilled out of the warlock's mouth almost of its own volition. He described the foul spells that Toma had imprinted on the minds of his son and Ssarekai, then proceeded to tell of the tragedy that had befallen the kingdom of Penacles.

Darkhorse was still when Cabe at last finished. The icy eyes glowed with much less fury but more frustration.

"I am . . . sorry . . . about Toos. He was an interesting human, Cabe. Such an end was hardly fitting. So his assassins also are dead?"

"By the same manner as their leader. He was a wolf raider, probably an officer."

"Wolf raider. . . . " Darkhorse glowered as only he could. "Even without an empire, they still manage to meddle. This explains such a fanatical mission. Only an Aramite officer would see to it that neither he nor his men would survive if the plot failed. Good in one respect, for it means less to hunt down afterward. May the Lords of the Dead have no pity on their souls. It's over, then?"

Cabe could not prevent a sigh this time. He hoped that his companion would not read too much into it. The warlock was not certain that he could maintain the lie if pressed. "This is. There may be repercussions, though. Kyl was quite shook up."

"So I would think." Darkhorse scuffed the soil, sending large chunks of earth flying. "I am still not certain about this matter, Cabe. I think someone else was behind this."

"You do?" He tried not to reveal his anxiety.

The eternal dipped his head in an equine nod. "I would not be surprised to find the talons of *Toma* sunk deeply into this travesty!"

Seizing the notion and turning it to his own use, Cabe agreed. "You may be right."

"We need to find that reptilian fiend and put an end to his misdeeds! I will not rest until that has happened!"

This time, the warlock had no difficulty agreeing. Even if the renegade drake had not been involved in Darkhorse's capture, which was still not a notion that Cabe could entirely dismiss, he had much else to answer for.

"We'll find him, Darkhorse. Somehow we will."

The nightmarish stallion again pawed at the ground. The spark in his eyes rekindled, becoming a blaze. Yet, his form noticeably wavered, as if he still did not have complete control over it. The pupilless eyes peered down at him. "Do you intend to return to the Manor now?"

Cabe gently touched the box in his robe. He hoped his own presence shielded the artifact from Darkhorse's senses. Despite the shadow steed's manner, it was clear that he was weak, which was the only reason that the warlock hoped he could keep the box concealed. Darkhorse would want to destroy the box and, in truth, Cabe would have been hardpressed to prevent him from doing so without revealing just exactly why it was necessary to keep it in one piece. The mage himself was not exactly certain why; he simply felt that the sinister device would prove a damning bit of evidence when he faced the one responsible. "Yes. I want to look around here a little first, then I'll be returning to the Manor."

Again the shadow steed's form wavered. This time, when Darkhorse spoke, his voice was muffled, as if someone had in part succeeded in gagging him. Yet, his tone was still one of unbridled self-confidence. "Then I shall trust to your safety since all the villains are dead. In the meantime, there is a hunt that I must begin. *Toma* must needs be taught a proper lesson for this!" The eternal began to turn away. "If I find anything of significance, I shall come to the Manor; I promise you."

"Are you . . . are you certain that you'll be all right, Darkhorse?"

The ebony stallion swung his head and chuckled. "Of *course*, I will be! I *am* Darkhorse, am I not?"

Cabe could only smile and shake his head. No matter what dire straits the shadow steed faced, it seemed that there were some character traits forever ingrained in his rather eccentric personality. On the one hand, the sorcerer would not have wanted Darkhorse to change, but on the other hand, it likely would have been better for all concerned if the shadow steed *was* better able to restrain himself when it came to certain matters. Certainly, Cabe would sleep easier. Unfortunately, Cabe was aware that nothing but imprisonment or destruction would sway the injured stallion from his chosen path.

"Fare you well, Cabe, and my thanks. . . . " The massive equine began to trot . . . and was suddenly nowhere to be seen. Swifter than the wind was a phrase that failed to describe the eternal's speed.

He doesn't realize, the master mage thought as he stared where his companion had stood not a breath before. *Hopefully, it'll remain that way.*

Alone, Cabe finally turned and gave the dusty remains of the conspirators one last cursory glance. Already Cabe knew that there was nothing to be learned from these. Even the leader's empty armor and cloak left no secrets. After a minute or two of futile searching, the warlock turned his attention to the horses, but a thorough examination revealed that the saddlebags contained only some food, water, and a few other necessities for travel. The contents told him only one interesting thing; the sparsity of food meant that either the hooded figures had planned to locate supplies elsewhere, or they had not expected to ride much further after this. Cabe knew of nothing nearby. They could not hope to catch sufficient game in this area, either.

The evidence would have been circumstantial to most, but to the uneasy spellcaster, what he knew was sufficient to condemn. He dared not deal with the matter this night, though. *Best to return home and face this when I've rested. Maybe I'll still find another answer. Maybe.*

He remained long enough to send the horses through a blink hole, one of the large, magical portals a spellcaster could create, that would leave them in the royal stables of Penacles. One of the animals carried a note on its saddle, a missive from the warlock to the Gryphon explaining what had happened. As with the explanation to Darkhorse, it left some things unsaid.

Satisfied that the Gryphon would know best what to do with the dead assassins' things, Cabe prepared for home. A good night's sleep was what he would need, especially if he planned to go through with his accusations. He would need *all* the strength he could when it came time to reveal what he knew.

Even then, Cabe was not certain that he would be strong enough.

XVII

Despite his determination the night before, the new day found Cabe ensconced in his study, his mind a raging maelstrom of doubt and contradiction. He had been there since his return from tracking down the assassins. Neither Gwendolyn nor the children had been able to stir him from the emotion that bespelled him, and they had finally resigned themselves to allowing him to find his own way back.

Cabe could not explain to them, not without revealing what he felt should not be revealed. There had been enough tragedy and violence already; the knowledge . . . the suspicions . . . he entertained were enough to start a new war.

The damning box sat on the table before him, a dark thing both revealing and mysterious. No one knew it was here; he had cast a cloaking spell around it at first opportunity. Since no one here had known of the box in the first place, the few moments it had been unshielded had not mattered. Besides, there were so many other concerns already being dealt with that it was doubtful anyone else had had the time to even notice the brief existence of the foul artifact.

"What do I do about you?" Cabe muttered not for the first time. He prodded the box ever so slightly. "I should destroy you now, that's what I should do." Destroying it was not truly the answer, however. That would only leave the incident unresolved, possibly forever. The box was proof.

He knew that, but the warlock could still not bring himself to take it to its former owner. *This could set kingdom against kingdom . . . create civil wars. . . .* Cabe wondered if the one responsible for the box had foreseen that. Had they actually *wanted* that?

Cabe? The voice that suddenly echoed in his head made him grateful he had also taken the precaution of shielding part of his mind. Despite the fact that she was now linked to her husband,

230

Lady Bedlam would *not* be aware of the thoughts running through his head. She, especially, could not be told just yet.

It was possibly the first time he had kept something of such importance hidden from her. Cabe struggled with the shame as he responded to her mental summons. *Yes?*

At last! came her response. *I was beginning to fear for you, you know! This isn't the first time I've tried to contact you.*

He grimaced. Cabe did not even know how long he had been sitting here, save that the small breakfast he had forced down no longer was enough to sustain him. At present, his stomach was sounding much like a volcano preparing to erupt. *I'm sorry.*

Where are you?

In my study.

The surprise was almost vocal. *Still? Darling—*

Before she could ask the question that he would again be forced to ignore, Cabe interjected, *What is it? You sound as if you have some news.*

I do. It was clear that she did not like her questions being shunted aside again, but knew better than to argue at this point. For that, the frustrated mage was happy. *This morning there was a missive from the Green Dragon.*

He straightened. "What does he want?" he asked out loud before recalling the link. Fortunately, asking the question was the same as framing it in his mind.

The master of Irillian by the Sea is demanding to see Kyl sooner than we'd planned. In fact, the missive clearly indicates that we can expect him to leave his kingdom tomorrow or the day after.

Of all the things that the missive might have contained, the meeting between Kyl and the Dragon Kings' chosen representative had been the only matter the warlock had *not* worried about. Yet, it should have not been so surprising. Of course the Dragon Kings would know almost instantly about the botched assassination; they would be justly concerned about the state of affairs at this point. This alteration in the schedule was as much to assess the change the attempt might have had on the heir's mental state as it was anything else. Cabe could not blame the drake lords, but he certainly wished that they had not reacted so. It meant one more terrible concern to add to the mountain already looming before him.

Is the meeting place still the same or has he changed that, also?

That's what makes this even more important. The Blue Dragon is coming here.

Cabe grunted. There really had been no reason to think that the Blue Dragon might have wanted to change the location of the meeting, but the warlock had wondered. Now he was being rewarded for that curiosity.

There is no stopping the Blue Dragon. Therefore, Lord Green would like one of us to come see him. There are some details that he would like to go over; things we might have to do differently now that the Manor is the location. I think he might have some concern about Penacles and its stability, too. The Dragon Kings might be anxious about the Gryphon resuming control. That may be one reason that Blue will not wait. I know that doesn't quite make sense, but the message indicated such a fear.

Toos only died the other day, the somber mage noted to his wife. *Does the entire continent already know?* There really was no reason to be concerned about the return of the lionbird to the throne of Penacles; the policies of the general and his former commander were of a like nature. If the Dragon Kings had not been overly fearful of the regent's rule, then the return of the Gryphon should not be bothering them that much. They could certainly not be thinking that the monarch of Penacles had war in mind. Cabe found the Green Dragon's fears questionable.

Will you go or shall I, Cabe?

He realized that he had drifted away from the silent conversation. The warlock tapped a finger on the arm of the chair. He knew what he wanted to say, and he also knew it was the coward's way. After some deliberation, Cabe finally sighed and replied, *I'll go.*

There was a still moment as she obviously waited for him to continue. When it evidently became clear that he had finished, the enchantress returned, *All right. I hope everything goes well.*

Her concern, her love, was quite genuine, as it always was, and knowing that only served to make him feel even more guilty for hiding what he knew from her. Not for the first time, he was amazed that she still loved him so after all these years.

It'll be fine, he promised.

Please hurry back.

"I won't stay any longer than need be," he promised out loud. A breath later, the link was broken. Left alone once more, Cabe at first resumed his pensive staring, but then guilt forced him to sit up. Guilt and the glimpse of some figure at the very edge of his vision. Using his body to shield the box from the newcomer, he quickly cast a spell that sent the artifact to one of the chests in which he stored objects. The chest was protected by other spells, so Cabe knew that the box would be secure there.

That left the intruder to deal with. The warlock finished turning around. "Who is—yes, scholar? Did you want something?"

It was indeed the form of Benjin Traske, but the huge man was acting in a peculiar manner. First, he did not respond to the mage's question. Second, the tutor appeared obsessed with the books just to the side and above where Cabe presently sat.

"Scholar Traske? I asked you a—"

Through the massive girth of the man the warlock could see the opposing wall.

The Benjin Traske before him was nothing more than one of the Manor's ghosts. Even as the realization sank in, the bearded figure, hand outstretched toward the shelf of tomes that Cabe kept in the study, ceased to be.

Knowing that the tutor had been in the study more than once in the past, Cabe's interest in the phantom dwindled somewhat. Out of habit, he located the notebook in which he kept track of all sightings and wrote down this latest addition to the parade of images. Cabe eyed the list, briefly wondering if he would ever discover the pattern or reasons for any of the ghostly intruders, then replaced the tome among the others. His gaze rested on some of the titles.

Aurim was still not free of Toma's spell. Cabe knew that he would not rest easy until that problem was also dealt with, but he had run out of ideas . . . of his own. It occurred to him now, though, that he had not consulted any of the books in his small collection here. Perhaps there was something he could quickly thumb through. It would but take a few minutes of his time to decide whether the books would be of any use. The Green Dragon could wait that long. Certainly Cabe could, if only for his son's sake, he told himself.

The master mage scanned the titles. To his disappointment, he knew almost immediately that he could eliminate virtually all of them. There was, however, one volume that he decided might offer some hint of what he sought. Cabe reached up, but as he took hold of the tome, the notebook, several volumes to the left, suddenly slipped and fell onto his desk. The book flipped open before him, revealing the page upon which he had just recorded his sighting of the Traske ghost.

Cabe took the book he was holding and set it aside. Then, with more care than he had apparently used the last time, the annoyed mage returned the notebook to the shelf, this time making certain that it would not slip again.

A quick glance through the book he had chosen revealed that it held no clue to a swift and safe manner by which to unbind the spell Toma had cast. In point of fact, it held *nothing* of use. Disgusted, the warlock rose from his chair and returned the tome to the shelf. As he pulled his hand away, Cabe happened to notice that the notebook was now a good third of the way over the edge. Quietly cursing himself for the carelessness with which he had undoubtedly returned the last book to the shelf, the warlock pushed the notebook back into place.

That took some doing. It was like trying to squeeze a watermelon into a wine goblet, but at last he managed to accomplish his task. *I'll have to transfer a few of these to the Manor library. This shelf is far too overladen.*

Giving up his quest for the time being, he turned from the shelf and mentally prepared himself for the journey to the Green Dragon's domain. It was not a meeting he looked forward to for many reasons, but Lord Blue's sudden decision made it necessary that alterations in the plan be made and made with swiftness. Gwendolyn had too much to contend with already; Cabe could not place this on her shoulders, too.

Steeling himself, the warlock pictured the lair of the lord of Dagora . . . and vanished.

Had he not been so engrossed in his thoughts, had he looked back even for a moment, Cabe Bedlam would have perhaps noticed one peculiar thing. The notebook that he had so carefully returned twice now was already slightly over the edge of the shelf . . . and *moving*.

"I have been thinking, Grath," announced Kyl. The heir to the dragon throne was visibly calmer than he had been previously—a good sign. For Kyl to fall to pieces this late in the game would have been tragic. Everything that had been planned depended upon his ascension to the throne. Grath had been ready to drag his brother to the throne if that was what it took to see the coronation done. After that, the younger drake would take his just due. That was fair enough, he thought. Grath deserved much for enabling things to have gone this far. Even his mentor had praised his efforts.

"What've you been thinking about, my brother?" He hoped that Kyl had not devised yet another insane plot for dealing with invisible assassins and the like. Kyl put on a devious front, but he lacked Grath's depth in cunning and subterfuge. Besides, the heir had a hidden ally who was working even now to prevent a reoccurrence of the travesty perpetrated in the regent's arena.

"Benjin Trassske."

"And what about our tutor?"

The two of them were in Kyl's chamber. Grath had been reading while his brother, becoming more daring since yesterday, had wandered to the balcony. Granted, the Manor was the one place where even Grath was certain nothing could happen, but the hours just after the assassination had left his elder brother in such a state that he had secluded himself in his bedchamber, not even deigning to eat his meals with the Bedlams, specifically Valea. The younger drake had been annoyed by such cowardice, for it had ruined a perfect opportunity to play on the beautiful witch's sympathies.

Kyl turned from the balcony, every inch the dazzling emperor-to-be he had been trained from birth to become. The improvement was remarkable and could easily be traced to the visit by the very person the heir now spoke of. "We have known Ssscholar Trassske for many yearsss, from the day he firssst came to educate us. How many yearsss isss that?" He waved aside the response that Grath was about to make. "I do not need the exact count. What I mean isss that throughout ssso long a period, the man hasss tutored usss well and guided usss as much asss any other. Hisss knowledge isss great and hisss ssskillsss many. Yesterday, I know that I sssaid he could not undersssstand all that I face, but today I sssee thingsss in a new light. Asss ever, he hasss been a steadying force." Kyl eyed his brother. "You ressspect him greatly, do you not?"

"More than you could ever know," replied Grath, suspecting where this was going but afraid to reveal his enthusiasm.

Unseen by the smiling Kyl, Faras and Ssgayn exchanged brief, unreadable glances.

"Asss I thought. My own admiration for him isss alssso very high. That isss why I think that I shall apologize to him for my earlier wordsss and asssk him quite sssincerely if he will join me after I become emperor and . . . and become a trusssted advisssor, sssecond to you, of course, brother."

Inside, Grath was fighting back the urge to cry out his triumph. The seed he had planted long ago had finally taken root: Kyl wanted his former tutor as a counselor. Keeping his voice properly restrained, Grath nodded his approval and replied, "I could not have made a better suggestion myself, Kyl."

"The only trouble may lie in whether he will accept." The heir paced back and forth, a habit that his brother secretly found very irritating. Kyl finally paused and looked again at Grath. "You have much influence with our dear teacher. Perhapsss if you presssented him with the offer, he might be more willing to agree. He isss human and a sssurvivor of Mito Pica, which definitely will be wallsss needing to be sssscaled—"

"No wall is too high for a dragon." It was an old drake saying, one which his mentor had taught him long ago. "I think that I can do it, Kyl. I think that he might be interested."

His brother's eyes drifted from his to fix upon the empty air. "It'sss almosssst time, Grath. Only the confrontation with Lord Blue remainsss asss a sssstumbling block." A hint of nervousness tinged his words. "That will prove an interessssting meeting."

"But one not to be fearful of." Grath put down the book he was reading and rose. He met Kyl's glare with a confident expression. "I am not insinuating that you are afraid, Kyl. Simply that you will so impress Lord Blue that none of the others will question him when he gives you his support. The rest will fall in line then, especially when they learn that the daughter of Cabe Bedlam follows you to Kivan Grath."

"Valea . . . " The look in the heir's emerald-gold countenance made it clear that the elder drake had completely forgotten about the enchantress he had been courting. "She may not come."

Grath walked over to his brother and straightened the narrow collar of Kyl's tunic. "You're wearing one of her favorite outfits. She finds you almost irresistible in it." He pretended as if an idea had just struck him rather than had been simmering since earlier in the morning. "You should look for her. Lead her to a place where the two of you can be alone. Now would be the best time to strike, to ask her to be *yours*."

Kyl looked uncomfortable. "She'll be expecting marriage. Asss emperor, I could only take one of our own kind asss a mate. You know that."

"Do you have to mention the word? A bonding is all you need talk about, Kyl, if you don't wish to lie. She *will* be bonded to you."

That brought a hiss of anger from the heir. "I would rather that she came *willingly*. I am not ssso loathsssome that I mussst ressort to a ssspell, am I?"

"Of course not, but we are rushed for time! When your position as emperor is more secure, then you can release her from the spell if you so wish." *By that time you will dare not, brother, and we both know it,* Grath silently added. Again, he knew that Kyl would tire of her as a female and see her only as a tool. The bond would allow her to keep her personality, but prevent her from disobeying her masters. Valea Bedlam would still need comfort . . . and giving that comfort would link her with Grath in a way that would grow stronger as the spell grew weaker. *You'll bring her with you for my interests alone, if nothing else. After all of this, I will have my rewards, too, and she will be my most prized!*

Slowly, the emperor-to-be agreed. "You are correct asss usssual, Grath. With you and Ssscholar Trassske to advissse me, I will make the throne of the Dragon Emperor once more the ultimate power in all the Dragonrealm!"

It will certainly have the proper flair for the dramatic! the younger drake decided, stepping away. "Speaking of our tutor, if I am to persuade him to join us, I must first talk to him. The sooner the better. You should do the same with Valea, Kyl."

"Yesss, you are correct, of course." As Grath started for the door, Kyl turned away from it. "But firssst, I should make certain that I am my very bessst. Then, she will not be able to help but be ssswept off her feet, asss the humansss sssay."

Grath held back a groan. There was, it had to be said, something for the way Kyl was behaving, but over the years he had grown weary of his brother's preening. Grath knew that he himself was considered quite fascinating to both human and drake females, but his role did not allow much time for making full use of his charms. It was Kyl who was supposed to be the mark of perfection.

But, in the end, she'll be mine. That's what matters. I will have the sorceress and I will be the true *lord of all the land!*

In only a matter of days. . . .

Only a matter of days left and I still haven't talked to him, Valea thought morosely as she walked the halls of the Manor. The ancient structure seemed so cold, so oppressive to her. She had not seen Kyl since he had retired to his chambers after the attempt on his life. Grath and Benjin Traske had both said that he was well, but clearly the botched assassination had had some effect. The young Lady Bedlam wanted dearly to go to Kyl and see if there was any comfort she could give him, but that would be throwing herself at him. She had her pride, after all.

That was *all* she would have if he left without speaking to her. While on one hand it was clearly ridiculous to think that he would remain in his rooms until his ascent to the throne, Valea could not help imagining that it might be so.

Ursa had been of little assistance in assuaging her fears, mostly because she had hardly been around. The female drake and Aurim were up to something in his room. Nothing romantic, of course. The two might as well have been brother and sister as far as Valea was concerned. They got along better at times than Valea and Aurim did. No, the young enchantress suspected that they were attempting to find the key to releasing her brother from the spell on his mind. Valea would have been worried if Aurim had tried to do this on his own, but with the more pragmatic and patient Ursa to guide him, it was possible that the two would succeed where even the Gryphon had so far failed.

Which still meant that she had no one to talk to about her situation. Mother was busy with some preparations and, as far as she knew, her father was still ensconced in his study, being moody over who knew what. She could not have talked to either of them, anyway, not about this.

Valea sighed and abstractly created a flying ring of roses that she then made spin slowly around and around. She bored of the sight very quickly, however, and changed the flowers to paper birds, who fluttered about and danced in some sort of aerial ballet her subconscious had decided upon.

There was only one person that she could turn to, only one person who would understand: Benjin Traske. She had tried to avoid disturbing him, for he, too, had seemed pressed since returning from Penacles. Twice Valea had tried to talk to him, but both times he had seemed preoccupied with something else.

I can only try. I have to talk to someone.

She turned down a hallway that would take her toward the scholar's chambers, the paper birds vanishing in little puffs of smoke as the young Lady Bedlam's concerns turned to what she would say to her tutor. He might not even have time to speak with her, but Valea had to try. She was fairly *bursting*. She needed someone close to talk to, and Scholar Traske had already more than proven himself in that regard. Had he not been the one to tell

Valea that Kyl loved her? Had she not discussed her quandary with him several times since then? If he could just give her a minute, it would at least make Valea feel a little better. Perhaps he would even have a solution.

It certainly could not hurt to ask.

There were times when the Manor seemed larger on the inside than it did from the outside, but Valea was fairly certain that the feeling was an illusion more than any magic inherent in the ancient edifice. There was no denying that the unknown builders had been great craftsmen. The enchantress did not even mind the long walk this time, for there were still things that she had to resolve with herself.

Along her path she met few others. Most of the people were outside, either working or enjoying the weather. The Manor itself was a surprisingly easy place to care for; it practically cared for itself. Valea had often thought that the true purpose of the many servants in the house was to give it some life. Granted, this had been her home since birth, but the Manor could seem very lonely when no one else was about.

She hated to think what it would be like if she was left behind after Kyl headed north to his throne.

Valea turned down yet another corridor and, because her mind was engrossed in her terrible problem, she did not at first see the figure at the other end of the hall. Only when she heard the sound of boots did she stir from her contemplations.

To her surprise and pleasure, it was Benjin Traske himself. The scholar had evidently not been in his room after all, but the direction in which he was heading indicated that he was likely on his way there now. The young woman wanted to call to him, but she had been raised not to do such mannerless things as shout across halls, so Valea had to content herself with increasing her pace and hoping that she might attract his attention before he entered his chambers.

Valea reached the intersecting corridor and followed after the scholar, but despite his immense girth, Benjin Traske was a swift man. Already he was nearly to the door of his chambers. She tried to hurry more, feeling somehow that to disturb him after he stepped inside was a greater inconvenience to the tutor. Benjin Traske had been so kind to her, she wanted to be as little trouble as possible to him.

Concentrating on reaching the scholar, Valea paid no attention to the side corridors and alcoves. There was no reason to do so.

That was why when the draconian figure stepped out from around a corner she did not at first notice him. Only when he rushed silently toward Traske's unprotected back did she pay him any heed.

Only *then* did the enchantress see the curved blade rise.

Her reaction was instinctive, the memory of the regent's death and Kyl's near assassination still fresh. She raised a hand in the direction of the would-be killer and cried, "Nooo!"

The assassin hesitated, obviously surprised to have been discovered. Valea was never able to unleash her spell, however, for with reflexes surprising even for Benjin Traske, the heavyset scholar whirled around to protect himself. The two figures became tangled together. Uncertain as to the effectiveness of her spell, she dared not use it for fear that the tutor would also suffer. Hoping for a better opportunity, Valea rushed forward. If the two separated for even a moment, she wanted to be ready.

Traske and his attacker spun about. For the first time, Valea saw the countenance of the assassin—saw it and stumbled to a halt as she tried to make sense of what was happening.

It was *Ssarekai*. As difficult as it was for most humans to recognize individual drakes from a distance, she knew the stable master too well not to know it was him now. Dear sweet Ssarekai, who had helped train her to ride her first horse and, later, her first riding drake. Ssarekai, who listened to her stories and told fascinating ones of his own about the days of the Dragon Emperor. Servitor drakes saw much that their superiors did not realize.

Dear sweet Ssarekai was trying to murder Scholar Traske?

She remained where she was, caught up in her confusion. Valea could think of no reason for the drake's behavior at first, but then her chaotic thoughts happened to touch upon the spell that Toma had woven into the minds of both Ssarekai and her brother. Was this attack the result of that?

The two hissing combatants seemed not to recall her at all as they spun back and forth, the blade dangling between them. Ssarekai still held it, but Benjin Traske had his wrist and was trying to push the blade toward the face of his adversary.

"I know you again!" Ssarekai suddenly hissed. "I should have sssmelled your foul . . . foul ssscent and recognized it! You were alwaysss ssso certain of yourself!"

Traske did not reply, but his bearded face had taken on a most—*evil*, was the only word Valea could find that fit—look, and as he pressed his counterattack, he appeared almost inhuman.

His eyes seemed to blaze. His lips curled back in what reminded her of the toothy reptilian "smile" of an angry drake.

She still did not know what to do. Somehow, the young sorceress could not bring herself to try to bring down the drake, no matter that he had tried to murder her teacher. There was something about the desperation in Ssarekai's voice and the increasingly dark visage of Benjin Traske that prevented her from doing what should have seemed obvious. Summoning aid did not even enter her mind, so ensnared was she in the situation. Two of those who had been a part of her life from the beginning were fighting to the death, and she could not decide which one to save.

The blade inched closer to the drake's half-concealed face. Ssarekai evidently saw the inevitability of its path, for suddenly he released the knife, sending it clattering to the floor. At the same time, Valea felt a tug on the powers from which all mages drew, a sign that a spell of great magnitude was being formed and executed in rapid order.

Ssarekai opened his mouth as if to scream, but no sound emerged. The drake froze in place and his entire form turned a mottled gray.

It was Benjin Traske who had released the spell, the novice sorceress realized: Benjin Traske, who was supposed to have barely enough ability to raise a *feather* a few inches from the ground.

It was Benjin Traske, a man who, still engrossed in crushing his opponent, was also beginning to melt.

More and more he looked less human. His mouth was open in a triumphant smile, but the teeth within were noticeably jagged even from where Valea stood. The scholar's skin had taken on a peculiar coloring, one that was faintly . . . *green*? He looked taller, thinner, and beneath his robes it seemed as if he might be wearing armor. Even the blade he always wore on his belt had changed, for now it gleamed as if it had become a source of light itself.

Benjin Traske was a drake.

He could be only one drake, but Valea tried to deny it. Tried and failed, for too many things were falling in place, many of them involving her.

The stern but understanding man who had taught her and the others over the years was in reality the most hated creature in the Dragonrealm. He was Duke Toma, the renegade.

He began to turn her way. His face and form were again solidifying into the one she was so familiar with, but it would be impossible for Valea to ever believe that what she had just witnessed had been some illusion.

Traske/Toma fixed his gaze on her. "Valea—"

She transported herself away without even thinking of where it would be best to go. The hallway before the tutor's chamber door became another corridor. At first, the enchantress was uncertain as to where she had chosen to flee, but slowly Valea recognized her location. She was near Kyl's room . . . only a few yards from his door, in fact.

It was impossible to move. The realization of what she had just witnessed was finally catching up to her. Valea stood where she was, gasping for air and shaking. Only now did guilt touch her; guilt for leaving poor brave Ssarekai to Toma. It mattered not that she could have done nothing, but the weary sorceress felt that she should have been able to do *something*.

Ssarekai must have recalled what it was the spell Toma had put on him had made him forget. That suppressed memory had probably concerned the horrible truth about Benjin Traske. Something had stirred the stable master's memory enough to break the spell. Why Ssarekai had chosen the path he had, a daring assassination attempt, she did not know, but it likely would have succeeded if Valea had not chosen to be there at that moment.

I have to warn everyone. Stirring, she tried to recall where her mother and father were. Father had been in his study. Perhaps he was still there. Valea tried to focus on the blue-robed figure. Father would make things right; he had always managed to overcome what she had often considered impossible odds. He would save them all from Toma.

Perhaps he would have, if he had been in his study. Valea called to her father, but sensed only that he had been in the Manor but recently, which helped her not in the least. Toma could only be moments behind her. Valea knew what sort of chance she stood against the renegade. Toma was a spellcaster on a par with her parents. Aurim, whose skill and power were greater than hers at the moment, had easily fallen victim to the drake.

She was almost ready to begin an attempt to contact her mother when the door to Kyl's chambers swung open. The scarlet-tressed woman paused as the tall, elegant figure of the heir stepped into the corridor.

"Valea?" Kyl's mouth broke into a dazzling smile, making Valea almost forget what was happening. "Thisss *isss* a pleasssant sssurprise, I mussst sssay! I wasss jussst—"

The sound of his voice stirred her to action. She seized him by the arms and cried, "Kyl! Toma's in the Manor! Toma, he's right behind—"

Confusion and dismay spread across the drake's exotic visage. He looked at her close. "What'sss that? What are you sssaying?"

Before she could answer, however, an armored drake stepped out of Kyl's chamber. Whether it was Faras or his counterpart Ssgayn, Valea could not at that moment have said. "My lord! We heard her ssspeak of Toma!"

"She sssays that—"

The guard did not wait for him to finish. He took hold of each of the two by an arm and began to steer them inside the room. "Bessst not to talk out here, my lord! What Toma cannot see he may not find! Hurry!"

Valea wanted to protest, but Ssgayn—she had recognized his voice at last—already had them through the doorway. As he led them through, Faras, standing nearby, closed the door and bolted it.

"We can't simply wait here!" the sorceress finally shouted. "Toma will come here before long!"

"I agree." Kyl hissed in obvious nervousness. "Toma! I was jussst ssspeaking of him, wasss I not?"

The two guards nodded solemnly.

Valea had no time for this. Again she took hold of Kyl. Another time, such close contact would have thrilled her, but now what mattered was their lives. "Listen, Kyl! I tried to contact my father, but I couldn't find him. I'll try my mother, but you have to know something first. He's *Benjin Traske*, Kyl! Benjin Traske!"

The heir apparently misunderstood her. "Toma hasss the ssscholar? Where? How?"

"No! Benjin Traske *is* Duke Toma! I discovered it by accident. He caught poor Ssarekai, who tried to kill him."

Kyl simply stood there, as if unable to accept what he was hearing. "Ssscholar Trassske isss *Toma*?"

The two guards said nothing, but both had grown very tense. Valea could hardly blame them; how many times had they left their lord with the tutor, not realizing the truth? "I have to try my mother. Everyone is in danger! I think he dares not hide any longer, Kyl! He had to fight Ssarekai and he knows that I saw him!"

"No more talk, then, my enchantress! Do what mussst be done." He gave her an encouraging smile.

Strengthened by that, Valea put as much will as she had left to muster into the magical summons. She had no idea where her father must be, but her mother was usually in the same place at this time of day. If she failed to contact Lady Bedlam, Valea then planned on trying a scattered call, which, theoretically, would send her message to all parts of the Manor. Valea had trouble with that method, though, which was why she hoped that she was successful with her first attempt.

However, a peculiar thing happened when she tried to reach out and make contact with her mother. Valea felt the summons stretch forth from her mind, felt it building in strength, but when she tried to reach out beyond Kyl's chamber, it was as if she had run into a mental wall. She tried to push harder, but still could sense nothing beyond the room. Valea tried again, but the results were the same. Try as she might, she could not have contacted her mother even if the emerald enchantress had been standing on the other side of the door to Kyl's suite.

Toma knew where they were. It was the only answer.

"What isss wrong? Why are you shivering?"

Shivering? Valea had not even noticed that she was shivering, but under the circumstances, she did not think that she could be blamed for doing so. Quickly, Valea explained what had happened.

After she was done, Kyl glanced at his two guards, but their faces betrayed nothing. Valea simply assumed that they would follow whatever command he gave them. She had never been close to either Ssgayn or Faras, but then, they had never tried to be more than what they were. It was as if they had been born to be bodyguards all their lives.

"Perhapsss . . . " Kyl began. "Perhapsss if we pool our abilities, Valea. I have alwaysss thought that between the two of usss, we could accomplish mossst anything!" He gave her a brief smile. "But talk of that can wait. What do you think? If your power and mine were combined, we might be able to contact one of your parentsss or, if need be, even deal with the renegade."

This at last caused the two guards to move. It was clear that they did not relish the idea of Kyl fighting Toma.

"My lord—" Faras began.

"Sssilence! Well, Valea?"

Someone rapped on the door. A moment later, a familiar voice hissed, "Kyl! Let me in!"

Grath! Valea had completely forgotten about Kyl's brother. She had simply assumed that he was in one of the connecting rooms. If Grath had been elsewhere all this time, then he, too, had been in danger. In fact . . .

The heir hissed. "I sssent him to talk to Benjin Trasssske! Thank the Dragon of the Depthsss that he isss safe! Open the door! Quickly now!"

Faras had almost unbolted the door when Valea called, "No! You can't!"

The drake paused, then looked to Kyl for guidance. "My lord, your brother isss in danger while he is out there. You know that your chambersss are alssso spelled against intrusion by sssorcery."

Kyl waved aside Valea's protests. "I know my own brother's voice . . . and his mind." He turned to face the door. "Grath! Did you ssspeak with Ssscholar Trassske asss I asked you?"

"No!" returned the voice. "I— Kyl, you would not believe what I have to tell you! Let me in!"

"Let him in," whispered the emperor-to-be to Faras. "But I want all of you ready. Even Toma would not think to take the four of usss on, now would he?" The last was obviously for Valea's benefit. She was certain that he was making a mistake, but there was nothing that she could do. Besides, it was cruel to let Grath remain out there. If he *was* alone, each second he was forced to wait left him vulnerable.

Faras unbolted the door and peeked around it. Ssgayn and Kyl stood ready, the guard with a sword and Kyl with a spell of some kind. Valea readied a crude but powerful spell of her own. If Grath was the puppet of Toma . . .

Slowly, Faras swung the door back just enough for a single person to slip through. Grath, or at least someone who looked exactly like him, did just that. Once the figure was through, the draconian guard immediately shut and rebolted the door.

"There isss sssome reasssonable concern that you might not be who you look like, Grath." Kyl's tone was incredibly apologetic. "I hope you will forgive usss for having to determine the truth."

Grath stood still, his arms hanging at his sides. "I am me, but if you need to verify my honesty, please do so in whatever way you feel most suitable, Kyl."

Kyl looked at the guards. "Are you ready, jussst in cassse?"

The two nodded. Satisfied, the dragon heir stepped in front of the one who might be his brother. He carefully reached out and put one hand on Grath's shoulder.

Valea felt the power that passed between them. All those with even the most minor tendency for sorcery had a special magical signature, a particular touch, that other mages could sense if they knew how. For two with as strong a bond as the brothers, it was virtually impossible to fool either one of them with a false signature. Even Toma would be hardpressed to mask his own magical pattern as that of Grath.

Kyl exhaled as he removed his hand. "You are Grath."

"Of course I am."

"We could not be certain. We could not trussst that it wasss you, brother."

Grath eyed him, an enigmatic expression on his face. He glanced Valea's way very briefly, then returned his gaze to Kyl. "*Do* you trust me, Kyl?"

The heir was surprised by the question. "With my life!"

"And you should know that I want nothing more than to see you on the throne. That is why you must trust me now."

Valea did not care for Grath's tone. She took a step toward him, not quite certain as to why he was making her nervous. "What do you have in mind, Grath? Do you have some sort of plan in mind for dealing with Toma?"

He looked at her. "You have tried to contact your parents?"

"I couldn't find my father and something prevented me from contacting Mother." Grath's calm was annoying her. Did he not realize how dire a situation they faced?

Grath reached up and put a comforting hand on her shoulder. "That's what I wanted to know. Thank you."

She wanted to ask him what he meant by such an odd response, but then she noticed the buildup of power within him. Too late did she realize that she had yet *again* been betrayed. As she tried to pull free of his grip, a grip suddenly tight and painful, her body refused to follow her desires. Instead, Valea found herself unable to move, unable to even speak.

"What have you done to her?" snarled Kyl, realizing too late that his brother had cast a spell on the startled witch.

Grath looked beyond his brother. "Faras. Ssgayn."

She could still see, and so at the edge of her vision Valea was able to watch as Kyl's two trusted bodyguards seized hold of their emperor-to-be and kept him pinned by the arms no matter how much he struggled.

"We are sssorry to do thisss, Your Majesssty," Faras added with much anxiety.

Grath stood before his brother. "If you will calm down and listen, I can have them release you that much sooner. I am sorry about this, but you didn't look as if you were going to wait for me to explain. Will you please do that now, Kyl?"

"I ssseem to have little *choice* in the matter, *brother*!"

"Actually, you have much choice. Do you remember our conversation just a short while ago? How we talked about the throne and the troubles it has brought? We talked about Toma, didn't we?"

Grath's transformation dismayed the frozen Valea. She had always known him to be a studious, somewhat shy person. He had always walked in the shadow of his brother, although even she would have been willing to admit that Kyl had always benefited from his advice. Now, however, Grath more resembled a smooth, cunning courtier, like some of those the young Lady Bedlam had met among the aristocracy of Penacles or Talak.

Kyl did not reply to his brother save to reluctantly nod.

"We've talked about Toma, our *brother*, before. You and I both know that he wasss loyal to our father and remained with him long after the other Dragon Kingsss had abandoned him. You know that he wasss there to rescue us from Lord Ice when we became caught between the machinations of the mad lord of the Northern Wastes and Master Bedlam. Among all the drakes, Kyl, you will have to admit that no one hasss been more loyal to the throne than he."

That was not quite the history that Valea had grown up knowing. It was close enough to the truth, however, to disguise itself as fact. Her father would have been able to relate the entire tale, but she doubted that anyone but she would have listened.

"I remember the Northern Wastes, I think," Kyl admitted with reluctance.

"Toma can never be emperor. You know that. I know that. *He* knows that. He has known that for years. Therefore, only one path was left open to him. Despite the need to hide, despite the enemies who have sought to kill him because he represents the might of the emperor, the duke has continued to work to see the day that a new, stronger leader will bring our kind back to the preeminence we once held."

Slowly, Grath stepped back to the bolted door. He reached for the bolt. "No one is more regretful than he that all his work had to be done under the guise of another. He had hoped to present himself to you after your crowning. His life would have been yours to take or end there. At least the goal he has sought for the last several years would then be secure."

Valea tried her best to break the spell that held her, but Grath had cast it too well. She doubted that even Aurim would have been able to escape.

Unbolting the door, the younger drake seized the handle. He looked so very apologetic to his brother that Valea wanted to spit in his face. "Kyl, I present to you one who isss not your enemy, has never *been* your enemy, but rather has been your most loyal servant . . . even moressso than I, I have to admit."

The drake swung open the door. Valea's heart sank as Benjin Traske entered.

"Ssscholar . . ." Kyl muttered, more awestruck, the sorceress was sad to see, than fearful.

"Not scholar, my lord," said the massive figure, and even as he strode forward, he resembled less and less the bearded tutor and more and more something terribly inhuman. Then the scholar began to melt. The heavy girth became a river of glowing liquid that faded as it poured away. Yet, while Benjin Traske grew thinner, he also grew taller still.

Traske's clothing also changed. Quickly the scholar's robe became armor, scaled armor that covered the teacher from head to toe. His hands twisted and the fingers lengthened, becoming much like those of either of the brothers.

Kyl gaped and Grath smiled as the face also became something different. The stern, bearded visage pulled in and the head reshaped itself, at last forming a partial shell. The shell defined itself into a helm within which the last vestiges of Benjin Traske reformed into the flat, incomplete features of a drake warrior. Yet, unlike most drake warriors, the helm of this one had as elaborate a dragon head crest as any of the drake lords themselves.

Crossing the little distance that still remained between the two of them, the immense drake warrior stopped, then knelt before the dragon heir. Within the false helm, the lipless mouth curved into a toothy smile.

"Your Majesssty," announced Grath as he shut the door and bolted it again. "It pleases me to presssent your mosssst humble and *loyal* sssservant, *Duke Toma* of Kivan Grath."

XVIII

Cabe wound his way through the vast underground cavern of the Green Dragon, his escorts trying their best to keep pace with the hurrying warlock. Having known the Dragon King for as long as he had, Cabe could have transported himself directly to the main hall of the subterranean labyrinth without asking permission, but he had needed the time to think. Think and plan.

"This way," he muttered, turning down yet another corridor. The guards and guide stumbled after him. None of them thought to order him to slow down, for everyone who followed the master of the Dagora Forest knew of the warlock and how powerful he was said to be. He was also known to be a friend and ally of their lord. If there *had* been some question as to his motives, then they would have tried their best to either capture or kill him, but it would not have been something any of the guards would have looked forward to with eagerness. They were quite aware of their chances against the robed figure stalking ahead of them.

Only at the end of the corridor did Cabe at last pause. Here at last was the great central chamber that the Green Dragon utilized as his throne room and hall. Here the Dragon King met his guests.

Unlike the caverns of most of his counterparts, that of the Green Dragon was covered with lush plant life, most of it of the kind that should not have been able to thrive so far from the sun. Yet, thanks to the power and skill of the drake lord, vines, shrubs, and flowering plants made the chamber resemble more a forest than a cave. Over the past few years, the Dragon King had re-designed this hall, adding further to his vast collection of foliage.

In the midst of the underground grove and seated upon his throne was the armored form of the Dragon King himself. He was flanked on each side by the fiercest pair of guards that Cabe could recall ever having faced. As was typical of Lord Green, one of the guards was a drake, but the other was a human. It was debatable which was the more terrible of the two. The Green Dragon prided himself in carrying on the ways of his predecessors; here, humans and drakes were almost as equal as at the Manor. What made things different in Cabe's home, however, was that it was a human who ruled there, not a Dragon King. The experiment at the Manor represented the first time that drakes had ever coexisted peacefully with humans in a place where they did not dominate. The idea had been the Green Dragon's.

There was so much about his host that the warlock had always admired.

"Thank you for coming, Friend Cabe." The reptilian knight indicated a chair that had been set near his throne. The chair was set on a level with the Dragon King's own, which was supposed to indicate the drake's long-standing belief in the equality of the two races, but the mage had always noticed that both Lord Green and his throne stood *taller*. He had often wondered whether that was intentional, or whether the Dragon King had simply never noticed it.

"Thank you, but I prefer to stand." Behind him, his escorts vanished down one of the other tunnels.

The Green Dragon straightened a bit. "As you desire. You know the contents of the missive, then?"

"Gwendolyn informed me, yes. It's not surprising when you think about it. Not even the fact that Lord Blue is coming here. Of all the Dragon Kings, other than yourself, of course, he is the only one I would trust enough to allow entry, *temporary* entry in his case, into the Manor."

"Yesss, I trust him, too. The others are upssset, Friend Cabe, although none of them would be able to give you the same reasons."

Cabe frowned. "Imagine what they would have been like if the assassins *had* succeeded in murdering Kyl. Thank goodness for Grath, if that should happen."

It appeared to take Lord Green time to translate what he was saying. "Yesss, we may be thankful that if some tragedy did seize the life of the heir, may the Dragon of the Depths prevent such, there would be Grath to step in and take hisss place."

"We've often commented to one another that he would make just as good, possibly *better*, an emperor as Kyl."

The Dragon King shifted position. "That we have, which is not to say that Kyl isss not already coming into his own. He will do sssplendidly, I am sure."

Cabe walked around the chair set aside for him. He stared the drake lord in the eye. The warlock heard the guards suddenly straighten but paid them little mind.

"*You* are the one who sent the assassins to murder Kyl. *You*, my Lord Green, tried to have your new emperor killed. We both know that, don't we?"

The guards readied their weapons and started for the warlock, but the armored tyrant raised a mailed hand. Both warriors paused, but the glares they gave Cabe Bedlam were dark and murderous.

"Friend Cabe, are you aware of the wordsss you jussst spoke? We have known each other since you firssst were forced to acknowledge your heritage. I consider you and yours not only close allies but close companionsss as well."

"Which doesn't change the fact that *you* tried to murder Kyl and ended up murdering *Toos*."

There was an edge to the Green Dragon's voice. "How could you sssay something like that?"

"You captured Darkhorse," the bitter sorcerer went on, ignoring both the questions of his host and the seething faces of the guards. "As good as tortured him by using that box. I think that you had confidence enough to handle everyone but Darkhorse . . . and you found a way to make use of his power, too. You forgot one thing, though. I know you as well as anyone does. We've discussed the history of the Vraad over and over. I've seen your collection, and I know from my own researches some of the tricks and toys that my unesteemed ancestors devised, especially when they realized that most of them were losing their vast powers." Cabe folded his arms. "There was also the band of assassins that I was supposed to think was part of an Aramite plot. Drakes and humans working together on this? Did you *want* to be discovered, my lord? Was that why you made it so obvious to me?"

He knew that he had really said little that could directly be tied to the Dragon King, that would have been considered proof by anyone, but to the warlock's sad surprise, the Green Dragon slumped back in his throne. He glanced back at the guards and commanded, "Leave usss, pleasssse."

With obvious reluctance, the two obeyed.

When they were alone, the lord of Dagora finally spoke. "I do not know whether I desssired to be found out, Cabe Bedlam, or sssimply wasss so full of anxiety and horror at what I was doing that I did not take more care. Yesss, I *am* the one responsible for nearly assassinating Kyl and inssstead killing the brave and honorable regent of Penacles."

Try as he might, Cabe could no longer stay angry. Instead, disappointment was all he felt. Great disappointment. It was as if the world he had known had proven to be a falsehood. In some ways, it was even more terrible than when he had been torn from his uninteresting existence as a server at an inn and thrust into a world of sorcery and intrigue. He had learned so much from the Dragon King, shared so much with him. There were few beings that the warlock felt comfortable with; in the small circle of true friends he had thought he had, the Dragon King had been one.

Yet, after what the drake lord had done . . .

"I did what I felt was necessary, warlock. Kyl was an arrogant, conceited creature who threatened to repeat the mistakes of hisss sire. Grath, who the powersss that be had brought to this world *after* his brother, wasss by far a more level sssort. He would deal with the relations of both races fairly, evenly. Kyl might suddenly be of the mind to reconquer the continent, plunging usss all into a war none can afford. He might even be the great enemy of hisss own kind, for I know that he still holdsss much bitterness toward sssome of the surviving kings for abandoning his predecessor. Kyl isss even the sort who might find the renegade, Toma, more of an ally than a danger."

"I find *that* hard to believe."

The Green Dragon rose from his throne and looked down at the human. Cabe did not flinch, much less back away. "*I* do not."

The warlock matched his counterpart's gaze. He was not pleased, however, when the Dragon King finally looked away. Things should not have deteriorated to such a point that the two had to attempt to stare one another down. "Kyl had Grath to guide him."

"But our esteemed emperor-to-be doesss not have to *listen* to hisss brother. Should Kyl grow furiousss at something Grath suggests, he has only to order his brother from hisss sight. Then, the voices that whisper in his ears will become those of my fellow kings' spiesss. Where would the Dragonrealm be then? No, the only certain method by which the stability of the throne could be assured was to remove Kyl and replace him with Grath."

"I don't agree." Cabe shook his head, still unable to completely believe that the figure before him had created so much chaos and tragedy. "That also doesn't condone what you did to Toos and

Darkhorse—or the Gryphon. Toos was a brother to the Gryphon, my Lord Green; you saw what the general's death meant to him. He wants the one responsible. So does Darkhorse."

The inhuman knight started to turn away. "I did what I knew *had* to be—"

"Don't turn from me!" roared Cabe. Without meaning to, he almost unleashed a spell on the recalcitrant monarch. Cabe barely contained it in time, and the power was such that his body glowed red for several seconds afterward.

The Green Dragon stared at him, jaw hanging. The warlock calmed enough to see that, for the first time, the Dragon King was truly afraid of him.

"I should tell them the truth, you know! Both Darkhorse and the Gryphon *deserve* to know. Do you realize the extent of Darkhorse's claustrophobia? He existed in a place without time or end. I know that the Vraad used a box very much like that to capture him! He's never told me everything, but I've never seen as much terror in his eyes as when he is reminded of that!"

"What did you do with the box?" interrupted the drake lord.

"I still have it. It damned you more than anything else; I could recognize your knowledge in it. No one else had access to such an artifact, and no one else would have understood it the way you do!" Again, the accusations were flimsy, but now that Cabe had had confirmation of his suspicions from the Green Dragon himself, the claims had weight. "There was so much. The spells that masked one magical trace with another. The cloaks of the assassins—men you callously assured would not live so that anyone questioning them would discover the truth. They died too easily, Lord Green. Even the Aramite. *More* futile deaths on your shoulders."

"I will take no blame for their deaths, Cabe Bedlam! They were condemned criminals, one and all. They would have been executed. I am not like Black, who would carelessly send his enchanted human legions against the walls of his enemies again and again until the mindless unfortunates either overran the foe or died to a man!"

The warlock, his face carefully neutral, shrugged. "I don't know *what* you're like anymore."

"I am as I have *always* been."

"That worries me even more, then. What will you decide next serves your needs? The deaths of me and my loved ones?"

The Dragon King hissed and his talons unsheathed. "Of course not!"

"How can I believe that anymore?"

For several seconds, the tall, armored tyrant stood there, eyes burning embers, claws at the ready. Then, the talons slowly sheathed and the fire in his eyes died. Lord Green returned to his throne and slumped back into it again. "There isss no promise that I could give you that you would believe, isss there?"

Cabe slumped, too. This had taken more out of him than the drake lord knew. "No. There isn't."

"Will you tell the others, then? Shall I prepare to receive the visitations of either the eternal or the lionbird?"

"It would mean only more chaos and tragedy, neither of which we can afford these days."

It was clear that his reply puzzled the Dragon King. "Are you saying that you will keep what you know a sssecret?"

Some of Cabe's anger returned. "Not because of the friendship we once had, but because if peace is to work in the land, nothing else can go wrong. I may not even tell Gwendolyn, although I probably will. I know that she'll think as I do, that we can't afford another war." He paused. "What she'll think of you, I couldn't say."

His host nodded slowly. "I understand what you sssay. I understand your view of thisss. You will do nothing else?"

"There's nothing I can do that wouldn't make the situation worse than it is. I'm more concerned now with seeing this coronation through to the end . . . with Kyl assuming his *rightful* place. When he's emperor, then we can judge his abilities. No sooner. Prejudgment is no one's right, however often we *all* fall prey to it."

Silence filled the chamber for several seconds. The Dragon King finally looked up into the eyes of the warlock and quietly asked, "Isss there more? I had assumed you would be gone the moment your piece had been sssaid."

Cabe took a deep breath and smoothed his robe. "We still have Lord Blue's change in plans to talk about. We still have to make all of this work. Are you prepared to accept things the way they are?"

"After Penaclesss, I swore that I would do nothing else to risssk this peace. I desire it as much as you, even if it meansss Kyl on the throne."

With a small flicker of power, the exhausted warlock brought the other chair to him. He also enlarged it slightly, this in order to allow him to look directly into the eyes of his host, not *up* at them. "Then we should begin. Tell me what I need to know about the Blue Dragon and what he might have planned for Kyl."

The Dragon King began to discuss his counterpart, but although the conversation became more comfortable as they went on, Cabe knew that his relationship with the drake lord would never be the same.

Aurim sat cross-legged on his bed while Ursa sat next to him. His fingertips were pressed against his temple and his eyes were shut tight. Although he could not see her, he knew that the drake watched him with concern. Neither of his parents knew what he was doing. That was fine with him; they had far too much on their minds already. He had relied on them and their friends far too long. It was time to prove that all the talk of potential meant something.

The young warlock intended to break Toma's spell on his own.

Not *completely* on his own. Ursa was assisting him, albeit with reluctance. Some of the paths he had tried required more manipulation than he could muster by himself. She was also there in case something *did* go wrong . . . which he had assured her several times would *not* happen.

His methods of search bordered on the unorthodox. Aurim had already observed his parents and the Gryphon going through most of the more normal paths, and not a few unusual ones they were familiar with, which left him only the ones he was taking. One of those methods, he was certain, had to be the key to unraveling the renegade's spell.

The past few minutes had left him encouraged in that respect. It was difficult to be certain, but Aurim almost felt as if the web Toma had spread over his mind had weakened a little more. It *felt* different.

"Are you all right, Aurim?"

"Yes." He dared not answer further. At the moment, the tiny magical probe he was guiding was slipping past one of the multiple safeguards Toma had planted. This was his first *major* triumph over the spell. The warlock felt the pressure in his head ease just a bit more as he removed the safeguard and weakened the spell further.

Images flashed in his mind. Ssarekai, a look of shock on his face that even the dim light of night illuminated all too well. A figure halfway between two forms, and although neither had been recognizable, he had known that one of them was Toma.

There was something more, but it remained just out of his mental reach.

"I've broken through," he whispered, glancing up briefly at Ursa. His throat felt astonishingly dry. "Just a little, but I've made more progress than they did the other day."

She clapped her hands together. "How *wonderful!*"

"It gets harder here, though. I think that I might need for you to—" Aurim was interrupted by a knock on the door. The sound shattered his concentration, which, in turn, shattered his probe. The warlock was frustrated, but at least he had forged further than anyone else. Once he dealt with the interruption, Aurim intended to try a stronger probe in an area near the location he had just freed. If the safeguard Toma had planted there also fell to him, Aurim suspected that he stood a good chance of completely dismantling the spell before it was time for dinner.

"I'll see who it is," offered Ursa.

Aurim was glad to let her. The moment he tried to rise, the room began to whirl.

The drake opened the door. "Yes? Scholar Traske!"

Aurim glanced toward the door to see the huge tutor waiting in the hallway. A shiver went down his spine as he met the eyes of the man.

Now why—he started to think, but then Benjin Traske spoke, interrupting Aurim's train of thought.

"My apologies. I expected to find you alone, Master Aurim."

"Ursa was just helping me with something." He hoped that the scholar would not ask what it was with which she had been assisting. Aurim was fairly certain that Traske would not have approved. Likely the tutor would have reprimanded him and then informed his parents.

"I see." Benjin Traske took a step closer. "May I enter?"

Ursa quickly darted aside. Aurim slid over to the edge of the bed, lowered his legs, and started to stand, but Traske raised a hand to stop him. "Sit, please. There's no need to stand, boy."

Ursa started to move for the open door. "I should leave you two alone. If you will excussse me, Scholar Traske, then I—"

"No, I think it's best at this point that *you* stay also. Yes, that would be for the best, indeed. Why don't you close the door and sit down next to Aurim. That will make everything much *easier* for me."

Puzzled, she nonetheless obeyed his suggestion, closing the door, then settling down beside the curious warlock.

It seemed to Aurim that Benjin Traske was apprehensive about something. There was just the slightest hesitation in his movements and his breathing was a bit fast. "Are you all right, Scholar Traske?"

"Sssome decisions had to be made at the proverbial spur of the moment, Master Aurim. They are not decisions that I am comfortable with, but there really is no other choice that I can see at this time."

"What do you mean?"

The tutor advanced so that he was within arm's reach of both of them. He looked down at the two with what Aurim believed almost fatherly concern. Why not? Benjin Traske had watched all of them grow up. Surely he must sometimes think of them as his own children?

Putting a hand on each of their shoulders, the tutor sighed, a sound that was almost a hiss. A slight smile peered out from within the beard. "I mean that I can take no chancesss."

Aurim felt the power swelling within Benjin Traske, but the comprehension was too late in coming. A thick malaise suddenly enveloped his mind. Somewhere distant, he heard Ursa gasp. Traske himself seemed to shift, becoming something else briefly, something that stirred memories.

The warlock *remembered*. It did him no good to do so, but nonetheless, he remembered. He remembered seeking out with his power and, through it, discovering something terrible happening. Ssarekai, his mind pleading, had been put under some spell. The other mind, that of the caster of the spell, had been two minds. On the surface, it had been Benjin Traske. Below, it had been a creature most vile.

Toma. Aurim had discovered that Benjin Traske was Toma.

He managed to rise to his feet, but that was all. Even that made the false Traske hiss in surprise. Then, however, the golden-haired warlock's strength gave out and he fell back onto the bed.

Consciousness fled.

Although she had no control over her movements, Valea found that she could still shed a tear. Her world was in tatters. Benjin Traske was—possibly had always been—Duke Toma, the deadly renegade. He had listened to her as she had revealed all her deepest secrets to him. He had betrayed the trust her entire family had placed in him. Now, evidently in part because of her, Traske/Toma was going to seize control of the Manor by making one last use of his false identity. The drake intended to use the face of Benjin Traske to get close enough to each member of the family, whereupon he would catch them unaware with his power.

She had no idea why he did not kill them all outright. She did not even have any idea as to why he had left her frozen like a statue in Kyl's room, her mind still very much functioning.

None of that completely explained the tears. Valea was well aware that much of the reason for her crying concerned Kyl. Kyl and his betrayal of her.

The other drakes remained in the room, awaiting Duke Toma's return. They were all highly anxious, especially the traitorous heir himself. Valea hoped that Kyl was feeling pain. She hoped all of the drakes, Grath, Faras, and Ssgayn included, were feeling pain and remorse, but most of all she hoped that Kyl did. The enchanted witch wanted him to feel so much pain that it would make his heart burst.

"Where isss he?" muttered Kyl as he paced.

"You know very well where he is," responded Grath, looking up from a book. The younger drake sat in one of the chairs, hands steepled, eyes keeping track of his brother's movements. "If the spell on Ssarekai has failed, then it stands that Aurim, too, is near recalling. That hasss to be the first thing that is dealt with and the duke must do that on his own. It would look too suspicious for all of us to go with him."

"I want them handled with care, that isss all." Kyl glanced rather guiltily at Valea. "They dessserve that much."

"I know that. Our brother only does what he has to do. They would kill him instantly if they knew he was here, Kyl. Do you think *that's* fair? Toma will fight to preserve his life, that is all. Look how long he has lived among us, yet never has he tried to harm anyone. *That* more than anything lese, isss proof of his intentions."

He's killed no one here because that would mean chancing discovery. It was enough just risking the spell on Aurim and Ssarekai. Toma wants Kyl to give him a place at his side, one where the Dragon Kings can't touch him! She wondered how long Kyl's reign would last once the renegade had a secure power base again. With the confederacy of the dragon clan survivors to back him, the duke would have enough influence to perhaps alter the law that said he could not be emperor himself.

Despite her bitterness over Kyl and all else, Valea could not help but admire Duke Toma's incredible patience. All those years of masquerading so that he could be an influence on the life of the young emperor-to-be. He had helped mold Kyl—and Grath, too—had learned the innermost secrets about his greatest enemies, and prepared the way for his return to power.

She tried to speak, but, as before, Valea might as well have not even made the attempt. There was no movement whatsoever. She could see, blink, swallow, and breathe, but nothing more. The witch remembered the stories her mother and father had told her about her mother's imprisonment by her grandfather. Azran had left her sealed in amber for . . . what? One? Two centuries? At least Gwendolyn Bedlam had not entirely known what was happening around her. The few minutes that Valea had been helpless were already driving her close to the edge.

Concern for her family was what kept her going. She knew that Toma had no intention of letting any of the Bedlams live. Kyl and even Grath might believe otherwise, but she knew too much about the history of the renegade to think he would do otherwise. The Bedlams would always be a threat to him.

There was a quiet knock on the door. Faras, who stood nearest to the door, unbolted and opened it.

Aurim stepped through. Valea's spirits rose, then sank. Behind Aurim came Ursa, but behind her followed Toma, the renegade once more clad in the form of the tutor.

"You see," said the duke after the door had been closed. "As I promised, my lord, here are your friend and your sisssster, both unharmed."

"Why did you bring them here?"

With no warning, Traske melted into Toma. The transformation continued to both fascinate and horrify Valea. "If anyone saw them after I had bespelled them, they would have realized something was amiss. I could not simply make them forget. As I said earlier, Your Majesty, things must now be resolved with ssswiftness." Toma looked properly upset, an expression Valea knew was as false as his words. "Thisss is hardly the way I wanted it. I would have preferred your transition to the throne to be peaceful. If you like, I will sssurrender myself to the Bedlams and take their brand of justice. If you think it will benefit your ascension, that isss."

Accept his offer! Valea wanted to shout. It was not that she believed that Toma would follow through on his promise, but rather that she wanted Kyl to understand the dark creature with whom he was dealing.

Kyl, however, shook his head. "No, I know what will happen. Jussst . . . jussst ussse care."

"That I will, my brother. I have promisssed that from the beginning, have I not, Grath?"

The younger drake looked at the heir. "That he has, Kyl. Toma has only worked to serve you for all the time I have known him."

"Now that I have the opportunity to prove myself to you persssonally, I dare not fail to live up to your ssstandards."

Kyl stepped away from the others and out of Valea's view. "What will you do with them?"

Indicating the emperor-to-be with his hands, the draconian knight returned, "As I sssaid earlier, it isss my hope to capture them all and, once that is accomplished, place the entire family under a more subtle, more thorough forgetfulness spell. Already, the children—and, regrettably, sister Ursa—are mine. As Benjin Traske, I should be able to approach both Lord and Lady Bedlam and take them without warning."

"And *kill* them? I'd imagine that you hate them dearly."

Again, Toma looked properly subdued. "My hatred hasss dwindled away over the years here, Your Majesty. I've seen them doing both good and ill. Now, I hold no grudges. I cannot say that I have come to love them; I simply understand them better. If they can be convinced to leave me be, then I shall leave *them* be."

"And if they won't?"

"I would rather not think about that unlessss it becomesss necessary to do so."

"There is no time to discuss this further," Grath interjected. "We must deal with Lord and Lady Bedlam asss soon as possible."

"There is a piece of news that I have not informed either of you about yet." As Toma spoke, he began to shift once again to the scholarly shape of Benjin Traske. This time, Valea clearly saw that the belt blade, the only item true to both Toma and Traske, glowed. She was fairly certain that it was what allowed the renegade to so well retain the form of the tutor. Drakes generally had two shapes. The first was the dragon form that they were born with, the latter was most often the reptilian knight, such as how Duke Toma looked when he was not being Traske. While the renegade was, by her parents' own admissions, more versatile, there were still limitations. The enchanted knife was apparently a way around those limitations.

"And that news is?" asked Kyl. His tone was so matter-of-fact, so calm now, that Valea wanted to scream. He was, in her opinion, worse than the rest of them, for Kyl, as heir to the emperor's throne, should have been strong enough to withstand Toma's ploys. Instead, he had accepted every word as easily as a sheep would have accepted a handful of grass. It made the imprisoned witch furious, which only served to fuel her frustration.

"The master warlock is not in the Manor nor is he on the Manor grounds. He had gone to speak to Lord Green. It seems that the monarch of Irillian will be here in only two, at most, three days."

Valea, unable at the moment to think of any drake save dear Ssarekai as trustworthy—and Ssarekai might be dead, although no one had told her so—did not see the visit as any buffer against the renegade's plans. Toma knew the Dragon Kings well. They would be easier to fool than her mother or father.

"Ssso sssoon? I'm not ready for him!" Kyl stepped back into her field of vision. The veneer of confidence had been stripped from his face. He was openly nervous.

"You will be. Grath and I shall see to it that Blue himself will become one of your most ardent supporters by interview's end."

"Have *we* failed you so far, Kyl?" asked Grath, almost mimicking Duke Toma.

"You know that *you* have not, Grath, however—"

"Much of what I did, what suggestions I made, originated from Toma, Kyl. He has guided you more than anyone else, both as Benjin Traske and as himself."

Traske/Toma moved toward the door. "We will have time to talk later. For now, I mussst locate and deal with the Lady of the Amber before her mate returns home." He bowed. "With your permission?"

"You may—" Kyl began, but then he glanced at Grath. "One moment. You should take Grath with you, perhapsss. The better to occupy Lady Gwendolyn's attention while you prepare to take her. What do you sssay?"

Valea saw the merit in the heir's plan, which made her hate him all the more. Grath found it of interest, also.

"An interesssting notion," returned the renegade, his smile more open. He was no doubt pleased by this sign of Kyl's cooperation in this foul venture.

If I only had a few seconds of freedom! She had already planned and replanned how she would have dealt with the drakes. As to whether or not her ideas would have succeeded, Valea did not care. Trapped, the mental images of Toma and the others, especially *Kyl*, at her mercy was the only thing she had to keep up her hopes.

"Interesting," Traske/Toma continued. "But unnecessary. I have thingsss worked out, Your Majesty. Besidesss, your safety isss as great a concern. The humans tried to assassinate you once; they may try again. Grath'sss place should always be by your side."

"Surely I am sssecure here."

The false scholar indicated himself. "Where I can enter, who can sssay what others might have followed?"

Kyl quieted instantly.

Traske/Toma bowed again. "Once more, with your permission, I shall now leave." His eyes darted from Kyl to Valea. The glance was only brief, but the hatred she felt in that look would have been enough to make her stumble away had the spell not prevented her from doing so. "Before thisss day isss done, Your Majesty, I promise you that the Manor will be secure." He returned his gaze to the heir. "Then, your future may begin in earnessst."

XIX

Cabe left the caverns of the Green Dragon feeling drained and still more confused. He did not know how to behave toward the Dragon King and was aware that he might possibly never resolve that problem. Eventually the warlock would also have to tell his wife. She would know that something was wrong.

He had left the matter of the Dragon King's relations with the Gryphon and Darkhorse in the claws of Lord Green himself. The only thing that Cabe had promised was that he would not permit war. Somehow, if the truth came to be known to either of the two, Cabe would have to see to it that they did not attempt to seek justice—or *vengeance*—against the master of the Dagora Forest. That would be only the beginning, for the drakes would see such an attack as an assault on their race. Even the more level-headed Blue Dragon would likely join the fray.

Why is it that justice and right aren't always necessarily the same thing? Cabe pondered as he exited the cavern mouth into the forest. *I can see why the Green Dragon did what he did and I can see why he should be punished for doing so. Yet, to punish him would create an even greater conflict and accomplish nothing good. Might as well punish the drake guards who, trying to rescue Kyl, pushed Toos into the path of the bolt.* No one intended to do the last. The drake bodyguards had only been performing their function. They had not known about the assassin with the bow until it was too late.

There was only one thing good about this situation. The Green Dragon was very remorseful about what he had caused to happen. He had known Toos well; Cabe knew that the Dragon King was already punishing himself for the assassination. Behind the false helm, the reptilian eyes stared too often into empty space.

The only Dragon King who would feel remorse in the first place over something like this. It's almost ironic. If Black or the Storm Dragon had been behind this, they would have shrugged their shoulders in disappointment that more had not died.

He took a moment to simply stand in the midst of the forest, drinking in the peacefulness of his surroundings. Cabe would have liked to have stayed longer, but Gwendolyn would be expecting him and there was much to do before the Blue Dragon's arrival. They might have as little as a day and a half before the drake lord showed up. Someone would have to see to Kyl so that he would be prepared when the time came. That might take some doing, Cabe thought, for the last he recalled, the heir had still been secreted in his chambers.

The warlock did not intend to argue about the Dragon King traveling to the Manor, even though it went against his earlier wishes. Under the circumstances, Lord Blue could hardly be blamed for wanting to come so quickly. Had it been any other drake lord, Cabe would have remained adamant in his refusal, but Blue he trusted, if only because of the Gryphon's friendship with the Dragon King's son, Morgis.

Knowing he could delay no longer, Cabe pictured the main hall of the Manor. With a sorcerer of his skill, thought was as good as action. Cabe's surroundings faded away to be replaced but a moment later by the very location he had just imagined. The warlock was pleased by the smooth transition. Sometimes, when his thoughts were as scattered as they felt now, his travel spell either took more time or left him more weary. On a rare occasion, he even ended up in a different location.

With his sorcery, he sought out his wife. Unlike the travel spell, this proved more troublesome, for, although he found her with little effort, she seemed not to notice him at first. At least, the sorceress did not *respond* immediately. Only when Cabe pressed for contact did the link establish itself.

Gwen?

Cabe. You're back.

Her thoughts did not reach him as intensely as they should have had. *Are you all right? You don't sound very strong.*

She took a second or two to respond. *There has just been so much to do, so many things to keep track of.*

I understand. Now was not the proper time to tell her the truth about the Green Dragon and the assassination. That suited the exhausted mage. He was very much tempted, in fact, to simply wait until Kyl was on the throne and he and Gwendolyn finally had some time for themselves again. *You're in the library?*

Yes, I am.

I'll come to you, then. He broke off contact with her. Cabe was almost ready to transport himself to the library when a terrible ache in his stomach reminded him that he had still not eaten. Not wanting to disturb his wife again, the warlock decided to make an unscheduled stop in the kitchen.

When he materialized in the kitchen but a second later, the familiar smells of herbs and spices almost overwhelmed him, so hungry had he become. Cabe looked around, intending to apologize for his entrance, but neither Mistress Belima nor any of her helpers were present. The kitchen was completely empty. There was not even anything baking or cooking at the moment, a truly rare occurrence. Mistress Belima *lived* in the kitchen. She had once informed the master warlock quite testily that cooking was how she relaxed. Considering the delicious meals that the woman organized, Cabe no longer even brought up the subject.

"Hello? Is anyone in here?"

His question was greeted with silence. Cabe studied the room again, but other than the fact that no one was here, there was nothing unusual to see. He finally shrugged it off and began searching for something to eat. It would have been easier to conjure up bread and fruit, but with Mistress Belima's kitchen, it paid better to search. One never knew what delight she had concocted and set aside.

Sure enough, besides the fresh bread that the woman always had ready, Cabe also found fresh oatmeal and raisin cookies, cheese, and a small bowl of some sort of vegetable mix. The warlock made himself a quick, makeshift meal, then bolted it down. He would have liked to have savored it more, but Gwendolyn would be wondering where he had gone. He located some milk to wash down the food and finally, because it was a rule no one dared break for fear of incurring Belima's wrath, cleaned up after himself. Cabe was just about to shift to the library when he noticed that he was no longer alone.

Aurim stood across the room from him. The younger Bedlam looked rather bleary-eyed, as if he had not had much sleep in the past few days. The sun-tressed warlock stood on unsteady legs, gripping one of the tables. He blinked two or three times at his father, but said nothing.

"Aurim!" Cabe rushed to his son's side. "Are you well?"

"Father, I . . ." He shook his head. "I don't remember what I was going to say. . . ." A sickly yet somehow triumphant grin crossed Aurim's countenance. "But I know that there's something else to rememb—remember. . . ."

The master sorcerer slipped an arm around his eldest. "You shouldn't even try to speak right now, Aurim. Let me take you back to your room."

He blinked again. "No . . . I have to tell you . . . the spell, I played with it. . . ."

The spell? Toma's spell? What had his son done to himself? "You shouldn't have worked on it on your own. I'd better bring you directly to your mother. She'll better understand what you've done. Hopefully, she'll also know what to do about it."

"Mother?"

"She's waiting for me in the library," Cabe explained, but his son no longer appeared to be listening. Aurim's brow was furrowed in an attempt at deep thought, although the attempt was already looking to be a failure. "You relax. Don't try to think about it. There'll be nothing to worry about."

"Yes, there *is*."

"Sssh! Hold tight."

Aurim obeyed without protest. Cabe cleared his thoughts and transported the two of them from the kitchen to the library.

The room was immaculate, as always. The Bedlams treated the collection—and books in general—with respect. Volumes were always carefully returned to their original locations. Pages were never bent; bookmarks were always used. A preservation spell kept the books from deteriorating, but Gwendolyn had laid down a rule that no unnecessary light enter the room, for sunlight still damaged books over time. Instead, carefully positioned reading chairs were spread throughout the library. Some caught the light from the one window allowed for circulation while all had candles nearby. However, most of the Bedlams, being spellcasters one and all, provided their own illumination in the form of tiny spheres that they conjured. The magical light did not harm the books and generally gave better illumination than either the candles or the narrow stretch of sunlight. In truth, the library had been well-kept before their coming, but Cabe and his wife had felt that they should not allow the Manor's ability to fend for itself cause them to become careless and slovenly.

He did not see Gwen at first, not until he turned halfway around and discovered her standing only a few feet from him. She looked mildly surprised at the sight of his companion.

"What's wrong with Aurim?" she asked quietly. The enchantress made no immediate move to aid Cabe with his burden.

"I think that he's been trying to free himself from Toma's spell. I think he's done something worse now." Cabe began helping Aurim to the nearest chair.

"He should be in his room, then."

"We can look him over just as easily here," the warlock returned, just slightly annoyed. He could not shake the sudden feeling that he had missed something. The enchantress spoke much too calmly, and the only times that Cabe could recall when she had spoken in such a way was when she had either been ill or angry with him. Glancing her way, he noticed no sign of sickness, but neither did she seem upset with him. Gwendolyn simply seemed . . . detached.

"I can't right now." She gave no explanation.

He started to straighten. "What do you mean you can't d—?"

"Is everything all right here?" asked a voice from the doorway of the library. Cabe looked up and saw Benjin Traske standing there. "I thought—" His eyes alighted on Aurim and his mouth shut. After a breath or two, he finally added, "Master Aurim . . . are you well?"

Cabe was about to answer for his son when Aurim quietly asked, "Father, will you help me to my room?"

The scholar stepped toward the Bedlams. "Allow me to do that, my Lord Bedlam. I am certain that you and the Lady Bedlam have much to do. Is that not correct, Lady Gwendolyn?"

"Yes, let Benjin help him, Cabe."

The warlock gaped at his bride. Could she not see how disoriented their son was? Benjin Traske, for all his offer of assistance, could hardly aid Aurim in this. The situation called for a knowledge and skill in sorcery. Traske barely had even a glimmer of ability.

From his chair, Aurim leaned toward his father. "Would *you* help me, please?"

That was enough for Cabe. The younger man was almost pleading. Aurim was probably afraid that he had caused more harm than good to himself, which was the way his father also felt. That Gwen could not see it astounded Cabe. Later, he would have a word with her, but for now, it was best that he brought Aurim back to his room and did what he could to help.

"Take my arm," he ordered his son. To Traske, he added, "I thank you for your concern, but I'll take care of this."

The massive tutor's face grew expressionless and he bowed. "As you wish, my Lord Bedlam. Then, if I may have but a word with your wife, I'm certain that she will be along shortly to help you."

"Of course," replied the enchantress.

Cabe had no more time to consider Gwendolyn's behavior. With Aurim holding onto him, albeit unsteadily, he simply turned to her and said, "Please hurry."

Her reply was a rather disinterested, "I will."

He was still frowning when Aurim's bedchamber took the place of the library. The tired mage helped his son to a sitting position on the edge of the bed. Aurim looked around as if he had lost something. Cabe scanned the room, but saw no object that might have been what the younger sorcerer was seeking.

"She . . . they . . ." Aurim let loose with an uncharacteristic snarl. "Just a little *more*! I only need a little more and then I'll have it!"

"Aurim, what *are* you talking about?" Cabe knelt by his son and tried to meet the latter's gaze. Aurim stared past him, however, a haunted look in the young man's eyes.

"*Benjin* . . . he's the key . . . Traske with a 'T' . . . that's how I remember it. 'T' also stands . . ."

"Son . . ."

The other waved him silent. "The spell didn't . . . didn't set right. Not this time. Traske with a 'T' . . ." Aurim suddenly looked up. A smile slowly grew. At last, he met his father's gaze. This time, the haunted look had been replaced by one of weary triumph. "Father! Benjin Traske—"

"How is he doing?"

Startled, they both looked up to see Gwendolyn standing by the door. Cabe had not noticed her materialize, and he was certain that neither had their son.

Aurim was pleased to see her. "Mother! I was just about to tell Father! I remember! I think he must have not known that I'd worked on destroying the original spell. When he tried to cast it again, he only turned it into something even *more* haphazard."

The warlock turned his back on his wife. Something that Aurim had just said had struck him almost dumb. "Aurim! Did you say that it was cast *again*?"

"Yes! Listen! He's been here all the time, laughing at us! Father, *Benjin Traske is Duke Toma!*"

He stared at his son, unable to make sense out of the pronouncement. Benjin Traske . . . *Toma*? "Aurim, you can't mean that, can you?"

His son grabbed him by the arms. "Father, we have to act! He's taken Ursa and I think he must have Valea!"

It was still inconceivable. "But we just left Traske at the library, Aurim!"

"I know, but it wasn't quite clear to me, then. I only knew that I had to get away from him! I—" Aurim looked past him to his mother. Cabe saw his eyes widen.

If I may have but a word with your wife . . .

"*Look out!*" shouted the young spellcaster. One arm thrust forward in a defensive maneuver as Cabe was suddenly thrown to the side.

The room was suddenly aglow with emerald green flame. Intense heat buffeted Cabe, but he knew that it should have been far worse. The spell should have killed him instantly, killed him and Aurim, too.

At the hands of Gwen.

Cabe rolled over just enough so that he could see what was happening. Before him, the doorframe outlining her, stood the scarlet-and-emerald enchantress. Her hands were outstretched, and even behind the magical shield that Aurim had managed to just barely create, the master warlock could sense the incredible river of power being thrust at them.

Gwendolyn's face was still indifferent, almost blank. How long had she been under Traske's . . . *Toma's* cursed spell? Not for very long, but definitely before the disguised renegade had entered the library. Traske had been surprised to see Aurim there, too, which meant that he had thought that he had already dealt with Cabe's son.

The library had been a trap, one set to snare him in particular. Had Aurim not been with him, Cabe would have gone there alone to talk with his wife. Toma would have no doubt entered when he had anyway, thus giving the warlock too little time to realize what was wrong with his mate. Then, with Cabe unsuspecting, the renegade would have struck from both sides.

He would have made Gwen Cabe's murderer.

Cabe held his anger in check, realizing that the situation now required thought, not emotion. Aurim's shield was still holding, but he did not have the experience to keep pace with his mother. Fortunately, it appeared as if the witch did not have the full use of her senses, else she would have gotten around her son's defenses by now.

The warlock added his own power to the shield. Toma had expected the enchanted sorceress to catch both her son and her husband off guard. Under his spell, she was only a puppet, which meant that the knowledge and cunning of Lady Gwendolyn Bedlam was almost completely lost.

Engrossed as he was in trying to understand what had become of his wife, he barely sensed the black tentacles coming from behind him.

They darted toward him, but the warlock had already shifted position, materializing just a foot or two out of the way. The tentacles struck the floor, then immediately sought him again.

Evidently not *all* of her cunning was lost. The mage cast his own spell, severing the tentacles from their source. The magical extremities dropped to the floor and wiggled around once or twice before they dissipated.

"Father! How do we fight her? I *can't* hurt her!"

There lay the gist of their problem—and Toma's final ploy. Gwendolyn would continue trying to kill them unless they defeated her, but doing so might cause her injury, or worse, *death*. For the renegade, that would be as great a victory as it would be if she succeeded in her mission.

I swear that you'll pay for all of this somehow, Toma! It was so easy to swear oaths, though. Fulfilling them, however, was another matter, one which would first require a resolution to the situation at hand.

The ensorcelled Gwendolyn chose that moment to look at the ceiling. Cabe did not understand until the room began to shake.

"The ceiling! Aurim! You take care of it! I'll watch her!"

It was possible that a look of relief and gratitude crossed his son's countenance, but things were moving too swiftly to take the time to be certain. *At least he won't have to worry about harming his mother.*

Aurim also looked up. The shaking slowed, but did not cease. Out of the corner of his eye, Cabe saw the younger warlock squeeze his fists tightly together in an attempt to force his will on the weakening ceiling.

The quake became imperceptible.

That left Cabe to deal with his wife. He dared not attempt a direct attack. As desperate as his own predicament was, to harm her was out of the question. Knowing that she would probably die at Toma's hand if he *did* sacrifice himself did not make things easier.

Part of Gwen had to be in there. It was the only way by which the drake could make some use of her skills. Otherwise, she would have been no more than a statue. For Toma to twist her to his bidding, he would have had to keep a flicker of her soul awake. All Cabe had to do was find something that would shock her enough to weaken the spell holding her in thrall.

The deaths of her husband and son would do that, but faking such a scene would require too much concentration. It would leave the shield weakened, something that his bride, even in her present state, would be unable to miss.

The true deaths of her husband and son *would* awaken her.

He needed something else, but it had to be something stunning or a fear or even possibly—

A fear? Cabe knew of one. It was a fear so powerful that as hard as she had tried in the past to hide it from him, he had noticed the tension, the shaking, time after time.

It would have to be that. The warlock gritted his teeth and whispered to his wife, "I'm sorry for this, Gwen. Another thing that Toma owes us for."

It was easy in one sense. All Cabe had to do was picture the enchantress as he had first discovered her.

A golden glow materialized around the sorceress. She did not pay it any heed at first, focused as she was by Toma's command on the process of trying to kill her family. Then, as the glow condensed, took form, a slight look of uncertainty flashed across the otherwise emotionless face.

Beside him, Aurim tried to watch while maintaining his counterspell on the ceiling.

Cabe continued to solidify the glow. It now had a rocky, translucent look to it. He knew that what he was creating was an illusion, but he doubted that Gwendolyn's mind in its present state would be able to make the distinction.

The Lady of the Amber. That was the name by which she had been known in legend. The story of her imprisonment by Azran had become folk legend. Azran had worked his spell well and only Cabe had somehow managed to shatter it. Perhaps it had been because he was of the mad mage's bloodline. Whatever the reason, release her Cabe had. Yet, the memory of her imprisonment remained rooted in her mind, haunting her dreams on occasion and filling her with a dread whenever she saw even a small piece of the substance. She feared being entombed again, and while that was not likely to happen, it was impossible to rid Gwendolyn of that dread. The amber prison had become a demon to her. It was why she insisted that no one, without exception, use the title in her presence.

Gwen's eyes abruptly rounded. Her face twisted from disinterest to outright horror.

She screamed as Cabe had never heard her scream.

Her spells died at the moment of her cry, much to Cabe's relief. Aurim, groaning, slumped onto the bed, but the warlock could see that his son was merely exhausted. This was the first time the younger Bedlam had been forced to use his power on such a level. Practice would make it easier.

Still his wife screamed, but Cabe could not stop now. She was not yet free of Toma's control. Only when her mind was completely her own could he dare cease his attack. The sorcerer only prayed that she did not lose her mind in the process of recovering it.

At last, the enchantress ceased screaming and dropped to her knees. She began to cry. Cabe heard his name and those of his children amidst her sobs. Immediately, he dismissed the illusion of the amber prison and rushed to her side.

"Gwendolyn!" Cabe put his arms around her.

The distraught woman gradually looked up. "Cabe?"

He held her close. "It's all right. The amber wasn't real. I had to do it to break you out of Toma's spell."

"Toma? I don't . . . I don't *think* I remember. . . ."

Of course she would not, the warlock realized. His wife had never actually seen Toma. "Gwen . . . Traske came to you, didn't he?"

It was clear that, as with Aurim, it was an effort for her to think. "Yes . . . he did. I don't recall what he . . . what he wanted to talk about, but . . ."

"Gwen . . . Traske *is* Toma. He may have always *been* Toma."

Cabe felt her body grow perfectly still. For a brief moment, he began to fear that she had slipped back into panic, but then she spoke. Her voice was steady but filled with growing hatred. "All this time we've cared for a *viper* in our midst? All this time he's walked among us, laughing inside?"

"I don't know if he's always been Traske, but he has been for some time, I think."

"Rheena!" The oath was one that the disheveled enchantress used rarely these days, which to Cabe revealed just how horrified his wife felt. "He would have made me kill . . . kill . . ."

Cabe silenced her. "He *didn't*. He failed."

"But not for my lack of trying. . . ."

He dared not let her collapse now. "You're not to blame! Toma's to blame!" Cabe made her look him in the eye. "He's still *here*, Gwendolyn. He's still here and he may have Valea."

"Valea!" The enchantress tried to rise, but her legs would not support her. Toma's spell and Cabe's illusion had combined to drain her completely, both emotionally and physically. "We . . . we have to save her!"

"You'll do nothing but rest here."

"I *can't* leave my daughter to that demon!" Straining, the weary sorceress tried to rise again. This time, she almost fell over.

Cabe helped her to the bed, where he put her down next to Aurim. His son sat up. Aurim's face was drawn.

"I'll go with you."

The master warlock shook his head. "No, you stay with your mother. This is something that requires gradual recovery and we can't leave her defenseless. *I'll* take care of Toma."

Aurim wanted to argue, but he knew better. He frowned, however. "Father, I think Toma must also have Ursa. She was in this room, helping me with the spell, when Tra—*Toma* came."

Another hostage. Another life to worry about. Toma, however, was not one to indiscriminately take hostages, which meant that he would hesitate before doing something to them. Cabe knew that at the very least the renegade had Valea in order to confound him, and Ursa had probably been taken because of her bloodline. Grath? He was the one that the warlock worried about most. Kyl was no doubt allied with Toma, but did the heir need his brother? Did he really care that much for Grath?

Maybe it would've been better if your assassins had managed to kill him, Lord Green! If Kyl *was* Toma's ally, then he would pay along with the renegade duke, emperor or not.

Although only a few minutes had elapsed since the beginning of his battle with his ensorcelled wife, Cabe knew that he had delayed too long already. Leaning over quickly, he kissed the worn enchantress and patted his son on the shoulder. "I have to go. I have to get Valea."

"You'll need help," insisted Gwen, trying to rise again.

Cabe briefly looked away, his gaze drifting to empty air. After a moment, he turned back to his family. "I'll get it. Don't worry. Toma *has* to be stopped."

"Good—" the witch began, but Cabe was already gone.

He had no doubt where they would be. Cabe Bedlam had been able to sense the renegade and the others all the time he had been in his son's chambers. Toma, Valea, Kyl, Grath, and at least three others occupied the chambers set aside for the heir, his brother, and their bodyguards.

The odds were very much against him; the warlock was aware of that. Yet Cabe was concerned only about Toma. The others would be more hindrance to themselves. Kyl was possibly a threat, if Cabe was correct in his assumption. Toma, however, would have his hands full keeping Valea, Ursa, and likely Grath under control. The drake duke would insist on doing so himself. Toma trusted no one enough, not even his supposed emperor.

He materialized just a few feet from the royal chambers. The spell that prevented magical intrusion was still in place, another reason why Toma would have chosen these rooms rather than his own. The drake had dared not place such a spell on his own suite, for someone would have noticed and questioned why a tutor needed such safeguards.

How best to do this? Toma was making Cabe come to him. Despite Cabe's intentions otherwise, the warlock was once more being played with by the renegade. Duke Toma had always excelled at manipulating others, but his game of the past several years had been his crowning achievement. Even now, he simply had to wait for his adversary to come to him.

Well, I am *coming to you, you damned lizard and, believe me, you* will *regret that!*

Cabe sent a probe toward the doorway, the obvious entrance into a place protected by sorcery, but he also sent out two more subtle probes to seek out the windows on the other side of Kyl's bedchamber. He doubted that either the door or the windows would do him any good, but it was always a wise idea to investigate.

The probes finally informed him of what he had already assumed. None of the obvious entrances were available to him. There were spells crisscrossing them, spells whose intentions were to assure his immediate death. He could not fight both Toma and the traps the renegade had laid, not at the same time. That was far too much for even Cabe, with all his power, to concentrate on.

It became clear to Cabe that he could either stay here and hope that Toma would tire of waiting—or try to fight his way through the drake's traps. Neither was a particularly attractive choice. He could not take long in deciding, either, for Valea's life lay in the balance. Kyl did not likely want her killed, but Toma might. Whatever master plan the renegade had hatched all those years ago, when he had first donned the mask of Benjin Traske, had been shattered, likely by Aurim's appearance in the library. Traske *had* seemed visibly startled. With Gwen having failed him, Toma now had to revise his moves.

Which did not mean that the drake had not already planned for this somehow.

He could not wait out Toma. Cabe *had* to assault the magically defended suite. He had to do it alone, too, for neither his wife nor Aurim were—

There was a sudden *tingling* in his mind. The tingling was followed by the intrusion of a familiar, albeit ever unique presence. *I am here, Cabe! Let me in!*

Darkhorse! Enter freely! Come to the hall beyond Kyl's suite! Quickly!

"What is it?" rumbled the eternal, suddenly beside him.

With the tension so great already, Cabe fairly jumped at the abrupt appearance of his old friend. He quickly scanned the shadow steed. Darkhorse did not look as powerful as he generally did. His presence was just a bit less imposing, as if not all of him was there. "Are you well enough? Can you help me?"

The eternal looked insulted. "*Can* I help you? I am Darkhorse, Cabe! I am your *friend*! To not help you, to do less than I am able . . ."

"Toma's in there."

That silenced the ebony stallion. The icy orbs that were his eyes narrowed. "*Is* he now?" Darkhorse started toward the door. "Then I think that we should *join* him . . . so that we may *tear* him apart!"

"Wait!" Cabe leapt in front of the eternal. "Listen! Toma is Benjin Traske. He used that identity to draw us to him. I think he has Valea and Grath in there, and I *know* that the doors, the windows . . . *everything* . . . are bespelled!"

"Bespelled against *you*, Cabe!" snorted the shadow steed. "I am Darkhorse! Move aside! I owe the renegade for much and I will see him pay now!"

Somehow, the hulking form of Darkhorse slipped around him. Cabe cursed, reminding himself for the thousandth time that what the eternal resembled was *not* what he was. It was too late by that time. Darkhorse was already at the doorway.

The massive black stallion rose on his hind legs and struck out with his hooves. The warlock felt a rush of sorcerous energy encompass the eternal. Cabe shielded himself, but nothing struck him. He heard Darkhorse laugh and knew then that his companion had absorbed the sorcery and was now mocking the one who had cast the spell.

"I am *coming* for you, bloody duke!" Darkhorse kicked the door again. It still stood, a testament to Toma's own skills, but Cabe estimated that one, perhaps two more kicks would shatter it. He readied himself to enter the fray the moment the way was clear.

It took only one more kick. The door splintered, bits flying this way and that. Again, spells were unleashed. The wary sorcerer was amazed at the preparation his adversary had made. Once more, however, all the preparation went for naught, for Darkhorse absorbed all the power with only a slight glow to show that he had noticed the attacks at all.

The eternal did not wait. He charged into the suite. Cabe prayed that the Manor would be able to withstand all the damage. It would not do to have the ancient edifice come down around them just as they were about to capture Toma.

"What in the name of the Void?" roared Darkhorse in absolute confusion.

Cabe, just entering, paused. He stared at what had so confounded the stallion, his heart sinking as he realized the latest ploy the duke had played on him.

Huddled together like frozen statues were Lady Belima and six of the household staff. They stared without seeing, but Cabe could at least tell that they were breathing.

"Look what hangs on their chests," Darkhorse muttered.

Stepping forward, a demoralized Cabe saw that each person wore a simple loop necklace from which hung an object. Mistress Belima, a graying, busy-looking woman, wore a small dagger. Another woman wore a ribbon that resembled one worn often by Valea. The warlock studied the other items, finally muttering, "Those are personal items. Something from Valea, something from Kyl . . . something from everyone in Toma's little group, including himself."

"We have been *tricked*!"

He nodded. Darkhorse had the right of it. Toma had played the warlock as a master bard played his harp. Kyl, Grath, Ursa, Valea—they were all gone. Frustrated, the warlock stalked through the suite. He knew that the renegade had departed, but desperation made him hope that perhaps he was wrong. This had to end here and now, not drag on and on and on. . . .

In one of the side rooms, the warlock made a grisly discovery. Whereas Mistress Belima and the others were simply under an enchantment, this poor soul had been murdered most horribly. He forced himself to walk up to the figure, whose features were frozen in a scream, and touch it.

"Gods, Ssarekai . . ." he whispered. "You, too. . . ."

Perhaps this murder had been the beginning of the end of Toma's patient waiting. The drake servitor had not simply been frozen or made to forget again; he had been turned into *rock*. Solid rock. There was no bringing him back to life, not from this particular spell. The spark that had been the stable master's essence was gone.

General Toos, the real Benjin Traske—if he had ever existed—and now Ssarekai. More names to add to Toma's list. More things to condemn the duke, already many times condemned.

Cabe did not like to kill, but he knew that it was up to him to see to it that Toma caused no more deaths.

Cabe? came a weak voice in his head.

Gwendolyn?

It was clear that she was still in no shape to help him. *Is it . . . is she . . . what's happening?*

The warlock sighed and told her. She relayed nothing back to him as he quickly described what had happened, but Cabe could sense her growing despair.

When he was finished, she asked, *Valea? He still has Valea and we don't know where he is now?*

Cabe started to shake his head, recalled that his wife would not be able to see him do so, then suddenly paused before answering her.

Perhaps he *did* know where Toma had gone. Considering the renegade's past, considering his companions and his manner, it seemed to the warlock that there was only one place that the duke *could* go. Toma's arrogance would permit him to go no place else.

"I know where he has to be," he said out loud.

"Where is *that*?" asked Darkhorse, trotting into the room. The shadow steed's eyes narrowed thoughtfully as he noticed what remained of poor Ssarekai. The stable master, after getting over the typical drake's fear of the eternal, had pleased Darkhorse to no end with his constant compliments concerning the stallion's magnificent appearance.

In his head, the enchantress echoed the eternal's question.

Cabe's hands balled up into fists as he thought of the place. It was appropriate, for it had been, in a sense, the birthplace of Cabe Bedlam, master sorcerer. From there, the harbingers of fate, in the form of Dragon Kings, had gone out to seek an unsuspecting young man.

"We have to go to Kivan Grath."

XX

Although the wind and cold could not touch him, Cabe Bedlam nonetheless felt a chill as he stood on a ledge high atop one of the smaller peaks of the Tyber Mountains. In the distance, Kivan Grath stood above all else. Somewhere within, the warlock knew, Toma and the others waited. The spells that now enshrouded the citadel of the Dragon Emperor made it impossible to locate those inside. They also made it impossible for Cabe and Darkhorse to simply materialize there.

"We are not alone," remarked Darkhorse. The shadow steed had insisted on joining him in this confrontation and, despite Cabe's awareness of the fact that the eternal was not entirely well, the warlock had been unable to turn down his offer.

Cabe nodded. Besides the creatures who inhabited the Tybers, he could sense two other forms in the direction of Kivan Grath. Two monstrous forms. *Dragons.*

"Are you ready?" he asked the eternal.

Darkhorse chuckled and kicked the edge of the ledge. A portion of it broke off and tumbled down to the valley below. "Of course!"

"Then let's see what Toma has waiting for us. You know what I want of you?"

The ice-blue orbs flashed. "I will watch for Valea; you may rest assured on that, Cabe. I will take her from this place and bring her safely back to the Manor. Grath, too?"

"Please. It's not his fault Kyl is allied with Toma."

"I wonder. The young drake is clever; I find it amazing that he could be so ignorant of his brother's doings."

Cabe tried to fix on the two hulking figures he could sense near the mouth of the Dragon Emperor's sanctum. They were most definitely keeping guard. He sighed. "Follow my lead."

"As you say."

With a thought, the warlock sent the two of them forward. They materialized only a short distance from the very mouth of the cavern, but still far enough so that its two immense guardians were not on top of them.

Even still, the sight of the two dragons *was* an impressive one.

Green they were, but mixed within was a trace of gold that made them glitter a little even in the cloud-enshrouded Tybers. Their wings, presently folded, looked to have a span at least equal to the length of their bodies. They were a pair of the largest dragons that Cabe could recall encountering, and he had encountered some of the greatest. Each drake guarded one side of the massive doorway. The warlock glanced between them and noticed that someone had repaired the entrance but recently.

"Come no farther, Master Bedlam!" rumbled the dragon on his left.

"Faras?" the warlock asked, slightly disoriented. The two leviathans were almost identical in appearance, but something in the first one's voice reminded him of the drake.

"You have not been given leave to enter," hissed the other.

"Ssgayn." Cabe nodded to each of them. He had never seen the two drakes in dragon form, not since they were hatchlings. In truth, it was almost as surprising that they could actually shift to such shapes, not having practiced it . . . or had they? "You know why I'm here."

Faras dipped his huge head. His teeth were jagged spikes as long as the human's arms. Ssgayn's were no less impressive. Even for dragons, these two were giants. "Duke Toma hasss given us strict ordersss."

"Duke Toma? Is he emperor now?"

The dragons snapped their heads back in discomfort. Faras hissed, "Duke Toma *ssspeaks* for the emperor!"

"Does he?" The warlock's eyes darted over the forms of the two dragons. He had seen almost all he needed to see. Faras and Ssgayn were not as comfortable in their present shapes as they would have liked. Their movements were sightly awkward, as if they understood the functions of their bodies but had not had enough practice. Still, knowing dragons as well as he did, Cabe did not doubt that they would be swift and deadly foes.

"So Toma speaks for Kyl now. Does Kyl know that?"

Ssgayn hissed. "You would be wissse not to mock, Master Bedlam."

"Let me through, Ssgayn. I want my daughter."

"We cannot. We have been charged to protect thisss entrance from all intrudersss. We mussst obey."

They would, too. It saddened Cabe, because, knowing the two as he did, the warlock understood that Faras and Ssgayn truly saw this as their duty.

"I'll have to enter. I won't be kept from Valea."

The two dragons simultaneously raised their heads. Ssgayn opened wide his maw while Faras simply replied, "Then you mussst pass *usss* first, Massster Bedlam!" The dragon lowered his eyes. "I *am* sssorry."

Cabe started to raise his hand toward Ssgayn when the green-and-gold leviathan called out, "Wait!"

The warlock paused, but did not lower his hand. "Why?"

Both guardians had distant looks in their eyes. Cabe Bedlam recognized that look; someone was speaking to them through their minds. He glanced at Darkhorse, who dipped his head in understanding. They would wait for the dragons to listen, but no longer.

Faras was still listening inwardly when Ssgayn finally returned his attention to the warlock. "Fortune sssmiles upon us all, Massster Bedlam." The massive dragon almost sounded relieved. "You have been granted entrance."

Without pause, the two guardians began to shift aside. Faras, too, had broken contact with whoever had spoken to the two of them. He dipped his head in what might have been construed a draconian bow.

"This is a trick," rumbled Darkhorse softly. "They shall let us pass and then try to catch us from all sides."

Eyeing the dragons, Cabe scratched his chin. "I don't know. They *look* as if they're telling the truth," he whispered back.

"How would you *have* them look if they wanted you to believe their story?"

"Good point, but there's only one way to really find out whether they're lying or not, isn't there?"

"And if they are, we shall easily take them, won't we?" The eternal chuckled, which made the dragons, who had been unable to hear the conversation, tense.

The warlock and the shadow steed started forward, but then Faras, who more directly faced Darkhorse, hissed and shook his head. "Noooo . . . only *you*, Massster Bedlam! Only you. Ssso the emperor hasss *spoken*."

"Through Duke Toma, no doubt," muttered Cabe.

"I will *not* accept this!" roared his companion. "We go together!"

The two dragons shifted nearer one another, effectively cutting off any glimpse of the entrance to the Dragon Emperor's sanctum. "That isss not permitted," added Faras.

Darkhorse looked ready to charge both scaled titans, but Cabe quickly put out a hand to halt him. "No, Darkhorse. If we fight, then we certainly endanger Valea. I'll go in alone."

"You cannot walk blindly into such an obvious trap!"

"But I *won't* be blind, will I?"

Ssgayn moved a stride closer, a great distance when one considered that he was a dragon. Darkhorse thought it *too* great, for he suddenly darted ahead of Cabe, becoming, in effect, a shield between the warlock and the leviathan.

The drake did not retreat, but he did pull his head back. "I only convey my liege'sss promissse that this will be a proper, peaceful audience." Ssgayn's reptilian eyes met the sorcerer's own. "Thisss my *emperor* sssswears!"

Whether or not he truly believed the guardian, the warlock had no true choice. Valea needed him. "Very well. I'll enter alone."

"Cabe! I—"

"You'll be near enough, Darkhorse," Cabe interjected, glancing at his companion. "If this *is* a ploy, do whatever you have to do."

Neither dragon looked comfortable with that notion, but they did not appear ready to back away. *I hope it doesn't come to that,* Cabe thought. *Darkhorse isn't as strong as he generally is and . . . and I've known Ssgayn and Faras so long.*

The ebony stallion settled down, albeit with reluctance. He glared at the two huge drakes. "Very well . . . but I shall be waiting for your summons, Cabe. Do not hesitate in the least, and rest assured that I *will* come to you . . . no matter what or who I must go through."

From the expressions on the draconian visages of Faras and Ssgayn, Cabe knew that Darkhorse would have to fight both of them if he did try to pass. The warlock shook his head as he started toward the guardians. If this was the path to peace, then perhaps the old days *were* better.

The two behemoths again moved aside, making a clear path for the warlock. Faras kept one eye on Cabe while Ssgayn studied the shadow steed carefully. The warlock paid no further attention to the guardians; his gaze was on the great bronze gate before him. It *had* been repaired recently, possibly by the Dragon Kings in preparation for the ascension. Toma would not have had the time or patience, not even if he had been willing to use sorcery. He could also not have replaced it during his long exile, for the other drake lords would have investigated immediately. That the gate had been repaired interested Cabe. It meant that at least someone had been fairly certain of Kyl's success, and since only the Dragon Kings ever came here, it *had* to have been one of them.

That was something he could think about later . . . always providing there *was* a later.

He was just about to reach forward and knock on the gate when it swung open to receive him.

There was no one within. Cabe stepped into the gloom of the cavern and looked around.

A figure suddenly stepped out of the darkness, a figure who the warlock knew quite well.

"Ursa!"

Her sorrowful smile told him that she was not under the sort of spell that Toma had cast upon Gwendolyn. Cabe was glad to see that, but at the same time, he felt worse because Ursa was clearly a slave. She was clad in fine emerald-and-gold raiment worthy of her status as drake dam of the royal line, yet being here was clearly not by her choice.

"If you will follow me, Master Bedlam, they are waiting for you."

She started to turn away, but he caught her arm. "Ursa, can you tell me if—"

"We have to go to them, Massster Bedlam," the beautiful drake insisted, turning anxious. "I cannot sssay anything."

"Toma?"

The look in her eyes was answer enough. Cabe quickly released his hold on her. With Ursa in the lead, they began the trek through the dark cavern entrance. Creatures fluttered about above them. The warlock heard something fairly large scuttle away.

"May we at least have some light?"

The words were no more off his tongue when a dim, golden sphere materialized before them. From Ursa's gasp, he gathered that she was not responsible. Toma was keeping a very keen eye on his old foe.

It was the longest short walk in which Cabe had ever partaken. He knew that the distance to the main cavern was but three or four minutes, yet time seemed to slow during the journey. It felt more like an hour. That might have been due to his own anxiety concerning Valea or, knowing Toma, it *might* have been a spell.

Certainly, his first glimpse of the main cavern when he and Ursa finally emerged seemed to be the product of a spell.

When last Cabe had left here, the throne room of the Dragon Emperor had been a fallen ruin. The huge stone effigies that lined the path to the throne had been in total disarray, with many of them tipped over and shattered. Vast portions of the ceiling had collapsed. While the massive stone throne itself had more or less survived, the steps of the dais it stood upon had been cracked and broken. All around, the Gold Dragon's treasures had been crushed.

Here, too, someone had tried and succeeded in repairing much of the damage. Now there were barely any signs that the destruction created in the process of bringing down the mad emperor had ever taken place. Only a few telltale cracks and some missing fragments gave any indication that the warlock's last visit had not been a delusion.

On the throne once occupied by his sire sat Kyl.

To his left stood Valea.

At the sight of his daughter, the mage started forward. Ursa shook her head and tried to grab hold of his sleeve, but Cabe moved too swiftly for her. He stalked toward the path and the effigies, his only concern being to get Valea safely away.

"*That* . . . will be far enough, warlock."

From behind the statues nearest to the dais stepped Toma. The renegade duke wore the form of the knight, but instead of his more normal green coloring, the drake was a resplendent gold and green. Cabe had seen him like this only once before, when Toma had invaded Talak and had captured both Gwendolyn and him.

A movement near Valea tore Cabe's gaze from the deadly drake. To the sorcerer's shock and amazement, he watched as Grath, materializing out of the shadows, seized hold of the young witch's arms. Kyl's brother bore an expression of interest in the proceedings, nothing more. Cabe did not even have to utilize his skills to know that Grath was no prisoner, no enchanted victim. He was a willing participant in Toma's madness.

It was all the mage could do to keep his fury under control.

"It isss cussstomary to kneel before the emperor," Toma announced.

"I am not a drake, as you know," returned Cabe. He gave the renegade a slight smile. "Besides, I recall the ascension being some days away still . . . if it still comes after what you've done."

At that, Kyl leaned forward. There was something in his manner that the warlock thought bespoke of built-up tension. The heir resembled a trap set much too tight, so that the slightest touch would set it off. Cabe thought it an interesting contrast to the attitude of the other two drakes. "What do you mean by that?"

"He meanssss nothing by it, Your Majesty. He isss seeking to undermine you, to ssstir phantom fears in the hopesss that you will be a less able monarch becaussse of them." Toma took a few steps upward as he spoke. Almost midway to the top, he turned to again study the human. "He hasss never desired a *strong* ruler for our race. That would be too much a danger to growing *human* control. That would be too much a danger to the power that he and hisss friends wield."

Cabe wanted to laugh, although the duke's words were anything but humorous. "I'm hardly *you*, Toma. I never asked for or desired *my* power the way that you covet not only yours but everyone else's. Neither I nor any of the others have tried to seize the entire land . . . unlike you."

"I did what I did in the name of my father, the *emperor*."

"And now you do it in the name of your brother?"

"Of course," replied the duke in all solemnity. "Ssserving the emperor hasss always been my duty . . . but perhapsss you cannot fathom sssuch thinking, warlock."

Cabe took a defiant step forward. Kyl leaned back in the throne, his eyes darting from the warlock to Toma and then back to Cabe again. Grath tightened his hold on Valea, who was clearly under some spell that did not allow her to move of her own accord. Cabe was, however, fairly certain that she could both hear and see him. "Oh, I can fathom such thinking, as you say, but not in regards to *you*, Toma. I know you. I remember. Perhaps you did have some loyalty to the Gold Dragon, but I wonder just how much of that has been transferred to the one who, because he bears the markings that you feel life cheated you of, sits on the throne that *would* have been yours, otherwise."

The duke hissed in anger, but said nothing. Cabe noted with interest how Kyl studied his supposed champion. It was not the type of look that he would have expected. The heir was not so pleased with Toma as the warlock had first imagined. *What else have I been mistaken about?*

"You have ssstill not anssswered my question, Massster Bedlam. What do you mean when you sssay that my ascension to the throne isss now in jeopardy?"

He had Kyl listening. That was more than Cabe could have hoped for under the circumstances. Toma clearly wanted to find some reason to prevent the warlock from answering, but to interrupt again would only serve to indicate the danger the duke felt Cabe's response represented.

"First, I must assume that it was not the duke's original intention to cause such chaos so close to the culmination of his plans. I must assume that he wanted you to be firmly ensconced on the throne . . . with Grath beside you acting as his mouth." The last was only a guess, but from the way Kyl's brother behaved, Cabe had to assume that he had spent most of his life misreading Grath. The younger drake was no innocent; he was definitely allied with Toma. The reasons behind that alliance would have been interesting to know, but now was hardly the time to pursue such questions.

Toma laughed, a harsh, raspy sound containing little humor. He turned partially toward the heir and pointed an accusing finger at the warlock. "You see how hisss mind works! You need to forget whatever supposed friendship he extended to you, my liege, and recall only hisss dissstaste for you whenever you were near hisss daughter." The renegade's eyes burned bright as he returned his attention to Cabe. "Hisss Majesty isss well aware of the circumstancesss that forced me to abandon a plan ssso well conceived and executed that I walked *among* you for years! An accidental encounter that could have been forgotten if not for your precocious ssson! No one would have had to come to harm or trouble. You would have all sssimply been made to forget. What your get did to my ssspell I do not know, but by meddling when he should not have, he forced me to defend my emperor."

Now it was the sorcerer's turn to laugh. " 'Defend my emperor'? Nothing would've happened to Kyl if you'd left. In another day, he would've simply met with Lord Blue and, I've no doubts about this, Kyl would have gained his support without trouble." Cabe's expression turned grim. "I wonder, too, how you planned to make us forget Ssarekai's death on top of matters, Toma. He remembered you, didn't he? Poor Ssarekai. Knowing him, he tried to stop you himself. You didn't have to kill him, especially not the way you did, but that's typical of you—"

"Toma!" hissed Kyl. "You told me that Ssssarekai wasss alive but bessspelled!"

The duke's taloned hands folded into fists. Cabe felt a mild tug on the powers around them. Toma was doing something, but it was too weak to be a spell of any danger. *What* then?

"An accident, my liege," replied the sinister drake. "I acted without thinking, for a knife wasss at my throat. I assure you, I did not want the ssstable master's death—"

"I've told you about Toma, Kyl," interrupted Cabe. "Others tend to die around him."

"I will have you *sssilent*!" roared Toma. This time, there was the definite buildup of power. Cabe quickly threw up a magical shield, all the while silently praying that he had not underestimated the intensity of the duke's assault.

The area surrounding the warlock flared bright orange.

"Toma! Ssstop! I forbid you!"

The renegade did cease his attack, but was otherwise paying little attention to Kyl. He descended to the last step, eyes wide with hatred and lipless mouth open to reveal the sharp, predatory teeth. Cabe strengthened his shield again, but Toma unleashed no new spell.

"Ssso much *planning* wasted after ssso much success! Daysss from my goal and *children* ruin everything! Ever hasss there been a Bedlam acting as a thorn in my hand! The cossst of the ssspell that allowed me to masquerade as the tutor left me without physical ssstrength for days and little ability to touch upon the powers for *monthsss*." Here, Toma clasped a hand over the blade that Cabe recognized as the one Traske—*the drake*—had always worn. Now the sorcerer knew what it was and the knowledge made him curse himself for never noticing. Small wonder that Toma had been so weakened after endowing the blade with his spell. The complexity of such a design staggered Cabe. Toma would have to look, act, sound, and even *feel* like Benjin Traske, a human, at nearly all hours. He could never be certain that someone might need to speak to him in the middle of the night. More dangerous was the fact that, with so many others around him, the drake would have to be concerned over an accidental touch by a passerby. Yet, despite living among his enemies for so very long, Toma had been able to succeed with his masquerade. Cabe had shaken his hand on many occasions. He *should* have been able to note the difference. Worse, the warlock *should* have sensed the sorcery at work.

Something must have happened that night that Aurim had noticed Toma. Perhaps Toma had lost control of the knife. Aurim probably recalled now. If Cabe survived . . .

"Jussst a little *longer*," Toma continued, oblivious to the intense interest Kyl now had in what he was saying. "Jussst a little longer and then he would have been emperor. I could have been introduced to him ssslowly, firssst as Benjin Trassske, his advisor, and then asss myssself."

Someone would have had to pave the way for that to happen. Cabe looked up at Grath, who was growing uncomfortable. That was why Toma needed Grath. Kyl had always looked to his brother for advice; if the younger drake recommended leniency, even a position of importance for the renegade, Cabe did not doubt for one moment that the new emperor would eventually grant the duke both.

How long after would Toma be all but emperor? Could Kyl not see what Toma's plans would ultimately mean?

Cabe was not quite certain how he hoped to end this situation, but he knew that much of it rested on Kyl now. The heir was obviously neither the steady ally nor the outright pawn the mage had expected him to be. If Kyl no longer supported Toma . . . "Kyl, the Dragon Kings will never accept Toma. Ask Blue what they think of him. You already know how Lord Green feels about him. When I spoke of the danger to your ascension, I was referring to this. If you support Toma—and have no doubts that even if I should remain silent, the Dragon Kings *will* discover what happened today at the Manor—they will reject *you*." The warlock shrugged. "Some might not—I suspect that Toma has support from some quarter—but that will only mean a potential civil war among your kind. I can't allow that to happen. The fate of the drakes is tied to the fate of my kind as well."

Kyl brooded on this in silence, which Cabe took as a good sign and Toma, it appeared, took as the opposite. The drake turned toward his supposed emperor and, forcing himself to remain calm, again pointed at the warlock. "Subtle wordsss in their own way, my brother, but surely you sssee what lies *beneath* them?" At the heir's puzzled look, Toma quickly continued, "He says give in to the Dragon Kingsss in this and give in to the Dragon Kings in *that*. He tellsss you not to be a ssstrong emperor, but rather a weak *puppet* of theirs, fearful of offending them. Let them sssee you back down once and they will make you back down again and again! You will be an emperor in *name* only. A mockery to be paraded around whenever they have need to impressss the humansss. It will be Black, Ssstorm, and the others who will dictate and it will be *you* who obeysss!"

As opposed to you giving him sage advice, Toma? The trouble was, there *was* something to what the duke had said, just enough, in fact, to lend credence to his warning. It was clear that Kyl thought so, too, for his face took on a troubled expression, as if Toma had reminded him of something he had already feared.

The renegade drake saw that he had touched a nerve and pushed his advantage. "It wasss what they tried to do to our father, Kyl, but he persssevered . . . at leassst until they entirely abandoned him." Toma's tone grew sad. "They tried to overthrow him, but when that failed, they turned their backs on him in his hour of need. Left him to be driven *mad* by the very human before you! *That* isss the thing you mussst truly remember, my brother and my liege! The creature resssponsible for the fall of our father, our emperor, ssstands before you now spouting *lies*!"

Kyl raised a hand, silencing everyone. He rose from the throne and peered down at both the duke and the warlock. The heir's expression was unreadable. He clasped his hands behind his back, then glanced at Grath, who had remained by Valea all this time. Cabe did not like the way the younger drake held his daughter so possessively. He was almost willing to swear that Grath was *obsessed* with her, which would be yet another thing he had failed to notice during the past several years. *What have I been doing all this time?* There were obviously *many* things he had failed to notice and realizing that now did not in any way assuage his guilt. Should this situation somehow be resolved, Cabe swore that he would be more careful . . . and more caring. How much of what Toma had accomplished might have been avoided if the warlock had not suffered from his own prejudices against drakes?

Kyl faced him again. "There isss much merit in what you sssay, Massster Bedlam, but at the sssame time, there isss much, even you will admit, to what the duke sayss. Asss emperor, I will have to make decisions on matterss far more complex than even thisss. I mussst consider what ssserves bessst. I cannot be weak, but I cannot try to be too ssstrong, for that, alssso, hasss itsss dangers. I mussst learn to heed the advice of many," here the heir indicated Grath, Toma, and Cabe, "but make the final choice basssed on my own evaluation of the sssituation."

Triumph returned to Duke Toma's expression and Cabe could not blame him for reacting so. While Kyl's words impressed upon the warlock the fact that the drake would make a more able emperor than he had once supposed, the tone left little guesswork as to his decision regarding Toma.

"I will *not* bend to the Dragon Kingsss. With or without an official coronation, they mussst learn that *I* am emperor. They mussst accept *my* decisions. Lessst they think that I will have no sssupport without them, the duke hasss informed me that the legionsss of the drake confederation will act as my handsss. They are more than a match in number to any Dragon King's army."

At this revelation, Toma hissed in dismay. Cabe, on the other hand, found it interesting that Kyl would reveal such a secret. It was almost as if he was trying to warn the warlock.

The confederation. After the debacle with the Silver Dragon, survivors of those clans without a Dragon King had finally banded together, first slowly and then quicker and quicker as the benefits of an independent "clan" became clear. They held lands to the west and, if the rumors were true, kept on fairly good terms with the human kingdoms there. However, among the clans of their kind, they had no recognized status. The backing of the emperor, even an embattled one, would give them some recognition in the eyes of both the drake and human races.

No doubt Toma had presented it to their leaders in much that way.

Kyl looked at his brother, who appeared almost as upset as the renegade, then returned his gaze again to Cabe. He nodded slightly to the wary sorcerer. "I have made my decision. If you have no other reassson for being here, then thisss audience isss at an end."

That suited Toma. Recovering from his consternation, he started to point at Ursa, no doubt to tell her that the warlock was to be escorted out *now*. Cabe, however, did not give him the chance to speak.

"You know that I can't leave yet, Kyl. Even if I grant you all that you say, I can't leave here without my daughter."

Grath held Valea's arm in an even tighter grip. Toma backed up a step. Kyl, oddly enough, did not seem put out by the demand.

"I once thought to make her mine," he began almost apologetically. "She doesss fassscinate me, Massster Bedlam. I would have treated her like a queen."

"But not an empress. At the very least, Kyl, as emperor you would *have* to take one of your own kind to be your prime mate, the matriarch of the hatching chambers." Dragon Kings took several mates, mostly because many eggs were either sterile or were damaged before the young could hatch. Young drakes also often perished in their first several months.

"True." Kyl stared long at Valea. There *was* something more than fascination in his eyes. Cabe was unnerved by the notion of the heir actually *caring* for his daughter.

"Give me back my daughter, Kyl, and I promise you I won't interfere in whatever comes of your fight for the throne. Leave my family alone—make *him* leave my family alone—and we will remain distant."

Toma gave him a mocking look. "I find *that* a—"

"I agree to your termsss."

Duke and warlock stilled. Cabe could hardly believe his ears. Kyl was giving up one of his strongest cards so easily? Without Valea as his prisoner, his hold on the Bedlams was almost nothing. Under the same circumstances, Toma would have laughed in the warlock's face and threatened the young witch unless Cabe and the rest of his family agreed to obey the renegade.

The differences between Toma and Kyl were becoming more and more evident with each passing moment.

Grath would have none of his brother's promise. "Kyl, are you insssane? Give her up? I—you cannot do that! Think of what you are saying!"

Toma, too, was incensed. "Lisssten to your brother, Your Majesty! If you give up the female, what's to ssstop the mage from trying to bring you down next?"

"His *word*." Kyl, sounding a bit tired, gave Cabe a polite smile. "In all the yearsss I have known Massster Bedlam, he hasss rarely broken his word, and thossse times were not generally by choice. Thisss time, I know he will hold to his word, becaussse he truly does want peace. Ssso do I, Massster Bedlam. After all this, I mossst definitely do." He reached a hand in the direction of the ensorcelled woman. "She isss yoursss, with no ssstrings, no *tricksss*, involved. I ssswear this by both my sssire and the throne of the Dragon Emperor."

Cabe found that he believed him. It hardly seemed possible, but he could find nothing in the heir's manner to make him suspect a ploy of some sort. Kyl *wanted* to release Valea to him.

Unfortunately, the emperor-to-be's brother did not feel so. Still holding Valea by the arms, he turned with wild eyes to Toma. "He can't do that! It would ruin everything!"

Toma was seething, his breathing an audible hiss. Yet, he restrained himself where Grath could not. In a very quiet, overly calm voice, he told the young drake, "He isss our emperor, Grath. He may do asss he pleases. Release the female from the ssspell and let her go to her father."

Grath was aghast. He had clearly not expected such words from the duke. It was only with effort that Kyl's brother slowly released his grip on Valea. He did not step away, however, instead continuing to stand uncomfortably close while he began to unravel the spell he had cast on her.

For the first time since Cabe had followed the drakes to the cavern, his daughter was able to act of her own accord. He expected her to come running to him, but instead, she suddenly whirled on Grath, who resembled, of all things, a forlorn lover, and *slapped* the drake hard on the cheek.

"*That* is the least you deserve!" she snapped. Ignoring him from there on, Valea turned to Kyl. Unlike her tone when speaking to Grath, the young witch's manner was now cool yet polite. "Thank you for doing this, Your Majesty."

Judging from Kyl's countenance, he would have preferred a slap.

Moving a bit unsteadily, Valea made her way to the steps of the dais. She carefully avoided descending anywhere near Duke Toma. The drake clasped both hands behind his back in a manner reminiscent of Kyl's earlier stance, but in the renegade's case, it was evidently more to assure that she need not fear him trying to grab her.

As she neared the bottom, Valea's expression finally turned to joy. Cabe could not keep the happiness from his own face.

"Father!" Valea cried as she began to hurry across the remaining distance. At the edge of his vision, the warlock caught Kyl staring directly at him. His attention was pulled somewhat away from his returning daughter. Had he not known better, he would have sworn that the drake was trying to tell him something, but it could *not* be what Cabe thought it was.

Valea stretched out her arms to hug him. Forgetting Kyl for the moment, Cabe opened his own arms to receive her.

"No! You cannot!"

The horrified voice was Grath's, but he was not protesting his brother's decision again, rather something that Toma was doing.

Cabe cursed silently for forgetting the duke even for as long as the blink of an eye. As his gaze snapped back to the renegade, something flashed in his direction.

His first thought was *Toos!*, despite the differences between what had happened in Penacles and what was happening now. Cabe only knew that a knife—no, *the* knife—was hurtling toward his daughter. Everything around him slowed as the warlock threw Valea to the ground. He knew that his shield would not hold against the ensorcelled blade. Toma would not, of course, have forgotten the original use of the object that had controlled his shaping spell. A knife was made to be used. Trust Toma to ever remember that.

Cabe tried to transport them away, but for some reason, his spell failed. He had no time to consider the reason. Cabe Bedlam now fully expected the blade to strike him and knew that, at long last, Duke Toma would have his death. The drake would not have thrown the knife if he had not been certain of the results. Cabe threw himself onto Valea and closed his eyes, wondering just what form his death would take. From a blade magicked by Toma, it would not be a painless one.

Valea gasped as she struck the floor. Cabe's shoulder scraped against stone, but the pain was muted by the realization that he had suffered no other injury. No knife had sunk into his side.

Rolling onto his back, he discovered the sinister blade frozen in the air above him. From where it floated, the warlock estimated it would have struck him squarely in the back. The thought was an unsettling one even despite the knowledge that he had in some way escaped.

The reason for his survival stood gasping at the top of the dais. Grath, face covered in sweat, had one hand stretched toward the blade. From the look on his face, he was struggling with something. It slowly dawned on the warlock that Kyl's brother was still battling the magical knife.

Kyl, furious, had taken a step toward Toma. "Ssso *thisss* isss an example of your *loyalty*! Ssso thisss isss a sssign of your *complete* obedience!"

Toma said nothing, but abruptly glanced at the dark blade.

The knife spun around and flew toward the top of the dais.

Kyl gasped and raised a hand to protect himself, but too late he realized that he was *not* the intended target.

Grath stared round-eyed as the blade sank deep into his chest, too stunned by the swiftness of what had happened to scream.

"Interfering little fool!" growled the renegade.

Bright orange flame enveloped the younger drake. Grath was outlined but a moment as he started to fall . . . then the knife pulled away and flew back to the claws of Toma, leaving the unfortunate drake a sprawled form on the dais.

"You . . . *murdered* . . . Grath!" Kyl, his eyes darting from the corpse of his brother to the knife nestled in the renegade's hand, clenched his fists and took yet another wary step toward Toma. "I gave you sssanctuary! I *protected* you and thisss—"

Duke Toma gently wiped the blood from his blade. He eyed the heir and hissed. "No more *gamess,* Your Majesty. Do you think that I do not know what you were planning? Have you forgotten how well I know all of you? I know how you think; I know how you plot. I saw your eyes when you ssspoke to the human. I read the truth in there." Toma toyed with the knife. "I know just how secure my place with you would have been once *she* was safe in the care of the warlock."

Cabe and Valea had risen, with the mage shielding his less-experienced daughter. Ursa joined them. Watching the duke, the warlock whispered, "Valea, get ready to transport the two of you away when I say to. We don't dare do it until Toma's fully occupied. Otherwise, he could easily pull you back."

She looked astounded. "I'm *not* leaving you, Father!"

"We don't have time to argue! He—"

"Hasss heard everything, Cabe Bedlam!" Duke Toma backed away from them all, the knife still at the ready. There was a strained look in his eyes and Cabe, who had already wondered about the renegade's instability, knew that Toma had nearly reached the brink. He could no longer tolerate the slightest interference with his dreams. Grath's death was proof of that, and now the duke had even turned on the one being who might have given him succor.

"Ssso much work for nothing. . . ." muttered Toma. "So many *yearsss* wasted on raising an *unfit* hatchling for what should have been mine in the first place. I had my doubtsss time and time again, but the promissse was still there."

Kyl worked to keep his own temper in check again. "Toma, if you sssurrender now, I will give you a jussst judgment."

"A 'just judgment'? With my *lissst* of crimes? I think not."

It was now or never. Cabe leaned toward his daughter and whispered. "Leave! Now!"

She hesitated for a moment, but knew he was correct to send Ursa and her away. It was fast coming to the point where Toma would talk no more, and that left little other choice but battle. Valea was aware that she especially would be more hindrance against the drake than help. At least she could go for aid.

The only trouble was . . . she did *not* disappear. Neither did Ursa.

Toma ignored Kyl for the moment and smiled at the two humans from within his false helm. "Did you think I had not consssidered thisss eventuality? I am *Toma*! *I* led my father's forces. *I* planned his campaigns! How sssimple, then, to consider the possibility that a wavering, would-be ruler would waver the wrong direction or that my foes might come to this very sssanctum! How simple, alssso, to plan ahead, come here, and leave a few sssurprises. You will not be leaving."

Darkhorse! Cabe called in his mind. *Darkhorse! I need you!*

His silent cry could not go beyond the cavern walls.

"You are alone. Cut off," Toma informed him needlessly.

"What do you hope to gain by this? You've lost everything already, Toma! Kyl's offered you a fair judgment. It's the best you can do now."

"Not quite." The renegade held up the knife. At first it appeared that he was going to throw it, but then Toma did a strange thing. He took the dark blade by the grip and replaced it in his belt. "There will be a terrible battle in here, yesss. Alas, only one will sssurvive. Toma will have killed the daughter of Cabe Bedlam, but the warlock and his arch foe will die together in a blaze of power that will leave few remains. Caught up in that sorcerous conflagration will also be the perhapsss not ssso trustworthy heir to the throne and the female called Ursa. Only one will sssurvive, a young lad who hasss alwaysss been more of a favorite to some of the Dragon Kingsss than his own brother."

"What are you babbling about?" hissed Kyl. "What sssort of fanciful ssstory isss that? You have—"

The dragon heir swallowed the rest of his words as a horrific transformation took place. Toma melted, growing smaller. The massive dragonhelm crest shriveled to nothing and the helm itself pulled away. A handsome, almost *human* face took the place of the broad, flat visage of Toma.

Moments later, where the drake duke had been, *Grath* now stood. In every way, in every movement, Cabe would have sworn that it was Kyl's brother and not the renegade.

"Did I do well, Master Bedlam?" asked Toma in Grath's voice. An uncharacteristic sneer crossed the golden-green features. "I contemplated a masquerade like this in the beginning, but there were many reasonsss why the other path wasss better." Toma/Grath tilted his head to one side and gave the others an innocent look. "Still, I think that I can easily fool those great drake lords. I have done so before. I'm sure that Lords Green or Blue will even give me sssanctuary when I tell them that I do not trussst my safety at the Manor. For obvious reasssons, of course."

The knife gave him the power to create such a thorough masquerade. Cabe knew now that there *had* been a Benjin Traske at one time and that Toma had killed him as he had killed so many before. His present plan had merit, too, for none of the Dragon Kings, not even the Green Dragon, knew Grath well enough to see the difference. Toma had probably studied everyone of importance living in the Manor, all the better to know his enemies. The warlock was certain that, given the opportunity, Toma's new form *would* fool the drakes. How the duke planned to rule through illusion for possibly the next few centuries, Cabe did not know. What he *did* know, however, was that if there was one creature capable of succeeding in such madness, it was Toma.

There was still one question, though. . . .

As if reading his mind, which for Toma might be possible, the false Grath added, "And surely you mussst be wondering how I plan to make all of thisss work."

Toma blinked once. It was, to Cabe's eyes, a very deliberate blink. Cabe felt a mild tug of the surrounding powers and recalled when the duke had earlier done the same thing.

A signal. He's summoned someone . . . someone inside!

A peculiar, almost mournful howl echoed through the chamber from within the deeper parts of the cavern system. By the echo, whatever had made the cry was not far. A second wail indicated that it was drawing nearer at an incredible pace.

"What in the name of the Dragon of the Depthsss *isss* that?" whispered Kyl, so stunned he had temporarily forgotten his rage.

Toma/Grath smiled. It was a smile that told Cabe he should recognize the sound.

The warlock did. It was a cry that he had not heard since a day years ago when he and Gwendolyn had fought a frenzied Gold Dragon. It was the call of a monstrosity, a thing that should not have survived its time in the hatcheries of the drakes but somehow had. Only through a combined effort had it been defeated last time, to go fleeing deep into the vast underground system. Cabe had hoped that it had died there.

A misshapen form lumbered out of the tunnels and into the throne room of the Dragon Emperor. It caught sight of the warlock, and there and then Cabe knew that, as he had remembered it, so had the beast remembered *him*.

The monster started toward him, jaws wide.

XXI

Darkhorse paced, and as he did, he eyed the two great dragons guarding the entrance into Kivan Grath. They returned his gaze with steady ones of their own. He knew that this pair would not be stared down, however much that would have been preferable to the other choice. If it came to battle, the eternal was certain that he would be victorious, but any combat would leave him even weaker than he was now. Darkhorse had not yet had the time to recover from his imprisonment; whatever his captors had done with him while he had been a victim of the box had sapped much of his strength.

He did not want to endanger his friends. Better he remain here and do nothing than become a detriment during a possible duel with foul Toma.

What made the situation more worrisome was the silence that greeted Darkhorse every time he attempted to reach Cabe. He was aware that the sanctum of the Dragon Emperor likely had spells that kept whatever was said within a secret, but both dragons had received commands from someone inside. That meant that it *was* possible to forge a link with Cabe. Certainly, his human friend had intended to send him word of the conditions of Toma's captives. The warlock knew how much Darkhorse cared for his children; there *should* have been some word. He was certain of it.

Had there already been a battle? Had Cabe been prevented from summoning him?

Darkhorse ceased his pacing and turned to confront the two mammoth guardians. The dragons studied him with wary eyes.

He tried to look his most impressive. "I must know what is happening in there."

Their responses were the same. Both dragons hissed and readied their claws. The eternal felt each guardian draw power in possible preparation of a magical assault.

Darkhorse gouged a ravine in the rocky soil beneath him. His pupilless eyes glittered. "Yes, I did not *think* you would like that statement."

"You will have to passs *ussss* to gain entrance, demon sssteed!" snarled the one Cabe had identified as Faras.

Sighing, the shadow steed started toward them at a trot. He tried to ignore the vast reservoirs of power the two behemoths were gathering. Between the two of them, they did have sufficient ability to end his existence. He told himself that he would just have to learn to ignore that particularly unsavory fact. Otherwise, thinking about it might be the death of him. "I still have hope that you *might* reconsider the necessity of that. . . ."

"Halt!"

At the sound of Duke Toma's voice, the monstrosity paused. It looked, absurd as the image was, like a puppy that had just been forbidden its favorite chewing bone. As he was to have been that bone, Cabe appreciated the reprieve, but the warlock also knew very well that the drake had not protected him out of any sudden change of heart.

Duke Toma, again resembling himself, looked from the creature to his adversary. "I think he *remembers* you, Master Bedlam!"

"Father!" whispered a horrified Valea. "What *is* that?"

"Misfit . . ." muttered Ursa, breaking her silence. "Freak of nature . . . they usually don't live this long. . . ."

It only remotely resembled a dragon. The thing was several times taller than a human, but that was in part because it stood on two legs instead of four. The tail that dragged for several yards behind was all that allowed it to balance. Even still, the monster teetered at times, in great part because its head was far too large for its body. Strange follicles almost resembling whiskers hung down from above its maw. Two spindly, almost useless arms waved back and forth in agitation.

It should have been dead. It should have died of starvation or *something* after Cabe and Gwen had forced it into the depths of the immense cavern system. *Trust my luck that not only did it survive, but Toma found it first!*

The renegade was laughing, no doubt in part because of the expression that had crossed the warlock's countenance when the beast had first started toward him.

"Yesss, I think you recognize each other. He isss more than a dumb beasssst like a riding drake, human. He is very much like usss, a thinking—to a point, that is—creature. Doubt not that he recalls what you did to him and the one who gave him care and purposesss. Doubt not that he remembers well when you took his provider from him."

At the comment, the thing howled. Everyone but Toma was forced to put their hands to their ears until the monster ceased.

The duke silenced his pet with a glare. Had he not known what the creature was capable of, the mage would have felt more sympathetic toward its plight. It craved guidance. It needed *someone* to command it. Unfortunately, that someone had first been the Gold Dragon and now was the renegade.

"How did you find it?" Cabe asked Toma, not so much because he wanted to know but because he was desperately trying to think of some way to defeat the monster before it literally destroyed him with a glance.

To his relief, Toma was willing to explain. After so many years of silently coordinating his various plots, it was not surprising that the renegade might desire to boast of his success to his enemies. "After the death of my sssire in the Northern Wastes, I returned to this cavern. Although I dared not leave signs of my stay in the upper system, I was still able to spend quite some time here recuperating and thinking." There was a distant look in Toma's eye. "I know the cavernsss of Kivan Grath better than anyone. I explored their depths asss no one before me or sssince. There are few sssecrets here that I am not privy to." He pointed at the waiting monstrosity. "He is one. Who do you think firssst noted the potential and informed the emperor asss to the possibilitiesss? I am *always* looking ahead, plotting for every circumsstance . . . but then, you know that now, don't you?"

Kyl moved a step, but Toma's pet turned and eyed him, causing the young drake to grow still once more. The monster seemed a bit confused by Kyl, Cabe noted. Why that was, he did not know, but it was something definitely worth considering . . . provided that Toma gave him the time to do so.

The duke gave Kyl a mocking smile. "It would be ill-advisssed to move much, *Your Majesty.* Asssk Master Bedlam. He knows what this creature can do. A magical marvel! A fire-breathing dragon in reversssse! Let him fix his baleful eye on you long enough, and suddenly the world will feel like an *inferno.* It will be asss if all the heat of the world isss building up within you and there is nothing you can do to douse those fires. All thisss will happen in but the blink of an eye, too.

"You will burst into flamesss and be consumed from within. A truly novel death, at the very leassst. Our sssire found him to be a very useful tool, much to the *permanent* regrets of the traitorousss kings Bronze and Iron."

Everyone knew that something had happened to the two Dragon Kings who had sought to usurp control from their counterpart, Gold. What the emperor had done had been a mystery. The only thing that most knew was that there had been little left of either drake lord. The deaths had, for a time, quelled any further notion of rebellion by the surviving monarchs.

"Massster Bedlam!" whispered Ursa in as quiet a voice as possible. "I remember that thing . . . I sssaw it once; heard our sire talk about it. The . . . the creature was blindly obedient to the emperor!"

Blindly obedient? To the Dragon Emperor? A plan, admittedly thin in substance, came to the warlock. At the very least, it would throw Duke Toma's plans into chaos . . . hopefully *all* of them, this time.

"The emperor must've taken good care of it for it to have survived at all. It must've been very loyal to him."

Toma was visibly amused by the continuing conversation. He was clearly prolonging it only to give his foes desperate hope. In the drake's eyes, he held all the cards.

Cabe hoped that did not prove to be true.

"Only my sssire had greater control over him than I did . . . and now, only *I* am his massster!"

The monster's attention strayed to Toma while the renegade spoke, but then the head slowly swung toward Kyl again. It was not simply the young drake who seemed to interest him, though, but also Kyl's proximity to the throne.

"But if Gold—if the Dragon Emperor were here," persisted Cabe, "it might not even look at you."

Toma now only looked annoyed at his comments. Cabe dared not look at Kyl, for fear that the renegade would realize what he was attempting to do. The drake duke folded his arms and stared at the warlock. "I think that this missserable attempt to drag out the last few momentsss of your lives has come to an end, human." He had eyes for no one other than Cabe. "I think that it isss time to end our long and colorful association, don't you?"

The renegade turned to the monstrous creature, who seemed to shiver in anticipation.

"Stop!" roared a commanding voice that echoed throughout the caverns. "I, your *emperor*, command it!"

Even Toma could not help but turn.

Cabe thanked the Dragon of the Depths and whatever else might be watching out for Kyl and the others. The heir had picked up on what the warlock had been hinting at . . . picked up on it and taken it farther than Cabe could have believed possible.

Kyl no longer stood near the throne. Instead, impossible as it was to believe, there loomed before them a dragon as had not been seen in years. To Cabe, it was as if time itself had stepped backward, resurrecting for all to see the glory of the Dragon Emperors in the form of the drake lord Gold.

He had confronted the emperor only in the final moments, when that glory had been, in great part, tarnished by madness. Kyl, on the other hand, was a sleek, gleaming leviathan, the epitome of glory and command.

For several seconds, even Toma was speechless. He gaped at the dazzling sight, then recalled himself. Hissing loudly, the duke whirled to his pet beast and pointed at the sun-drenched form atop the dais. *"Slay him!"*

In response, the monster emitted a mournful howl. Duke Toma stepped back as if slapped. The creature took a few tentative steps toward Kyl, then paused to glance at the renegade.

It remembers the Dragon Emperor as its guardian! It did not matter that this was not the same dragon. Kyl was similar enough in form that even Cabe had had to look twice to see the differences. Toma's pet had evidently sensed the kinship from the beginning. Moreover, to it, the throne represented the emperor, the one who had given it a place. The beast was understandably torn in its loyalties. Kyl had solidified that impression by taking on the form of his sire.

The heir had done something more than simply copy the appearance of his father. Cabe doubted that Kyl had ever so completely changed form before. What everyone saw now was the form that the drake, had he not been influenced by human presence, would have certainly worn when he had reached adulthood. What stood before them was truly Kyl, *emperor* of the drake race.

It was a realization that did not sit well with Toma.

"What are you waiting for, you misssguided monstrossity? That isss not the one who gave you purpose! That isss an enemy of hisss in disguise! *I* am the only one you can trusst here!"

The beast wavered, again unleashing its mournful howl.

"How horrible!" whispered Valea. Cabe glanced at her, thinking that she meant the misshapen drake, but his daughter's eyes were fixed on Kyl. It occurred to him then that Valea had never considered the heir's other form. Not truthfully. She had no doubt realized that as one of the drake race Kyl had another form, but imagining it and *seeing* it were two entirely different things. Kyl was a handsome dragon, but he was still a *dragon* and not the exotic young man the witch had grown up knowing. It mattered not that she had seen Ursa change, either. Ursa was not Kyl.

"You will obey *me*," roared the heir to Toma's pet. "Obey me and I will protect you."

That was all the monster evidently needed to hear, for it started to trot toward the dais much the way a small, lost animal that has finally found its mother might have.

No one betrayed Duke Toma. Grath had learned that, much to his misfortune. The renegade evidently intended Kyl to learn that, too, for the warlock barely had time to act as he saw Toma pull the deadly blade from his belt and stretch his arm back in order to throw it at the heir, who was preoccupied with guiding the monster to him.

As quick as Cabe was, Ursa was even quicker. She leapt toward the turned Toma, already shifting her form. Yet, if the female drake had hoped to catch the renegade off guard, she had not counted on Toma's propensity for survival. Somehow, the drake always had some response ready, even if circumstances warranted it to be a swift one.

Toma barely succeeded in maintaining a hold on his blade. There was, much to Cabe's relief, no time for the duke to turn the knife directly on the attacking drake, but he was still able to bring down the hard handle on the side of her head. As she had not yet completely altered her form, her head lacked the scaly armor and thick skull of a dragon. More importantly, the spark that flew off when blade met skull was clear proof that the dark knife was ensorcelled on many levels.

Ursa struck the floor already unconscious. All vestiges of her change dwindled away, leaving her in the human form she had always so much preferred.

"Ssstupid, *ussseless* female!" sneered Toma.

Unable to act before without possibly harming the brave drake, Cabe attacked the moment Ursa was out of his line of sight. The spell was not an intricate one; the warlock's only intention was to permanently part Toma from his blade. The weapon was the key to much of the renegade's work, including, Cabe suspected, the spell that surrounded the cavern.

Near the dais, Toma's monster had turned back at the sounds of struggle. Now the creature wanted to join its former master, but repeated commands by Kyl were so far keeping it in check. It continued to howl, frustrated by the two conflicting loyalties.

Cabe did not strike at the blade itself, suspecting that among the powers that Toma had imbued it with was some sort of shield. Grath had been able to hold it a short time, but that was because he had simply been trying to halt its flight, not affect the weapon itself. Instead of the blade, the warlock chose to strike at the renegade. Granted, Toma was probably also protected, but what Cabe planned was not exactly a direct attack.

Without warning, the duke's hand opened wide. The drake's expression was indication enough that he had not *wanted* to open his hand, especially as that meant he no longer had a grip on the knife. Toma tried to seize the falling weapon with his other hand, but it was too late.

The blade struck the cavern floor point first and bounced a foot or two away. Cabe noted no change in the conditions around them, despite Duke Toma having no direct control of his toy. Of course, he had not had any such control when Grath had attempted *his* spell. *The blade's tied to him. It has to be destroyed to be stopped.*

That was something easier said than done, especially with the renegade now turning his attention to his old adversary. The drake stretched forth one hand toward the knife while the other he balled into a fist and pointed in Cabe's direction.

As the knife rose from the floor, the warlock felt his shield buckle under an unseen but incredible force all around him. Cabe strengthened the shield, but doing so drew his concentration from seizing the blade. He watched with frustration as it neared Toma's open hand.

Then *another* hand thrust upward from the floor and snared the knife by the handle. Ursa, not so unconscious as Duke Toma had supposed, reversed the blade so that it pointed toward its master. At the same time, she tried to plunge the weapon into the belly of Toma.

There was no doubt that it would have sunk deep, armor or no, but the renegade drake was swifter than Ursa had evidently hoped. Although taken unaware by her sudden revival, Toma recovered quickly. This close, he did not have time to protect himself with a spell, not against such a powerful device as his own magical blade, but he could still move. Toma's hand came down on the female drake's own, forcing the blade lower and to the side. Ursa gasped in obvious pain as the duke squeezed.

The knife missed his stomach, but Ursa was evidently stronger than he had supposed. Stronger *and* swifter.

A hissing cry burst from the renegade as his own dagger plunged almost halfway into his thigh. Armorlike skin failed to slow the sorcerous weapon.

Pulling away, the knife still in his thigh, Duke Toma cursed. The knife and the wound glowed a peculiar green. Fueled by his pain, he struck Ursa as she tried to rise and finish what she had begun. It was quite clear from the angle at which the female drake fell that this time there would be no trick.

From the dais, the dragon Kyl turned to the monster and roared, "Kill him!"

The creature remained where it was, looking confused and almost panic-stricken. It could no more destroy Toma than it could the one it believed was the previous emperor. Distraught, the beast looked up to the ceiling and renewed its howling.

The ceiling shook. A rain of tiny and not-so-tiny fragments buffeted everyone. Even Toma paused in his pain to cover himself as one particularly large chunk of rock fell within a few feet of him.

Cabe tried for what seemed the thousandth time to focus on Toma, but again something prevented him from unleashing a new spell. The something this time proved to be Kyl, who, realizing that there would be no victory through his new pet, charged toward the wounded renegade.

Toma looked up to see several tons of dragon converging on him. He did not seem panicked, however, but rather *furious*. Foregoing the removal of the enchanted blade, which still glowed, the duke faced his awesome foe and clenched his fists. Kyl was already almost upon him, frustrating the warlock's attempt. Only a powerful spell could take down Toma, but such a powerful spell would likely include the heir as well. *So much power and I stand around like a dithering fool!*

There was, however, one thing he could do. That was pull Ursa away from the vicinity of Toma and Kyl. With a glance, he raised the still form of the female drake and brought it swiftly toward himself. At the same time, he whispered, "Valea! Take hold of Ursa the moment she's near enough. Bring her to the gateway. You have to find some way to open it and summon Darkhorse."

"But Father, that will leave you alone!"

"Do as I say! Quickly!" Although the tasks he had given her were of great importance, there was a part of the warlock that admittedly desired Valea to be out of harm's way. Even if she failed to open the gates or contact the eternal, the simple fact that Valea was no longer in here would allow Cabe to fully concentrate on Toma. It was his daughter more than anything else that made it almost impossible for Cabe to completely commit himself to battle.

Even as she took hold of the floating form of her friend with her own sorcery, Cabe's attention returned to the battle before him. Kyl had reached Toma . . . almost. The majestic golden drake stood above the tinier figure of the renegade, one massive paw attempting to squash Toma. Unfortunately, some unseen barrier prevented Kyl from closing the last two or three feet above the duke's helmed head. The emperor-to-be roared and attempted to smash through the shield, but the result of his attack was a shriek of pain as the barrier proved even stronger than his full draconian might.

Kyl raised his paw to try again . . . and was enveloped in a ball of lightning.

Above the combined din created by both the crackle of the lightning and the roar of agony unleashed by the dragon, the voice of Duke Toma hissed, "Impudent little fool! *You* challenge *me*? You dare think yoursssself a match for me becaussse you wear that color? Becaussse you wear a few *sssuperficial* markings that in no way determine your power or your cunning?"

Still holding the dragon at bay, Duke Toma reached down and seized the blade in his leg. With obvious strain, he plucked out the deadly toy. The renegade wobbled a little, but did not fall.

There was at last distance enough between the two dragons for Cabe to utilize his master spell. He stared directly at the knife and concentrated.

The knife flared white but was in no other way changed. In fact, the only other result of his attack was that Toma now turned to him. "And *you*, human! That you could *ever* think yourself my equal! That I have tolerated you for ssso long isss to laugh!"

Kyl took the brief moment of inattention to attempt a new and more daring assault, this time in the form of an attack on the ground around Toma's feet. The golden dragon tore at the earth, obviously trying to undermine the renegade's footing.

Pointing the blade toward Kyl, Toma muttered something under his breath.

Blue lightning turned the emperor-to-be into an azure inferno. Cabe watched in horror and stupefication as Toma's spell raised Kyl's overwhelming form several feet above the ground and tossed him toward the far side of the vast cavern.

The huge, gleaming form crashed into the hard, rock surface of the chamber wall. Kyl's shocked roar became, for a brief moment, an immense grunt of surprise and pain. The grunt was followed by another crash and then silence, as the dragon crumpled to the floor. As with Ursa, Kyl suddenly reverted to his more human form, a transformation that did little to improve his battered look. Unlike his sister, however, it was clear that the heir was not playing at unconsciousness.

The monster started toward Kyl. Toma called to it, but the beast paid him no mind. With its oversized head, the beast nudged the heir's still body. When Kyl did not move, it squatted next to him and began once more its mournful howling.

"Your plans are crumbling, Toma," taunted Cabe, a spell at the ready. He wanted the drake just a little farther away from the direction of the entrance. Valea had finally slipped past with Ursa's floating body, but if the duke realized what was happening, he stood a good chance of taking the two women before the warlock would be able to stop him. "Just like they always do."

"If there hasss been any any fault in my plansss," hissed the renegade, forgetting all else save the robed figure, "it isss because I have been naive enough to trussst the competence of *others*. In the end, I mussst always rely on *myself*."

"Yourself?" Cabe took a step back and away from the entrance. To his relief, Toma matched his steps, unconsciously moving farther from where Valea had fled. "It was *your* incompetence that destroyed your plans. It was *your* incompetence that forced you to abandon the Manor mere days before your plot would have seen fruition."

Reptilian eyes blazed within the false helm. Toma was finding it difficult to restrain himself. "That was the fault of trusssting *children* and bumbling fools!"

"Maybe, but who was it who was *truly* to blame for bringing down the Dragon Emperor in the first place? Who was it whose *ambition* pushed Gold to make the decisions he did?" The warlock straightened and stared Toma in the eye without blinking. "Who was it who secretly urged the kings Brown and Black to hunt down one lone human boy and kill him because of what his grandfather had been? If not for *you*, I might not be here to stop you now and, perhaps more important to you, Toma, Gold might never have fallen."

"I will have your *tongue*, human!"

Cabe had drawn the power that he needed. There was but one more thing that he wanted to say, one more fact he wanted Toma to know, whatever the outcome. "You've always desired to be the shaper of the Dragonrealm, Toma, but have you ever considered that you already *are*? You've done more to make the land what it is today than almost anyone else. You brought down the Dragon Emperor, put the drake lords into disarray, and helped make humans and drakes equals." Cabe Bedlam bowed humbly before the renegade, but his tone, he hoped, held just the proper level of ridicule. "For that, you deserve the thanks of all of us, especially *me*."

"You arrogant little vermin!" Toma raised the knife toward Cabe. "You . . . *human*! I will have you ssstuffed and mounted! I will have you made the centerpiece of a collection of thossse who fell before my glory!"

The sinister dagger blazed.

Cabe released his counterspell just as Toma committed himself.

The warlock was buffeted by an incredible wave of sorcerous energy. He stumbled back and fell to one knee, but then the pressure eased, becoming less and less with each passing breath.

Toma did not understand at first, so caught up was he in the intended destruction of the mage. He did not comprehend until the blade began to shimmer in an odd fashion, alternating between a glow as bright as the sun and a blackness as dark as the night.

"What are you—" was all the renegade managed. Then, Duke Toma hissed in pain.

The dagger dropped from his hand. The palm of his hand was black and blistered.

The knife struck the cavern floor, but this time it did not bounce. In fact, it struck more with a *splatter*, for the blade was already half-melted.

"Nooo!" Reaching down with his good hand, the renegade attempted to retrieve what was left. He was too late. All that remained was the lower half of the handle, and that melted even as Toma tried to pick it up. The duke snarled and rubbed his fingers.

Around Cabe, it suddenly felt as if a vast barrier had been lifted . . . which, in truth, had happened. Against the power of the blade, Cabe's options had been limited. Toma had worked his magics all too well in creating the knife. Not only had it helped the drake defeat Kyl, but it also still shielded Darkhorse from the knowledge of what had transpired in the cavern.

Cabe could have wasted his own strength fighting against the shielded walls, the knife, and Toma himself, but there could have been only one outcome to such an unbalanced struggle. Therefore, the sorcerer had instead concentrated on the blade and one of the weaknesses its very function forced upon it.

Only one power was certainly equal to the task of defeating Toma's plaything. That was the power of the blade itself. It was a trick he had made good use of several times in the past. Cabe's spell had not been an attack on the knife nor had it been a simple shield against the weapon's might. What the warlock had instead cast was a conduit of sorts, a magical path that would turn the power of the blade to another purpose. Cabe had refocused the deadly force of the knife against the invisible barrier that cut off all communication between those in the cavern and those in the outside world.

The blade had worked against itself, feeding more and more of its power into the attack on Cabe, which was then turned on the barrier that it projected. In order to strengthen that barrier from the sudden attack, the magical dagger had been forced to further drain itself. Yet, it could not do so for long because Toma's will continued to force more power into his battle against the apparently impervious shield of his warlock rival.

The result had been too much for Toma's toy to handle.

He did not wait for the renegade to recover, attacking while the duke still clutched his injured hands. Crimson loops formed around Toma's legs and torso and attempted to bind his arms together. However, the drake proved to be less disoriented than Cabe had hoped, for suddenly a green aura formed, an aura that proceeded to melt away the loops covering each arm. The aura spread over Duke Toma's body, dissolving the loops as it touched them. Only when the last of the loops faded to nothing did the green glow dwindle away.

"You *continue* to pessster me like a flea biting at my flesh!" Toma held his hands palms forward so that Cabe could see them. A haze formed briefly over each palm. As it passed, the burns healed, until there was no sign of the injuries. The renegade hissed again, his forked tongue darting out once. "But that isss *all* you are, Cabe Bedlam! A flea! A *flea!*"

Duke Toma's shape twisted. His form was quicksilver, fluid and changing. He began to expand, as if filling with air. Hands arched, becoming taloned paws. Arms and legs bent at angles that should have broken them. From the renegade's back tremendous wings sprouted and with them a tail. The savage, leering dragon's head crest began to sink down and merge with the half-hidden countenance behind the false helm. In but the blink of an eye, Toma grew to several times his original size and continued to expand.

He was not as huge a beast as either Kyl, Faras, or Ssgayn, but Toma the dragon was possibly the most ferocious drake that Cabe had ever encountered. The jaws opened wide as the transformed duke roared, revealing an impossible number of long, sharp teeth. The forest green and sun gold form was lithe and swift in appearance. Toma's eyes burned with such hatred that the warlock half-expected to drop dead simply from the rage he saw in them.

The dragon rose on his hind legs, obscuring all sight of the dais and the throne. He hissed again, the long, snakelike tongue darting about like a frenzied whip.

"It isss time you learned, flea, what a dragon is *truly* capable of!" Toma inhaled . . . then exhaled an inferno.

Flames licked the area all around Cabe. His robe burned and the heat seared his flesh. He held in check the scream he wanted to release, instead turning the pain into power. His shield strengthened, cutting off both the flame and the heat. A simpler spell doused the fires on his clothing. The burns he healed just enough to ignore. It would take all his will and ability to fight back. A little pain would have to be endured.

Toma inhaled again. Cabe chose the respite to attack in turn, severing a number of the largest and sharpest of the stalactites from the ceiling. The rain of missiles came down on Toma just as he was about to unleash a second firestorm. The barrage caught the dragon by surprise. One stalactite pierced a wing, while several others battered the outraged leviathan's head.

Cabe's success was short-lived. A barrier formed around Toma, a barrier that seemed adept at deflecting the stone missiles. Cabe brought a hand up and turned the swarm aside. The deadly rain pummeled the restored effigies and created a second massive shower of rock that further reduced the area to the wreckage it had been after the warlock's previous battle here, the one with Toma's sire, Gold.

The dragon laughed and a malevolent smile crossed the reptilian features. "Flea bitesss! Nothing but flea bitesss! I shall scorch you, rend you, and crush you, human! Then I shall take your precious *daughter*! Perhapsss I shall make her one of my dams! Humansss and drakesss *are* capable of procreating, you know. I have . . . sssseen it. Then, I shall take your son and your lovely bride—*all* of your companionsss—and, one by one, teach them the meaning of ssslow death! I should be able to keep myssself amusssed with them for *months* at a time!" Toma laughed again, loosening a few more stalactites that fell harmlessly around him. "And, knife or not, as *Grath,* I shall look on, properly mournful but unable to end the terror!"

He would do it, too. Everything that Toma had just promised, even without the baleful dagger to aid him, he would do. Cabe knew that, and a cold, ever so cold, fear overwhelmed him. Yet, instead of being left numb and paralyzed, the fear stirred within him a rage, a need to react and overcome that very fear.

His voice was surprisingly calm as he started toward the malignant drake. "You won't be doing anything to anybody, Toma. I can't allow that. I can't let you leave to cause more horror. It has to end here."

Toma laughed again and, raising one huge, taloned paw, caused a storm to form above and around the tiny figure that dared to defy him. Wind and rain rocked Cabe, while thunder deafened him and lightning sought to strike him down.

Gritting his teeth, the warlock somehow found the wherewithal to continue forward. Fueled by his fatalistic determination, Cabe's shield spell held against the onslaught of the magical storm. Toma roared and increased its fury, but still his foe advanced.

Within only yards of the leviathan, Cabe at last attacked. He raised his hands before his chest, and from between them there suddenly formed a sphere of blinding blue light. The sphere grew to twice the size of a man's head, then flew forward as if shot from a catapult.

Wings stretching, the dragon snorted his disdain and nodded almost minutely at the oncoming projectile. A second sphere, this one a dark, decaying green, formed instantly and flew to meet its blue counterpart.

The two balls of light collided.

Toma had already forgotten Cabe's sphere, assuming that his counterspell had eradicated it. His gaze had already returned to Cabe when the dragon became aware that, instead of dissipating the moment it had touched its emerald counterpart, the blue sphere had exploded into a thousand fragments. A thousand fragments that continued on toward their intended target with no loss of velocity.

Skilled as he was, it took the dragon little effort to strengthen his shield, but Cabe's spell was stronger in intensity than anything Toma had yet faced. Most of the glittering fragments faded as they met the magical wall, but several burst through.

Toma howled in pain as dozens of tiny, fiery avengers assailed him. Several scored hits on his torso while a few lucky ones burned through the membranes of one wing. The dragon staggered back, knocking over yet more of the ancient statues and coming to a halt only when the floor gave way to the steps of the dais. Cabe raised his arms toward Toma to give his attack better focus, ignoring, as he had so many times in the past, the agony caused by an old wound suffered facing the Aramites. None of his pain mattered now; it was secondary to keeping the dragon at bay.

The battle had at last drawn the attention of the monster, although it still made no attempt to leave Kyl's side. Toma noticed its attention and, pointing a claw at Cabe, roared, "Kill him now! Kill him before he leavesss you once more without anyone! Kill him before he leavesss you *alone* again!"

No! Cabe swore as he heard the creature's howl take on a new, deadlier tone. A furtive glance informed him that Toma had at last managed to stir the beast from its stupor. Rising, the monstrosity began to lumber toward the warlock, who was quite aware that even at his best he could not possibly take on both the wily dragon and the baleful monster. All the creature had to do was fix his gaze on Cabe long enough . . .

He was caught between the two of them. Worse, with Cabe forced to spread his attention between the dragon and the monster, Toma was also recovering from his terrible onslaught. There would be no hope whatsoever if the weary mage allowed that to happen, but he could foresee no way to prevent it.

I've failed. . . . Toma would find some way to escape the caverns and eventually Grath, possibly even Kyl, would return to claim the throne. No one would realize that it was Toma making use of some new devious spell.

A second howl nearly deafened him. With an awkward leap, Toma's pet covered much of the remaining distance between them. It could have easily dealt with him before this, but Cabe guessed that it was debating between using its inherent magic to destroy him or simply seizing the human morsel in its mouth and swallowing him whole.

"Kill him!" hissed Toma once again. Still weak from his wounds, which this time he did not instantly heal, the renegade appeared to be satisfied with keeping his adversary occupied enough so that Cabe could not deal with the other threat until it was too late.

The beast paused. It howled again, but moved no closer. Its horrible eyes focused on the haggard mage.

A curtain of absolute darkness covered the warlock. At first he thought that this was the prelude to death, but then the curtain moved, and for the first time since the beginning of the struggle, Cabe's hopes rose high.

"I have seen some ugly drakes in my time," boomed a welcome voice, "but you, my misbegotten friend, are positively the most repulsive thing I have *ever* come across!"

"Darkhorse!" gasped the thankful warlock. Destroying the blade had worked better than he had hoped. Valea must have made her way through the gate once the spell surrounding the cavern had been broken and warned the shadow steed of what was happening.

Whether it was due to the eternal's derisive comment or simply because of Darkhorse's sudden presence, the creature forgot the warlock and fixed his deadly gaze on the ebony figure confronting him.

Cabe remembered that Darkhorse knew nothing of the beast's frightful abilities. "Don't stand still!"

It was too late. The horror stared and howled. The warlock could not recall whether it was the stare or the cry or a combination of both that caused the victim to burn from within. Whatever the cause, it was too late to help his companion. The eternal had arrived in time to do nothing but die.

Yet, even after the creature had long stopped howling, even after it had blinked in confusion more than once, Darkhorse still stood.

A child of the Void. That was how legends had often described the eternal. He was not like any creature in the world, simply because he was *not* from this or any other world.

The power of Toma's pet was useless against the black stallion. Perhaps there was no inherent heat within Darkhorse upon which the monster could work its horrible spell.

Even Toma briefly forgot about his part in the battle as he and Cabe stared at the stunning tableau.

"Well?" mocked Darkhorse. "Was *that* supposed to mean something?"

Outraged, the monstrosity howled and charged the eternal.

"No!" Toma snarled. "Ssstop!"

His words went unheeded. The creature leapt as it came within range of its motionless prey. Not once did it hesitate to perhaps wonder why the massive horse did not try to flee or fight. It was too furious, too filled with a bloodlust. A victim had survived its power; that could not be allowed.

Jaws opened and talons flashed as the beast fell upon Darkhorse . . . and continued to fall *into* his would-be prey. There were those who would have described the eternal as a living hole, a dark abyss with no bottom. Darkhorse was that and so much more. He was and was not the very emptiness in which he had been spawned.

The howl of anger became a cry of fear. Darkhorse's form grew distorted from effort; as Cabe had suspected, his companion had not yet completely recovered from his captivity. The stallion persevered, however. It was a strange sight—it was *always* a strange sight—to behold. Despite the fact that the beast had stood far, far taller than Darkhorse, the monster's entire form was dragged into the body of the shadow steed. Smaller and smaller the shadow steed's adversary became, until at last it vanished within. The howling ceased but a moment after.

Despite all the times he had seen Darkhorse do this to his enemies, Cabe could not help but feel unsettled.

There was something different about this particular instance, however, for Darkhorse made no immediate move to take on Toma. He did not move at all, but rather stood where he was. His body literally rippled, but it did not collapse as it had done once in the past.

With effort, the shadow steed finally turned to face the renegade. The dragon eyed him warily.

"You . . . have attacked my . . . friends . . . monster! You made me a prisoner . . . and tortured me. For that . . . I will make you pay."

It was clear that the comments concerning Darkhorse's imprisonment only puzzled Toma, but the stallion paid that no regard. He started toward the renegade at a somewhat irregular pace.

This Toma noticed and a calculating look crossed his draconian features. "Come to me then, old nag, and show me what you can do!"

His form still shifting, the shadow steed prepared to attack.

Cabe gestured. A wall of energy appeared between Darkhorse and Toma. The shadow steed turned in confusion. "Cabe! What do you do?"

The warlock took a deep breath. His fear and rage had not been quelled, and now that he had committed himself to his present course, the two emotions began to burn with renewed force. "Take care of Kyl, Darkhorse. Forget Toma. He belongs to *me*."

"What care have I for that traitorous young—"

Cabe cut him off. "Kyl helped us, Darkhorse. Grath was the traitor. Now do as I say and take Kyl from here. He needs the aid of a healer badly. If you don't hurry, I'm afraid he might die."

"But—"

"Take care of Valea and Ursa, too . . . please." He had been about to say *especially if I fail,* but Cabe did not even want to acknowledge that likely possibility. "Now."

Toma absorbed the exchange with something approaching amusement. "Have I given permission for thisss, human? Do you think that I will jussst let him depart with the heir?"

The warlock was grim-faced. "Yes."

"You are mistaken, then."

The dragon raised a paw toward Darkhorse, who, obeying Cabe, had backed toward Kyl. Dust began to rise around the shadow steed, dust that somehow clung to the eternal's form.

"Let him be."

The force of Cabe's blast threw the great dragon against the steps of the dais. Toma thundered in new pain, his spell dissipating as he lost control. Smoke rose from his form. There was now a gaping hole in the already injured wing.

Darkhorse paused. "Cabe, if you and—"

"Do what I said, Darkhorse." The mage dared not reveal just how weakened he already was. Each new assault drained him, but he could not relent. Toma was his. Toma had *made* himself Cabe's. He would take the dragon whatever the cost. Whether that was the right thing or the wrong thing to do, the warlock did not care. Toma was *his*.

"You *insolent* mortal!" raged the wounded leviathan. "Who do you think you *are*?"

The exhausted sorcerer pulled himself up to his full height and quietly responded, "I am *Cabe Bedlam*."

His next assault forced Toma partway up the dais. The renegade drake roared. Once again Cabe was awash in a storm of flame, but this time the heat and pain were barely noticeable. He pushed his way through the inferno until Toma could maintain it no longer.

The dragon was breathing heavily when the warlock again looked him in the face. For the first time, there was uncertainty in Toma's eyes.

Cabe took the opportunity to look Darkhorse's way. He was relieved to see that the stallion had obeyed him, for both Darkhorse and Kyl were no longer there. One weight lifted from his heart. Whatever happened here, the others were safe. Kyl and the others would spread the truth about Toma if Cabe failed.

"We're all alone now," he informed the renegade.

"A pity. Then no one will be able to die with you."

"You'll do."

The huge head suddenly dropped toward Cabe. The warlock belatedly noted that he had never estimated the length of Toma's neck. The world above Cabe became the wide maw of a slavering dragon.

Toma's jaws snapped shut on the place where his rival had been, but the sorcerer had been able to dive aside at the last moment despite the dragon's swiftness. The dragon tried once, twice, three times more. Cabe rolled over, bouncing again and again against the rock floor. He was bruised from head to toe, but at least he was alive to fight.

The knowledge did not much encourage him.

"Ceasssse hopping and bouncing, flea! You only prolong what musssst be!"

"You . . . have a . . . point there," Cabe gasped. It was now or never. If he allowed this battle to go on, Toma would defeat him through sheer stamina. The warlock could hardly keep up his present pace much longer.

Again, the human struck, choosing force over subtlety. Toma recast his shield, but while it held, the dragon was still driven to the top of the dais. Toma tried to exhale another river of flame, but only a gust of heat greeted his efforts.

Cabe pushed on, knowing that he had to be relentless. A second bolt and then a third pushed Toma nearly to the throne. The mage ascended the steps, pausing only two or three from the top.

Toma straightened, unsteady but hardly defeated.

"What does it take to put you *down*, warlock?"

Cabe wanted to ask him the same question, but chose to save the energy for the combat. He attacked again, and this time the dragon's shield failed him.

Toma nearly fell upon the throne. His entire form crackled with the power that his adversary had unleashed on him. The dragon righted himself, but now he twitched from pain. His breathing was irregular.

"You *cannot* defeat me! I am *Toma*!"

Again, a taloned paw rose.

The steps around and beneath Cabe Bedlam sizzled. Bolts of blue lightning rose from the rock and assailed the warlock. They were not like ordinary lightning, for each one that assailed him remained attached like a parasite, drawing his power away and nearly forcing him to his knees.

"You are *mine*, warlock!" Toma the dragon roared his delight.

Gwendolyn, Valea, Aurim, Darkhorse, the Gryphon . . . all the faces formed before Cabe. They and others looked to him, called to him. Whether it was true or not, the warlock again felt that if he gave in to Toma, he would open the way for all their deaths at the renegade's claw.

The warlock fought the lightning, even managing another step up. Toma's cries of triumph faded as he eyed with disbelief the continued existence of his tiny bane.

Cabe drew everything he had into one last effort, aware that by doing so he might kill himself where Toma had so far failed. He met, for what he hoped was the last time, the eyes of the renegade. Cabe tried to imagine the faces of all those close to him whom Toma had already killed. Even Grath, despite the young drake's secret allegiance. Grath *had* saved Cabe and Valea from the duke's black blade.

"From the beginning," he called to the sinister behemoth, "you've desired that it be *you* and you alone who sat on the throne as Dragon Emperor."

"It *should* have been mine! I was the most *worthy! I, Toma!*"

Cabe ignored the outburst. "I can't make you emperor, Toma, but the least I can do . . . is give you the *throne*."

The attack that Cabe had prepared was fueled as much by his own life force as it was by the sorcerous power at his command. He reached forward with his right hand and pointed at where he knew the dragon's heart to be. So ensnared was he by his own spell that he no longer even noticed Toma's own withered assault.

His last view before his bolt hit Toma in the chest was the dragon's absolute refusal to accept what was happening.

Toma's shield was nothing to Cabe's spell. Neither was the thick, tough, scaled hide of the deadly leviathan. The bolt burned through all, piercing the dragon completely through and not dissipating until it struck the wall far behind him.

The dragon stiffened, transfixed by the lethal assault. Toma's massive form shivered as Cabe continued to pour his life into the effort.

"*Fall, damn you!*" he cried, unconsciously mimicking Toma from but a few moments before. "*Why don't you fall?*"

Toma did.

With a last, pain-wracked roar, the renegade dragon fell back upon the very object he had so long desired to control. Toma's huge body was too much for the throne, and as he fell upon it, the throne crumbled under his weight. The drake's head swung back in a horrible arc and smashed against the rock wall to one side of the dais. A burst of fire shot briefly ceilingward as Toma exhaled.

Cabe did not move. He could not believe that, after all this time, Toma was defeated. Surely, the warlock thought, there must be some last trick.

There was none. Even as he watched, the dragon twitched feebly once or twice. The head slowly came round so that Toma could see Cabe, but the renegade's eyes were already clouding. Even still, Toma attempted one last sneer.

It was the expression that would remain frozen on his face as he died.

Cabe Bedlam crumpled on the steps, the knowledge that Toma was dead finally giving him release. He struggled to remain conscious, but the effort of his victory had drained him too much. His eyes closed. He forced them open again, only to find an anxious

Gwen peering down at him, a vision which made no sense since not only was his wife not here but he would have had to have been lying on his back to see her so. Clearly, the haggard mage thought not so clearly, he had worn himself so thoroughly that he was suffering delusions.

Then the delusion told him to go back to sleep and Cabe, knowing that he could fight the darkness no longer, finally gave in.

XXII

"Are you feeling better?" asked Gwendolyn.

Cabe lowered his cup and peered at his wife from the bed. She looked concerned, as she had since he had first been carried back to the Manor from Kivan Grath, but she also looked preoccupied with something else.

"Better than yesterday. Better than the two weeks I don't remember."

His last, fairly clear memory before waking in his bed but two days ago had been of his wife leaning over him, fear dominating her expression. It had not been a delusion, as he had thought, but rather a brief awakening just after Darkhorse had brought him to the Manor. The shadow steed had returned to the cavern the moment that he had assured the safety of Kyl, Valea, and Ursa.

The eternal had joyfully greeted his human friend yesterday, ecstatic to discover that the warlock had finally recovered. No one knew exactly what had happened to Cabe, only that he had hung between life and death for two weeks, then abruptly recovered almost completely.

Darkhorse had described the surprise with which he had viewed the cavern upon his return. He had expected a battle of epic proportions still raging, only to find the dragon Toma dead on the dais, maw still curved in what seemed a cruel smile, and Cabe sprawled on the steps. At first, the shadow steed had feared that his friend had died alongside the devilish drake, but then he had noted the thin thread of life remaining.

"Praise be that it was not yet time for you to journey down the Final Path!" the stallion had rumbled yesterday. Darkhorse, too, had recovered. He had recovered so much, in fact, that he had made the rare transformation and given himself a pair of long, tentaclelike arms with which to hug the weary mage.

Everyone had come to give Cabe their best and express their pleasure at his survival . . . everyone except one young drake. Even Ursa had come, although when Cabe had pressed her about Kyl, the female drake had quickly excused herself.

No one would even tell him what had happened to the meeting with the Blue Dragon. It had, of course, not taken place due to Kyl's own injuries. The heir, however, had suffered much less than Cabe and had recovered some days ago.

After Kyl's heroism in the cavern, Cabe had not wanted to think ill of the emperor-to-be, but again doubts crept into his mind. Kyl *had* looked willing to join forces with Toma when it had seemed the renegade would win.

Toma. The Manor had been trying to warn them in its own way about the truth concerning Toma and Traske. The warlock knew that now. He wondered if the other images had any such meaning. He also wondered just how sentient the Manor was. More than Cabe had ever imagined? It would bear looking into once things calmed down.

"Do you want anything to eat?" asked Gwendolyn, stirring her husband from his thoughts.

"No, Mistress Belima's lunch should do fine for the next few days." The cook had been so gratified by the mage's recovery that she had made him a bit of just about every specialty she knew. Of course, with Mistress Belima, that was almost everything. Cabe's lunch could have easily served the army of Penacles. Despite all he had eaten—and his days of sleep had made him ravenous—he had hardly even made a dent in the vast meal. Gwen had used her power on Cabe, but that had only allowed him to survive. He looked forward to digging further into the pile of food later, but now he could only dream of eating.

"Then, do you think you can handle another visitor?"

"Another one? The Gryphon's been here despite now officially being recrowned monarch of Penacles. Troia couldn't make it because of the nearing birth and the somewhat abbreviated coronation ceremony. Erini and Lynnette paid a visit yesterday . . . at the same time Darkhorse showed up, of course." It had not been surprising to find the trio depart at the same time. This way, Erini could visit with all of her friends without Melicard becoming disgruntled at the shadow steed's presence. Melicard could never seem to make up his mind about Darkhorse. At least the king had sent his own regards. "I think that everyone in the Manor has been here, including Master Ironshoe several times to thank me for, as he put it, 'putting down that mad riding drake once and for all for poor old Ssarekai.' "

"I'm sorry you missed Ssarekai's funeral." Despite the drake having been petrified by Toma, everyone had agreed that it would only be polite to his memory to bury Ssarekai as soon as possible.

"I'll visit his grave later. He deserves so much more than the end Toma gave him." *Who does that leave?* the warlock pondered. *Could it be . . . the Green Dragon?*

"Shall I tell him to come back?" The enchantress grew more concerned.

Cabe realized that she thought he was growing weary again. "No. Who is it?"

She stepped toward the door, giving him only a cautious look. "I think I'll just let him introduce himself."

The sorceress quickly departed through the doorway. Cabe heard her whispering to someone, but could not hear what was being said. Heavy footfalls announced the coming of the visitor.

"I am glad to sssee you better, Massster Bedlam."

It was Kyl, but Kyl as Cabe had never seen him. The young drake was clad in resplendent dress armor that glittered like the noonday sun. A dragonhelm, a *real* dragonhelm, lay crooked in his arm.

Cabe straightened. "Congratulations, Your Majesty. I would gather that the meeting with Lord Blue went well and that he's thrown his support behind you."

"Only just thisss morning."

That made the warlock's eyes widen. "This morning?"

Kyl looked him straight in the eye. "I informed the massster of Irillian when I first woke after the battle that I would not even consssider a meeting until I knew that you were going to recover." The heir looked embarrassed. "I have been here every day for asss long asss the Lady Bedlam would permit, awaiting your return to usss. Each day, I thanked you for all you've done."

That stirred a vague memory. Kyl, kneeling by him. Kyl's voice, apologetic and promising to make amends.

"She will vouch for the truth of my words, Massster Bedlam."

"I don't doubt you. You have *my* best wishes, also, Kyl. I've evidently been wrong about you."

"Not entirely." The emperor-to-be hissed. "Pleassse alssso relay my apologiesss to Valea. She will not ssspeak to me and I can hardly blame her. I *did* intend to ussse her asss a pawn, and for that I shall never be able to forgive mysssself. She deservesss ssso much better."

"I'll talk to her."

"That isss all I asssk."

Cabe was silent for a time, then quietly said, "Kyl, I'm sorry about Grath."

The heir shrugged and took his helm in both hands. His countenance was neutral, but his eyes bespoke his misery. "I cannot sssay that Grath—or I—were innocents caught up by Toma's sssubtle teaching, but . . . thank you."

"What will happen to Faras and Ssgayn?"

The drake placed the helm on his head. Even clad so, he resembled more a legendary human king than the emperor of the drake race. "They chossse in the end to ssserve their emperor, not the beguiling renegade. Their greatest crime isss a narrow view of loyalty. They will be punished, but if they remain repentant, I will find a place for them."

Cabe had been relieved to discover that the two guardian dragons had not joined the lengthy list of those who had fallen because of Toma's obsession. They had decided in the end to stand aside and let Darkhorse pass when it became apparent that not all was as it had seemed in the cavern. "Good."

"I mussst go now. There are preparationsss to be made. Lord Blue isss waiting to essscort me to Irillian, where the final sssteps before the coronation can take place will be made. There isss alssso the matter of cleaning up the throne chamber again. The largessst refussse has been taken away and burned, but damage still remains. Also, a petition from the lord of this new drake confederacy demands my eventual attention."

So much for the grand designs of Toma. Still, something else Kyl had just said . . . "Lord *Blue*?"

Kyl walked to the doorway before answering. When he did respond, there was a note of question in his voice. "Lord Green hasss requesssted that his brother in Irillian take over the matter.

He expressesss hisss apologiesss, but sssays that he believesss Blue will be better able to handle the event. Perhapsss when you are fully recovered, you could ssspeak with the lord of Dagora and find out what ailsss him."

"Perhaps."

Kyl bowed, indicating his intention to depart. "May I expect you to be at my ascension?"

"The Dragon Kings might not care for that."

"They will endure it if it isss what their emperor desiresss. I promissse you that."

"Then, we'll be there."

The heir unleashed an uncharacteristically childlike smile. "Thank you."

He departed, leaving Cabe temporarily alone. The warlock stared out the window of his bedchamber, thinking that the coronation would certainly be interesting at the very least.

"I asked Aurim to see Kyl and the Blue Dragon out of the Manor. I thought you'd like some company."

Cabe looked at the doorway to discover his wife had returned. Gwendolyn came to the bedside and sat down next to him. The two kissed. "Thank you. How is Aurim? Has there been any aftereffect?"

"Still nothing. I think he's safe. Once he succeeded in remembering, the spell apparently dissipated completely. Both the Gryphon and I have checked carefully for the past two weeks. Nothing remains."

"So no last vestige of Toma to haunt us." The drake and his evil *were* dead. Cabe sighed in relief for the first time. It had still been difficult to accept that the duke would trouble them no more.

"Hard to believe that it's finally all over," she whispered. "Peace has a chance . . . and through *Kyl* of all drakes."

"Peace has a chance," he agreed, "but it's hardly all over. There's a lot to do. The Dragon Kings will accept Kyl as emperor, but that doesn't mean they'll cease plotting. Then there's Zuu and the new generation of mages growing up. This confederacy of drakes . . . they were allies of Toma. There's a hundred other things that I can think of that will delay peace long past even *our* lifetimes."

She gave him a playful frown. "You are without a doubt the most pessimistic optimist I have ever met. Let's at least enjoy what we've achieved so far, all right?"

Cabe took her in his arms and kissed her again. He *did* feel more hopeful, despite his own words. Perhaps the path was still fraught with rocks and pitfalls, but there was definite hope . . . and who could ask for anything more than that?

The Dragonrealm at peace . . . it was finally possible.

ABOUT THE AUTHOR

RICHARD A. KNAAK lives in Bartlett, Illinois. Besides the Dragonrealm novels, among which are the titles *Firedrake, Dragon Tome,* and *The Crystal Dragon,* he has also been a longtime contributor to the Dragonlance® series, having penned several short stories and two novels including the *New York Times* bestseller *The Legend of Huma* and its sequel *Kaz the Minotaur.* His other works include the Chicago-based fantasies *King of the Grey* and the forthcoming *Frostwing.* In the future, he plans more fantasy, science fiction, and also mystery. Those interested in finding out more about future projects may write the author care of Warner Books.